grim
adjective

1. Ghastly, repellent, or sinister in character
2. Having a harsh, surly, forbidding, or morbid air

The Grim Fugue

A Third Floor Mystery

By Alfred M. Struthers

 Escape Hatch Books

escapehatchbooks.com

ISBN 978-0-9976397-9-7

1 2 3 4 5 6 7 8 9

Printed in the U.S.A.

For Bill Perry

"But in your dreams whatever they be,
Dream a little dream of me"

Ella Fitzgerald

Prologue

Cambridge, Massachusetts
October 12, 1850

Daniel Hammond stood at the front window of his newly opened bookshop, Hammond Books, watching the sky darken. A steady breeze, the herald of an impending storm, pushed the early morning stragglers down the sidewalk.

The shop had been an immediate success in the weeks that followed his arrival from England. With him aboard the ship was the bookcase built by his older brother, Thomas Hammond, who was wrongfully convicted of conspiring with a revolutionary group plotting to overthrow the British government. Thomas' urgent words, spoken the day after the trial that sealed his fate, still burned in Daniel's memory.

In my shop you'll find a bookcase. Hidden inside it is part of a secret that must be safeguarded at all costs. Due to the extreme danger it poses, I can't reveal what it is, nor should you try to pursue it on your own. There are dark forces at work who will stop at nothing to ensure the secret is never revealed. An identical bookcase holds the other half of the secret, and as I tell you this, arrangements are being made to ship it to America aboard a ship called the Greenwich. You must do the same with the bookcase in my shop. The further away from London it is, the safer it will be. It's imperative that you take every measure of caution possible. Maintain secrecy at every turn, and trust only those closest to you. Your life depends on it.

Following his brother's public hanging, along with other members of the group he was suspected of collaborating with, Daniel quietly arranged for a brigantine ship, owned by a trusted friend, to leave for Boston under the cover of darkness with the bookcase safely hidden below deck. As an added precaution, the bookcase was off loaded onto a smaller ship a mile before reaching Battery Wharf in Boston's North End. It now sat in the furthest corner of the back room, beneath a heavy tarp, and obscured by a makeshift wall of wooden shipping crates.

What troubled him the most wasn't the unknown secret hidden within the bookcase, but the cryptic instructions that Thomas had given him.

Keep the bookcase hidden at all times and speak of it to no one. Once you're settled, you'll be approached by a man who will know what to do next. Trust this man, and do as he says without question. He'll identify himself with a single code word—Châlucet

That was four months ago. In that time, no one had approached him, certainly not in the manner his brother had described, and with each passing day he became more concerned. Despite his subtle inquiries, news of the *Greenwich* was nonexistent. Either the ship had been swallowed up by rough seas after it left the West India Docks on the Isle of Dogs, or foul play was involved, perpetuated by the same dark forces his brother had warned him about.

He was watching a young mother steer a three-wheeled pram past the window when the front door to the shop opened and a woman ducked inside. She was dressed in a mid-length brown coat that was wrapped in an ivory colored wool shawl. Her thick calico skirt fell just above hobnailed leather boots that were scuffed and dirty, and her linen cap was held on by two maroon ribbons tied neatly beneath her chin.

She quickly closed the door and looked back out the window.

"May I help you?" Daniel asked, walking toward her.

The woman pulled a hardcover book from inside her coat. "Quick, take this," she said, panic in her voice. She pressed the book against his chest and then checked the street again, this time peering nervously through the front window. They were getting closer. In another few seconds they would burst through the door and take her. After that, there was no telling what they would do with her. Whatever it was, she had no intention of finding out.

"Ma'am, is everything all right?" Daniel asked, ignoring the book in his hands.

She stepped back from the window and surveyed the room. "Is there a back way out of this place?"

"Yes, it's through that door," he said, pointing to the opposite end of the room, "but why—?"

"You never saw me," she said, cutting him off. She bolted across the shop floor, making a beeline for the narrow door that led to the office.

"Wait!" Daniel said. "What about your book?"

"Hide it," she shouted over her shoulder. "And whatever you do, don't let them find it. I'll come back for it later."

"Them? Who are you talking about?" he asked.

But she had already slipped through the doorway and was gone. Seconds later, two hulking figures burst through the front door. The first had a square face, with a protruding chin and a crooked nose that had been broken and reset on more than once occasion. The second man had ratty brown hair and deep-set eyes that professed a penchant for all things evil.

Daniel casually shifted the book behind his back. "Good morning, gentlemen," he said brightly. "How may I help you?"

"Where is she?" the crooked-nosed man barked.

"To whom are you referring?" Daniel asked.

The dark-eyed man stepped forward, did a quick sweep of the shop floor. "She's not here," he said.

The first man considered Daniel with a menacing look, debating how much he knew about the woman and ready to beat it out of him if necessary.

"Let's go," his partner said impatiently. "We're wasting time." They left as abruptly as they had entered, hurrying down the street to the next shop.

Two days later, the woman returned. She appeared at the front door as Daniel was locking up for the day, her wool shawl pulled up over her head to hide her face. When Daniel saw her, he immediately let her in.

"You gave me a start," he said as he locked the door behind her.

"Do you still have it?" she asked, the words spilling out of her mouth in a single, frantic breath.

"The book?" Daniel asked. "Yes. I put it in a safe place, just as you requested."

Hand to chest, she breathed a sigh of relief. "Thank you."

"My name is Daniel Hammond," he said. "And you are?"

"Maria Garza," she replied, removing the shawl from her head. She instinctively turned back to the door, checking to see if she'd been followed.

Seeing that, Daniel said, "Uh, why don't we talk in my office."

He ushered her to the back room where he retrieved her book from the bottom drawer of his large rolltop desk—a cherished possession handcrafted by his older brother, Thomas.

The book was a collection of watercolors, exquisite renderings of the city of Venice by the famed Italian painter Francesco Bassetti. On the cover was his depiction of the Grand Canal in the early morning, the glassy surface of the water reflecting the tall palazzos lining either bank, and the cloud-filled sky that hung overhead like a tufted baby's blanket.

"This book is quite special," Daniel said, eyeing it with admiration. "I'm sure I could sell it for a handsome profit. If you're interested in selling it, that is."

"Its value to my family exceeds any monetary sum," Maria replied. She took it from him and held it firmly against her body, as she would her own child. "That's why I stole it."

"*Excuse me?*" Daniel blurted out.

"I had no choice," she explained. "This book is the only way I can save my father."

1

Days of War

Tuesday, 4:35 P.M.

It was over in 18 seconds.

With chilling precision.

On a summer day like so many before it, 12-year-old Nathan Cole had spent the afternoon sorting books for Richard Abbott, a long-time family friend and renowned bookseller, at Abbott's barn in North Cambridge. The part-time job, initiated earlier in the year by Nathan's mother, Elizabeth Hammond Cole, was intended as a distraction, one that would keep him out of the attic on the third floor, well away from the old bookcase hiding in the shadows.

Passed down through the Hammond family for generations, the bookcase was shrouded in mystery, with a dark past and a potentially darker future. From the first time Nathan stood before it, the bookcase called to him. What followed was a series of enchanted encounters, and over time, as he learned the truth about the bookcase and the legacy it held in his family, he was powerless to ignore it.

And now there was another one.

An identical twin.

Stolen nearly 165 years earlier while being smuggled out of England aboard the brigantine ship *Greenwich*, its whereabouts had been unknown until Nathan accidentally discovered it two months earlier in the back room of a small shop in Portland, Maine. In the hours that followed that discovery, the shop's owner, Dan Perry, along with the *Greenwich* bookcase, seemingly vanished into thin air.

Compounding the mystery was the fact that clues to a monumental secret lay hidden within each bookcase, put there by Thomas Hammond, a master craftsman who built the twin bookcases in 1850. What that secret was, and why he divided the clues between the two bookcases was unknown. But according to family lore, the secret was rumored to be as troubling as it was potentially lethal, and only with the combined clues could the secret be revealed.

Nathan finished sorting books at 4:15pm. As he rode home, the late afternoon heat clung to his body like a second skin, making every turn of the bike pedals that much harder. He was a mile from home when a white delivery van pulled to the curb fifty feet ahead of him.

As he rode toward it, a man climbed out the passenger-side door holding a road map the size of a small tablecloth. He had a slight build with close-set eyes, and was known simply as Foss. As he turned the map one way then another, trying to make sense of it, he called out, "Hey kid…help me out, would ya?"

Nathan came to a stop three feet away.

"This is North Cambridge, right?" Foss asked.

"Yup," Nathan replied.

Foss inched closer, showing Nathan the map. "Where the heck is Rindge Avenue?"

Before Nathan could respond, the van's driver, a beast of a man named Romero, walked up behind him and pulled him off his bike. With force.

"HEY! WHAT ARE YOU DOING? LET GO OF ME!" Nathan shouted. He fought desperately to break free of Romero's powerful grasp, but to no avail. Romero dragged him toward the van as Foss hurried to the side door and slid it open. With one hand clamped on Nathan's shirt collar, the other on his belt, Romero picked Nathan up like a bag of dirty laundry and flung him inside. While he was doing that, Foss went back for the bike.

"What are you doing?" Romero shouted.

"We leave nothing behind, remember?" said Foss.

Nathan lay on the floor of the van, momentarily dazed. His head and shoulder ached and he blinked hard several times as he tried to get his bearings. He was pushing himself up off the floor when his bike came sailing through the open door and knocked him back-ward into a wall-mounted shelving unit.

After that his whole world went dark.

Angie Falco was in a mood. She gathered her long black hair, put on her baseball cap, and pulled her ponytail through the opening in the back. "All I'm saying is, why keep one of your best hitters at the bottom of the order?" she asked Kendra, who was pushing the speed limit even more than usual, trying to avoid being late to batting practice for a second straight day. "You've seen me hit," Angie said. "I should lead off, right? But no! Every time I say something to coach—"

"Whoa! Are you seeing this?" Kendra blurted out.

"Seeing what?" Angie asked, checking the road ahead.

"Up there," Kendra said, pointing. "Those guys...with that kid..."

Angie leaned forward. "What the...?"

"Wait a minute! NATHAN?" Kendra shouted, as Romero wrestled him toward the van.

"You know who that is?" Angie asked.

Kendra gritted her teeth and stomped on the accelerator. "Hold on," she said as they rocketed around the Mini Cooper in front of them. When she swerved back into the right lane, narrowly missing an oncoming truck, she looked up and saw the van pulling away from the curb. It raced to the stop sign at the end of the street, then turned right and sped away.

"Did we just see what I *think* we saw?" Angie said.

Kendra accelerated again. When she came to the stop sign, she cranked the wheel and took the corner hard, the tires squealing as they left a long black ribbon of rubber on the pavement.

"We gotta call the police," Angie said, struggling to dig her cell phone out of her pocket as the car bucked and swayed.

"There's no time," Kendra said, her face flush with anger. She saw the van at the far end of the street, pulling away. Suddenly, its brake lights flared as it slowed for a four-way intersection that was snarled with late afternoon traffic. She watched the traffic light as she drove. "Come on...come on...change!" she growled.

Seconds later, as if the traffic signal gods had heard her plea, she got her wish.

The light turned red.

"Go around!" Foss shouted, waving his hand wildly at the landscaper's truck directly ahead of them in line. It was pulling a long trailer packed with tall thin maple saplings.

"I can't," Romero yelled back. Thinking the landscaping truck would run the light, he had ridden its bumper, leaving himself no room to maneuver around it. He reached for the gearshift and checked his side mirror, when Kendra's faded blue Volvo came to a screeching stop just inches from his rear bumper.

"Nowhere to run to baby, nowhere to hide," Kendra muttered as she twisted around and grabbed two baseball bats from the pile of softball equipment strewn across the back seat. "Here," she said, handing one of the bats to Angie.

Angie took the bat, confused. "What's this for?"

"You say you're a hitter?" Kendra said. "Prove it."

"Excuse me?"

"I'll take the driver," Kendra said, cracking the door open, "you take the other guy." She started to get out of the car when Angie grabbed her arm.

"Wait! Take the other guy? What's that supposed to mean?"

"If he tries to get away," Kendra said impatiently, "hit him with the bat." Before Angie could object, Kendra jumped out of the car and ran to the van, praying the light wouldn't change before she got there. When she reached the driver's door, she pounded on the window with her fist and shouted, "GET OUT!"

Romero sized her up briefly, then checked the traffic light, hoping it would change. But through the small forest of trees on the landscaper's trailer, all he saw was a sinister red circle, like the eye of a demon, staring back at him.

"I'm outta here!" Foss yelled. He pushed the door open and jumped out.

Where Angie Falco was waiting.

As Foss started down the sidewalk, she stepped out from behind the van, set her feet, and launched a home run swing at his mid-section. He saw her at the last second but it was too late. The force of the bat knocked the wind out of him and he buckled. She hit him again and he collapsed on the ground.

Romero froze, unsure what to do. That's when his side window exploded into a thousand tiny pieces, pelting his face and chest with the force of a January nor'easter.

"I SAID…GET OUT!" Kendra bellowed.

The standoff was broken by the shrill whine of sirens. Kendra turned to her right and saw a police cruiser come to a screeching stop twenty feet away. She looked left and saw a second cruiser pull into the intersection, stopping directly in front of the landscaper's truck. She grinned at Romero. "End of the line for you, pal," she said, then turned to the officer as he climbed out of the cruiser. "Those guys abducted a friend of mine," she shouted, pointing at the van.

The officer, a senior member of the department named Hollins, drew his gun and shouted, "PUT DOWN THE WEAPON!"

"Weapon? What weapon? It's a *bat!*" Kendra yelled back.

"PUT IT DOWN! NOW!"

"You're kidding me, right?" Kendra grumbled as she laid it on the pavement.

Hollins holstered his gun and ran toward her, pulling a pair of handcuffs from his belt.

"Hey, easy does it," Kendra said, as he spun her around and pushed her to her knees. "I'm not the bad guy here."

Hollins cuffed her and then pulled her to her feet.

"Look in the van," she shouted, as he walked her back to the cruiser. "There's a kid in there. He's a friend of mine. Those guys abducted him."

"Don't worry, miss, we'll check the van," Hollins said as he eased her into the back seat of the cruiser. "I'll be back to take your statement."

Beside the van, Angie stood over Foss, bat raised high in the air, ready to hit him again.

"DROP IT!" a voice boomed from fifteen feet away.

Angie looked up and saw the second officer, Tanner, a fire hydrant of a man, was kneeling next to the landscape trailer, his gun trained squarely on her.

"All right, all right," she said, quickly laying the bat on the ground.

Tanner hurried to her side and began cuffing her when Foss

emitted a low moan.

"Oh, shut up you baby," Angie whined. "I didn't hit you that hard."

"That's enough," Tanner warned her.

"Well, it's true," she said.

As Tanner walked her to his cruiser, a crowd had formed all around the intersection. Many were taking pictures and videos with their cell phones.

Hollins hurried over to the van, gun drawn, and eased up to the driver's door. When he looked through the jagged opening where the window used to be, the front seat was empty.

Tanner walked back up the sidewalk and paused next to the landscape trailer.

Foss was gone.

Hollins came around the front of the van. "Did you see the driver?"

"No," Tanner replied. "Did you see the other guy? He was right here a second ago."

Hollins went to the side door of the van and slid it open. In the dim light, he saw Nathan propped up on one elbow, dazed, his bike lying at an odd angle atop his body.

The ambulance showed up five minutes later. One of the EMTs, a young woman with short hair and a navy-blue uniform, sat Nathan down on the back bumper and started her examination.

Through it all, he sat perfectly still, staring straight ahead, anger churning in his gut. His elbow ached from the gash he'd gotten when the bike landed on top of him. His hands were blackened from the grime on the floor of the van, and there was dull throb in the back of his head. But the thing that pained him the most was the ease with which he'd been taken: the van appearing out of nowhere; the man with the map seemingly genuine in his confusion, and the brute force used by the driver.

The sound of his mother's voice washed the dark images from his mind. Ten minutes earlier she'd gotten a call from Officer Hollins and had rushed to the scene.

"Nathan!" she shouted, running toward him. "Are you hurt?"

"No," he lied.

She bent down and gave him a hug.

Ten seconds passed.

Then, ten more.

She didn't let go.

"Mom, stop," he groaned. "People are *watching*!"

"Let them watch," she replied.

Five more seconds ticked by.

"All right, all right," he said, pushing her away. "It's okay. I'm fine."

"No, it's not okay," she said firmly, releasing her grip on him. She took his face in her hands, staring at him as if inspecting a priceless Ming vase. "Nothing about this is okay," she said.

From nearby came a familiar voice. "Hey, back off! I told you, I'm a friend of the family." Kendra appeared, looking angry enough to start swinging her bat again. "There you are," she said to Nathan. "Are you okay?"

"Yeah, thanks to you," he said. "Did they get those guys?"

"No, but Angie clipped one of 'em pretty good," Kendra said proudly. "We would've had both of them if not for the cops."

"What do you mean?" Elizabeth asked.

Kendra explained how she and Angie had Romero and Foss trapped in the van, but then the police arrived and mistook *them* for the bad guys. Hearing that, Elizabeth shook her head in disgust and surveyed the street in search of Hollins.

"Ma'am?" the EMT said to her.

Elizabeth spotted Hollins 50 feet away, standing next to the van, talking to Tanner.

"Mom," Nathan said, nudging her with his knee.

"What?"

He nodded toward the EMT. *She wants to talk to you.*

"I'm sorry, did you say something?" Elizabeth said to the young woman.

"We're going to take your son to the hospital for a more thorough examination."

"Oh, yes, of course," Elizabeth replied. When she saw the look of concern on Nathan's face, she gave him another hug and said, "Don't worry. You're safe now. I'll meet you at the hospital."

"I'm going too," Kendra said. She feared the two men from the van were still nearby and might make a second attempt to grab Nathan. Elizabeth waited until Nathan was secured in the ambulance, then walked over to Hollins and Tanner, just as their conversation was coming to an end.

"Officer Hollins," she said. "You have information for me?"

"No," Hollins replied.

"No?" she said, eyebrows raised "I'm afraid that's not good enough. Two men forcibly abduct my son and you have nothing to tell me?"

"Ma'am—"

"From what I was told, you had both of them right here," she said, cutting him off. "And then they escaped? Right before your very eyes? How did *that* happen?"

"If you'll let me explain…"

"Yes, by all means, explain. I assume by now you've questioned the witnesses?" she said, motioning at the assembled crowd across the street. "And what about my son? He must've given you a physical description of the two men. Surely that will help you track them down."

Hollins shook his head. "No, ma'am."

"No, what?" she fired back.

"We didn't question your son."

"You didn't question my son," she repeated, loudly.

"That's correct."

"When were you planning on doing it? Sometime today, I hope."

"No. We're not going to question him."

"Excuse me?"

It couldn't have worked out better for Romero and Foss. When Officer Hollins cuffed Kendra and walked her back to the cruiser, Romero eased out of the van and walked along the side of it, using it as a shield from Angie. When he got to the back, he turned sideways and squeezed between the back of the van and the Volvo, then ducked down and peeked around the taillight.

He saw Foss lying on the sidewalk, conscious but clearly in pain. When their eyes met, Romero nodded toward the alley several feet away—a narrow corridor no wider than a shopping cart that separated a small laundromat and an even smaller cigar shop. Foss nodded his understanding, then Romero made a beeline for it. Angie Falco was standing guard over Foss, and with her back turned she never saw the big man slip away.

When Tanner hauled Angie back to his cruiser, Foss struggled to his feet and made for the alley. He caught up with Romero behind the laundromat and they didn't stop moving until they were two blocks from the intersection. They were passing a city parking garage when Foss ducked inside and began checking each car, running his hand along the underside of bumpers and inside wheel wells, looking for a spare key case.

On the fifth car, he hit the jackpot.

Kendra shadowed the ambulance all the way to the hospital, as if their bumpers were fused together. As she drove, she pulled her phone from the center console and dialed Jameson. "Dad, it's me," she said, before he could utter his usual greeting.

"What's wrong?" he asked, sensing the urgency in her voice.

"Before I tell you," she said, "I need you to know, he's okay. Understand? He's okay."

"Before you tell me what? Who are you talking about?"

"Nathan."

"Nathan? What about him?" Jameson asked, his heart starting to race.

"He was abducted about an hour ago on his way home from Richard Abbott's house."

Jameson grabbed the back of the desk chair to steady himself, then eased down into it.

"Luckily, I was nearby and saw the whole thing go down,"

Kendra explained. "Long story short: we got him back, but the two guys who grabbed him got away. I'm in the car, on my way to the hospital. Elizabeth is headed that way too."

"Which hospital?"

"Mount Auburn."

"I'll meet you there," Jameson said. "Wait for me outside."

"But…who's going to drive you?" Kendra asked.

"Just meet me outside the front entrance."

Click.

Foss drove, one hand holding his sore gut, while Romero struggled to get comfortable in the passenger seat. The charcoal gray Toyota Camry was technically a mid-size car, but Romero was folded up in the front seat like a beach chair. "You couldn't find a bigger car?" he grumbled.

Foss ignored the question and pulled out of the garage. "Where to?" he said.

"Just drive," Romero growled. "I gotta think."

Minutes later they were stopped at an intersection when an ambulance crossed in front of them, followed by Kendra's blue Volvo.

"Look!" Foss said, pointing.

Romero leaned forward to get a look at the driver. "That's her," he said. "Go!"

Foss took a hard right, ignoring the traffic light, and jammed his foot on the gas pedal.

"Not too close," Romero warned as they closed in on the Volvo.

They followed the procession to Mt. Auburn Hospital, staying far enough behind to keep from being recognized. When they saw the ambulance turn into the emergency room entrance, Foss pulled to the curb. Romero dug the phone from his pocket, stared at it momentarily, then made the call he'd been dreading since he slipped down the alleyway.

But he had no choice.

Not making it would only make matters worse.

Much worse.

Dan Perry had been awaiting Romero's call for over an hour. Not something he liked to do. When given a job, he expected it to be completed in a timely manner. Failure to do so was simply not tolerated, as those who came before Romero and Foss would attest. At least, the ones that still had the capacity to speak.

"You're late," Perry said in an eerily calm voice, something that always unnerved Romero.

"It couldn't be helped," Romero told him. "We hit a snag."

"Did you acquire the package?"

"Yes and no," Romero said. "We had it, but on our way back we got ambushed."

"Ambushed," Perry repeated. He lowered the phone and looked away, thinking of his next move. He wasn't interested in the details of Romero's failure: who had ambushed the van, how they'd come to learn of his plan to take Nathan Cole, or how Romero and Foss had managed to escape. That information held no value to his current dilemma. The boy who could bring about his undoing, along with the empire he oversaw, was still at large. And while Nathan Cole had no idea of the enormity of the information in his possession, Perry had no interest in waiting around for him to figure it out.

"Hello?" Romero said.

Perry pressed the phone to his ear. "Where are you now?" he asked.

"Across from the hospital."

"Hospital?"

"The package was a little roughed up."

"Stop!" Perry cut in. Hospitals meant restricted access, mandatory identification, and far too many witnesses. "Make no attempt to secure the package," he said, his mind already shifting to an alternate plan. "Do you understand?"

"Yeah, but—"

"Say you understand."

"I understand," Romero said.

The line went dead.

Romero dropped the phone in the center console and uttered an obscenity. They had pulled it off, easy as you please—even easier than they had anticipated. But then the whole thing went sideways, all because of the woman in the blue Volvo. Despite what had happened, he knew they could reacquire the package. He was sure of it. He'd done some of his best work in hospitals.

"Well?" Foss asked. "What did he say?"

"He said not to pursue the target."

"Okay, so what do we do now?"

"We go back," Romero said begrudgingly. He looked over at the hospital. *So close*, he thought.

Foss gave him a look like he was crazy. "Go back? Are you sure?"

"Of course, I'm sure," snapped Romero. "You know what'll

happen if we don't."

Foss knew all too well.

He'd heard the stories.

He said nothing and started the car.

Perry pushed his anger aside and dialed a number he'd programmed into his phone many years earlier. It belonged to a longtime associate, one whose building skills were known the world over, by smugglers, thieves, and underworld figures alike, along with his flair for the dramatic and the cruel.

It rang several times before a husky voice came on the line.

"Trask."

"There's been a slight change," Perry said. "The package won't be delivered as originally scheduled."

"Understood," Trask said. "When do you expect it?"

"Uncertain," Perry replied.

Trask bent down and rummaged through the tool tray sitting on the floor next to his boot. "That's probably for the best," he said, pulling a pair of needle-nose pliers from the tray. "It'll give me time to fix a few things."

"What things?"

"There's some faulty wiring. A few hinges need to be replaced. It wouldn't hurt to install a couple more cameras."

"Proceed," Perry said. "I'll let you know when the merchandise is ready for storage." He disconnected the call and went to his desk. From the center drawer he pulled out a small leather address book. Each entry in it was encoded using a complex cipher, and he quickly found the one he wanted.

His calls to this person were sporadic, but had a singular purpose. The man was a meticulous planner, a master of disguise, and his execution was second to none. Simply put, he got results, which made him the ideal candidate for the job at hand. And while no formal names were ever used during their phone conversations, Perry had learned through trusted sources that the man had once gone by the name Odom. Over time, as his reputation grew, along with the increased demand for his unique skills, he went by no name. He spoke to only a select few people worldwide, and was never seen in public.

Perry worked through the cipher, then dialed the number. Two rings later, a male voice answered, his greeting, as always, limited to a single word.

"Code?"

Perry's reply was equally brief. "Chevron," he said, reciting the name of the ancient French castle he'd visited as a young child with his father.

"Verify."

"Mercury," replied Perry, saying the town where the Château de Chevron was located.

The two-part authentication system had been put in place by Odom. Without it there was no conversation. Only when he was satisfied that the caller was reliable would he continue.

"The job?" he asked.

"Pickup and delivery," Perry answered.

"Difficulty?"

"Five," Perry said, using the 10-digit numeric scale they'd

adopted years earlier—numbers that increased with the urgency of the job, or its degree of difficulty. It was understood by both parties that as the numbers escalated, so too did the price.

"Time frame?" Odom asked.

"Ten."

Elizabeth sat in the waiting room while Nathan was being examined. She hadn't been sitting there long when she was approached by a young woman in her mid 40s, dressed in a short slate-blue blazer with a matching skirt and a teal blouse. "Excuse me," the woman said. "Are you Mrs. Cole?"

Elizabeth eyed her briefly. "Yes, I'm Elizabeth Cole."

"Dr. Archer," the woman said, reaching out to shake Elizabeth's hand. "Please call me Carolyn. I believe Officer Hollins gave you my name?"

"Yes. You're the forensic examiner?"

"Forensic psychiatrist," Dr. Archer said. "I'll be interviewing your son."

"Officer Hollins was a bit vague on why you were called in to speak to my son," Elizabeth said. "I thought the officers would've done that at the scene."

"A perfectly logical assumption," Dr. Archer replied as she sat down next to Elizabeth. The tone of her voice was soothing, almost hypnotic. "In years past, that's exactly what would've happened. But now, with cases involving children, specifically, traumatic situations like the one your son experienced, a forensic specialist is brought in as a precaution."

"Precaution?" Elizabeth asked.

"Should this case end up in court," Archer explained, "the information your son shares with us can't be deemed to have been coerced or manipulated in any way."

"Because the case might get thrown out and the perpetrators would go free," Elizabeth offered.

"That's correct."

"How long will this take?"

"Not long," Dr. Archer said, then stood to go.

After she left, Elizabeth considered the pile of magazines on the table next to her chair momentarily, then went outside. Walking in the fresh air helped to clear her mind, and gave her time to think about what she'd say to her husband, David, who was returning from a business trip later that evening.

To date they had kept to the plan, and it had worked.

But now, everything had changed.

It was time to tell Nathan the truth.

2

Safeguards

After Nathan was taken into the emergency room, Kendra positioned herself at the front door of the hospital and waited for Jameson, as instructed. She was eyeballing every person who came and went when she saw Elizabeth appear at the far end of the sidewalk that skirted the front of the building. Her head was down and her arms crossed, deep in thought as she walked.

"How's Nathan?" Kendra asked, as Elizabeth approached.

"A little banged up, but other than that he's fine."

"Nathan's a tough kid," Kendra said. "He's survived worse." *Be glad you don't know the half of it*, she thought to herself.

On Mt. Auburn Street, a bronze-colored Chevy Caprice slowed, then turned into the hospital's main entrance. Kendra watched the vehicle approach, putting its date of manufacture right around 1987. It came to a stop at the curb and she and Elizabeth watched as the passenger door opened and Jameson got out. As an old and trusted friend of the Hammond family, one who had worked in Henry Hammond's bookshop years earlier, his was a welcome face to see. He pushed the door closed and stepped up onto the sidewalk as the driver of the car emerged—a behemoth of a man that neither woman recognized. As he walked toward them, he seemed to grow steadily larger, like the oncoming curl of a tidal wave.

"How is he?" Jameson asked.

He was as tense as Elizabeth had ever seen him.

"As good as can be expected," she said. "He's still inside, talking to a forensic psychiatrist."

"Did he tell you anything?"

"No. There wasn't time."

"Don't worry," Jameson said, seeing the worried look on her face. "We'll have plenty of time for discussion."

Kendra's eyes drifted slowly to the driver. Of particular interest to her were his black military-grade tactical boots and his razor-sharp brush cut. *No hair gel in his bathroom,* she thought.

"Oh, forgive me," Jameson said, realizing his mental lapse. "Kendra, Elizabeth, this is Beck. Beck, this is my daughter, Kendra, and our close friend Elizabeth Cole, Nathan's mother."

Beck gave each of them a single nod, then tapped Jameson's arm. "I'll be right back," he said, then went to the car and pulled it into the visitor's parking area.

"I need to speak with Elizabeth," Jameson said to Kendra. "While I'm doing that, I need you and Beck to wait here and watch for anyone or anything suspicious. We're at war now and we need to be ready for anything."

"Go," Kendra said confidently. "We got this."

After they'd stepped through the doors, Jameson pulled Elizabeth aside. "How are you holding up?" he asked.

"Not well," she replied.

He did a quick sweep of the foyer, then guided her over to a sitting area along the far wall. "First off, let me apologize," he said. "We should've seen this coming. The warning signs were there but we ignored them."

Elizabeth closed her eyes and lowered her head, haunted by the mistakes she'd made with Nathan and the bookcase. Each failing had been a trigger for the next, like a cascading row of dominoes, but with several near-fatal outcomes. "This is why I didn't want Nathan to go near the bookcase in the first place," she said, the stress of the day's events bleeding from her every pore. "It's why I hid it in the attic after my father died. I thought if it was buried in that mess, no one would bother it. What I should've done was remove it altogether."

"And do what with it?" Jameson asked, giving her an obvious look.

"I don't know," she said softly.

"You can't blame yourself," Jameson insisted. "Nathan was going to find the bookcase sooner or later. You know that. Not only was it unavoidable, we both know it's what your father wanted."

Elizabeth reluctantly nodded her agreement. "You're right, but what now?"

"We need to match deed for deed."

"What do you mean?"

"This afternoon, Perry upped the ante," Jameson said, his firm expression revealing the anger he was feeling. "We need to respond in kind."

Elizabeth looked over at him, confused. "And how do you propose we do that?"

"He needs to be eliminated."

"Well…yeah!" Elizabeth blurted out.

The receptionist sitting at the main desk looked over at them and frowned.

Jameson motioned to her…*sorry*…then leaned in. "Not Perry," he said softly. "I'm talking about Nathan."

"You want to *eliminate* my son?" she exclaimed.

The receptionist cleared her throat. Loudly.

Jameson stood and ushered Elizabeth toward the front door. "What I meant was, we need to eliminate him from the equation," he whispered. "Not permanently."

"Oh," Elizabeth said. She checked her watch. "I should go get him. They're probably done."

"Let's meet back at the house," Jameson said. "Kendra and I will take the lead. Beck will follow directly behind you."

"You really think that's necessary?"

"Yes," Jameson said with a firm look. "Whoever did this may still be in the area. And going forward we can't take any chances…with anything."

"This guy, Beck," Elizabeth said. "Who is he?"

"You remember Ray Sullivan? My friend with the Portland Maine Police Department?"

"Sully? Yes, of course."

"Beck is one of his associates."

"An associate?" Elizabeth said with a suspicious look. "You mean, a fellow officer?"

"No."

"I see," Elizabeth said. "And he's here to do what, exactly?"

"Provide security."

"You really think one man is going to keep Nathan safe?" Elizabeth asked, the tone of her voice making the answer obvious.

"Beck is more like a one-man army," Jameson replied.

Per Jameson's plan, Kendra took the lead out of the hospital parking lot. Elizbeth was next, and through the Volvo's rear window she could see Jameson sitting in the passenger seat, his phone tight to his ear. Who he was talking to was anyone's guess.

"So, how did it go?" she asked Nathan.

"I don't know…all right, I guess." He glanced at the side mirror and saw a car following closely behind them. The bronze hood glistened in the late afternoon sun like a polished copper kettle.

"What did you tell her?" Elizabeth asked.

"There wasn't much to tell. I was riding home when two guys appeared out of nowhere. They stopped me on the sidewalk, acting like they were lost, then threw me in their van." As he spoke, his eyes were glued to the side mirror, watching Beck's car mimic their every turn. "She asked me if I'd ever seen them before, or if they said anything that might indicate why they abducted me."

"And you said…?"

Nathan gave her a pathetic look. *What do you think?*

"All right, dumb question," she said, trying to lighten the mood.

He turned in the seat, looking nervously out the back window. "We're being followed."

"Don't worry," Elizabeth said. "He's with us."

"Are you sure?"

"Positive. He's one of Sully's friends. His name is Beck."

Sully's friend.

To Nathan, that meant he was either a current or former policeman. Maybe even ex-military. Judging by the hulking size of the man, clearly visible a full car length away, Nathan settled on ex-military.

"He's another layer of protection," Elizabeth explained.

Good, Nathan thought. The way Romero had yanked him off the bike and muscled him into the van was a memory he couldn't shake, and something he never wanted to experience again. Still, a complete stranger helping them posed the unavoidable question. "What about Dad?" he asked. "What do we tell him?"

Elizabeth let out a troubled breath. "He's flying in later tonight, which gives me a few hours to figure that out."

"What's to figure out?" Nathan asked, frowning. "You tell him *nothing.*"

The previous year, his mother and Jameson had made it painfully clear: any discussion of the bookcase, or anything related to it, with his father, was strictly forbidden.

"Tell him nothing?" his mother repeated.

"Yes," Nathan insisted.

"I can't do that, Nathan. He's your father. He needs to know what happened today."

"No, he doesn't," Nathan countered.

"Okay, fine, then answer me this," she said. "What if he sees you on the news? Or me for that matter? Or Kendra? How am I supposed to explain that? You saw all the people watching from across the street, holding cell phones, recording the whole thing…"

Nathan tipped his head back against the headrest and stared at the roof. She was right. Someone was sure to post a video of Kendra smashing the window of the van, shouting at the driver, or the police dragging her and her friend away in handcuffs. It was too juicy not to post online. And once that happened, it would go viral.

They rode the rest of the way home in silence.

Sully was having an early dinner at a small dockside restaurant in the Old Port when his cell phone vibrated on the counter next to his plate. He recognized the number, with a Massachusetts area code, and answered at once. "Jameson, to what do I owe the pleasure?"

"Perry's men tried to grab Nathan today," Jameson said, forgoing his usual greeting.

Sully dropped the fork on his plate and stood. "Where?"

"A mile from his house. Luckily, Kendra was nearby and saw it go down."

"What happened?" Sully asked. He pulled a handful of bills from his wallet and tucked them under the plate, then hurried outside.

"Kendra followed them and managed to detain them until the police arrived."

"She *detained* them?" Sully repeated. "Let me guess. She had her bat."

"She always has her bat," Jameson said.

"Say no more," Sully told him as he walked to his car that was parked nearby. He climbed in and slid the key into the ignition, but didn't start the engine. "Where's Nathan now?" he asked.

"With Elizabeth, in the car directly behind us," Jameson said. "He went through a forensic interview at the hospital. We're headed back to the house to discuss where we go from here. As a precaution I brought in Beck. I hope you don't mind."

"Mind? Why would I mind?" Sully asked. "Tell him from now on he doesn't let Nathan out of his sight."

"Will do. How's it going up there?" Jameson asked, referring to Sully's ongoing search for Dan Perry and the *Greenwich* bookcase.

"We're combing every street and every neighborhood from Kittery to Old Orchard Beach," Sully said. "If this lunatic is really in southern Maine, like Nathan believes, we'll find him."

"Okay, stay in touch," Jameson said. "In the meantime, is there anything you need me to do?"

"Yes. Keep Nathan out of sight. That goes for his friend, Gina, too. We need to start thinking like Sun Tzu."

"Meaning?" Jameson asked.

"Know thy enemy."

"Agreed."

Jameson clicked off the call and immediately dialed Ellie's number.

"Jameson," she said brightly, picking up after the second ring. "How are you?"

"Ellie," he said without fanfare, "how soon can you meet me at Nathan's house?"

"Uh, I don't know…fifteen minutes? Why? Is everything okay?"

"Nathan's house. Fifteen minutes," he replied. "Sooner would be better. And Ellie?"

"Yeah?"

"Bring Gina."

Less than a minute after his conversation with Odom, Dan Perry sent him an encrypted file via a secure link. Odom took a moment to decipher the contents, then began his preparations. First, he brought up a map of each address on Perry's list, places that Nathan Cole was known to frequent. Odom studied the maps carefully, committing every street, public walkway, or footpath to memory. Another curious item in the file was the description of a bookcase that Perry believed resided at the Cole's residence in Arlington. Included in the information was a diagram of the bookcase, and a description of the item it held—an item that Perry desperately wanted to obtain.

Next, he assembled the various tools he would need for the job, packing them in a rugged black canvas bag with a heavy-duty zipper and wide, leather-reinforced, canvas handles. In a matching bag he packed extra clothes and a few bathroom essentials—enough to last him three days.

Finally, he walked through his palatial home, past priceless pieces of art that adorned the walls, to a short flight of stairs that led to a 10-car garage. Each bay held a different vehicle, each expertly maintained, fueled to capacity, and ready to use at a moment's notice. He walked past each one, pausing momentarily to assess its suitability, before moving on to the next.

The steel-gray Aston Martin DB9 coupe was tempting, but much too flashy. He needed something inconspicuous. The jet-black Chevy Suburban had the power and the storage space he needed, but the tinted windows gave it a government-vehicle look. Not flashy as much as daunting, the kind of thing that would get people talking.

The forest-green Mini Cooper was plenty quick, but much too small. The nondescript white commercial van, on the other hand, was too big and too slow. The silver Range Rover was a possibility, as was the pearl-white Chrysler Town & Country. Both were very common, family-style vehicles, and a regular fixture in most grocery store parking lots and at little league games. Either one would allow him to easily blend in.

After careful consideration, he settled on the Range Rover. It offered all the interior space he'd need, and the beefed-up engine would come in handy if he needed to evade a pursuer. Official or otherwise.

With that decided, he loaded everything in the back seat, then checked the Range Rover's hidden gun safe in the center console.

Weapons. *Check.*

Ammunition. *Check.*

He glanced at his watch, making note of the time, then went to the weight room at the opposite end of the house to shadow box and work the heavy bag.

At Nathan's house, Kendra and Jameson took a seat on the couch while Elizabeth went to the kitchen to round up drinks for the group. Nathan stood at the window, watching the street. Beck was parked at the curb near the mailbox, keeping an eye out for anything or anyone that looked suspicious.

Elizabeth came back from the kitchen and was setting a tray of

41

soft drinks on the coffee table when the front door opened. Ellie had just stepped inside when Gina pushed past her and tore into the living room.

"Nathan?" she exclaimed, looking frantically around the room. She spotted him at the window and ran to him. "I just saw it on TV," she said, wrapping both arms around him. "Are you all right?"

He struggled to break free but Gina wasn't having it. She continued to hold him as if a giant hand might smash through the window at any moment and pluck him from her grasp.

"I'm fine," he said calmly. "You can let go now."

As her arms fell away, her hand brushed his elbow.

"Oww!" he said, grabbing it gingerly.

"What is it? Are you injured?" she asked, when she saw the pained look on his face. "What did those monsters do to you?"

"I'm okay," he said. "It's just a scratch."

Ellie appeared at Gina's side and gave him a cursory inspection. "You gave us quite a scare there, buddy," she told him.

"Yeah, tell me about it," he muttered. His eyes instinctively wandered back to the window and he leaned closer to the glass, checking the street in both directions.

Ellie and Gina exchanged a worried look.

"Uh, if I could have everyone's attention," Jameson said. "We have much to discuss."

Gina took hold of Nathan, making sure not to touch his elbow, and gently eased him away from the window. "Come on," she whispered. "They're gone. You're safe now."

Safe, Nathan thought. *Yeah, right.*

Ellie took a seat on the couch next to Kendra. Nathan and Gina sat in the large overstuffed chairs that looked like two giant red peppers. Elizabeth paced the floor in front of the fireplace.

"What Nathan went through today never should've happened," Jameson began. "Dan Perry has been systematically observing this house for the past two weeks, using a variety of means. We underestimated his intentions, which was a critical mistake. That ends, starting now."

"Is this about the bookcase?" Ellie asked.

"*Two* bookcases," Nathan said.

"Oh, right," Ellie said softly.

"Perry obviously knows the secret that the two bookcases contain," Jameson said. "We know he has the *Greenwich* bookcase and that he wants its twin. Why? We don't know."

"What's his play here?" Ellie asked. "Why try to abduct Nathan?"

Gina bristled at the thought.

"I'm not exactly sure, but I've got a pretty good idea," Nathan said. "Perry's been trying to lure me back to Maine, using Richard Abbott and his love of rare books as bait."

"What are you saying?" Ellie asked. "He wants to use you as a bargaining chip for the bookcase?"

Nathan looked at her and nodded. There was a more permanent possibility, one that he didn't want to mention, let alone even think about.

"This is insanity," Elizabeth muttered. "We need to find him, and fast."

"Yeah we do," Kendra said, nodding, her face awash with anger.

Jameson addressed Nathan directly. "Since Perry tried once, and failed, we have to assume he'll try again. And because he had no problem attempting to take you in broad daylight, the next time could be even more brazen."

"What do you mean?" Gina asked.

"He might try something here at the house," Jameson said, "which is why we're going to institute a series of safeguards for Nathan, and for you too, Gina."

Gina's face went blank. "You think he'll try to take *me?*" she said.

"I do," Jameson replied. "You're just as much a part of this as Nathan, and like I said, we can't afford to underestimate Perry's intentions again."

"What safeguards?" Elizabeth asked.

"For starters, Nathan needs to vanish. If Perry and his men can't find him, then we'll avoid a repeat of what happened this afternoon."

Nathan flopped back in the chair. *Vanish? To where?* he wondered. *Who's going to protect the bookcase if Perry tries to break in? Russ McCullough? All by himself? Right.*

And then it came to him.

The perfect solution.

It was so simple, so painfully obvious, that it took every bit of restraint he could muster to keep from jumping up from the chair and running upstairs to the third floor.

Darkness had just begun to fall when Odom climbed out of the shower, got dressed, and went to the kitchen to fix his dinner. It was later than usual, but for this job that was actually a good thing. He'd eat a leisurely dinner, clean up, then make the trip north. The darkness, like a heavy cloak in a storm, would provide him with ample cover as he began the crucial first task— surveillance.

Tuesday 11:50 P.M.

Nathan dozed off, then awoke. Dozed off, then awoke. Each time, he was jolted from his sleep by the same nightmarish image: a pair of burly hands grabbing his shoulders; the powerful fingers digging into his flesh, pulling him from his bike and dragging him toward the van. Just after midnight, he threw back the covers and went to the window. The street was empty, every house dark, the only light coming from a few dim streetlamps and the milk-white moonlight breaking through the clouds. It was time.

He went to the door, eased it open a few inches, and listened. The eerie stillness beckoned to him: *sleep time is over—it's time to get to work.*

Moving quickly and quietly, he grabbed his flashlight from the bedside table and tiptoed down the hallway to the attic stairs. He grasped the handrail tightly and made his way up to the third floor, gently placing his foot on each stair tread before slowly applying his full weight. *Easy does it,* he told himself, moving in super-slow motion. The wooden treads were old and dry, and creaked softly, but not loud enough for anyone downstairs to hear.

At the top of the stairs, he paused, then inched his way across the landing to the attic door. After a painfully slow turn of the doorknob he pulled the door open and stepped inside. The dry air, heavy with the stale odor of old cardboard, brought back memories of the previous year and the seemingly innocent visit to the attic that started him down the dangerous path where he currently found himself.

He couldn't help but wonder how his life would've proceeded had he not entered the room that day; if he'd never seen the stray book lying on the floor, the one that led him to the mysterious bookcase hiding in the corner.

It took him an eternity to reach it, squeezing past crooked stacks of cardboard boxes, and ducking dust-covered garment bags that hung from the rafters. With each step, the floorboards gave out a painful creak, like a nail being pried from a plank.

Standing before the bookcase, he ran the beam of his flashlight over each shelf. Top to bottom and side to side. To anyone else, it would appear to be an ordinary bookcase. Only a chosen few knew that it held a secret rumored to be as immense as it was deadly, put there by his ancestor, Thomas Hammond.

Dan Perry knew the secret. What's more, Nathan knew he'd do anything to obtain it, including breaking in and stealing the bookcase altogether. If he somehow managed to do that, the secret would be lost forever, and everything Thomas Hammond had worked and died for would've been for naught.

Nathan had no intention of letting that happen. Not if he could find the secret and remove it first. After that, let Perry come and take the bookcase. All he'd have is another antique to add his collection. But he wouldn't have what was hidden inside it. With any luck, they'd catch him in the process.

By Nathan's estimation, it was five hours until daybreak. Shortly after breakfast, according to the safeguards Jameson had put in place, Beck would take Nathan to a remote location. "A safehouse," Jameson had called it, a place where Nathan would be virtually invisible while Sully and his team searched for Dan Perry in southern Maine.

Gina, on the other hand, would stay home under the watchful eye of Ellie. Gina would have to stay out of sight, but how hard would that be for a girl who spent her free time reading and vanquishing puzzle books with her trusty pencil?

He peeled a spider web from his face and began his search. Starting at the top of the bookcase, he ran his hands along the front and underside of each shelf. He imagined Thomas Hammond, a skilled woodworker, crafting a hiding place that would be naked to the eye. But to hold what? Given the simple construction of the bookcase, what possible hiding places did it offer? Nathan figured he'd know when he saw it.

He finished checking the shelves and knelt down to inspect the Doric columns that adorned either side of the front. After that, he examined all four bun feet, shining his flashlight into the narrow opening beneath the case. Other than spider nests, there was nothing.

He moved to his left and studied the side of the case, then did the same on the opposite side, running the light over every inch of the dark wood, looking for an indentation, a dent or a ding—any seemingly innocent imperfection Thomas Hammond may have fashioned for a fingertip to slip into and trigger a hidden compartment.

When his search produced nothing, he aimed his flashlight at the three-inch space that separated the bookcase from the attic wall. It was another jungle of spider nests and webs, and after a deep breath he pushed his hair back behind his ear and slipped his hand into the narrow opening. "It's got to be back here," he said, running his fingers over the back side of the case.

Just then, the attic door swung open. He froze, his heart pounding as a bright beam of light swept across the room, slowly creeping toward the bookcase. When it reached him, it stopped, instantly blinding him.

"Nathan?"

He held up his free hand, trying to block the light. "Dad?"

David lowered the flashlight and plowed through the mess, twisting and turning and bumping into stacks of cardboard boxes and plastic totes along the way.

Nathan quickly pulled his hand from behind the bookcase and began brushing webs and grit from his shirtsleeve. Seconds later, his father appeared at his side.

"I heard about what happened today," David said. "Are you okay?"

"Yeah," Nathan mumbled with a shrug, like it was just another day in the life of 12-year old Nathan Cole.

David moved closer and hugged him for several long seconds, then stepped back. He eyed the bookcase briefly, then looked at Nathan. "Are you packed?" he asked.

"Packed?" Nathan replied.

"For your trip."

"What trip?" Nathan asked, playing dumb.

David ignored the question. "I know it feels extreme, but it's just for the time being."

"Who told you that?" Nathan asked.

"Your mother."

Nathan's eyes went wide. "She did?" he blurted out, "uh... I mean...oh."

David took him by the shoulders and looked him straight in the eye. "Now listen to me," he said. "I don't want you to worry. Hiding you is the smart thing to do. It's the only way we can ensure your safety."

We? Nathan thought.

David saw the confused look on his face and said, "He's not going to stop. You understand that, right? He's going to keep coming for you."

"I don't know who you're talking about," Nathan lied.

"You know *exactly* who I'm talking about."

"Seriously, Dad…I have no idea who—w"

"STOP! You think this is a game? You think he's just going to quit pursuing you?"

"I…uh…" Nathan mumbled, struggling to think of a response.

"Dan Perry will not stop," David said forcefully. "Not until he gets what he wants."

Nathan's eyes went wide. "You *know* about Dan Perry?"

3

Eddie

Nathan grabbed the side of the bookcase to steady himself. *This can't be*, he told himself.

David brushed a spider out of his hair, then swatted at another one scurrying up his arm. "This place gives me the creeps," he said, looking up at the web-covered rafters. "Come on, let's get out of here. We can talk downstairs."

Nathan followed him out, stumbling toward the door amid a fog of questions. *He knows about Dan Perry? How can that be? Did Mom tell him? She must have. But why? What was she thinking?*

They went into the living room and Nathan plopped down in one of the large red chairs. David took a seat directly across from him on the couch. "You must be asking yourself a number of questions," he said, when he saw the bewildered look on Nathan's face.

Nathan remained quiet, eyeing him suspiciously. Something wasn't right here. In fact, something was very *wrong* here.

"You know that your Aunt Sarah and I attended the same college, right?" David said.

Nathan nodded sadly at the mention of his long-lost aunt, a woman he never knew, but with whom he shared a common bond—the discovery of the *Greenwich* bookcase.

"And you know that we were seeing each other, outside of school?"

Nathan gave another nod. *How does he know that I know that?* he wondered.

David leaned forward and rested his elbows on his knees, his hands clasped together, staring at the floor as he spoke. "What you don't know is that after she died, your grandfather asked for my help. He was very insistent. He made me promise."

"Promise what?"

"That I'd protect your mother."

"Protect her against what?"

"He believed that dark forces were behind Sarah's untimely death, and that they were somehow tied to the *Greenwich* bookcase. There was no proof of this, but your grandfather—"

"Wait!" Nathan blurted out.

"What's wrong?" his father asked, looking up.

"You *know* about the *Greenwich* bookcase?"

"Yes. As I was saying, your grandfather suspected it was linked to Sarah's death. For years he and I searched for proof but we couldn't find a connection. Now, however, thanks to you, we know that she found the *Greenwich* bookcase."

"You're telling me you *know* about the *Greenwich* bookcase," Nathan said, the idea still not firmly rooted in his mind.

"Yes. Sarah told me about it during our time together."

"Then, you know about both bookcases... and their...uh... secret?"

"I know everything you know," David said. *And more.*

Nathan's jaw fell open.

"It's true," David said.

"Hold on," Nathan fired back, still grasping at reality. "You know about last year, and the boxcar?"

"Yes."

"And Charles Warren?"

David nodded. *Yup.*

Nathan looked away, shaking his head. "Unbelievable," he muttered. "All this time, you *knew?*"

"Yes."

"But wait," Nathan said. "Mom, and Jameson...they told me—"

"Not to talk to me about the bookcase on the third floor?" David cut in.

"Not *ever,*" Nathan said.

"Because, in my grief over Sarah's death, I might overreact and destroy it?"

"Yeah."

David stifled a grin.

"What?" Nathan asked.

"That was my idea."

"Your idea," Nathan confirmed, his face growing hotter.

"Yes."

Nathan stood up and paced the length of the room. This was crazy, and the simple act of walking helped to ease the anger that was welling up inside him. It took nearly a minute, but when he spoke again, his emotions had shifted. "Why?" he said softly, unable to hide his feelings of betrayal.

"Why what?" David asked.

"Why the lie?"

"Come. Sit," David said, gesturing toward the red chair.

Nathan walked back, reluctantly, and sat down, resting his elbow on the arm of the chair as he cradled his head in his hands. *They lied to me*, he thought. *All of them. They lied!*

"Your mother and I..." his father began, then paused.

Nathan looked up. "You and Mom what?" he snapped.

His father let out a long breath. "Our job, first and foremost," he said slowly, "is to protect you. I think you know that." He paused again. "For that reason, we knew that..." he said, his words falling off again.

His mother appeared in the doorway. She was wearing her long blue robe and her hair was unbrushed and ragged. "What your father is trying to say," she said, "is that we knew this would happen." She walked over and sat down next to David on the couch.

"You knew what would happen?" Nathan asked.

"That once you discovered the bookcase in the attic, you would eventually learn the deeper truth behind it."

"That it has a twin?" Nathan said. "And together they hold a deadly secret."

"Yes."

"And what? You thought it would be wrong for me to know the

truth?"

"It's not what we think, Nathan, it's what we know," David said, looking at him intently. "We knew that once you found out the full story behind the bookcase, your life would be in danger."

"And we knew you'd have questions," Elizabeth said. "Lots of questions. But given the potential danger, and for the safety of everyone involved, we needed to keep a lid on it. That meant less talk, not more."

"Less talk," Nathan said. "Great."

"That's the way it's been in our family for generations," his mother explained. "We assumed that whoever stole the *Greenwich* bookcase would want its twin, given what the two bookcases are rumored to contain. And because we didn't know who they were, until now, we couldn't risk anyone overhearing us talk about it. Not after..." she began, then looked away, emotions choking her words.

"Not after what?"

David nudged her with his knee. *Tell him.*

She hesitated momentarily. "Your grandfather had an older brother. His name was Kenneth Hammond."

"You never said anything about him having a brother," Nathan said.

"That's right. He was long gone before you were born."

"Gone? You mean...?" Nathan began.

"Vanished," his father replied.

"Huh?"

"Kenneth was the first one to locate the *Greenwich* bookcase, but in his haste to get it back, he made a number of critical mistakes."

"What kind of mistakes?"

"For starters, he spoke of it openly," his mother said. "Not only around the family, but with strangers as well. Then, to make matters worse, he set out to retrieve it alone, without the help or protection of anyone in our family."

"What happened?" Nathan asked.

"We don't know," his father said.

"What do you mean, you don't know?"

"He disappeared," Elizabeth said.

A deafening silence fell over the room. The only sound to be heard was the soft *tick-tick-tick* of the mantle clock.

"This is why I came up with the story about…you know… destroying the bookcase on the third floor if I were to learn the truth about it," David said. "By doing so, it took me out of the loop, so to speak. I figured, if you couldn't talk about it with me, your own father, you'd understand the seriousness of it."

"And you'd be less inclined to discuss it with others," Elizabeth added.

"So, all this time, you've been playing dumb," Nathan said.

"Pretty much."

Nathan turned to his mother. "And you," he said. "Your concern about Dad finding out was all an act? The bookcase, the mysteries I solved, the camera that Russ installed outside?"

"Yes. It was done for your safety."

"My safety," he repeated, like that wasn't a good enough reason.

"You've *seen* what Dan Perry is capable of," Elizabeth said. "And it's only going to get worse. Ever since you found the *Greenwich* bookcase in his shop, you've become a target."

"Oh, so this is *my* fault," Nathan said, flopping back in the chair.

"No, that's not what we're saying."

"Is that the real reason you're making me leave? Not for my own safety, but as punishment…because I found out the truth?"

"No, that's not it at all. You know it isn't."

Nathan stood, his anger surging. "I can't believe it. You both lied to me."

"Nathan—"

"You know? Sometimes I wish I'd never found that bookcase!" he exclaimed, then stormed out of the room.

"Nathan, wait," his father called out.

"Just forget it," Nathan growled as he marched up the stairs.

"Let him go," Elizabeth said. "It's late, and he's going to need some time to process all of this."

"We have to tell him the rest," David said.

"No," Elizabeth said firmly. "Absolutely not."

Standing on the lawn, keeping several feet back from the window where he couldn't be seen, Odom watched as Elizabeth turned off the lamp and followed David out of the room. The sound of an approaching car made Odom move closer to the house. Standing upright, his body pressed tightly against the clapboards, he watched a red Dodge Neon speed past. He was starting across the lawn when a glint of light from the tree at the corner of the property made him stop short. He cut a wide arc around the tree and came up directly behind it. On one of the branches he saw the camera, a thread of moonlight reflecting off its plastic housing.

Installed weeks earlier, by Russ McCullough, a family friend and former officer with the Brookline and Cambridge Police

Departments, it had proven useful in monitoring the activity in front of Nathan and Gina's house.

Odom made a mental note of the camera's location and angle, knowing he'd have to adjust his approach to the house when he returned to collect the package.

Nathan got as far as his bedroom door, then paused. It was late, but in just a few hours he'd be whisked away to some unknown location. Where that was, he had no idea. It was the one detail Jameson had left out. Wherever it was, it would effectively end any chance he had of finding what was hidden in the bookcase. That meant, if he was going to find it, he had to do it now.

He pushed his bedroom door open, then pulled it shut. Hard. The sound echoed up and down the hallway, sending a clear message: I'm mad and I don't want to talk to you; leave me alone. Then, like before, he eased down the hallway and made his way up the attic stairs.

After finding nothing on the outside of the bookcase during his initial search, it was clear that whatever was hidden in the bookcase was on the inside. So, this time, he decided to try another approach. Starting with the bottom shelf, he'd remove the books and stack them in short piles on the floor. After that, he'd inspect the inside of the case. Every inch, every surface, checking for anything that looked suspicious.

He stepped into the attic and fought his way back through the maze of junk again, all the while pulling rubbery spider webs from his face. When he reached the bookcase, he knelt down and got right to work. The books were packed tightly on the shelf, and using the tip of his finger he reached in to pry one out. When it wouldn't move he tried another one. Same thing. He tried a third time, using both hands, but it still wouldn't work. He went shelf by shelf, but each time he got the same result.

Every book was stuck in place.

Wednesday, 7:00 A.M.

"Nathan! Wake up!"

Nathan was lying face down across the bed, his feet hanging off the edge. He was still dressed in his clothes from the previous day, looking like he'd been steamrolled.

"NATHAN!" his mother said again, louder.

His head came up off the pillow like it weighed a thousand pounds. "Huh?" His eyes felt like they were glued shut.

"Get up," his mother said. "Beck is waiting, and you need to eat."

Nathan flopped his head back down on the pillow. "Do we *have* to do this?"

"Yes. We already talked about it. Now, let's go."

He didn't move.

"NATHAN?!"

"All *right*," he grumbled.

He rolled over and draped his arm across his eyes, trying to block out the light. The last thing he remembered was sneaking up to the attic— a visit that was cut short by the strange behavior of the bookcase. In all his time with it, he'd never had a problem removing a book. Quite the opposite. The first book had literally thrown itself at him, refusing to stay on the shelf.

Through half-opened eyes he checked the clock on his bedside table. 7:00 am. "You've got to be kidding me," he groaned. He climbed out of bed and got dressed, and when he walked into the kitchen several minutes later, his father was hard at work at the stove, stirring a large pan of scrambled eggs. On the counter was an oval platter heaped with crispy bacon, a casserole dish loaded high with home fries, and a pitcher of orange juice.

"Good morning," his father said. "I hope you're hungry."

Nathan looked at the clock on the stove. 7:20 am. By this time his parents were usually rushing out the door to go to work. "This is Wednesday, right?" he asked.

"Yup."

"You're not going to work?"

"Your mother and I are both taking the day off," his father said, scraping the eggs onto a waiting plate.

Nathan stared at the counter. Something was off. Next to the food was a stack of plates and a pile of napkins, each rolled tightly around a fork, knife, and spoon. "Are we expecting company?" he asked.

"Yes," his father said. "Do me a favor. Beck is outside. Go tell him it's time to eat."

"What's he doing outside?"

"Watching."

"Watching what?" Nathan asked.

"Everything."

Nathan went out the back door and circled the house. When he came around to the front, he saw Beck standing next to one of the columns on the front porch. His face showed no emotion as his eyes swept slowly from one end of the street to the other.

"Time to eat," Nathan said, from the bottom of the front steps.

Beck went to the screen door, held it open, and gestured for Nathan to go inside. As Nathan made his way up the steps, a late model Chevy Nova came down the street. It slowed as it passed the house, then pulled to the curb directly across from Gina's mailbox.

"Inside," Beck said, his eyes tracking the car.

Nathan reached the top of the steps and turned to look. "What is it?"

"Go," Beck said, firmly.

"All right, I'm going," Nathan grumbled. He went inside and stopped to look back, watching through the screen as Beck walked down the steps and made a beeline for the car. It was a reclamation project by all appearances. The original green paint had faded, and various sections of the body had been replaced and were coated with gray primer. A cowl induction hood had been installed but was yet to be painted.

Beck approached the driver's side window and saw the driver, a boy in his late teens, talking on his phone. The kid nearly jumped out of his skin when he turned and saw Beck's hulking shape. After eyeing him briefly, he resumed talking on his phone.

Beck rapped on the glass with his knuckle.

The kid scowled...*go away*...then waved him off with the back of his hand like he was swatting at a fruit fly.

That's when Beck pulled the door open.

Odom was parked in a driveway at the far end of the street.

Fifteen minutes earlier, he'd watched from the corner as the owners left for work. Once they were out of sight, he pulled into their driveway. Using a high-end pair of Zeiss binoculars, he had a clear view of the proceedings in front of Gina's house. Clearly, the $50 bill he'd slipped the kid at the gas station to drive his Nova past Nathan's house and pull to the curb had paid handsome dividends. Now he knew that the family had brought in extra muscle. But were there more? Only time would tell, not that it really mattered. For Odom, more bodies, no matter how big they were, were a minor wrinkle. He'd faced similar opposition on countless occasions, without serious consequence.

He checked his watch—it was time for breakfast. He packed the binoculars in his travel bag, then sat back in the seat, watching Beck through the passenger-side window, waiting for the right moment to back out of the driveway without calling attention to himself.

Beck walked back to the house as the Nova sped away. The driver, a wanna-be tough guy named Eddie, wouldn't be driving down this street again any time soon. Beck had seen to that. But the kid's lame excuse for being there in the first place had given Beck an uneasy feeling. His gut told him it was a set-up, a ploy designed to test the vulnerability of the house, and by association, Nathan. If that were the case, then it had worked to perfection. The thought of being played by an unknown adversary made Beck's stomach burn. From now on he'd be more careful.

"Who was that?" Elizabeth asked him when he walked into the kitchen. She'd been upstairs in the bathroom when she heard a commotion out in the street. When she came downstairs to see what it was, she'd found Nathan standing at the front door, his jaw hanging open in disbelief.

"Nobody you know," Beck said in a guarded tone.

"Why was he parked across from Gina's house?"

"He was lost."

The tone in his voice told her there was more to it than he was letting on.

Just then, the front doorbell rang. Nathan went to answer it and came back moments later with Russ McCullough, who'd been recruited to keep an eye on the house, should Dan Perry attempt to break in and steal the bookcase from the attic. Perry's name and detailed history with the Cole family had been purposefully kept from McCullough, who only knew of a vague threat.

"Hope I'm not late," he said, nodding to the assembled group. When he saw Beck, he did a double take.

"Russ, this is Beck," Elizabeth said.

"Russ McCullough," Russ said, extending his hand.

As they shook, Beck offered his customary nod. *Sir.*

The sound of shuffling footsteps and chatter erupted in the back hall, and seconds later Ellie and Gina appeared. Following right behind them were Jameson and Kendra.

"Ah, perfect timing," Nathan's father said. He set the plate of eggs on the counter and said, "Everyone, grab a plate and dig in. Coffee will be ready in just a minute."

Nathan's parents sat at the kitchen table with Russ, Jameson, and Beck. Kendra and Ellie sat at the counter, taking turns eyeing Beck's massive frame and chiseled good looks. Nathan was in no mood to eat and went to the living room. Gina followed, plate in hand, and they took a seat on either end of the couch.

"Did they tell you where he's taking you?" Gina asked, folding a piece of toast in half before taking a bite.

Nathan frowned and kicked at the leg of the coffee table.

"I'll take that as a no," Gina said.

Nathan gave the coffee table another kick.

"What's the matter?" she asked.

He looked out into the front hallway to make sure no one was standing there, then said, "I can't go. Not now."

"What do you mean, you can't go?" she said, attacking the pile of bacon on her plate. "Of course you can. You have to. Or do you want a repeat of what happened yesterday?"

"It's not me I'm worried about," he said. "It's the bookcase."

She dropped the bacon and looked over at him, dumbfounded. "What is *wrong* with you?" she said loudly.

"Quiet," he hissed, checking the hallway again.

"No, I won't be quiet. You want to hang around here where Dan Perry can find you? Then what? You'll fight him off?" She stabbed at the air with her fork, mocking him. "Get back, or I'll jab you. I mean it. Take one more step and I'll do it!"

"Go ahead, make jokes," he said. "But I need to find what's hidden inside the bookcase before he tries to take it…and he *will* try to take it. That's what this is all about, remember?"

"Then, go upstairs and get it…whatever *it* is."

"I tried," he said, looking away. "Twice."

"And?"

63

"I couldn't find it," he mumbled.

"I'm sorry, what was that?"

"I couldn't find it," Nathan said, only slightly louder.

"What do you mean you couldn't find it?" Gina snapped. "It's a bookcase. Did you check everywhere? The top? The sides? The back?"

"Yes."

"Underneath?"

"Uh-huh."

"Well, you obviously overlooked something."

"No," he insisted, with a firm look. "I checked every square inch."

"How about inside?" she said. "You know, *behind* the books?"

"I thought of that, but…"

"But, what?" she said impatiently.

"They were stuck."

"They were *what?*"

"Stuck."

She gave him a look. "What's that supposed to mean?"

"Just like it sounds," he said. "I tried to pull the books off the shelf but they wouldn't budge."

"Oh brother," she sighed, picking up another piece of bacon. "Here we go again."

Elizabeth circled the table with a carafe, offering refills of coffee. As she was filling Beck's mug, she said, "What was it that you didn't want to tell me earlier?"

Jameson looked at both of them, confused.

"We had a visitor today," Elizabeth explained.

"Yes, I saw that," Russ said, an indication that he was still monitoring the feed from the remote camera he had installed in the tree at the corner of the property. He looked over at Beck. "You have a very…uh…interesting way of dealing with strangers."

"Had to be done," Beck said, scooping up the last of the scrambled eggs on his plate.

"What visitor?" Jameson asked, suddenly concerned.

"His full name is Edward Waller," Russ said. "He lives on Dunbar Street in Medford." As he had done on several previous occasions, he had checked the plate number captured on the camera feed.

"He was just a punk kid," Beck explained.

"But…?" Elizabeth asked, knowing there was more to the story than he was telling.

"He said he was lost."

"Lost?"

"It was a lie," Beck said. He set his fork on the empty plate and pushed it away.

"How could you tell?" Jameson asked.

"People who are lost don't act like that."

"Like what?"

"Cocky."

"Go on," Jameson said.

Beck sat back in the chair, making it creak softly. "I think someone put him up to it, to see what would happen."

"You think he's testing us," Jameson suggested.

"Yes."

"And you didn't think Nathan needed to know that?" Elizabeth asked.

"No," Beck said. "Not after everything he went through yesterday."

"Wait a minute," Russ said. "What happened yesterday?"

Elizabeth looked at David, then at Jameson. "We need to tell him" she said.

"Tell me what?" Russ asked.

Jameson and David both nodded their approval.

"You heard about what happened in North Cambridge yesterday afternoon?" Elizabeth asked.

"I didn't actually see the news report, but, yeah, I heard something about it. Somebody tried to abduct a kid?"

"That kid?" Elizabeth said, "was Nathan."

"What?" Russ blurted out, dropping his fork on his plate.

"It's true," Jameson said. "If not for Kendra, they might've succeeded."

Russ thought for a moment, then addressed Elizabeth directly. "The threat you told me about when you brought me in to help watch the house, is this the same group? Because if it is," he said uneasily, "this is a clear escalation of their intent. I think it's time you brought in the authorities."

Elizabeth looked across the table at Jameson. *Do you want to take this or should I?*

Jameson tapped his chest. *I'll do it.* "It all comes down to what we can prove," he told Russ. "At the moment, all we have are theories."

"All right," Russ said. "But if you do get something you can prove, the police will want to know. You understand that, right? They'll be conducting their own investigation into what happened yesterday and anything you could share could help prevent this from happening again. Not just to Nathan, but to other children as well."

"Of course," Jameson assured him.

Russ pointed at Beck. "Is that why *he's* here?"

"Yes. I asked Beck to help us. From here on out he'll be guarding Nathan. As soon as we're done here, he'll take Nathan to a secure location."

"Smart," Russ said. "What about Gina? Awhile back you told me this threat could affect her as well."

"I'm staying with her," Ellie said.

"Good," Russ said. Then, to Jameson, "What would you like me to do?"

"You keep monitoring the camera feed. Let us know the minute you see anything suspicious."

"Will do. I'll also check with the Cambridge Police Department, see if they've come up with anything."

"You really think they'll tell you?" Elizabeth asked. *They wouldn't tell me squat.*

"I've still got a few friends in the department," Russ replied.

Jameson said nothing. McCullough could dig all he wanted, ask all the questions in the world, but the Cambridge police would have nothing to tell him. Dan Perry was too good. His tracks would be so well covered that nothing from the previous day would lead back to him. The two men from the van had vanished into thin air like the early morning mist. The van itself would turn out to be stolen, or rented under a fake name. The investigation would wither and die, but Perry wouldn't quit. He was coming for Nathan and the bookcase. Coming hard. It reminded Jameson that he needed to call

Sully for an update.

Odom finished his breakfast and drove back to the driveway at the end of Nathan's street. More cars were parked in Nathan's driveway, which was intriguing. Something was happening. But what? He discarded the question and called Dan Perry.

"You have news for me?" Perry asked.

"On site now," Odom replied.

"Evaluation?"

"Lots of activity."

"I expected as much," Perry said calmly. "Will it be a problem?"

"No."

"Estimated time of pick up?" Perry asked.

"Soon."

Nathan stared across the room, his mind hard at work trying to think of some last-minute excuse for not going with Beck— something, anything, that would give him more time to search the bookcase. Sadly, nothing was coming to mind. Nothing that would work, anyway.

"Have you considered that maybe there is no hidden secret?" Gina asked, breaking the silence.

Nathan snapped out of his funk. "Huh?"

"Maybe the hidden secret thing was just made up," she said.

He gave her a look. *Yeah, right…like my family would do that.*

"It could happen," she said defensively.

"Why would they do that?" he asked.

"Who knows?" Gina said, shrugging. "But you said it yourself—

you looked twice and you couldn't find it."

"Correction, I haven't found it yet."

"Well, I hate to break it to you, but you're out of time. You're going with Beck. Period. End of story." *Even if I have to drag you out of here kicking and screaming*, she thought.

Nathan opened his mouth to respond when his mother appeared in the doorway. "Ready to go?"

"Yes, he is," Gina said matter-of-factly.

Nathan gave her a disgusted look, then stood up and trudged out of the room like he was wearing concrete sneakers. When he reached the kitchen, most of the group were standing near the entryway to the back-hall stairs, talking amongst themselves. Missing from the throng were Jameson and Beck, who were over near the window. Beck was leaning down whispering something to Jameson, who was slowly nodding his head. When Beck finished, Jameson addressed the group.

"Okay folks, listen up," he said loudly. "There's been change of plan."

Nathan froze, eyes wide. "I don't have to go?" he said excitedly.

"Oh, you're still going," Jameson said.

Nathan's shoulders drooped. *Great.*

"We're all going to leave together," Jameson announced. He turned to Ellie and said, "That includes you and Gina."

"Me?" Gina asked, surprised. "Where am I going?"

"Actually, nowhere," Jameson replied.

"Huh?"

"Yeah, what are you talking about?" Ellie asked.

"If Beck's suspicion is right, and the house is being watched, we all need to leave together. Ellie, you take Gina and go…anywhere."

"Anywhere?"

"Downtown, the gas station, Kendra's coffee shop, it really doesn't matter," Jameson said. "Be back within 30 minutes, but when you leave, have Gina sit in the front seat where she can be seen. On the way back, have her lie down in the back seat, out of sight. When you pull into the driveway, park in the garage and close the door. Check the street. Then, when it's clear, bring her in the house through the back door."

"So it looks like she took me somewhere and dropped me off," Gina said.

"Exactly. You two will keep an eye on the house." He looked directly at Ellie. "Call me at the first sign of anything suspicious."

"Will do," she said.

To Nathan, Jameson said, "You go with Beck, and do *everything* he tells you. Understood?"

"Whatever," Nathan mumbled under his breath.

Elizabeth stepped forward and gently guided him into the front hallway. "You're angry," she said. "I get that. But it's like we told you already, this has to be done."

"Mom," he said, keeping his voice low. "I can't leave. Not now. Who's going to guard the bookcase? What if he breaks in and steals it? Someone has to be here to—"

"Whoa!" she said, gesturing with both hands. "The bookcase will be fine."

"You don't know that."

"Yes. I do. We've taken steps to keep it safe, and—"

"What steps?" he cut in.

70

"Steps," she said firmly, indicating she'd say no more about it. "Right now, the most important thing is keeping you safe. Now, go get your suitcase. It's time to go."

"Go? Go where?"

"You'll see."

Nathan studied the vague look on her face. "You don't know where Beck is taking me, do you?" he said.

"Actually, no, I don't. Jameson arranged it."

"And you're *okay* with that?" he blurted out.

Everyone in the kitchen turned and looked.

"Yes," she said calmly. "I trust Jameson completely. He has some experience in these matters."

"Experience?" Nathan asked, with a suspicious look. "In what?"

"Hiding people."

4

Braden Street

They all went outside at the same time. Single file. Walking slowly but with purpose, like a fire drill. One by one they piled into their respective cars. Then it was showtime.

Kendra and Jameson left first, the springs of the faded blue Volvo squeaking loudly as she backed out into the street, then chugged slowly past Gina's house. Russ McCullough was next. He followed Kendra down the street, instinctively scanning the neighborhood as he drove. Then it was Beck and Nathan's turn. The Caprice came to life with a low growl, and Beck drove north, past Nathan's house. Elizabeth and David took separate cars and drove in opposite directions. Ellie and Gina were last. Like Kendra and Russ, they drove south, past Gina's house.

Odom pressed the binoculars to his eyes and watched through the side window as the first car backed out of the driveway. That alone was nothing noteworthy. But then a second car backed out. Then a third. "Well, well, what do we have here?" he said. When he caught sight of Nathan in the bronze-colored Caprice, and Gina in the Subaru hatchback, each being whisked away in opposite directions, he knew better than to think they'd be returning anytime soon. This was all part of some elaborate show. The families sensed an imminent threat and were moving the kids to another location.

Odom shook his head, frowning. Could they make it any more obvious? Six cars? Each leaving within seconds of each other? Driving in opposite directions? Unless the house was on fire, which it clearly wasn't, there were playing the shell game. A short con. Now you see them, now you don't.

A grin crept across his face. "Amateurs," he said with disdain as he slipped the binoculars back into his travel bag. They had no idea who they were dealing with. In their foolish attempt to deceive him, they'd created the perfect opening. Perry wanted the kid. But even more than that, he wanted the item hidden in the bookcase. Odom assumed that Perry's plan all along was to use the kid to get the contents of the bookcase. But now the house was empty. So, Odom reasoned, why not just find the bookcase and retrieve the hidden item? It would be an easy in, easy out, just the way he liked it—much like Perry, a man who wielded considerable power and appreciated timely results above all else.

With his mind made up, he waited until the street was clear then started the Range Rover and backed out of the driveway.

Time was of the essence.

He had to move quickly.

At the end of the street, Beck turned right and headed downtown. He hadn't gone far when he abruptly spun the wheel and swerved down a narrow side street. He drove slowly, watching the rearview mirror, and when he was sure they weren't being followed he pulled to the curb.

Nathan checked the houses on both sides of the street. "This is it?" he asked, with a confused expression. "This is, like, four blocks from my house. We could've *walked*."

Beck ignored him and got out. He circled the car and stopped at the front passenger-side door. After a quick check of the street in both directions, he opened it. "Get out," he said.

"Out?" Nathan asked. "How come?"

"Just do it."

"Seriously?"

"Now," Beck said.

Nathan groaned, then climbed out.

Like a hotel valet, Beck opened the rear passenger-side door and motioned with his hand. "Get in."

"What?" Nathan said. "First you want me out, then you want me in. Make up your mind."

"I won't ask again," Beck said.

"All right, relax," Nathan moaned, then slid into the back seat. "There. Happy now?"

Again, Beck ignored the sarcasm and went to the trunk. He came back with a thick blanket that was folded tightly into a neat square. "Here," he said, handing it to Nathan. "Cover yourself."

Nathan looked at the blanket but didn't take it. "This is a joke, right?"

"No," Beck said, tossing the blanket in Nathan's lap. "Do it."

"This is ridiculous," Nathan muttered as he unfolded the blanket and covered his feet and legs.

"Down," Beck said.

"What?"

"Lie down."

"You've *got* to be kidding me," Nathan said.

"Do you need help?"

The calm in his voice was unnerving, and Nathan stretched out on the seat and pulled the blanket up to his chin.

"All the way," Beck said.

"Oh, come on!"

When Beck started to climb in the back seat, Nathan quickly ducked under the blanket. Beck closed the door, walked around the front end of the car, and climbed in behind the wheel.

"This blanket smells," Nathan said.

"Deal with it."

"Yeah…okay…thanks," Nathan grumbled. *Jerk.*

The blanket had been Jameson's idea. The less Nathan knew about where he was being taken, the less likely he'd be to do something reckless. Or so they thought.

Kendra was steering through traffic, passing slow-moving cars and mumbling obscenities, when Jameson pulled his cell phone from his pocket and called Sully. His longtime friend answered at once.

"Jameson, I was just about to call you. How did it go?"

"We had to make a slight adjustment," Jameson said, "but so far so good."

"What adjustment?"

Jameson explained the green Chevy Nova and Beck's assessment that it was a ploy by Dan Perry to test their defenses.

"Beck's right," Sully declared. "Perry's poking the bear."

"My thought exactly," Jameson replied. "You said you were about to call?"

"Yeah, I searched for Perry's known associates. Wives, family, girlfriends, you name it."

"And?"

"Well, I'm no computer genius," Sully admitted, "but from what I could find, he has no immediate family in the area. As far as associates, I only found a handful of shopkeepers in the Old Port, and a few local fishermen."

"Of course," Jameson said, excitement in his voice. "I completely forgot. He had a boat. Did you check with—?"

"On my way there now," Sully cut in.

"Good," Jameson said. "Let me know if you find anything."

"Will do," Sully replied.

Several minutes later, he eased his dark blue Crown Vic through the front gate of the South Portland Marina.

Nathan lay sideways on the seat, sweltering beneath the blanket, which was made from some kind of wool blend. The scratchy fabric made his nose itch, and try as he might to get answers, Beck wasn't forthcoming. The man simply refused to talk. About anything. Over the hum of the Caprice's engine, that seemed to resonate through every square inch of the car, all Nathan could hear was the sound of cars speeding past in the opposite lane and an occasional angry horn.

Even more frustrating was the fact that he had no idea where they were. After Beck pulled away from the curb, he made a series of curious turns that had Nathan completely disoriented. Were they still in Arlington? Had they gone as far as Lexington? His legs began to cramp and he shifted his position.

"Hey," Beck said. "Stay down."

"Why?" Nathan shot back. "Why don't you want me to see where we're going?"

Like before, Beck said nothing.

"Yeah, that's what I thought you'd say...nothing," Nathan griped. "Thanks a lot." He took a deep breath and tried to relax. *This will all be over soon,* he told himself. *They can't hide me forever. Sooner or later they'll have to let me go back home. And when they do, I'll find whatever's hidden in the bookcase, stuck books or no stuck books.*

The words hung in his mind.

Stuck books.

"Wait a minute," he said, picking his head up off the seat.

"Hey!" Beck snapped. "What did I tell you?"

Nathan set his head back down on the seat, his mind racing. From the very beginning, every book from his grandfather's bookcase had pushed and prodded him, guiding him to a hidden truth that his grandfather wanted him to discover. Over time, Nathan had learned that when it came to the bookcase, nothing happened by chance. Everything had meaning.

Beck stopped at another traffic light, but Nathan didn't notice.

There's a reason the books wouldn't budge, but what is it? he asked himself. THINK! Why didn't they just slip off the shelf like they had every other time? It's like he doesn't want me to see what's behind them.

77

And that's when it hit him.

The books were as good as a spoken message. Whatever secret Thomas Hammond had hidden in the bookcase wasn't on the inside. As was usually the case, Gina had called it. What he was looking for was right there in plain sight. Somehow, in his haste, he'd completely overlooked it.

Sully walked to the end of the 400-foot pier that led to the dock house, a small single-story building that served as the nerve center of the South Portland Marina. It was another typical summer day, with boats cruising lazily to and from their moorings, and boat owners coming and going, loading and offloading cartloads of supplies. All around them, a small army of young marina employees, decked out in shorts and their signature red tee shirts, monitored the flow of people and boats using hip-mounted radios. The steady wind off the water was a welcome relief from the blistering summer heat and gently rocked the boats in their slips, making their halyards ring out like the world's biggest handbell choir.

When Sully reached the dock house, he stepped up to the window and spoke to a strapping young man named Clay, who clearly spent his free time in a weight room. Sully imagined that the boy probably slept there. But as out of place as he appeared, Clay had an uncanny knowledge of every boat in the marina.

"I'm looking for information about one of your boat owners," Sully told him.

"Okay," Clay said casually. Challenge accepted. "Which one?"

"He goes by the nickname DP," Sully began, "but his full name—

"Dan Perry," Clay cut in.

"Yes, that's right. When was the last time you saw him?"

Clay flexed his shoulder forward and back, working out a knot in his trapezius muscle. "Saturday, three weekends ago," he said matter-of-factly, the bones in his back making a sharp cracking sound.

Sully wrote down the information in a small spiral-bound notepad that he kept tucked in his jacket pocket. "Nothing since then?" he asked.

Clay started in on the other shoulder. Flexing and cracking. "Nope."

"Which slip is his?" Sully asked.

"G-21."

Sully turned and surveyed the slips to his right. They were arranged along narrow docks called "runs" that extended outward from a larger dock at 90-degree angles. Each run was assigned a letter of the alphabet.

"Don't bother," Clay said, when he saw Sully looking. "He's not here."

"How do you know that?" Sully asked. "You said you hadn't seen him in three weeks."

"That's right," Clay replied, doing a slow neck rotation to the left, then to the right. "He left three weeks ago and hasn't been back."

After a drive into town, where Ellie stopped to get gas, and another stop at the grocery store, she drove back to Gina's house. "You okay back there?" she asked Gina, who was twisted like a pretzel on the back seat, out of sight, holding a small puzzle book inches from her face. Ellie had seen it at the checkout counter and decided to take a chance that *maybe* one of the puzzles would challenge Gina. But she'd already made her way halfway through it. "I'm good," she told Ellie as she turned to the next page. *Ah, a word puzzle*, she thought. Maybe there was hope after all.

When they reached Gina's house, Ellie pulled into the garage and shut the door, just as Jameson had instructed her to do. She walked back to the street and checked the mailbox, throwing a casual glance in each direction. Nothing seemed amiss, so she went back to the garage where Gina was waiting, leaning against the side of the car, nose buried in her puzzle book.

"Clear?" she asked, when Ellie opened the side door of the garage.

"Yup. Come on, let's get you inside."

They went into the house through the back porch. Gina sat down at the kitchen table, considered the puzzle book momentarily, then pushed it away and drummed her fingers on the tabletop. "So, what now?" she asked.

Ellie put the last of the groceries in the refrigerator and then went over to the table and sat down. "What now?" she repeated. She looked out the window to her left, surveying the front yard and porch of Nathan's house. "Now we wait, and we watch."

"Wait for what?" Gina asked.

Ellie checked the time. "You know, it's early," she said, ignoring Gina's question. "I think I'll go upstairs and take a shower." She got up from the chair and walked out of the room. "Let me know if you see anything," she called out over her shoulder as she walked down the front hallway.

"See anything? Like what?" Gina asked.

Ellie didn't answer.

"Ellie?" Gina shouted. "See anything like what?"

She was still waiting for an answer when she heard the shower start to run in the upstairs bathroom.

They were getting close now, Nathan could sense it. Beck was driving slower, and the drone of passing cars had been replaced by the sporadic drone of a lawn mower or the bee-like buzz of a string trimmer. The car came to a near stop and Beck made a sharp right turn. Seconds later, the car came to a full stop. Nathan heard a slow grinding metallic sound, then, nothing. As he lay there waiting to see what would happen next, Beck reached over the seat and pulled back the blanket. "We're here," he said.

"Finally," Nathan muttered as he pushed himself up off the seat and looked around. They were in a two-car garage, lit by a series of long fluorescent lights. Straight ahead was a workbench. Covering the wall behind it was a sheet of pegboard, home to a variety of tools that had been carefully arranged on peg hooks. To his right sat a mammoth jet-black Dodge Ram 2500 pickup truck with tinted windows. He climbed out of the car and stretched, breathing in the cool air that carried the faint smell of motor oil.

Beck retrieved Nathan's suitcase from the trunk and then walked over to a dark gray metal door. He punched in a four-digit code on a small numeric keypad, then pulled the door open. "Follow me," he said, then stepped inside.

The door opened into a large kitchen and adjoining living room. Beck flicked a switch on the wall and both rooms were immediately filled with soft light from a series of recessed high hats in the ceiling.

The kitchen was free of the usual household clutter. There were no dirty dishes littering the counter, no piles of unopened mail. Other than an electric stove and refrigerator, the only other appliance was a coffee machine sitting to the right of the sink. Across from that was a large rectangular island with an overhanging countertop along one side. Tucked underneath were three low-back swivel bar stools.

"This is your house?" Nathan asked.

"It's *a* house," Beck replied, indicating that the name on the deed wasn't his. "Consider it your home, for the time being, anyway. Your room is this way."

He crossed the kitchen and followed a narrow hallway that led past a laundry room and bathroom on the right, and a small office on the left. As he passed by, Nathan saw a large wooden desk, home to a pair of oversized computer monitors positioned side by side, and a wireless keyboard.

Beck continued on, to a guest bedroom at the end of the hall on the left. Directly across from it was another bedroom, with a king-size bed and a tall bureau. Other than that, the room was empty.

Beck pushed the guest room door open and turned on the light. There was a full-sized bed pushed up against one wall, a small desk and low bookcase across from it. Standing against the wall that faced the street, obscuring the only window in the room, was a tall antique highboy. Beck set Nathan's suitcase on the bed and then walked him back to the living room.

"Okay, here are the rules. Follow them, and we won't have a problem. Break them, and things are going to get very unpleasant."

Nathan said nothing as images of the green Chevy Nova flashed through his mind.

"Rule number one," said Beck. "Stay away from the windows. There's nothing to see and we can't risk anyone seeing you."

What if I wear a blanket? Nathan was tempted to say.

"Rule number two. Don't answer the door. If someone knocks, or rings the bell, you ignore it. Anyone we know who plans to stop by will call me ahead of time. Understood?"

"Understood," Nathan said.

"Rule number three, and this is non-negotiable. Under no circumstances are you to go outside. Is that clear?"

"Yes."

"Good. Rule number four. Eat whatever you want. Watch whatever you want on television. The refrigerator is full. So are the cupboards. The TV remote is on the couch. I'll leave it up to you to figure it out, which I'm guessing should take you all of ten seconds."

Uh, try five, Nathan thought. He surveyed the room, eyeing the monstrous 60" flat screen TV, and the huge leather sectional that looked big enough to seat an entire football team. Like every other room in the house, the drapes were pulled shut.

Beck went to the door and took a set of keys off a short metallic key rack. "I've got an errand to run," he said. "While I'm gone, remember the rules."

"Yeah, yeah, yeah," Nathan grumbled.

"What are they again?" Beck asked.

Nathan rolled his eyes and then rattled them off in a tired voice. "Stay away from the windows. Don't answer the door. No going outside. Eat whatever I want."

"And the TV remote?"

"On the couch," Nathan replied.

Beck was reaching for the door when Nathan asked, "What's the errand?"

"Springing the trap," Beck replied.

Not long after that, Nathan heard the garage door rattle open, followed by the roar of the truck's engine as it backed out into the driveway. The garage door closed again and an eerie silence filled the house. He walked over to the couch and picked up the remote. "Anything I want?" he said. "Okay, if you say so." He tossed the remote on the couch and made a beeline for the basement door.

Rules or no rules, he had to get out of there. The bookcase couldn't wait. And while leaving was sure to set off a firestorm with his parents, Jameson, and Beck, he figured once he unearthed the secret hidden in the bookcase, how upset could they get? If anything, he'd be a hero for finding it, not to mention the fact that he'd be preventing Dan Perry from stealing it.

At the bottom of the stairs he stopped and took in the dimly lit space. To his left was a large metal rack, lined plastic totes. To his right, on the front wall, was a workbench littered with an assortment of hand tools. On the back wall he saw what he was looking for—a set of stairs that led up to the bulkhead.

Sully sat at his desk, phone to his ear, waiting impatiently. He checked his watch and realized he'd been on hold for nearly five minutes. "Unbelievable," he muttered, then slammed the phone back in its cradle.

"Now, now…is that any way to treat your phone?"

The voice surprised him, and when he spun his chair around he saw Christine Reyes, the secretary for the detective division. At just over five feet tall, with close-cropped hair, and a youthful smile, she looked more like a kiosk employee at the mall, selling overpriced sunglasses or pastel-colored teddy bears. In fact, she was an 8-year veteran with the Portland Police Department. Sharp as a tack, and not someone you wanted to make angry.

"Oh, hey Reyes," he said. "I didn't see you there."

"They tell me I have a stealth quality," she quipped, pulling a manila file folder from the stack in her hand.

He looked back at the phone and scowled. "People who put you on hold and then forget about you should do hard time…at an Amazon call center…during Christmas!"

Reyes fought back a grin and slid the file folder on his desk. Inside was the incident report she'd typed for him. "Good news," she said, changing the subject. "You only spelled five things wrong this time."

"Wow, only five?" he said, smirking.

"That's a new record. But we should go over the difference between lay and lie."

Sully opened the file and glanced at the neatly typed report. Even if he had ten tries he'd never get it to look so good. "My grief lies all within," he said, in a dramatic voice. "And these external manners of lament—"

"Wait I know this one," Reyes said, cutting him off. "These external manners of lament are merely shadows to the unseen grief that swells with silence in the tortured soul."

Sully gestured for her to continue. *And…?*

"There lies the substance," she said.

"Bravo," Sully exclaimed. He pulled a pen from his shirt pocket and signed the report. "Hey, you're good with computers," he said, handing her back the folder. "How would you track down a boat?"

"What kind of boat are we talking about?" she asked. "Sailboat? Motorboat? Tanker?"

"Motorboat," Sully replied. "A 20-footer with a center console."

"Is it registered in Maine?"

"Yes." He pulled the notepad from his jacket pocket and read from his notes. "It's been moored at the South Portland Marina. Dock fees were paid for the year, but it left three weeks ago and they haven't seen it since."

"Did you contact the Coast Guard?"

"I did. They received no report of it missing, and there's no record of it being involved in any sort of mishap."

"Well, it is summertime," Reyes said. "Boaters go on sightseeing trips up and down the Maine coast, sometimes for weeks at a time. Have you tried calling around to other marinas?"

"That's what I was doing when, you know…"

"They left you for dead?"

"Uh-huh."

"May I?" she asked, gesturing at his chair.

He stood up at once. "Be my guest."

She sat down and pulled his keyboard closer, then began typing, her fingers flying over the keys at a dizzying speed. Within minutes she'd gathered a list of emails for marinas along the southern and mid-coast and had them arranged on an Excel spread sheet. "Per the state," she explained, "all boats manufactured after 1972 are required to have a 12-digit hull identification number."

"O-kay," he said slowly. *Good to know.*

"To find it, assuming the boat is still in Maine, you could call each marina, but that could take days. Me? I'd use an email blast."

"A what?" Sully asked.

"A mass mailing. One message, sent to multiple recipients. In this case, every marina from Kittery to Bar Harbor."

"Go on."

"Send the I.D. number of the boat you're looking for and ask them to check their registry. It may take some time to get a reply, but if this guy's boat is still around, someone saw it."

"And, uh, how exactly would I do that?" he asked. "The blast thing."

"Here," she said. "I'll show you."

Nathan emerged from the bulkhead, into a small yard. The grass was in desperate need of mowing, and much like the kitchen, it was missing the usual trappings. There was no swing set, no picnic table, no barbeque grill. A tall wooden fence lined the property, and just inside it, crowded together from years of neglect, stood a wall of towering arborvitae trees. He went to the corner of the house and exited the yard through a tall wooden gate. When he reached the sidewalk, he stopped and surveyed his surroundings.

It was a residential neighborhood. The houses were spaced at a comfortable distance, with thin lines of trees or large flowering shrubs offering a minimum of privacy. To his left, three blocks away, he saw a traffic light and a steady stream of vehicles passing by in either direction. To his right, the road continued for a short distance before ending in a small cul-de-sac.

He went left.

As he walked, he kept an eye out for anyone following him, but the only vehicle he saw was a postal delivery truck. Kids were playing in yards, men in sweaty tee shirts were mowing lawns, but none of them took notice of him. When he reached the intersection, he checked the road sign.

Braden Street.

He looked across the street and saw a strip mall with a pizza shop he'd been to with his dad on numerous occasions. "I don't believe it," he mumbled, then pulled his flip phone from his pocket and called Gina's house.

Gina was sitting at the kitchen table, grinning at the word search puzzle she had just completed. She checked the time. "Hah! Twenty-five words in seven minutes," she said triumphantly. It wasn't a personal best but it was close. Maybe one of these days someone would make a puzzle that would actually be hard. *Good luck with that, she thought.* She had just turned to the next page when the phone rang. Ellie was still upstairs so she went to the counter and grabbed the wireless extension.

"Hello?"

"Gina? It's me, Nathan."

"Nathan? What's going on? Are you okay?"

"I'm fine," he said. "I know where I am."

"Congratulations. So do I."

"Very funny," he shot back. "Remember when I told you that they didn't tell me where Beck was taking me?"

"Yeah?"

"Well, now I know why."

Gina shook her head, confused. "What are you talking about?"

"I'm in Arlington Heights," he said.

"Are you sure?" she asked.

"Yes...I'm standing on Mass Ave, right across the street from Ciano's."

"Wait. That's, like, three miles from here."

"Exactly. They didn't tell where they were stashing me because they figured if I knew how close it was, I'd try to sneak back home."

Gina got a bad feeling. "Let me guess," she said. "You snuck out."

"Yup."

"Where's Beck?"

"He took off to run some errand."

"What errand?"

"Who knows?" Nathan said. "He said something about springing a trap."

Gina's heart raced as she recalled Ellie's cryptic comment.

"Now we wait and we watch"

"Nathan, listen to me," Gina said. "Go back to wherever Beck took you. Do not go home."

Nathan didn't respond.

"Did you hear me?" she said. "Do NOT go home!"

Again, silence.

"Nathan? Hello?"

5

Anything Unusual

ina set the phone on the counter and marched over to the window. "Why does he always do this to me?" she griped. She pressed her face against the left side of the glass to get a better view of Nathan's garage. The door was closed and there were no cars in the driveway. Nothing unusual about that. Not on a Wednesday morning. She eyed the front porch, then the tree line that bordered the far side of the property. Nothing amiss there. So what did Ellie mean? *We wait and we watch.* What did she know that she wasn't sharing?

Upstairs, she heard the high-pitched whine of a hair dryer. She surveyed Nathan's yard one last time, then went to the back porch to continue her vigil. She would've preferred camping out on the front steps of her house where she'd have a clear view of the street in either direction, but that was out of the question. Jameson's deception had been designed to make anyone watching think she'd been hauled off to some unknown location. The only way to make that illusion stick was for her to stay out of sight. Not the easiest thing to do when you're trying to stop your best friend from doing something stupid. Again.

Nathan was fully prepared to walk. After all, it was a sunny day, and after being stretched out on the back seat of the Caprice under a stifling wool blanket, stretching his legs would be a welcome relief. But then he spotted the Arlington Heights Busway, a small single-story building sitting 200 feet down the street. "Hmm," he said aloud. "Walk or ride?"

Thirty minutes later he stepped off the bus at the corner of his street. As he approached his house, he saw no cars in the driveway. He knew that Russ' camera would record him returning home, but that was unavoidable, and he really didn't care.

He was about to be a hero.

Gina paced the length of the back porch as she calculated the numbers. "Arlington Heights is three miles away," she said. "Assuming a walking speed of 20 minutes per mile, that gets him home in one hour." She stopped pacing. "Then what?" she said. Would she try to stop him? To do that she'd need to go outside, the one place she wasn't supposed to go. Even if she did, would he listen to her? This was Nathan Cole she was dealing with. *I could always drag him back here*, she thought.

Of all the options, that one was the most appealing.

She went back to the screen just as Nathan was racing across the front lawn. "No, no, no…it's too soon," she said. She cupped her hands around her mouth and shouted, "NATHAN! WAIT!"

By the time she exploded out the back-porch door, he was already inside his house, sprinting up the attic stairs.

For Elizabeth Cole, the waiting was excruciating. She and David were parked in the vacant lot at the high school, side by side, their cars facing in opposite directions, driver's window to driver's window. She thought they must look like two state troopers on the median strip of a busy highway, comparing stories about the citations they'd issued, or telling jokes, or doing whatever state troopers did when they parked that way. "I hate this," she said, slowly shaking her head.

"Relax," David told her. He checked his watch.

"Worried?" she asked.

"No. A little anxious, maybe."

She exhaled nervously. "Are you sure we're doing the right thing?"

"Uh, it's a little late for that question, my dear."

"That's not an answer," she fired back.

He reached across the narrow gap that separated their cars and rested his hand on her forearm. "Don't worry," he said. "Everything is going to turn out fine."

Gina raced across the driveway, to the back door of Nathan's house. Once inside, she ran upstairs to the second floor, did a quick check of his room, then climbed the creaky stairs to the attic. At the attic door she paused. "Nathan?" she said, easing the door open. When there was no reply, she took a deep breath and let it out, then stepped into the room.

It was just a bad as last time. Musty air, heavy with the smell of mothballs and decaying cardboard. The gloomy darkness was worse than a cemetery at night. There were spiders and webs everywhere, but that didn't bother her so much. Spiders were okay. Cute, actually. She took another step forward when a beam of light erupted from the darkness and hit her square in the face. "HEY!" she shouted, shielding her eyes with both hands.

Nathan stood up from behind a pile of boxes. "Oh, it's you," he said, lowering the light.

"Of course it's me," she snapped. "What are you doing, trying to blind me?"

"Whoa, whoa, whoa, relax," he said. "I didn't know it was you."

She looked at the stacks of boxes to her left and right.

"What are you looking for?" he asked.

"Something to *throw* at you!"

"That can wait," he said. "Since you're here, you can help me with the bookcase."

She stared at him without speaking, debating whether she should stay or go. *Blinds me with a flashlight and then expects me to help him,* she thought. *Unbelievable!*

"Well?" he said impatiently. "Come on, let's go."

She stood her ground.

Time for a different approach.

"What we're looking for is in plain sight," he told her.

"And what makes you think that?" she asked.

"Something you said."

Her mood lightened, but only slightly. "Something *I* said?"

"That's right. It's a good thing you said it, too. If not, I probably would've given up all together."

"Huh," she said. "Well, in that case, I suppose I can help." She followed him through the mess, holding her arms tight to her chest so she wouldn't accidentally knock anything over, because if she did, she'd have to actually *touch* it.

When they reached the bookcase, Nathan aimed the flashlight at the middle shelf. "Do you remember what I told you about the books? How they wouldn't budge?"

"Yeah?"

"Go ahead," he said. "Try to take one out."

She eyed the bookcase warily. "Why?"

"Just do it."

"No. First, tell me why."

He grabbed her hand and pushed it toward the bookcase.

"STOP!" she yelled, jerking her arm back. She shot him a menacing look, then reluctantly reached out and pulled at one of the hardcover spines on the middle shelf.

It wouldn't budge.

"Try another one," he said.

She reached up to the next shelf and tried again. Same thing. The book felt like it was glued in place.

"It's a message," Nathan said. "He wants me to—"

"All right!" Gina blurted out, before he could finish. "You don't have to tell me." Hanging around in a room full of spiders was fine. The piles of old dust-covered junk were barely tolerable. But any mention of his grandfather, who he claimed was haunting the bookcase, made her feel like a thousand centipedes were crawling over her entire body.

"Fine, have it your way," he said. *Chicken.*

"Thank you," she sneered. *Creep.*

Elizabeth gazed at the football field in the distance, consumed by doubt. "Who does this?" she asked.

David said nothing. The plan had been his idea from the start.

"Seriously," Elizabeth said, looking over at him. "I want to know. Who in their right mind does something like this?"

David's phone sounded. Not a flowery chime or a curious electronic melody—it was the unmistakable popping sound a ping pong ball makes when it bounces off a paddle. "Hold on," he said. He tapped the screen, read the short message, then replied with a message of his own.

"What is it?" Elizabeth asked.

He finished typing and slipped the phone into the empty cupholder.

"We gotta go."

Nathan ran the flashlight beam up the right side of the bookcase and then down the left.

"What we're looking for isn't inside the bookcase," he said. "It's on the outside."

"And you have no idea what it is?" Gina asked.

"Nope. No one does," Nathan replied. *Except Dan Perry,* he thought.

"So how do you know what to look for?"

"I don't."

"Lovely," she said, eyeing the ancient relic. *Who would hide some-*

thing in a bookcase? she wondered. *Why not just hide it in a closet, or bury it in the ground?* She was fully aware of the answer to the question, but it still bugged her.

Nathan looked around the room and spotted an old metal trunk sitting several feet away. He slid it over to the bookcase and stepped up on it, then examined the top of the bookcase with his hand. The wood was caked with a thick layer of dust and grit, and more than a few insect parts, but he forced that out of his mind and ran his fingers over every square inch. When that yielded nothing, he stepped down, pulled the trunk to the side, and repeated the process with the front of each shelf. After that, he examined the base.

Gina stood behind him, peering over his shoulder.

"Uh, you could help, you know," he grumbled.

"Fine, where do you want me to look?"

"Check the side," he said.

"The side," she repeated, like it was a fool's errand. "And what exactly am I looking for?"

"Anything unusual," he said. "A button, maybe a small lever…"

"A button," she said, unconvinced.

"Yup."

A button on a bookcase, she thought. *Now I've heard everything.* She stepped around him and gave the dark wood a quick glance from top to bottom. It was just as she expected.

No button.

Jameson was sitting in the far corner of Kendra's coffee shop, sipping a cup of India ginger tea, when his phone vibrated. The aroma of fresh-brewed coffee and the loud chatter from the regulars filled the air and was punctuated by frequent blasts of steam from the espresso machine.

He snatched the phone off the tabletop and read the message, then stood and took his cup to the front counter. When Kendra turned to look, he nodded his head once...*time to go*...then walked to the door. Exactly one minute later she pulled up to the curb in her faded blue Volvo.

Jameson climbed in, and without a word spoken, they drove away. They hadn't gone far when he took out his phone and dialed Ellie's number. She was in the guest room, rifling through her suitcase for a change of clothes, but managed to grab the phone on the third ring. "Yeah?" she said, pulling a clean pair of blue jeans from the suitcase.

"It's happening," Jameson said.

Ellie walked to the window and scanned Nathan's yard and driveway. "Really? I don't see anything."

"That's okay," he said. "Just sit tight, like we discussed."

"I will," she said.

"I have your word on that?"

"Of course," Ellie said. "Why would you ask me that?"

"Because I know you," he replied. "I know how your brain works. Don't get me wrong. It's an amazing brain. Someday, a great statue will be erected in honor of your brain, carved from the finest Italian marble."

"I pity the stone cutter," Ellie quipped. "Don't worry. I won't move until I hear from you."

"Thank you."

He typed a quick text message, then looked out the window,

staring at the blur of passing storefronts as he struggled to see how the next 30 minutes could possibly unfold without someone getting hurt. Or worse. He looked over at Kendra, who gave him a snide look.

"What's wrong?" he asked.

"A marble statue? Of her brain? Give me break."

"Just drive," he said.

Gina stood at the side of the bookcase and extended her arm as far as she could reach, trying to feel along the top edge. It was out of sight, and by her way of thinking that was exactly where someone would hide a button, or a lever, or whatever. Taking a cue from Nathan, she slid an old plastic tub over to the bookcase. She had no idea what was crammed inside it, but that didn't matter. The question was: would it support her? She tested it by resting her foot on the cover and gradually applying more weight. When she was sure it was sturdy enough, she stepped up on it and reached for the top of the bookcase.

The tub's cover sagged.

Starting at the back, she ran her fingers along the top, feeling the end grain for any indentations or protrusions.

The top of the tub sagged a little more.

She continued moving her fingers along the top edge of the bookcase when the cover cracked, sending her foot plunging downward. She heard the sound of breaking glass and tried to pull her sneaker free, but the sharp plastic edges of the cover held her ankle like a vice, causing her to lose her balance. Instinctively, she hooked the fingers of her left hand over the top of the bookcase and grabbed hold of the wooden edging that separated the two halves of the bookcase with her right hand.

Nathan was busy examining the base when he heard a soft click. "Gina?" he said.

"I'm a little busy here, Nathan!" she barked, fighting to pull her foot free from the tub. The fingers of her left hand began to ache and she knew it was only a matter of seconds before she'd tumble backward onto the floor.

"What did you just do?" he asked.

"I didn't do anything," she snapped. "The top of the tub broke!"

Nathan's jaw fell open and he sat frozen, staring in disbelief.

"Uh, Nathan? A little *help* would be nice," she shouted.

"Gina?" he said again, awestruck.

"WHAT?"

"You found it."

6

Ushiro Geri

Nathan jumped to his feet and grabbed Gina around the waist just as her fingers slipped off the top of the bookcase. They teetered momentarily, like a dance routine gone bad, then toppled over onto a stack of old cardboard boxes that pancaked under their combined weight.

Miraculously, Gina's foot popped free of the plastic cover with only a minor scratch.

"You waited long enough," she crabbed as she climbed to her feet.

He ignored the dig and scrambled across the floor to the front of the bookcase. "This is it," he said.

She stopped brushing cobwebs and grit off her sleeves and looked over. "What are you talking about?"

"That," he said, pointing.

"That what? I don't see anything."

"Oh…right…hold on," he said, searching the floor for the flashlight. He found it poking out from beneath the bookcase, and when he tried to turn it on, nothing happened.

"Great, you broke it," Gina said. *Typical.*

"Hold on." He pounded the end of the flashlight into the palm of his hand and it flickered. He hit it again and the bulb came to life. "Right there," he said, pointing the light at the corner of the bookcase.

"What about it? It's a piece of wood," she said.

"Actually, it's called a Doric column. It's an architectural design from—"

"Yeah, okay, that's great," she said, cutting him off. "I'll be sure to remember that." *NOT!*

"Take a closer look," he said.

She knelt down and gave it cursory glance. "It looks broken."

"Not broken," he said. "Look again."

She moved closer and that's when she saw it. The column was at least 14" long and had been added as a decoration. But now, one side of it had separated from the bookcase, as if the glue holding it in place for over 160 years had finally succumbed to the ravages of time.

Nathan nudged the edge of it with his finger and it swung open with a whisper-soft squeak. "It's hinged," he said. "Whatever you did activated a hidden release mechanism."

I did? she thought. Unable to contain her curiosity, she wrestled the flashlight out of his hand and swept the beam up and down the side of the bookcase. Halfway up, she stopped.

"What is it?" he asked.

"I think I know what it was."

He got up at once, stepped around her, then knelt down again at the side of the bookcase. "Where?" he said. "Show me."

"Right there," she said, pointing with the flashlight. "See it?"

Thomas Hammond had built the bookcase in two sections. He started with a heavy base, which was essentially a waist-high bookcase with shelves, and a row of shallow drawers set just below a thick wooden top. He then added the upper section, a second bookcase of shelves. As a design feature, the wood that formed the top of the lower section extended outward beyond the front and sides of the bookcase by a scant half inch. Attached to the underside of it on either side was a hand-carved piece of cove molding that ran the full width of the bookcase.

Looking at it now, Nathan could see that the alignment was off. It had slid backward. He touched it with his finger and slid it forward again. "Gina?" he said. "You're a genius."

"You can thank the cheap plastic tub," she said.

He took the flashlight from her and went back to the front of the bookcase. With his heart racing, he aimed the flashlight at the hinged column and swung it open all the way, then peered into the narrow cavity that Thomas Hammond had carved into the frame.

Gina crouched down next to him and leaned in for a closer look. "What is that?" she asked.

"It looks like a piece of cloth," he said, his heart racing.

She looked at him, frowning. "Why would someone hide a piece of cloth in a bookcase?"

"Let's find out." He gave her the flashlight, then reached into the narrow opening with his thumb and forefinger and pinched the cloth, gently easing it out. It was a loose weave, the color of chalk, wrapped around what felt like a paper towel tube less than 2" in diameter and over 12" long. The rough edge of the cloth had been sewn from end to end with a simple whip stitch to keep it from unraveling, and both ends were tied off a short length of twine.

Nathan stared at it, awestruck. "What do you think it is?" he asked, turning it over in his hands.

"Why are you asking me? You're the expert on weird stuff, remember?"

He held it to his ear and shook it. Nothing. He held it up to his nose and inhaled. There was no smell.

"What are you doing?" she asked.

"I'm checking it out," he said, shaking it again.

"Oh brother," she groaned. She gently pried it out of his hands and studied it under the beam of the flashlight. "This is linen," she said, running her fingers over the cloth. She loosened the twine on one end and looked inside. "Huh."

"What is it?" he asked.

"See for yourself," she said, handing it to him, along with the flashlight.

He stood it on end and used one hand to hold the cloth open while he pointed the light inside. "It looks like a roll of paper."

"That's because it *is* a roll of paper," she said.

Nathan sat up, confused. "Why would Dan Perry want a piece of paper?"

Gina's eyes widened. "Maybe it's a map."

"Yeah, maybe," Nathan said. He pushed the Doric column shut and it closed with a soft click. "Come on," he said, standing up. "Let's get out of here. We need to show this to my mom and dad."

"And Jameson," Gina said.

"Yeah," he said, as he made his way toward the door. "Especially Jameson."

Seven minutes after David Cole got the call, he turned onto his street and pulled to the curb. Elizabeth had left her car at the high school and was sitting next to him in the passenger seat, talking to Jameson on the phone. "Yes, we can see you," she said, looking at Kendra's blue Volvo parked at the opposite end of the street.

Roughly halfway between them, Russ McCullough was parked in a driveway across the street from their house. From that vantage point he had a clear view of the front porch and the yard on either side. As he waited, he scanned the front of the house with his binoculars, pausing at each window, looking for movement of any kind.

So far, everything was quiet.

Nathan carried the scroll, as he was calling it, like an injured bird. He knew if he held it too tight he'd run the risk of crushing it. Too loose and he might accidentally drop it and step on it. It was a wonder that it was in such good condition, given its age, and the grueling journey the bookcase had taken to reach America.

He reached the bottom of the front hall stairs, Gina following three steps behind him, when a large figure suddenly appeared in the living room entryway. He was over six feet tall, with a muscular build that strained at the seams of his thin black tee shirt. His closely cropped hair and narrow eyes gave him a menacing snake-like appearance.

Nathan pulled back. "Who are you?" he demanded. "And what are you doing in my house?"

Odom didn't answer. Thirty minutes earlier, he'd parked his Range Rover two streets away, then cut through side yards, hopping over fences, skirting garden sheds, and ducking under clothes lines, until he arrived behind Nathan's garage. Approaching from that vantage point ensured that the camera at the front corner of the property wouldn't record him crossing the back yard and slipping quietly into the empty house.

With no one there, he figured he'd have plenty of time to hunt for the bookcase. Where it was, Perry didn't say, but Odom wasn't concerned. It was just a house, not some 7-story office building. How hard could it be to find a bookcase?

Now, as he stood five feet away from Nathan, he couldn't believe his luck. The very thing Perry had described was literally being hand-delivered to him. He extended his open palm and said, "I'll take that."

Nathan looked at the scroll, then back at Odom. Suddenly, he understood why this stranger was in his house. More importantly, who had sent him. "No," he said defiantly. This was his house. The bookcase belonged to *his* family, and they'd waited far too long to find the secret hidden within it.

"Nathan," Gina whispered. "Just give it to him."

"Uh-uh," Nathan said, shaking his head. He lowered the scroll to his side, keeping his eyes locked on Odom.

"Fine. Have it your way," Odom said calmly. The words were barely out of his mouth when he exploded at Nathan with blinding speed, crossing the void between them like he'd been shot out of a

50mm cannon.

Nathan anticipated the move and ducked down and to his right. Odom flew past him, on a collision course with the wall, but with cat-like reflexes he reached out and sprung off it like it was made of rubber.

Nathan started up the stairs when he saw Beck barreling down the hallway from the kitchen like a locomotive. He lowered his shoulder and drove Odom across the hardwood floor, smashing him into the front door.

"Come on," Nathan said, grabbing Gina's hand. "We're outta here."

"So, we're just supposed to sit here and do nothing?" Kendra asked. Her baseball bat was in the back seat and she was imagining the feel of the smooth wood in her hands, the balanced weight, and the exhilaration she got with every swing.

"Yes," Jameson said, watching the street ahead. "Beck wants us to stay out of sight, in case the intruder escapes."

"You mean, in case he can't overpower him and he escapes."

"Yeah, something like that," Jameson said. "But we've got him surrounded. If he does manage to get out of the house, one of us will see where he goes. My guess is, he's got a vehicle stashed nearby, or an accomplice waiting to pick him up in a different car."

Kendra turned to face him. "How about this?" he said. "You wait here and I'll move a little closer." As she spoke she nonchalantly reached over the seat, feeling for her bat.

Without taking his eyes from the street, Jameson calmly reached over with his left hand and pulled her arm back over the seat. "No," he said. "We wait here."

"Anything yet?" David Cole said into his phone, holding it over the center console so Elizabeth could hear.

"Nothing," Russ replied. "Is Beck sure about this?" he asked. "He actually saw the intruder enter the house?"

"Positive," Elizabeth said.

Following the plan, Beck had hidden in the garage. After dropping Nathan off at Braden Street, he switched vehicles and drove back to Nathan's house. As a precaution, he took an erratic route, looping through a maze of side streets, before parking his truck at a Cumberland Farms two blocks away. He jogged back to Nathan's garage, arriving there minutes after Gina had gone inside.

When he saw Odom enter the house, he called David Cole, who then called Jameson, who then called Russ McCullough. Beck gave them time to drive to their prearranged positions, then went into the house.

As Odom crashed sideways into the door, Beck slid his right foot forward and attempted to throw him backward onto the floor. But Odom grabbed Beck with both hands and slammed his knee into Beck's kidney. Beck spun away from the blow at the last second, lessening its impact, then flung Odom down on the floor. As he fell, he extended his elbow, aiming it at Odom's neck.

With a blinding two-handed motion, Odom slapped Beck's elbow aside with one hand, then slammed Beck's head into the door with the other. Beck was stunned momentarily, which gave Odom time to scramble to his feet. He set his body, then raised his knee in a short arc and delivered a powerful Ushiro Geri back kick, aimed at Beck's head.

Nathan pulled Gina, nearly dragging her, down the hallway toward the kitchen. Behind them, he heard Beck and Odom battling, but he didn't look back or slow down until he and Gina were safely outside.

"You had to come back, didn't you?" Gina griped as they walked along the back side of the house. "You couldn't stay away like I told you. And what happened? Exactly what I knew would happen!"

Nathan stopped walking. "You're *mad* at me?" he asked.

"What do *you* think?" she said. She brushed by him and kept walking, mumbling under her breath the whole way.

"Hold on," Nathan said.

She kept walking.

"Hey, what are you doing?" he called out, sprinting across the lawn after her. He caught up just as she cleared the corner of the house. "Stop," he said, grabbing her arm.

"Let *go* of me," she barked, struggling to break free.

He dragged her back behind the house, then released her arm. "Are you crazy?" he asked.

"You want to know if *I'm crazy*," she said. "Oh, that's good."

"You don't just walk out in the open," he said. "There could be more of them."

"That wouldn't be problem if you had just stayed away!"

"I couldn't, and I explained that to you, remember? If I hadn't come back then whoever was in the hallway would have *this*," he said, holding up the scroll.

She looked at it and shook her head in frustration. He just didn't get it.

"What?" he asked.

"You think this is over?" she said. "You think Dan Perry is just going to say 'Fine, you win, I'll leave you alone now'?"

An uneasy feeling washed over Nathan as the significance of her words sank in. They had both lived through some dark and dangerous escapades. But if what happened in the hallway was any indication, the days ahead were about to get even darker.

Ellie was peering out the second-floor window when she spotted Nathan and Gina standing at the back corner of the house. "NO!" she shouted. She hit a speed dial number on her phone, and one ring later Jameson answered.

"Ellie?" he said, pushing the speaker phone button so Kendra could hear.

"We have a problem," Ellie said.

"What are you talking about?"

"I'm *looking* at Nathan and Gina!" she said.

"What?" he exclaimed. "Where are they?"

"Standing behind Nathan's house."

"That's it," Kendra growled. She started the car and stomped on the gas pedal, sending the Volvo rocketing down the street. When she came to Nathan's mailbox, she slammed on the brakes, then backed up into the driveway, tires squealing the whole way.

"What is she doing?" Elizabeth yelled, as Kendra came tearing up the street.

David quickly dialed Russ.

"Yeah, I see it," Russ said.

"Is something happening that we can't see?" Elizabeth asked.

"Hold on," Russ told her. "She's backing into the driveway."

"We can see that," David said. "But why would she—"

"Wait," Russ said, cutting him off. "She's climbing out of the car. Now she's waving to someone."

"Waving?" David said, confused. From where they were parked, Kendra was out of their line of sight.

"It looks like she's motioning to someone," Russ said

"Motioning to *who?*" Elizabeth asked, her voice rising in volume.

"Oh, you've GOT to be kidding me!" Russ said.

Elizabeth snatched the phone out of David's hand and held it close to her face. "What's happening?" she shouted.

"It's Nathan and Gina," Russ replied.

"Are you sure?" David asked.

"Positive. They just got in the Volvo, and now they're leaving."

Beck blinked hard, shaking off the fog in his head, and managed to look over just as Odom was rearing back. In a flash, he ducked left and grabbed Odom's ankle with both hands and twisted in a clockwise direction. Odom rolled with it, doing a mid-air spin, before dropping to the floor. He was climbing to his feet when Beck bull rushed him, driving him backward into the living room. Odom stumbled, off balance, and fell onto the coffee table, snapping one of its legs in the process. Unable to stop their momentum, they tumbled over the tabletop and landed in front of the fireplace.

As Odom climbed to his feet, he pulled a stinger whip from the side pocket of his cargo pants. With the flick of his wrist, he uncoiled it then lashed Beck with the 17" industrial steel cable. Beck twisted his upper body attempting to roll away from it, but took a devastating blow to his shoulder. Hunched over in pain, he grabbed a cast iron poker from the rack next to the fireplace and swung it in a sweeping arc, smashing the hook into the side of Odom's knee.

Jameson turned in his seat, his face hot with anger. "Just what were you thinking, coming back to the house?" he said to Nathan.

Nathan ignored the question and looked out the back window.

"What's wrong?" Kendra asked, watching him in the rearview mirror.

"Keep going," Nathan said, "and whatever you do, don't stop."

"Why?" Jameson asked, fuming.

Kendra came to the end of the street, tapped the brakes once, then cut the wheel and took a sharp right, pitching everyone sideways.

Nathan continued to watch through the rear window. "Faster," he told Kendra.

"The two of you put yourselves in grave danger," Jameson said, his anger still raging. To Nathan, he said, "Why do you think we had Beck take you to Braden Street?" He looked at Gina. "And why do you think we had Ellie sneak you back into your house?"

Nathan and Gina said nothing.

"We know someone is watching the house," Jameson said. "The whole point of us leaving at the same time was to make them believe the house was unguarded, and that they could go in unchallenged."

111

"So, that was the trap," Gina said.

"Yes," Jameson replied, "and you two walked right into it!"

"Did you guys see the intruder?" Kendra asked.

"We saw him," Nathan said, turning to look out the rear window again.

"He was waiting for us when we came down from the attic," Gina said.

"So? What happened?" Kendra asked, anxious to hear the details.

"Beck happened," Nathan said.

"Hold on," Jameson said. "What were you two doing in the attic?"

Nathan held up the scroll. "Looking for this."

"What is it?" Jameson asked, like it couldn't possibly be anything of importance.

"This is what Thomas Hammond hid in the bookcase," Nathan said. "I came back to the house to find it before Perry could get his hands on it."

"*That's* what was in the bookcase?" Jameson asked, shocked.

"Yes," Nathan said. "It was hidden inside a secret compartment behind one of the columns. Gina was the one who discovered the release mechanism."

"By accident," she muttered.

Jameson's expression darkened. "Did the intruder see you with it?" he asked.

"Yes," Nathan said. "He wanted me to give it to him, but I refused."

"That's when Beck showed up," Gina added. *Thankfully.*

Jameson turned back around in his seat, processing what Nathan and Gina had said. Things had suddenly gotten much more complicated, and dangerous. They had to move quickly now.

"What is that thing?" Kendra asked, trying to see the scroll in the rearview mirror. When that didn't work, she hit the directional and slowed, preparing to turn into a grocery store parking lot.

"NO!" Jameson shouted. "Keep going."

"But…"

"We need to get off the street," Jameson said. He checked the side mirror, committing each car behind them to memory.

"That's what I was going to do," Kendra said.

"Not here," Jameson told her. "We need to go someplace safe, where no one can find us."

"And you know where that place is?" Kendra asked.

"Yes. Just keep driving." He checked the side mirror again. "I'll tell you when to turn."

Odom's left leg buckled and he grunted in pain. Still, he refused to go down. Holding his damaged knee with his left hand, he used his right hand to unleash a backhand swipe at Beck with the stinger whip.

This time, Beck met Odom's arm halfway, bringing the poker down on his wrist with a thundering tomahawk chop. The blow pulverized Odom's radial nerve, causing his wrist to go limp. The stinger whip fell harmlessly to the floor, but Odom was undeterred. He lurched forward and grabbed Beck by the throat. Using every bit of energy he could muster, and blocking out the searing pain in his knee, he pushed off with his good leg and drove Beck backward across the floor.

Weakened by the blow to his shoulder, Beck could only swat helplessly at Odom with his one working arm. Odom squeezed harder, restricting Beck's airflow, and as they neared the front window, Beck dropped to the floor, pulling Odom down with him. As they fell, Beck planted his boot in Odom's gut, catapulting him through the air and sending him crashing through the front window. He landed in a giant rhododendron bush, in a shower of broken glass and wood.

"What now?" Elizabeth asked, watching Kendra drive away. "Do we stay or go after them?"

"Russ, what do we do?" David barked at the phone.

"Stay where you are," Russ said. "The kids are in good hands. We need to hold our positions in case...WHOA!...did you see that?"

"What is it?" David asked.

"Someone just crashed through the front window."

"They did *what?*" David shouted.

Russ pushed the door open and hopped out. "It's the intruder," he said, running toward the street. "He looks hurt."

"What's he doing?" Elizabeth asked.

"He just went around the side of the house. Hold on," Russ said. He ran back to the truck and retrieved his service pistol from the glove box. When he turned around again, Odom was gone.

Beck rolled over on the floor and worked himself into a semi-standing position, then hobbled over to the window and looked outside. Through the ragged opening there was no sign of the intruder, which came as no surprise. Whoever he was, he was no amateur. His lightning-fast moves and his choice of weaponry were proof of that. It was curious that he didn't have a gun, but Beck assumed he wasn't expecting to find anyone home, which would make a gun unnecessary.

Beck heard footsteps on the front porch steps. Seconds later, the front door swung open and Russ McCullough appeared in the hallway. When he saw Beck standing at the window, hunched over and holding his shoulder, he ran to him. "Are you okay?" he asked. Then he noticed the tear in Beck's shirt, and just beneath it, a bloody gash. "You need medical attention," he said. He pulled out his cell phone and began dialing when Beck grabbed his arm.

"No," he said. "I'm fine."

"Who was that guy?" Russ asked.

Beck shook his head. "No idea." He moved closer to the window and examined the sill. From the rubble he picked up a shard of glass, then took out his phone and dialed Jameson.

"Beck, what happened?" Jameson asked. "Are you hurt?"

"A little roughed up but I'll be fine," Beck replied. "What happened to the kids?"

"They're with me and Kendra."

"What were they doing in the house?" Beck asked, letting his anger show. "If I had known they were in there I never would've waited as long as I did to go inside."

"Bad timing," Jameson said. "We'll address that later, trust me, but first we need to deal with another, more pressing matter. Tell me about the intruder. Did you get him?"

"No, he got away," Beck said, "but he left something behind."

"What is it?"

Beck held the shard of glass up to the light and examined the bloody smear. "DNA."

"Good," Jameson said. "You know what to do with it, right?"

"I do."

"Good. You stay there. Secure the sample and keep it safe. I'll make immediate arrangements for someone to pick it up."

He ended the call and dialed another number.

And after that, another.

Two different area codes.

Two different people he trusted to get the job done.

Odom limped back to the Range Rover, retracing his earlier route. Along the way he found a broken tree branch that he fashioned into a makeshift cane. Fortunately, the injury he sustained was to his left knee. With a fully functioning right leg, he'd be able to drive without any problem—a small victory in an otherwise failed mission. Not something he was accustomed to.

He eased himself into the driver's seat, checked to see if he'd been followed, then called Dan Perry.

"Status?" Perry said.

"Negative on the package," Odom said.

"I see," Perry replied, not a hint of concern in his voice.

"I did find it," Odom said, "but there was significant interference when I tried to acquire it."

"You found it?" Perry asked. He stood up, his pulse quickening. "Where is it now?"

"The boy has it."

"And do you know where he is?" he asked, sensing they were

close to completion.

"Negative," said Odom. "He ducked out of the house with it while I was distracted."

"Distracted?"

"Physically engaged," Odom said.

Perry's heart continued to race, but he kept his emotions in check. "Recommendations?" he asked.

"There's no way they'll bring the boy back to the house. Not after today," Odom said. "They're not that stupid. Odds are, they'll stash him somewhere else. As for the item, that's anyone's guess."

"What about the girl?" Perry asked.

"She was with him."

"Which means they'll hide her too," Perry said.

"Agreed."

Perry's eyes drifted across the room as he considered his next move. The boy had the item, but it was a safe bet that he wouldn't have it for long. That much was certain. Like Odom said, the family wasn't stupid. They'd pass the item on to someone else, someone who would try to determine its secret. The chance of anyone succeeding was laughable, still, recovering it was the only way he could be 100% certain that his secret would stay safely concealed, as it had been since the very beginning.

Given the state of things as they were currently constructed, the boy was still the key to everything. Second on the list was the girl—still a possibility if all other options failed. "Forget the item," he told Odom. "There's no telling where it is now and there's an easier way to find it."

"The boy?" Odom said.

"Yes. Once we have him, everything else will fall into place."

"Understood," Odom said. He ended the call, then started the Rover and began his trek home, ignoring the pain in his left knee, which had swollen to the size of a small watermelon. The pain he could work through, as he'd done numerous times before. But the person who caused it was another matter altogether. That score would be settled at a later date, and with a much different outcome. His first order of business: find the boy.

Jameson guided Kendra to Watertown, through a maze of secondary roads. They were cruising down Pleasant Street when he said, "Okay, slow down, it's coming up on the left."

Kendra slowed, then made the turn onto a street lined with tall condo units on one side, and industrial buildings on the other.

"There," Jameson said, pointing to a dirt lot up ahead on the right.

"You're not serious," Kendra said.

Jameson looked at her without speaking. *Just do it.*

"All right," she said. "I'm turning."

She pulled into the lot, drove a short distance, and stopped, the Volvo's draft stirring up a cloud of dust that drifted past the side windows. To their right was a towering mound of dirt littered with broken chunks of tar. Beyond that was a pile of pebble-sized stone, then another mountain of fill. To their left was a haphazard pile of construction debris, stacks of banded lumber, and a short tower of wooden pallets.

"Why did you stop?" Jameson asked.

Kendra looked at him, confused. "You want me to keep *going?*"

"That way," he replied, pointing straight ahead.

Kendra shrugged...*okay, if you say so*...then continued on, the springs of the Volvo squeaking on the uneven ground.

They passed more mountains of dirt and gravel, crooked piles of aqua-colored piping, and run-down excavation equipment that looked like it hadn't moved in years. The open pit gradually narrowed and came to a narrow dirt road lined on both sides by towering hardwood trees, their branches knitting a thick canopy that bathed the road in shadows. Kendra followed it to the end, where a square industrial building sat, sheathed in vertical metal siding. A single garage door occupied the front, with no other windows or doors visible.

"Wait here," Jameson said, then opened the door and climbed out.

"Where is he going?" Gina asked.

"Your guess is as good a mine," Kendra said. She looked to her left and right, following the line of trees that stood like sentries around the building.

Jameson walked up to the garage door, punched a code into the keypad mounted on the doorframe, and the door rose without so much as a squeak or a rattle. When it stopped, he waved Kendra forward.

"Okay," she said with a tentative look. "I guess we're parking *inside*."

Jameson waited until the Volvo's back bumper cleared the opening, then hit a square button on the panel next to the door and it slowly descended, just as quietly as it had risen. He started across the room as Kendra, Nathan and Gina were climbing out of the car.

"Wait, where are you going?" Kendra yelled, her voice echoing off the metal roof.

"You'll see," Jameson said.

Beck sat on the edge of the tub in the bathroom. Russ stood next to him, washing Beck's wound and gently overlaying it with gauze bandages. When David and Elizabeth came running up the back-hall stairway, Russ leaned out into the hallway, saw who it was, and called out. "In here."

Elizabeth took one look at the bloody bandages draped over Beck's shoulder and gasped. "I hope you don't mind, I helped myself to some of your medical supplies," Beck said.

"Don't be silly," Elizabeth told him, staring at the wound. "We need to get you to a hospital."

"No hospitals," he said. "What you can do is go get my truck. Everything I need is in it. I'd do it myself, but as you can see…" he said, pointing at his shoulder.

"I'll take her," David said.

"No, I'll do it," Ellie said, from the hallway.

They turned, as one, surprised to see her standing there. She had seemingly appeared out of thin air.

"You guys should stay here," Ellie said. "In case that guy comes back."

"I wouldn't worry about him," Beck offered. "He won't be returning anytime soon. If he does, it'll be on crutches."

"Where's your truck?" Ellie asked.

"At the Cumberland Farms, two blocks away."

"Keys?" she said, extending an open palm.

Beck dug in his pocket, produced a single key, and tossed it through the doorway.

"I need the other thing, too," Ellie said.

"What other thing?"

"The sample."

He looked at Ellie, confused. "Jameson told *you* to pick it up?"

"Yup."

Beck shrugged. *Okay.* If Jameson trusted her, that was good enough for him. Little did he know the full extent of their relationship, or the many times Jameson had employed Ellie's services over the years.

Oh, the stories she could tell.

He stood up, then took a plastic zip-lock bag from atop the medicine cabinet where he'd stashed it minutes earlier. Inside was the bloodied shard of glass, wrapped in a strip of brown paper that he'd ripped from a small lunch bag he found in the kitchen. "Take good care of that," he told Ellie as he passed it to her. "It's all we've got."

"That was my plan," she said.

"Before you go," Beck said to Elizabeth, "can I trouble you for a needle and thread?"

Elizabeth looked at his shoulder and grimaced. "You're not serious…" she said.

Beck nodded his head. "Don't worry," he said. "It's not my first time."

Jameson led them to the back of the building, weaving his way through a maze of automotive repair equipment and tall rolling tool cabinets. Nathan walked past a dolly holding an oxygen and acetylene tank. The long twin hose coiled around them was draped with cobwebs.

In the center of the back wall was a small office. Jameson pushed through the door and walked past a wooden desk that was set along the left wall. Directly across from it was a tall wooden bookcase, home to stacks of automotive catalogs, thick 3-ring binders, and service manuals for various types of vehicles, each dated and arranged in sequential order.

Kendra, Nathan, and Gina waited near the desk as Jameson went to the bookcase and reached under the middle shelf. There was an audible click, then the right side of the bookcase broke away from the wall as if shaken loose by an earthquake.

Nathan and Gina exchanged a look of shock. *Whoa!*

"This way," Jameson said, swinging the bookcase open all the way. As he stepped through the narrow opening in the wall, a series of lights came on, illuminating a small landing and a flight of steps that led to a lower level.

With each step they took, more lights came on. They were positioned at knee level on either side of the stairs, providing enough light to see the next step. At the bottom of the stairway was a steel-gray metal door. Like before, Jameson punched a code on a small keypad, the lock clicked softly, then he pushed the door open and motioned for the others to enter.

One by one they walked into the room and stopped. In the soft glow of the overhead lights, the room looked like a military command center. The walls were barren and a slate gray table with black edge molding ran down the center of the room. A pair of computer monitors sat atop it, their cables snaking down through a small hole, to a large storage cabinet with vented access panels.

On the facing wall was an array of large monitors. They were turned off with the exception of four smaller ones that were clustered together in their own grouping. Each showed a different view of the outside of the building. Front. Back. Left side. Right side.

"What is this place?" Gina whispered to Nathan.

Nathan shrugged. "Beats me."

"May I?" Jameson said, gesturing at the linen-wrapped scroll in Nathan's hand.

Nathan handed it over, then followed Jameson to the table where he gave the wrap a thorough inspection. He loosened the twine and glanced inside, studying the paper for several long seconds. "Interesting," he said, then promptly resealed the end with the twine.

"That's it?" Nathan asked. "You're not going to take it out?"

"No," Jameson said calmly.

"I don't understand," Nathan said. "I thought when we found it, we'd at least *look* at it. You know, try to figure out what it is, which might tell us why it was hidden in the bookcase?"

"Oh, believe me, we'll look at it," Jameson said. "We'll look at it a lot. But right now it needs to disappear."

"Disappear?" Nathan exclaimed. "But we just—"

"Yes," Jameson cut in. "It needs to vanish, and so do the two of you."

7

The Handoff

Jameson looked at his watch, then made the call. There was no guarantee that Poole would answer, especially if he was working in the solitary confines of his basement. But as luck would have it, he picked up right away.

"Jameson, my friend," he said. "How delightful to see your name on my call screen."

"Thank you, Fletcher," Jameson replied. "I hope I'm not getting you at an inconvenient time, but something of extreme importance has come up and it needs your immediate attention. I'm afraid it can't wait."

"Hmm, sounds intriguing," said Poole. "I was just preparing a cocktail."

Jameson glanced at his watch again. *A cocktail?* he thought. *At this hour?*

"These solvents are very tricky," Poole said. "They have to be mixed just right if you want them to work."

"Solvents?" Jameson asked.

"Yes, a custom cocktail of solvents to be precise. I use them for removing adhesive tape residue. If left alone it can oxidize the paper. In this case, an autographed manuscript of notes on physics and solid geometry, by Sir Isaac Newton. Quite a spectacular piece I must say. Written in Latin, no less."

Jameson waited patiently as Poole expounded. The man might be eccentric, but even in retirement he was a master of his craft. A former chemistry professor at Oxford University, his services were in constant demand by museums, auction houses, and law enforcement agencies. Which agencies those were Poole wouldn't say, but Jameson had a pretty good idea. Over the years, Jameson had worked with some of them as well.

"Now, enough about my project," Poole said at last. "What is this emergency you spoke of?"

"It's best if I tell you in person," Jameson said. "How soon can you meet me?"

"How soon? Well, let's see. It's nearly 1 o'clock. What say we meet at 4pm?"

"Let's make it 2:30…at the usual place," Jameson countered.

"Oh my," Poole exclaimed. "This really *is* important."

Elizabeth waited on the lawn while Ellie backed her car out of the garage. Once she was belted in, her questions came like a sudden afternoon downpour. "Jameson called you," she confirmed.

"Yes," Ellie said. "He wanted me to get the blood sample from Beck."

"What about the kids?"

"He and Kendra have them."

"Are they okay?"

"I believe so, yes," Ellie said, as she backed down the driveway.

"Where are they?"

"He didn't say," Ellie replied. She paused to check for traffic then backed out into the street.

"Didn't or wouldn't?" Elizabeth asked.

"Both. But trust me, they're fine," Ellie said, giving Elizabeth a confident nod.

Elizabeth tensed her fingers into a tight ball as Ellie sped down the street. "What were they *thinking?*" she said. "Going into the house like that? They could've been seriously hurt."

"Jameson said Nathan and Gina were upstairs in the attic when the intruder entered the house."

"They were up in the attic?" Elizabeth said, confused.

"Uh-huh," Ellie said, stopping at the end of the street. "Jameson said Nathan found something in the bookcase."

Elizabeth's eyes went wide. "He said *what?*"

Ellie turned right and headed into town. "Nathan found something in the bookcase," Ellie repeated. She spotted the Cumberland Farms up ahead and slowed to make the turn.

"Did he say what it was?" Elizabeth asked, anxious to hear the rest.

"No," Ellie said. She pulled into the lot and surveyed the vehicles parked along the side of the building. A handful more were parked directly across from them, in front of a tall chain-link fence. In the middle of the group, facing out, was Beck's truck. Compared to the cars on either side of it, the truck looked big enough to house a Shire horse. "Are you sure you can drive that thing?" Ellie asked, as she drove toward it.

"I'll manage," Elizabeth said. "You're sure Jameson didn't say anything else about what Nathan found?"

Ellie shook her head. "Nope. He was more focused on getting the blood sample to Sully."

Elizabeth sat motionless, staring at the glove box without speaking.

"What is it?" Ellie asked.

"I swear, I'm going to lock that kid in his room until he's eighteen," Elizabeth fumed.

"You're joking, right?"

"No, I'm not," Elizabeth countered. "If he found what I think he found, there's no telling what he'll do next. Knowing him, it'll be something extremely dangerous." She continued to stare. Then, as if touched by a live electrical wire, her body twitched and she said, "I have to get back to the house. Are you going to be okay?"

"I'll be fine," Ellie said. "It turns out Sully was in Saco checking out a marina. We're meeting in Newburyport."

"I'd go with you, but..." Elizabeth began.

"No," Ellie cut in. "You go. I'll be back in a couple of hours."

After she left the Cumberland Farms parking lot, she sped up I-95, making it to Newburyport in less than an hour. She found Sully waiting for her in the parking lot of the Cherry Hill soccer field, just off Storey Ave. He was leaning on the front hood of his Crown Vic, head up, eyes closed, basking in the warm afternoon sunshine, imagining himself aboard a cruise ship in the Mediterranean.

"Hey, kid," he said, as Ellie rolled to a stop next to him. "Long time no see."

"You're not going to suggest a trip to L.L. Bean again, are you?" Ellie joked, referring to the comments he'd made during their meeting in the Old Port two months earlier, when he was trying to dissuade her from questioning Reggie Griffin, a local boat captain and repeated problem child for the Portland Police Department.

"Maybe next time," he joked. He pushed off the Crown Vic and walked over to her open window. "You have something for me?"

She took the plastic bag from the cupholder and handed it out the window to him. "Careful with that," she said. "It's sharp."

Sully turned it over in his hand, inspecting both sides. "Tell Jameson I should have the results for him by the end of day tomorrow."

"Will do," Ellie said. "I assume he told you what happened this morning?"

"He did. How's Beck doing?"

"He took a pretty serious blow to the shoulder, but other than that I think he'll pull through. Sounds like the other guy got the worst of it."

Sully leaned down and spoke in a serious tone. "Today was nothing," he said. "Whatever that guy was looking for must be pretty important, or else Perry never would've sent such a heavy hitter. And because he didn't find what he was after, he'll be back."

"Or Perry will send someone else," Ellie suggested, recalling the crutches comment that Beck had made about the intruder.

"Exactly. And next time, it may not be just one guy. He could send a small army. What I'm saying is, things are going to escalate. Big time. We need to find Perry and find him fast. And until we do, you need to be very careful."

"Ehh," Ellie said, waving off the notion. "I'll be fine."

Sully gave her a look. *Oh, you think so, huh?*

"Don't worry," she told him. "I'll stay out of sight."

"Yeah, Jameson told me you're pretty good at that."

"He'd be right."

"Then do it," Sully replied. "I don't want to go to L.L. Bean alone." He gave her a pat on the arm, then stood and walked back to his car. As he was buckling his seat belt, he looked through the side window.

Ellie was gone.

Jameson clicked off the call with Fletcher Poole and walked to the far end of the room, to a tall metal cabinet pushed up against the wall. He opened the door and knelt down, rummaging through the items on one of the lower shelves for nearly a minute before he found what he was looking for.

"What's that?" Nathan asked, as Jameson walked back to the table.

"A storage tube," Jameson said. It was solid black, nearly 20" long, with a twisting end cap and a thin black shoulder strap.

"Looks like a small bazooka, if you ask me," Kendra said.

Jameson removed the end cap and carefully slid the linen-wrapped paper into the tube. He inspected the fit, then shortened the tube using the set of locking tabs that ran along the outer edge. When he was done, he tipped the tube one way, then the other, to ensure the contents wouldn't slide back and forth. With that done, he looked at Nathan and Gina, staring at each of them alternately for several seconds.

"What?" Gina asked.

"What, indeed," Jameson replied.

Nathan and Gina exchanged a confused look.

"What do we do with the both of you?" Jameson said. "You can't go back to your homes."

Gina frowned. "Hold on. Him, I understand," she said, pointing at Nathan. "But why me? Why can't I go home?"

"Did the intruder see you with Nathan?" Jameson asked.

"Yeah?" Gina said, shrugging. *So?*

"And was Nathan holding *this?*" Jameson asked, holding up the tube.

Gina nodded. *Uh-huh.*

"Then whoever he is, you just made his list. If he comes back looking for Nathan and doesn't find him, he'll turn his attention to you."

Gina swallowed hard. *Me?*

"Don't worry," Jameson said. "We're not going to let him find you."

He turned on one of the computers and typed in a series of commands. Seconds later, a giant monitor on the wall came to life. He composed a short message and hit send, then pulled his phone from his pocket and called Elizabeth.

"Jameson," she said, concern in her voice. "How are the kids?"

In the background, he heard the throaty growl of a truck engine. "The kids are fine," he said. "Where are *you?*"

"Driving Beck's truck back to the house."

"I see. How long before you get there?" Jameson asked.

"Five minutes, tops."

"Good. When you get there, turn on your computer and check your messages."

"Is it true?" she asked. "Nathan found something in the bookcase?"

"He did, and we'll talk about it, I promise you. But right now, I need you at home in front of your computer. And Elizabeth? Make sure the others are with you." He ended the call, then dialed Ellie's number.

"Jameson?" she said.

"How'd it go?" he asked her.

"Quick and easy, as expected. Sully told me he'd have results sometime tomorrow."

"Good. Do me a favor and stay on the line, will you?"

"Sure. What's up?"

"We need to draw up our battle plan. War is coming."

"Coming?" she said. "I thought it was already here."

Ten minutes later, Elizabeth was sitting in front of the computer in the living room. Standing behind her were David, Beck, and Russ McCullough. She found Jameson's email, with a video conference link, and seconds later she was staring at his face on her screen.

"Is everybody there?" Jameson asked.

"Here," they said, answering as one.

"I've got Ellie on speaker phone," he told them, "but before we start, there's someone here who wants to say hello." He stepped aside and Nathan's face appeared on Elizabeth's screen.

"Hey Mom," Nathan said, cautiously.

"Nathan!" she exclaimed. "Are you all right?"

"Mom, relax, I'm fine," he groaned.

"What about Gina?"

Gina leaned in front of the monitor and waved. "I'm good," she said. "Thanks for asking."

Elizabeth shook her head and let out an exasperated breath. "I don't know where to begin with you two," she said.

Nathan knew that voice. Her emotional rocket boosters had just ignited. Ten seconds to liftoff. Nine…eight…seven…six…

Jameson appeared on the screen again and eased Nathan aside. "We'll have plenty of time to discuss what happened earlier today," he said, "but at the moment, we need to figure out what to do with Nathan and Gina. As you're well aware, home is no longer an option. Our trap worked, but because the intruder escaped, the kids are more vulnerable now than ever before."

"Is there any reason Nathan can't go back to Braden Street?" David asked.

"I don't see why not," Jameson replied. "But that's something that you and Elizabeth need to sanction."

"The question is, will he stay there?" Beck asked.

"I'll stay there," Nathan said. "I have no reason leave. Not now." After seeing a stranger in his house, and the brutality that followed, he was keenly aware of the dangerous situation he was in. That they were all in.

"If I may," Jameson said. "We can keep Nathan at Braden Street for the time being. Should the need arise, we'll move him to a more remote location.

"Good idea," Russ offered.

"Agreed," said Elizabeth and David.

"That just leaves Gina," Jameson said.

"Let me deal with Gina," Ellie said.

Jameson adjusted the volume of the phone. "Say again?"

"Leave Gina to me," Ellie said. "I have the perfect place to take her."

"What about her parents?" Elizabeth asked.

"They'll be fine. I'll tell them we're going camping. I mean, it's summertime…and that *is* what people do, right?"

Gina looked at Nathan and grimaced. "Camping?" she whispered. *Yuck!*

He leaned closer and said, "A word of advice?"

Here it comes, she thought. "And what might that be?"

"Bug spray."

She gave him a sour look. "Gee, thanks."

"Don't mention it."

She reached over and flicked his ear. Hard.

"Oww!" he said, rubbing the side of his head. "What was that for?"

"Bug spray is two words, dummy, not one."

From Watertown, Kendra drove to the Central Square Parking Deck in Waltham to rendezvous with Nathan's parents. From there, David and Elizabeth would take Gina back to the house to await

Ellie's return. As agreed, they met on the ground level, in the back corner where they would be less conspicuous.

"Give us a minute," Nathan said, when he saw his father pull up next to Kendra's Volvo.

His parents were already out of the car by the time his feet touched the pavement. They rushed to him and gave him extended hugs, then guided him over to the concrete wall where the shadows offered them a thin cloak of privacy.

"Ellie told me you and Gina were upstairs in the attic," Elizabeth began. "Do you want to tell me what you two—?"

"Mom, I found it," Nathan said, cutting her off. "After all this time, I found it!"

"Whoa, hold on," his father said. "What exactly did you find?"

"A roll of paper," Nathan replied. "It's wrapped in a piece of linen cloth."

His parents shared a look of doubt.

"Where was it?" his father asked. "In a drawer? Behind one of the books?"

"No," Nathan said. "It was hidden in a secret compartment, behind one of the front columns."

His parents shared another look. This time it was amazement. *Could it be?*

"It's what Thomas Hammond hid in the bookcase," Nathan said. He didn't mention that the books wouldn't budge off the shelves, no matter how hard he or Gina tried to remove them. The thought that the bookcase had prevented him from removing the books, signaling him to look elsewhere, would scare the living daylights out of most people. A year ago, it would've scared *him* out of his wits, but he was well past that now.

"Where is this roll of paper?" his father asked.

"Jameson has it," Nathan said. "After we leave here he's going to give it to some guy he knows. For safekeeping, I guess."

"What guy?" his mother asked.

"Fletcher somebody."

Elizabeth nodded slowly, a pensive look on her face.

"You know who that is?" David asked.

"Yes," she said. "From a long time ago."

They walked back to the Volvo and spoke to Jameson, who stayed seated in the car with the window open, holding the storage tube in his lap.

"Did you look at it?" Elizabeth asked.

"Briefly," Jameson said. "It's very old and very delicate." He opened the plastic tube and eased out the scroll. "Here, see for yourself," he said, handing it to her. "Careful, now."

She held it in her open palms like an offering, staring at it in awe. From a very young age, she had heard stories about the secret buried within the bookcase. Her older sister, Sarah, had concocted fanciful tales about it—mystical accounts she would share at bedtime long after the light had been turned out. And now, here it was, after generations of rumor and speculation. *If only Sarah could see this*, she thought.

She loosened the twine on one end and peeked inside, spellbound by what she saw. "You're taking it to Fletcher?" she said.

"Yes," Jameson said. "I didn't think you'd object."

"Object?" Elizabeth said. "Is there anyone better?"

"No one I'd trust," Jameson replied.

"I'm sure my father would agree." She tied off the end of the wrap and handed it back. "You'll keep us informed of Fletcher's progress?" she asked.

"Absolutely," Jameson said. He slipped the linen wrap back in the storage tube then turned to Gina. "Ready to go?"

Gina managed a weak shrug...*whatever*...then reluctantly climbed out of the car. She stopped at the back bumper, where Nathan was standing like a sentry, monitoring the flow of people and cars in and out of the garage.

"So...Braden Street," she said.

"Yup," he said, watching a dark gray SUV creep down one of the aisles toward them.

"Do everyone a favor and stay there this time," Gina said sternly.

"I will," he said, as the SUV looped around and headed for the exit. He looked over at Gina then turned away, smirking.

"What?" she asked.

"Have fun camping," he said.

"Oh, you think that's funny?" She gave him a shove that sent him stumbling sideways.

Just then, David appeared at Gina's side. "Time to go," he said.

"See ya later," Nathan said, as she brushed past him.

It was everything she could do not to shove him again.

"Yeah, later," she mumbled.

Neither one had any idea when that would be.

After the meeting in Waltham, Kendra drove to Arlington Heights to drop Nathan off at the Braden Street house. When they pulled into the driveway, Beck was sitting in front of the garage door, in a folding aluminum-frame chair with green and white plastic webbing. In his hands was a small paperback book. He was dressed in camo shorts and a mud-colored tee shirt, and it wasn't until Nathan was standing next to him that he noticed the lump in Beck's left shoulder, caused by the thick gauze bandage covering his wound.

"So, back to stay, are we?" Beck said, without looking up from the book.

"Yeah, about before…" Nathan began.

"Don't bother," Beck said. He closed the book and stood, then led Nathan into the house using the same door as before. He tossed the book on the kitchen counter and went into the living room. "Sit," he said, pointing at the massive sectional couch. He lowered himself onto one end and sat back, the look on his face like chiseled stone.

When Nathan saw that, he sat down at the opposite end.

"Do we need to review the rules?" Beck asked.

"No," Nathan replied, meaning it.

"Good," Beck said. "Because the mystery intruder may have limped away, but he's not finished. If he returns, he won't just be looking for you. He'll also want another crack at me. A guy like that doesn't just quit after the first failed attempt."

"What do you mean, a guy like that?"

"He wasn't like those two clowns in the van. This guy was upper level. Ex-military. Special forces would be my guess. Definitely a mercenary. We'll know a lot more once we get the blood results back from the lab."

Nathan got a queasy feeling in his stomach and flopped back on the couch. *Ex-military? Special forces? Why would Perry bring in a guy like that to steal a roll of paper?*

Beck saw the color go out of Nathan's face. "Just remember Rule #3 and you'll be fine," he said.

Fine? Nathan thought. *Yeah, right,*

"Now, there's something else we need to talk about."

"What now?" Nathan muttered. *As if I don't have enough to think about already.*

"I want to know how you managed to get back to your house before I did."

With Nathan and Gina in safe hands, Jameson directed Kendra to the Tisch Library at Tufts University in Medford.

"*This* is the place?" she asked, as she drove down Professors Row, past the impressive construction of stone, concrete and glass.

"Let me out at the stop sign," Jameson said. "I'll call you when we're done."

"Okay, if you say so." She came to a squeaking halt at the stop sign, then watched as he got out of the car and started up the long walkway that snaked toward the front entrance of the library. Her concentration was broken by the blare of a car horn directly behind her. "OH, JUST RELAX!" she shouted at the rearview mirror.

The driver honked again.

"OH YEAH?" she yelled. She put the car in park and climbed out, just as the driver pulled around her. "YEAH, YOU'D BETTER RUN!" she shouted, as the car sped away. She got back in the car and slammed the door. "College punk."

Elizabeth and David took an indirect route back home, doubling back through quiet residential neighborhoods and side streets while keeping an eye out for anyone following them. Gina slouched down in the back seat, staying out of sight, like Nathan had done with Beck, but without the itchy blanket.

When they got home, Elizabeth's car was parked at the curb in front of the house, allowing David to pull up the driveway and straight into the garage. Gina waited until he closed the garage door, then sat up and got out.

"You wait here," Elizabeth told her. She stepped out the side door and nearly collided with Ellie. "I was just coming to get you," Elizabeth said.

"I saw you pull in," Ellie told her. "I've checked the street. We're good."

Gina appeared at the door.

"Ah, there she is," Ellie said. "My little wanderer."

Gina gave her a hard look. *Don't start with me.*

Ellie had plenty to talk to her about, but they were on the clock and what she had to say could wait...for now. She shepherded Gina back to the house, walking quickly, tension hanging between them like an invisible cloud.

Gina had just stepped through the back-porch door when she spotted her suitcase sitting off to the side. "Hey, that's my suitcase," she said.

"Yes, it is," Ellie said. "I took the liberty of packing some of your things. Grab anything else you need and meet me back here in five minutes."

"Hold on," Gina said. "You packed my things? Why would you do that?"

"Because we're out of time. We need to leave, right now."

"Right now? Why? Do we lose our campsite if we don't show up by 4 o'clock?" Gina snipped.

"We're not going camping," Ellie said.

"We're *not* going camping," Gina repeated. "Good. So where *are* we going?"

"I'll tell you on the way. It's someplace nice. You're gonna love it. Trust me."

"And we have to leave right now?"

"Yes."

"What's the rush?"

"I think the more pressing question is, why did you sneak out of the house this morning?"

"I went to talk to Nathan," Gina said casually, like it was no big deal.

"I see. And why would you do that?" Ellie asked. "You *do* realize the whole point of hiding you was to, I don't know, keep you *hidden?* As in, out of sight?"

"Look, I did it. It's done. Nothing happened. So can we just drop it?" Gina said as she stormed into the kitchen.

"Nothing *happened?*" Ellie said, falling in behind her. "You want to try that again?"

"I don't know what you're talking about," Gina mumbled. She went to the sink and poured a glass of water.

"Oh, I think you know exactly what I'm talking about," Ellie said.

"You're referring to the guy that broke in?" Gina asked.

"Bingo!"

"What am I, psychic?" Gina fired back. "How was I supposed to

140

know some creep was going to break in?" She took a sip of water and dumped the rest in the sink.

"If you'd just stayed put like you were supposed to…" Ellie began.

"Well, I didn't," Gina fired back. *So there.*

"Did you see him?" Ellie asked. "His face, I mean."

"Of course I did. He was standing five feet away from us."

"Do you think you'd recognize him if you saw him again?"

Gina nodded. In her mind she pictured the intruder's beady eyes and menacing expression. It was a face that would haunt her dreams for days to come.

"Did he say anything to indicate why he was there?" Ellie asked.

"Uh-huh."

"Was he looking for Nathan?"

"No."

Ellie rolled her eyes. "Was he looking for the thing Nathan found in the bookcase?"

"You know about that?" Gina asked.

"Yes," Ellie said, her patience waning. "Is that what he was looking for?"

"Yes."

"You're sure?" Ellie asked.

"Yes. He wanted Nathan to give it to him."

"Are you going to tell me what it is?" Ellie asked.

"I don't know," Gina snapped. "Am I allowed to?"

Ellie smirked. "Of course you are."

"Fine. It was a roll of paper."

"Paper," Ellie repeated, like Gina was mistaken.

"Yeah. It was wrapped in a piece of cloth and sewn shut."

"And the guy that broke in…he wanted it."

"Yes! He wanted it!" Gina groaned. *How many times do I have to say it?*

Ellie went to the window and did a quick scan of the street.

"What are you doing?" Gina asked.

"Being careful," Ellie replied. "That guy could be out there right now, planning a return visit."

"Don't *say* that!" Gina exclaimed.

When she saw that the street was clear, Ellie went to the door and paused, motioning for Gina to follow. "Come on," she said, "let's go."

"Right now?" Gina asked. "You told me I could get some things."

"Time's up," Ellie said, pulling her car keys from her pocket. "We're outta here."

Jameson was making his way along the asphalt walkway toward the library when his phone vibrated. He dredged it out of his pocket, checked to see who was calling, then punched the talk button. "Raymond," he said, using Sully's first name. "I understand the exchange went well."

"Piece of cake," Sully replied. "I'll call tomorrow when I get the results from my guy at the lab, but there's something else you should know."

Jameson stopped walking. "Go on."

"I went to the South Portland Marina this morning. According to the kid I spoke to, they haven't seen Perry's boat in three weeks."

"Curious," Jameson said.

"It gets better."

Jameson stepped off the asphalt walkway onto the grass,

stopping next to a tall maple tree. "I'm listening," he said.

"I sent out an email blast to marinas up and down the coast on the chance that someone might've seen it," Sully told him. He didn't mention that the idea came from Christine Reyes.

"That was smart," Jameson said. "When do you think you'll hear back?"

"I already did. I got a reply from a guy who works at Marston's Marina in Saco."

Jameson eyed the students meandering by on the walkway and turned away. "Saco? That would fit with Nathan's theory about Perry being in southern Maine."

"Yeah, chalk one up for the kid," Sully mused.

"Why?" Jameson asked. "What did you find out?"

"I visited the marina before my meeting with Ellie. Perry's boat was definitely docked there. Care to guess when?"

"Three weeks ago?" Jameson replied.

"You got it."

"Are you sure about that?"

"Yeah, they had a record of it," Sully told him.

"And now?" Jameson asked.

"Gone. The guy I talked to said he hasn't seen it since."

Jameson said nothing as he assessed the information. As he sorted through the possible interpretations, his eyes drifted across the spacious lawn to the Goddard Chapel. In the bright afternoon sun, its 100-foot stone bell tower stood above the tree line like a centurion guard.

"You still there?" Sully asked.

"Yes, I'm here. You said the boat's gone?"

"That's right."

"Well, it has to be somewhere, right?" Jameson asked.

"I'd say that's a fair assessment."

"If your emails worked once, let's hope they work again."

"I'll keep you posted."

Jameson ended the call and continued up the walkway, climbing two sets of stone steps before he came to the library entrance. He had just walked through the front door when he spotted Fletcher twenty feet away. He was standing in front of a map of the library that was mounted on the wall, studying it like a first-time visitor. In actuality, he and Jameson had met there on several occasions when Jameson needed the kind of help that only Poole could offer.

As always, Poole was dressed in baggy chinos, an untucked tee, and a wrinkled Campbell tartan shirt, also untucked. In one hand he held a bulky and battered leather briefcase with two outer pockets on the front, each held shut by a leather strap and bronze buckle.

"Fletcher," Jameson said, as he approached.

Poole turned and lowered his round tortoise-shell eyeglasses. "Ah, Jameson, you're looking well," he said.

Jameson fought back a smile as he eyed Poole's unruly mane. It never failed to elicit a mental image of Albert Einstein, hair askew, as if he'd just stepped out of a wind tunnel. Jameson couldn't help but wonder when Poole last brushed it, or if the man even owned a brush for that matter. "Are we all set?" he asked.

"That we are," Poole replied. As was the tradition, he'd secured one of the small study rooms in the Collections area where they could talk without being interrupted. Ordinarily, the library required advance notice, but Poole's notoriety was such that he was allowed to show up, unannounced, and use any study room that wasn't occupied.

He and Jameson followed the main hallway to the Collections area, then skirted the outer wall to the four small study rooms. They were arranged in pairs, two on the left, two on the right. Poole pushed open the door to 218C and stepped inside.

Jameson slid in behind him and promptly closed the door. When they were both seated at the small table, he removed the end cap of the plastic storage tube, eased out the linen wrap, and placed it on the table between them.

"Well, well, what do we have here?" Poole asked, eyes bright.

"That's what I was hoping you could tell me," Jameson said.

Poole picked up the wrap with great care and inspected it from end to end, taking special interest in the thread holding it closed. "Curious," he said softly.

"Yes," Jameson replied. "I'd put its date of origin somewhere around 1850."

Poole removed the twine on one end and looked inside. "Hello," he said, when he saw the roll of paper. He untied the twine from the opposite end, then found the end of the thread holding the wrap closed and tugged at it gently until it was free of the cloth. Working slowly, he unrolled the linen, stopping when the roll of paper became visible. "Remarkable," he said, then leaned down and sniffed, his face just inches from the tabletop.

The paper had a slight yellow tint, with subtle lines that ran both vertically and horizontally. In several areas he noticed dark brown spots that mushroomed outward, creating a halo of light brown color. He studied them for several seconds, thinking, then took his cell phone from his pocket and aimed it at the paper.

"No," Jameson said, pushing the camera aside. "No pictures."

"I always take pictures," Poole told him. "You know this."

"Not this time," Jameson said. "Trust me, it's for your own safety."

"My own safety?" Pool exclaimed. "Jameson, what have you gotten me into now?"

"Unknown," Jameson replied, staring at the roll of paper.

For several seconds neither man spoke.

"Very well," Poole said, as last. He set his phone on the table, then rested his fingers on the top of the roll and gently pushed down. Next, he picked it up, holding it in one hand while he used his other hand to peel back the edge. It gave slightly, but when he felt the paper resist he set it back down on the table at once. "Okay, then," he said.

"Thoughts?" Jameson asked.

"I have several," Poole said. He rerolled the paper in the linen cloth and slid it back into the plastic storage tube. "For starters, you're off."

"I'm off? What does that mean?"

"Your numbers," said Poole. "You told me the paper originated in 1850."

"To the best of my knowledge, yes."

"Well, it certainly *existed* in 1850," Poole noted.

"But?"

"By then it was already 100 years old."

8

The Press

Thursday, 4:45 A.M.

Fletcher's eyes snapped open and he bolted upright in bed. The first threads of daylight were weaving their way through the tangle of tree branches outside his window, and through the screen he could hear the faint flutter of wings and the chatter of the chestnut-sided warblers that nested nearby.

The woods had always been his favorite part of the property. It was set at the end of a narrow road in Lexington, just a stone's throw from the Munroe Tavern, offering privacy and a window into a world far less complicated than the one he navigated.

He climbed out of bed, not from a growling stomach or the need for a cup of hot tea. The tea could wait. Curiosity gripped him like a fever and he quickly got dressed and hurried downstairs to the basement, a room that had become more of a sanctuary than a lab.

It was a generous space when he first bought the house. But over time it became cluttered with benches and tables, stools, microscopes, sinks, a three-component water filtration system, tool boxes, and shelves lined with chemicals and assorted beakers, pipettes, and test tubes. An adjoining room, with its own museum-quality temperature and humidity controls, served as a storage area. In it were several flat file cases and a rolling storage unit. A third room had been set up as a ventilated chemical-storage area where he kept incompatible solvents, acids, bases, and oxidizing or reducing agents.

When he got to the basement, he made a beeline for the pressing packet he'd constructed the previous afternoon. He was tempted to break from protocol, dismantle it, and examine the paper again. Maybe by doing so, he'd find the answer to the question that had tormented him since his meeting with Jameson in the Tisch Library.

It began as a whisper, as he was pulling out of the parking lot. He pushed it aside and drove home to begin the delicate process of reviving the age-old roll of paper. To do that, he'd first need to make a humidification chamber. After searching his stores, he settled on a clear polycarbonate food storage box with a locking top, one of many he'd collected over the years for just such a purpose. With the roll measuring 13" from top to bottom, and the length as yet unknown, he chose a box that measured 26" x 18", with a depth of nearly 4".

As he worked, Jameson's words sounded again, stronger this time—the whisper turning into a full-throated caution. Again he dismissed it and moved on, layering the bottom of the container with three Tek-Wipe sheets, cut to size, which he then saturated with filtered water. On top of that he placed a sheet of common window screening, to keep the paper away from the water. Next came a layer of Hollytex, a spunbound polyester fabric that would add another layer of protection. With the bottom layering complete, he set the tightly rolled paper on the Hollytex and attached the box's locking lid.

When he returned 45 minutes later, the roll had begun to loosen. Jameson's cryptic warning, like a blistering shout, boomed through his mind, ultimately driving him from the basement. In an attempt to silence the voice, he went to the kitchen and busied himself with dinner preparations: peeling and boiling potatoes, then chopping and sautéing the onions and carrots. He soon fell into a rhythm, adding the garlic, then the ground lamb, the beef stock, and spices.

His professional curiosity began to burn at the edge of his thoughts, and by the time he put the meat sauce into the ovenproof dish, and covered it with the mashed potatoes, he could stand it no more. He slid the dish into the oven, washed up, and hurried back downstairs to the basement, drying his hands on a dish towel as he went.

As expected, the paper had loosened even more. At last, it was time. He removed the locked lid and picked up the roll, carefully testing the level of flex. When it offered little resistance, he slowly unrolled it. What he saw drew him closer and he breathed a sigh of relief, feeling like a massive weight had been lifted from his shoulders. Rejuvenated, he combed every inch of the paper, looking for any ink bleed. When he was done he carefully set the paper back down in the chamber, fully unrolled, and added a fresh layer of Hollytex, which he secured at the corners with flat gray beach rocks, each the size of a hockey puck, that had been worn smooth by the sea. After sealing the chamber with the locking lid, he went back upstairs and called Jameson.

"You were pulling my leg weren't you?" he asked, after Jameson picked up.

"I'm sorry, what was that?" Jameson asked.

"At the library. You were just having a bit of fun with me. That whole bit about no photos, how it was for my own safety. It was just some friendly kidding, right?"

"Fletcher, I'm afraid you've lost me."

Dan Perry asked Trask to meet him at the house at 6am. It was set at the end of a narrow road in Bartlett Mills, a heavily wooded township west of Kennebunk, Maine, with few homes, lots of trees, and very little traffic. Just what Perry needed if his plan was going to succeed.

By design, the house looked to be in a state of advanced decline. The yard hadn't been mowed in over a year. All along the property line, stray tree branches were left untrimmed and extended over the lawn, filtering out the sun and creating damp, dark areas that were overrun with fungus. The clapboards were in desperate need of scraping and painting. Even the fabricated realtor's sign at the front edge of the property was obscured by an invasion of mile-a-minute vines from the bank of the narrow brook that ran along the road.

When Perry arrived at the property, Trask was standing at the front door, his back to the street as he fiddled with the lock. His green and black camo pants were faded from years of wear, and his soot-gray tee shirt was torn in places, stained in others.

"Problem?" Perry called out as he walked up the steps.

"Nope," Trask replied without bothering to turn around. "Just double checking." He slipped the ring of keys into his pocket and stepped aside, moving his massive frame out of the way as Perry walked to the heavy wooden door and pushed it open.

From what he could see, the front hallway and center staircase looked completely normal. To the casual observer, this would look like any other house, on any other street, in any other town. In fact, every room had received a number of unusual alterations, each designed with a singular purpose in mind—containment.

That was Plan A.

Perfect in its conception and design, Perry was forced to scrap the plan after Romero and Foss failed to acquire the intended target: Nathan Cole. And now that Nathan had been stashed away at some unknown location, and was being guarded by a team of people, Perry had shifted to Plan B: the pursuit of the paper hidden inside the bookcase. When that attempt failed, he was forced to revert to Plan A, putting the house back in play.

"Looks good," he told Trask.

"Almost there," Trask said. He pulled a bug out of his thick beard and examined it up close briefly before crushing it between his fingers and flicking it away. "I still need to check the new hinges," he said, "and there's a loose support in one of the tunnels."

"What about the insulation?" Perry asked.

"Air tight," said Trask. "Nobody will hear a thing, even if they're standing right here on the steps."

"Perfect," Perry said. He leaned in again, surveying the front hall, then raised his foot to step inside.

"Whoa!" Trask shouted. He grabbed Perry by his belt and yanked him back. "What are you doing?"

"Having a look inside," Perry said.

"You don't want to do that," Trask warned.

Perry straightened and stepped away from the big man, bristling from the feel of another human's hand on his body. To those who knew him, or knew of him, it was understood: don't touch him. Ever. That meant no handshakes, no pats on the back, not even a fist bump. After all their years of working together, Perry assumed that Trask knew better. For such a transgression, a lesser man would permanently lose the use of his hand. Perhaps the rest of his body as well.

"Allow me," Trask said. He knelt down on the threshold, keeping one hand on the frame to steady himself. "You want to step there, or there," he said, gesturing toward the floorboards on either side of the small throw rug just inside the door. "Not there," he said, pointing at the center of the rug.

"And if I do?" Perry asked.

Trask clenched his fist, then leaned forward and brought it down on the rug like a sledgehammer, sending a deep thud echoing through the front room. He waited two seconds and pounded the rug again, several inches to the right, causing a three-foot square section in the floor to fall away, sending the rug plummeting down into the darkness below. Just as quickly, the panel swung back up and reset in its original position, looking like it had never moved.

"Impressive," Perry said. "But, why did you hit it twice?"

"Left foot, right foot," Trask said. "Whoever walks through the door will take one step, then another. It's the second foot that triggers the release. If the first foot activated it, they might grab the doorknob or the edge of the floor. This way, they're perfectly centered on the panel. Once it releases, the only option is to drop straight down. After that? Well, let's just say I wouldn't want to be that person."

"Indeed," Perry said, nodding approvingly.

As he climbed to his feet, Trask made a mental note to buy another throw rug. "I'd show you around," he said, "but I'm still testing the release mechanisms."

"Release mechanisms?" Perry asked.

"A safety precaution should one of us get trapped inside."

"You really think that's going to happen?"

"No, but why risk it?" Trask replied. "Without them, you'll be trapped inside with no way to get out, and no chance of anyone hearing your shouts for help."

"These are well hidden, I assume."

"Very well hidden," Trask replied. "Every room has one and no two are alike. You have to know the exact sequencing to make them work. After I test them, I'll give you the instructions for each one."

"Excellent," Perry said, feeling a surge of renewed hope. In another week's time, he'd take possession of the Hammond bookcase, which had eluded him for far too long, and he'd be done with Nathan Cole once and for all.

"Check back in a couple of days," Trask said, pulling the ring of keys from his pocket. "I should have everything ready."

"Very good," Perry said, marveling at what would undoubtedly be his greatest achievement. He was certain the others would agree.

Trask locked the door and the deadbolt slid into place with a heavy *click!* As he followed Perry down the steps, he asked, "Any update on when the package will be delivered?"

"You can say his name," Perry said. "There's no one else here."

"Nathan Cole," Trask said slowly, spitting out the words like they were covered with mold. He, as much as Perry, understood the danger the boy posed to them. "I look forward to the day when we never have to utter that name again."

"Agreed," Perry said, "but there's been a development."

"Is it serious?"

"No. Nothing insurmountable. In the grand scheme of things it will only delay us, not stop us. As far as Nathan Cole is concerned, the excellent work you've done here will be his ultimate undoing. Trust me, we'll have him soon. Very soon."

Thursday morning traffic was heavy and slow, and Kendra and Jameson didn't make it to Braden Street until 8:30 am. From there, the plan was for Kendra to drive, but when they arrived at the house, Beck suggested they take his truck instead. He had no interest in squeezing into the backseat of the Volvo, and the tinted windows in his truck would offer an added layer of anonymity.

Jameson was quick to agree.

Minutes later they met Elizabeth and David at the Sacred Heart Parish Center on Mass Ave. in Lexington. Beck watched the traffic for several minutes, and when he was sure they hadn't been followed he pulled out of the parking lot. David and Elizabeth waited, then did the same, keeping several cars back. Three minutes later they arrived at Fletcher Poole's house.

Standing in a loose group on his front porch, like a band of Christmas carolers, Poole eyed them with outward curiosity. *A giant, two women, and a boy?* he wondered. *What are THEY doing here?* It made no sense at all, not after Jameson's warning that the paper posed some sort of imminent threat. If that was true, then why were they being allowed to see it? Wasn't the whole point to keep it a secret?

Jameson handled the introductions, starting with Beck, then Kendra, then Nathan.

"Hold on," Poole said. "You're Nathan Cole?"

"Uh-huh."

"The grandson of Henry Hammond?"

"Yes."

He reached out and shook Nathan's hand. "I had the pleasure of examining the letter you found in the courthouse last year. Fascinating document. Simply fascinating."

Nathan gave him an uneasy look. *Yeah, it was fascinating all right.*

"Fletcher," Jameson said, continuing with the introductions, "you remember Elizabeth…"

"Elizabeth," Poole said, extending his hand. "Of course. So silly of me not to recognize you. Then again, it's been quite some time since I last saw you in your father's bookstore, stocking shelves and helping customers." Then, in a more somber tone, "I was saddened to hear of your sister's passing."

"Thank you, that's very kind," Elizabeth said graciously, bowing her head as she forced the painful memory away once again.

Poole turned his attention to David. "And you are?" he asked.

"David Cole. I'm Nathan's father."

"It's a pleasure to meet you, David." They were shaking hands when Poole looked past him at the sprawling maple tree in the front yard.

"What is it?" David asked, turning to look.

"An Eastern Phoebe," Poole replied. "Right there, see? On that large branch?" Everyone turned to look.

"Dark gray on top, white on the bottom?" Poole said.

When Nathan spotted it, he was surprised that Poole could pick it out from so far away.

"See how it flicks its tail?" Poole said. "That's a sure tell. She's probably waiting for us to leave."

"Leave?" Nathan asked.

"We're standing under her nest."

Nathan looked up at the porch roof but saw no nest.

"There," Poole said, pointing to one of the ceiling joists to his right. Tucked under the eaves was a ragged nest made of grass, clumps of moss, and mud.

"Oh, right," Nathan said.

"Well, let's not keep our feathered friend waiting any longer," Poole said. He opened the door and led the group on a long meandering journey through the house, pausing when they reached the basement stairs. "Now," he said, before going any further. "While you're here, feel free to look, but I must insist that you not *touch* anything."

Everyone nodded, then Poole continued down the stairs to the basement.

"Wow," Kendra said to Nathan, when she saw all the scientific equipment. "This feels like a James Bond movie."

"I assure you Mr. Bond was not as attuned to paper conservation as the rest of us," Poole said, seemingly put off by Kendra's comment. "His expertise was in, how shall I say, *other* areas?"

He walked them through the maze of benches to the table where the rolled paper was undergoing the next step in the process. As they neared it, Nathan darted around the others, making his way to the front of the line where he'd have a front row view. Poole stood next to him at the table while the others fanned out behind them in a line.

"What you have here is the second part of the procedure," Poole explained. "The first step began yesterday with the humidifying of the object, in this case, a sheet of paper that dates back over 250 years."

That brought a murmur from the group.

"The humidification stage lasts for 2-3 hours," Poole said, "whereby moisture is introduced into the paper by placing it inside an enclosed chamber with a water source. Water vapors then enter the fibers of the paper, allowing them to relax. Once that step is complete, the paper is removed from the humidification chamber and smoothed out with a brush. There are a number of brushes one can use, but I prefer a Hake brush."

He took the brush from the tabletop and held it up briefly for the others to see. "Next comes the pressing stage, using the materials you see before you. The top layer is glass, followed by matboard, two layers of thin blotter, and a ¼" thick piece of felt. Then comes the paper, followed by the same materials used on the top, only arranged in reverse order. Finally, weight is applied. As you can see, I'm using two short I-beams. They were a gift from a good friend in Boston who claims they came from the old Boston Garden.

"Nice!" Kendra said, nodding her head.

Nathan leaned down and studied the layers. Somewhere in the middle of it all was the paper Thomas Hammond had hidden in the bookcase. "So, what happens next?" he asked.

"We wait," said Poole.

Nathan looked up at him, confused. "Wait for what?"

"The purpose of pressing is to dry the paper and restore it to plane. That takes time."

"Restore it to plane?" Nathan asked, eyebrows raised.

"Make it flat," Poole said. "If we simply took it out of the humidifying chamber and set it on the table, the paper would buckle. You'd see multiple concave and convex distortions."

"You mean, like wrinkles?"

"That's right," Poole said. "Think of a wavy potato chip."

"Huh," Nathan said, nodding his head.

"So," Poole said, addressing Nathan directly. "The pressing process achieves what?"

"It dries the paper and makes it flat."

"Very good," Poole said, unable to control the professor that still lurked deep inside him. "Think of it this way. The paper has amnesia. It's been rolled up and bound by linen cloth since the mid 1800s, if not longer. Our job is to help it regain its memory, so to speak—to return it to its original state. More precisely, how it looked after its first pressing, when it went from slurry pulp to a cast sheet."

"How long does that take?" Nathan asked.

"Usually a week."

Nathan's shoulders slumped. "We have to wait a week to see

what's on the paper?"

Jameson stepped forward and tugged on Poole's shirt. "Could I speak to you privately?" he asked softly.

"Certainly," replied Poole.

Jameson walked him over to the base of the stairs and they spoke for several minutes. From across the room, Nathan watched the exchange, which resembled two seasoned tennis pros in a heated match.

Jameson calmly explained the situation.

15 love.

Poole shook his head.

15 all.

Jameson gestured toward the group, then offered more explanation.

30, 15.

Poole shook his head again.

30 all.

Jameson offered a compromise.

40, 30.

Poole thought for a moment, then held up five fingers.

Game.

Sully was sitting at his desk, reviewing the long list of emails he'd received that morning when one in particular nearly jumped off the screen. There were no words in the subject line, just a number. He recognized it at once as the hull identification number for Dan Perry's boat.

He opened the email, read the short message, then quickly

dialed the number listed at the bottom of the screen. Once he had verbal confirmation, he asked the dockmaster to send him a photo. Fifteen minutes later, with the photo on his screen, he called Jameson.

"Sully? Can I call you back?" Jameson said quietly, after connecting the call. There was a measure of nervous anticipation in his voice.

"Yeah, sure," Sully replied. "Did I wake you?"

"No, nothing like that. I'll explain when I call back. Is everything okay?"

"I found the boat."

"You did? Where?" Jameson asked, his words coming faster.

"Westport."

"Westport?" Jameson repeated. "That's at least, what, an hour from Portland?"

"Yup."

"Let me call you back."

"No problem," Sully replied. "You know, it's a beautiful day. I thought I might take a drive up the coast."

"I hear Lincoln County is nice this time of year," Jameson said, playing along.

"You read my mind."

Jameson ended the call and hurried over to the table. He got there just as Poole was removing the two I-beams from the press. "Five minutes, no more," he said to the group. "While I'm preparing new packing materials, you can *look* at the paper, but no one is to touch it or get close enough to breathe on it. Is that understood?"

"Yes, yes, whatever you say," Elizabeth said excitedly, speaking for the rest of the group.

"That goes double for you, Nathan," David said, giving Nathan a playful poke in the back.

Nathan shot his father a pathetic look...*very funny Dad*...then turned and watched as, one by one, Poole carefully removed the top layers of the press.

He made it as far as the felt layer when he paused and motioned for Jameson to come stand next to him. "Maybe you wouldn't mind telling me what's so dangerous about *this*," he said, then lifted the felt layer, exposing the pressed sheet of paper.

Nathan's jaw fell open, and he stood motionless, staring.

David and Elizabeth crowded in behind him, anxious to see.

Jameson leaned forward for a closer look when Poole extended his arm. "That's far enough," he said.

The only one that didn't move was Beck. At 6'5" he had a commanding aerial view of the entire table.

"Is that what I think it is?" Kendra asked, craning her neck to see.

"Yes," Poole replied. He turned to Jameson. "Well?"

9

Fuller

Despite the vapors that the paper had absorbed while encased in the humidification chamber for hours, the black ink showed no signs of bleed. The corners were curled up slightly, but Poole explained that it was still early in the process and that in another few days it would cease to be an issue. The good news was, the grand staffs were clearly visible, as were the musical notes and symbols.

"Sheet music?" Nathan said, bewildered. *This is the big secret?*

"Very old sheet music," noted Poole. "Mid 1700s sheet music to be exact. Judging from the paper's yellow tinge, along with some other factors, I'd say it came from a mill in Saxony."

"Germany," Jameson confirmed.

"Yes."

"You mentioned other factors?" Elizabeth asked.

"Yes. For one, you can make out a faint ribbed texture in the paper. A latticework pattern, if you will. This is characteristic of chain laid paper, which was very popular during the 1700s. It's caused by the wire sieve used during the papermaking process."

"Why is it called chain laid?" Nathan asked.

"An excellent question, Mr. Cole. In this particular example, the horizontal lines, those parallel to the short edge of the paper, are called chain lines. They're crossed at a right angle by vertical lines parallel to the long edge of the paper, called laid lines. Hence the term, chain laid paper."

Gina should be here, Nathan thought. *She'd eat this up.*

"Another tell is the ink," said Poole. "The ink used on this document is black carbon, also called carbon black. It was popular during the time period in question and can easily withstand the humidification process." He turned his wrist and checked the time on his watch. "Okay, we've reached the five-minute mark and I need to repack the press. So, if you'll excuse me..." he said, gesturing toward the stairs with both hands.

"Come," Elizabeth said, easing Nathan away from the table.

"Mom, stop," he said, squirming away. He went back to the table and watched as Poole carefully reconstructed the top layer of the press. Once the I-beams were in place, he slowly backed away, his mind trying to comprehend what he'd just seen.

As the group made their way up the stairs, Jameson stayed behind to talk to Poole. "Fletcher," he said, "thank you for your time and expert analysis. Excellent as always. Until we know more, I must ask you to keep this to yourself. My earlier words of warning still stand."

Poole dipped his chin and looked over his glasses, smirking. "I'll keep that in mind. You'll be sure to let me know if you learn anything more about this…uh…*danger?*"

Jameson ignored the sarcasm. "When do you think you'll be done?" he asked.

"Call me next Wednesday."

"That long?" Jameson asked.

"For a project like this? Most definitely," Poole said matter-of-factly.

Jameson knew the less time Poole had it, the safer he'd be, but that wasn't something he wanted to tell him. "Do me a favor," he said. "Work as fast as you can and get it back to me at the very earliest. Can you do that?"

"I can do a great many things," Poole announced, disapproving of Jameson's urgency.

"Yes, you most certainly can," Jameson said quickly, before Poole launched into another discourse about his amazing accomplishments. "Which is why I must insist on expediency. I mean, if anyone can do it…" Jameson said, letting the implication hang in the air.

"Oh, Jameson, you do know how to motivate me," Poole gushed.

"You'll move it along quickly, then?"

"Like the clappers," said Poole.

When Jameson got outside, Elizabeth and David were waiting for him at the bottom of the front porch steps. Beck, Kendra, and Nathan were already back in the truck.

"What do you make of it?" Elizabeth asked.

"Impossible to say until we find out what's hidden in the *Greenwich* bookcase," Jameson replied.

"If we ever do," David said quietly.

"To think," Elizabeth said, "we finally see what was hidden inside the bookcase and we're no closer to understanding why it was put there."

"Are you sure he's okay, all alone in there?" David asked, looking up at the front door.

"Oh, he's fine," Jameson replied. "It wouldn't hurt to have someone keep an eye on him, but he'd never stand for it. If he senses we're babysitting him, there's no telling what he'll do. He's been known to simply up and vanish."

"He would really do that?"

"Yes, he would really do that…and there's no telling when he'd show up again. It might be a month, it might be a year."

"Odd," David said.

"Oh, you don't know the half of it."

As they drove away from Poole's house, Jameson sat transfixed, struggling to understand why Thomas Hammond would hide a sheet of music in the bookcase, especially one that was so old. They were approaching Braden Street when he turned around and addressed Kendra. "Have you spoken with Elliot recently?"

"Elliot?" she said, surprised by the question. "Funny you should ask. I just talked to him. He flew into Portland for a few days."

"Perfect. Do me a favor, will you? Call him and see if he'd be willing to meet."

"You and Elliot? What, are you a fan now?" Kendra asked, with a skeptical look.

"What kind of question is that?" Jameson replied. "I've always been a fan."

Kendra rolled her eyes. "Yeah, right."

Gina was stirred from her sleep by the tinny whine of a motor boat. At first it was barely audible, like the faint buzzing of a mosquito up near the ceiling. But as it continued to grow louder, she pulled the pillow over her head and tried to block it out. When it became so loud that she feared the boat might crash through the wall at any moment, her eyes snapped open and she bolted upright in bed.

Something was wrong.

The room was different.

That's when the chain of events from the past 12 hours cycled through her mind in a series of rapid flashes.

Sitting in the kitchen at home.

Ellie's barrage of questions.

Leaving the house in a rush.

Driving north.

Falling asleep in the car.

Being jostled awake on a bumpy dirt road.

The cottage on the lake.

She climbed out of bed and went to the window. The sun was hanging halfway up the morning sky, making the surface of the lake shimmer like a sequined dress. She caught sight of the motor boat as it disappeared around the point, leaving a wake that gently lapped the rocks along the shoreline. When she walked into the kitchen moments later, she looked through the large sliding glass door and saw Ellie sitting on the deck in a plum-colored Adirondack chair, a cup of coffee in her hand.

"Good morning sleepyhead," Ellie said brightly, when Gina stepped outside.

"What time is it?" Gina asked, squinting.

"Ten o'clock."

"Seriously?"

"Seriously," Ellie replied. "But don't worry, after the day you had yesterday, I can hardly blame you for sleeping in."

"That's what I get for hanging around with Nathan Cole," Gina muttered as she sat down across from Ellie in a gray metal chaise with tan-colored sling fabric. The sun warmed her face and there was the hint of a breeze coming off the water. Across the lake she saw a number of small cottages dotting the shoreline. "Where are we?" she asked.

"Well," Ellie said, pointing straight ahead. "That right there is Merrymeeting Lake."

"Merrymeeting?"

"Uh-huh. And about 20 minutes that way," Ellie said, hitching her thumb over her shoulder, "is Lake Winnipesaukee."

"New Hampshire," Gina confirmed.

"That's right. Out here, none of Perry's goons will bother you."

Good, Gina thought. She looked back at the glass slider. "Whose house is this?"

"It belongs to a friend of mine. He's out of the country indefinitely and told me to use it anytime I wanted."

"He?" Gina asked like a protective mother.

Ellie smirked. "I know what you're thinking, and no."

Gina considered the lake again. "How long do we have to stay here?"

"That depends on what happens next," Ellie said. "I'm not sure if you heard, but after his battle with the intruder, Beck found some of the guy's DNA. I dropped it off with Sully yesterday. We should have the results today."

"DNA?" Gina asked.

"Blood."

Gina grimaced, imagining the amount of blood that must've been spilled from the fight.

"Beck heaved the guy through the front window, did you know that?" Ellie said.

"Through the *window?*" Gina exclaimed, eyes wide.

"Uh-huh," Ellie said. "Somehow he managed to get away, but with any luck the blood sample will help Sully and his guys find him." She paused briefly, then said, "Of course, that still leaves Dan Perry."

Gina shuddered. Just the sound of his name made her skin crawl. "They have a bunch of guys looking for him, right?" she asked.

"Actively," Ellie said. "And once they catch him, this whole fiasco will be over once and for all."

"It can't happen soon enough," Gina said. She looked left, then right, surveying the neighboring cottages through the veil of trees that lined both sides of the property. "So, what do we do here?" she asked.

Ellie closed her eyes and lifted her head to the cloudless sky, relishing the feel of the morning sun on her face. "Anything. Nothing. Take your pick," she said.

Gina thought for a moment. "Is there a bookstore around here?"

"Most likely."

"Will they have puzzle books?"

"I don't see why not."

Beck pulled his truck into the garage and closed the door. As everyone was getting out, Jameson felt his phone vibrate. He pulled it from his pocket, and when he saw who was calling, he motioned to the others. "You go ahead," he told them. "I'll be in shortly." As they filtered into the house, he tapped the talk button and pressed the phone to his ear. "Sully, I was just about to call you."

There was a sense of urgency in Jameson's voice that told Sully something had transpired since they last spoke. "What happened?" he asked.

"There's been a significant development," Jameson said.

"I'm listening."

"Well, before I get to that, I need to tell you why Dan Perry has been hunting Nathan."

"I just assumed it had something to do with his aunt," Sully told him. "Nathan was pretty sure Perry had something to do with her death."

"It's more than that," Jameson said. "Nathan's family has something Perry wants, and he'll stop at nothing to get it. The attempted abduction and the break-in at Nathan's house yesterday are just his latest attempts."

"Hold on. The break in I get. But why the attempted abduction?"

"We think Perry was planning to use Nathan as trade bait."

"Trade bait," Sully repeated. "For this thing Nathan's family has?"

"Yes. It fits with his earlier attempts to lure Nathan back to Maine."

"This item, do you know what it is?" Sully asked.

"Yes. Now we do," Jameson said, pacing in front of the workbench that lined the back of the garage.

"What do you mean, now?"

"Before yesterday, we didn't know what it was," Jameson explained.

"Wait, you lost me," Sully said. "Nathan's family has something Perry wants, but they don't know what it is? How can that be?"

Jameson's elbow clipped a 5-quart container of motor oil and he spun around and grabbed it just as it was falling to the floor.

"Jameson?"

"Yes, I'm still here," he said, setting the container back on the workbench. "Nathan's family knew approximately where it was, that's all I can tell you."

"What is it, buried treasure?"

"Not exactly. Nathan found it yesterday morning, but in the process of leaving the house, he encountered Perry's man, who somehow managed to sneak in without being seen."

"I thought Nathan was with Beck, at…you know…"

"He was."

"So, what was he doing at the house?"

"Looking for the item in question," Jameson said. "To make a long story short, Perry's guy broke in to look for it but Nathan beat him to it. He tried to get Nathan to give it to him but Nathan refused. That's when Beck showed up."

Sully thought for a moment. "You know what this means, right?" he asked. "Now that Perry knows Nathan has the item?"

"Yes. It takes things to a whole new level."

"Indeed," Sully replied, "which makes what I'm about to tell you even more troubling."

"What is it?"

"I drove up to Westport yesterday. Perry's boat was at the marina, just as the dockmaster reported, but the whole time it's been there no one's gone near it. Not Perry, not anyone."

"You think he just parked it there, to make us think he's in the area?"

"I do," Sully replied. "But he's pulled that stunt before, and I'm not falling for it again. My guys will continue their search along the south coast. As far as Perry's boat, I asked the dockmaster to contact me if anything changes."

"Good idea. Anything else?"

"Yeah. I heard from my guy at the lab about an hour ago. We got a positive I.D. on the blood sample."

Jameson stopped pacing. "Excellent!"

"Not so fast," Sully replied.

Nathan's parents returned home and found Russ McCullough's truck parked in the driveway. When they walked around the back corner of the house, they saw him standing on a ladder, affixing a small security camera just below the gutter.

"Good morning," he said, adjusting the angle of the camera, which would give him a panoramic view of the back yard.

"Another camera," Elizabeth said. "Good idea."

"I don't know what I was thinking," he said as he came down the ladder. "I should've done this when I installed the other one." He stepped off the ladder, pulled his phone from his pocket and checked the feed. Satisfied with the image, he shoved the phone back in his pocket. "So," he said, "what's the plan from here on out?"

"Plan?" Elizabeth asked.

Russ gave them both a stern look. "You've had people casing your house. An attempt was made to abduct your son. Now, you've had a break in, during which your son could've been seriously injured. Where does it end?"

"Why don't we go inside and talk," Elizabeth said.

She led him inside, to the living room, and Russ sat in one of the overstuffed chairs while she and David took a seat across from him on the couch. The front window was boarded up with plywood, giving the whole room the ominous feel of an impending storm.

"First of all, we appreciate everything you've done for us," Elizabeth said. "And I know it's been hard on you, not knowing... certain things."

"The more I know, the more I can help," Russ reasoned.

"Yes," Elizabeth said. "And we want you to help." She looked at David and nodded. *Go ahead.*

"This whole situation..." David began slowly, "centers around something we have in our possession."

Russ raised an eyebrow. "Something?" he said.

"Actually, it's been in my family for a very long time," Elizabeth explained. "Generations, to be more precise. The person behind these aggressive acts wants it. Why? We have no idea. All we can do is speculate."

"This thing you have," Russ said. "What is it, exactly?"

"It's a sheet of paper."

"A sheet of *paper?*" Russ repeated. "Seriously?"

"Yes."

"What kind of paper are we talking about? A legal document?"

"No," Elizabeth said. "It's a piece of sheet music."

Russ looked dumbfounded. "Sheet music?" he said. "*That's* what this is all about?"

"Yes."

"What is it, a rare original or something?"

"We have no idea," Elizabeth said.

Beck walked through the door and dropped the truck keys on the counter. "Anyone want coffee?"

"Sure, what'cha got?" Kendra asked.

Beck opened one of the cabinets over the counter and called out the choices. "Hawaiian Kona, Kenyan AA, or Indonesian Sulawesi."

"You have Sulawesi?" Kendra asked with an astonished look. "I own a coffee shop and even I have trouble finding it."

"You have to know the right people," Beck said, pulling the bag from the shelf.

"You know how it came to be, right?" Kendra asked.

When Beck shook his head, she explained the beginnings of coffee production in Indonesia by Dutch colonists in the 17th century. Nathan quickly lost interest and walked into the living room where he plopped down on the couch, the image of the sheet music rooted like a weed in his mind. During the meeting with his parents the day before, in the wee hours of the morning, his mother had called the secret hidden within the bookcase "deadly." But now that they knew what the secret was, her description hardly seemed accurate. *A piece of sheet music?* he thought. *Deadly? How could that be?*

Supposedly, since the time the two bookcases left England, only Thomas Hammond knew what secret they contained. Could it be that, over the years, speculation had magnified it, transforming it into some fantastical and forbidden item? There was a word for that, but he couldn't remember what it was.

The whole situation made no sense, and the more he thought about it, the more he believed there was something he'd missed in the attic—some detail to explain why Thomas Hammond had gone to such lengths to hide an old piece of sheet music in a bookcase, and then instruct his brother to smuggle it out of England, along with its twin, never revealing what secret they contained. Which raised another question: what was hidden in the second bookcase?

The fact that the ship that carried it, the *Greenwich*, had been diverted during its voyage, never to be seen again, only added another layer to the mystery. And then there was Dan Perry. Why was he coming for the Hammond bookcase now, after all these years? *There's something else, some part of this I'm not seeing*, Nathan thought. He closed his eyes and recounted his search of the bookcase, envisioning every square inch of wood. *What did I miss?* he asked himself.

Just then, the door from the garage opened and Jameson walked in. He didn't look happy.

"What's wrong?" Kendra asked.

Beck stopped what he was doing. "Who was that on the phone?"

"That was Sully," Jameson said, taking a seat at the island.

"Did he get the results from the blood sample?"

Jameson nodded.

"Well, did they I.D. the guy?" Kendra asked, impatiently.

"Yes," Jameson said softly, staring at the countertop, distracted.

"And?"

"He's a ghost," Jameson told them.

When Nathan heard that, he got up from the couch at once. "What do you mean...a ghost?" he asked as he walked into the kitchen.

"His name is Odom," Jameson said. "All we know about him is that he was born in Fort Dodge, Kansas. His father was in the Army, and as result, the family moved around quite a bit. The United States, Europe, you name it. When Odom graduated high school, he enlisted in the Marines."

Beck looked at Nathan. "What'd I tell you?"

Nathan felt sick all over again.

"What else? Beck asked Jameson.

"That's it."

"That's *it?*" Beck said.

Jameson nodded.

The two men shared a troubled look for several long seconds, then Beck went back to making the coffee.

After his call to Jameson, Sully dialed Eric Fuller at the U.S. Marshal's office at 1 City Square. Fuller was a member of the Special Operations Group, and had privately enlisted Sully's help on a handful of cases over the years. For that reason, Sully had no hesitation when it came to asking Fuller for a favor. The man was dedicated, efficient, and never failed to pick up after the first ring.

"Eric Fuller."

"Eric, it's Sully. Is this a good time to talk?"

"Sure," Fuller said. "What's up?"

"I'm looking for information on a guy, an ex-Marine," Sully explained. "I'm working off a DNA sample, but what I've been able to find so far has been pretty thin."

Fuller was sitting at his desk and pulled his notepad closer. "What's the name?"

"Odom. O-d-o-m."

"First name?"

"Karl, with a K."

"Middle name?"

"Dean. D-e-a-n."

"Karl Dean Odom, got it," Fuller said, tearing the note from the pad. "I'll see what I can find out."

"Much appreciated, Eric."

"Don't mention it."

When it was time to leave, Jameson had Kendra go outside to start the car while he spoke privately to Beck in the garage.

"What are you thinking?" he asked Beck.

The big man spoke with the certainty of a seasoned soldier. "I knew Odom was bad," he said.

"How so?" Jameson asked.

"You can tell a lot about a person by the way they fight, and by the weapons they carry."

"Right," Jameson said. "I asked Sully to check with some of his contacts, to see what they can dig up on this guy."

"It's not going to be good, I can tell you that right now," said Beck.

Jameson nodded his agreement. "Once Sully gets back to me,

we'll have to make a decision about Nathan. Does he stay here or do we move him to a more fortified location."

"Do you have someplace in mind?" Beck asked.

"I have a few options."

"Call me as soon as you hear anything," Beck said.

"Will do. But if I show up at your door unannounced…"

"We'll be ready to go," Beck assured him. He watched Jameson and Kendra leave, then closed the garage door and went inside where he saw Nathan pacing the length of the couch, muttering to himself like a mad scientist.

"What's wrong?" Beck asked.

Nathan stopped short and spun around. "There's something we need to do."

"We?"

"Yes," Nathan said. "You and me. Today. Now."

"Am I going to like it?"

Nathan shook his head. "No. You are definitely *not* going to like it."

10

N. Graf

"You want to do *what?*" Beck exclaimed.

"I need to go back to my house," Nathan said, with as much urgency as he could muster.

"Out of the question," Beck said. He grabbed his coffee mug off the counter and rinsed it in the sink.

"We won't stay there long," Nathan explained.

"No."

"20 minutes, tops."

"Doesn't matter," Beck said. "It's not going to happen."

"Come *on!*" Nathan pleaded.

Beck turned from the sink. "You're supposed to be gone, remember? Vanished. As far as Perry knew, you had somehow dissolved into thin air. But then you showed up again, and Odom saw you. Not only that, he saw you with the very thing he came to steal."

"Yes, I know…that was bad," Nathan admitted with an uneasy look. "And thanks again for showing up when you did. I really appreciate it. Gina does, too."

Beck eyed him momentarily, sensing a con, then refilled his mug with hot coffee. "The answer is still no."

Nathan tried a different approach. "I think there's something you're overlooking."

"Oh yeah?" Beck said. He took a sip of coffee then turned and faced Nathan. "Enlighten me."

"My house is the last place Odom is going to be."

"How do figure?"

"You said it yourself. He saw me with the thing he came to steal, but then I left before he could take it from me. What was the word you used…vanished?"

"Go on," Beck said. He took another sip of coffee.

"Odom knows the sheet music is no longer at my house. If he's the professional you claim he is, then he knows we're not dumb enough to bring it back there. That means the last place he's going to be is at my house. Right now, he's out *there* somewhere," Nathan said, with a sweep of his hand, "trying to hunt me down."

Beck took a slow sip of coffee, thinking. Then another. As the seconds slowly ticked by, silence filling the room, Nathan waited and watched, giving his words ample time to sink in. From out in front of the house came the groan of the postman's mail truck as it pulled away from the mailbox.

"Tell me why," Beck said.

Nathan's heart raced. He was almost home now—he could feel it. "Because none of this makes any sense," he said. "An old rolled-up piece of sheet music? That's what Perry is after? That's why he sent two guys in a van to abduct me? And when that didn't work, he sends an ex-military guy to break into my house to steal it?"

"He wants what he wants," Beck countered.

"Exactly. But why?" Nathan shot back. "There's something else, something I missed in the attic. Until I find it, the sheet music is useless to us. On the other hand, if I succeed, it may help us stop Dan Perry."

Beck stood perfectly still as if his brain had seized, his coffee cup inches from his lips. If he was a figurine in Madame Tussauds Wax Museum, the plaque would read: *Man Drinking Coffee.*

"Fifteen minutes," Beck said, at last. "No more."

Nathan clenched both fists. *Yes!*

He was almost to the door when Beck called out, "Hold on."

Nathan stopped and looked back. "What?"

"Just so we understand each other," Beck said. "When I say 15 minutes, I mean not one second longer."

"Yeah, 15 minutes," Nathan replied with a shrug. *That's what I said.*

Beck wasn't convinced. He set his coffee cup down on the counter. "Have you ever been handcuffed?" he asked.

"No," Nathan said, with a sour look. "Why would you ask me that?"

"Duct taped?" Beck asked.

"No!" Nathan replied, louder.

"Zip-tied?"

"Very much no."

"Well, just so you know," Beck said, "I have all those things, and if we have a problem, I won't hesitate to use them."

Jameson sat at his desk, his eyes fixed on the blinding wash of midday sunlight pouring through the large picture window on the far wall. It obscured the view of the finely manicured lawn and flowerbeds outside, and served as a stark reminder that, even though they'd discovered the contents of the Hammond bookcase, they were blind to the powerful threat it contained.

He was pondering that point when his phone vibrated. When he saw who was calling, he quickly snatched it up off the desk and punched the talk button. "Sully," he said anxiously, "tell me you have information."

"I do," Sully replied. "But first things first. Where's Nathan?"

"He's with Beck, at Braden Street, why?"

"We need to move him," Sully replied. "Immediately."

Jameson stood and began to pace. "What did you find out?"

"Nothing good. What I'm about to tell you came from the top, through a friend of a friend. So when I say it's accurate, I mean it's *certifiable.*"

"Understood," Jameson said, feeling a sense of dread building in his gut.

"As I told you before, Odom joined the marines right out of high school. He trained in North Carolina, at Camp Lejeune. By all reports, his military record is exemplary…at least, what we know of it."

"What are you saying?" Jameson asked.

"He was part of the Marines Special Operations Command. Beyond that, there's nothing. The rest of his record was scrubbed."

"Scrubbed?" Jameson said. "That can only mean one thing."

"Exactly," Sully replied. "Odom was involved in some very high-level stuff. As in, classified, the kind of operations they don't discuss on the nightly news."

Jameson had expected the news to be serious, but not like this. "Special Ops Command," he said softly, shaking his head in disbelief.

"The bottom line is, there's no telling what Odom is capable of doing," Sully explained. "If he broke in once, you can bet he'll do it again, or worse. Count on worse. For that reason, we need to move Nathan to a safer location without delay."

"I'll take care of it at once," Jameson said.

"You have a place?" Sully asked.

"I do."

"And you're sure it's safe?"

"Positive."

"Good. There's one more thing. It wouldn't hurt to have Beck sweep Nathan's house for listening devices. The girl's house, too."

"Understood," Jameson replied.

Beck decided to take the truck. With its tinted windows, he figured Nathan could sit in the back seat and be virtually invisible to any passersby. Nathan, for his part, readily agreed, only too happy not to be covered with an itchy blanket like the last time. As they drove back to his house, he was filled with nervous energy, fueled by even more questions.

How did Thomas Hammond acquire the sheet music?

Did he find it on his own?

Did someone give it to him?

Whose idea was it to hide it in the bookcase and smuggle it out of England?

Did he make that decision himself?

Was he instructed to do so?

If so, why?

What kind of person who make such a request?

As they approached his house, Beck saw no cars in the driveway and pulled all the way in, coming to a stop just inches from the garage. "Looks like your parents are gone," he said.

"Fine by me," Nathan muttered. *One less thing to slow me down.*

Beck turned off the engine and reached for the door handle. "Wait here."

"Why?" Nathan asked.

"Just wait," Beck replied. He got out of the truck and walked down the driveway. After an inspection of the street in both directions, he came back to the truck and opened the rear driver's-side door. "Okay, let's go."

"I told you," Nathan said, as he climbed out of the truck, "Odom's gone."

Beck said nothing.

"Are you coming inside?" Nathan asked.

Beck shook his head. "No….and your 15 minutes starts now."

"Suit yourself," Nathan said. He bolted across the lawn to the back door, then slipped into the house.

After Nathan went inside, Beck did a full sweep of the backyard, checking the garage and the perimeter of the property. When he was done, he took a position on the front porch where he could monitor the flow of traffic on the street. So far, things were quiet.

Nathan raced upstairs, grabbed a flashlight from his bedside table, and darted out of the room. As he hurried down the hallway he checked his watch.

Thirteen minutes to go.

No problem.

He scaled the attic stairs two at a time and charged into the attic, weaving his way through the assembled clutter. In his haste, he clipped a stack of cardboard boxes with his elbow, sending them toppling over onto the floor. The top box, filled with old skateboard parts, split open on impact and sent tires and bearings rolling in every direction. "Are you serious?" he shouted. He looked over at the bookcase, sitting fifteen feet away in the shadows, then checked his watch again.

Eleven minutes to go.

The mess can wait.

He continued along the narrow pathway, squeezing between the piles of junk, until he reached the bookcase. Standing on the left side, he grasped the thick wooden lip that separated the two halves and used the tips of his fingers to slide the molding sideways. No good. It wouldn't budge. He tried again and got the same result. "Come on!" he yelled.

He gripped it harder and tried again. Still nothing. He went to the front of the bookcase and checked the Doric column on the chance that it might've opened without him knowing it. It hadn't. He worked at it with his fingers, trying to pry it open but it wouldn't move.

Another time check.

Nine minutes to go.

Plenty of time.

He climbed to his feet and went back to the side of the bookcase. Using his flashlight, he studied the molding up close. No part of it stood out. No section was different. It was one continuous strip of wood, as ordinary as ordinary could be. But he knew better.

He thought back to his previous visit, reconstructing the chain of events that caused Gina to discover it as the trigger to the hidden cavity.

She was hanging from the top of the bookcase.

Her foot was stuck in the cracked lid of the plastic tub.

She lost her balance and as she fell backward...

"She grabbed the molding," he said aloud. Working quickly now, he set the flashlight on the floor and grabbed the wooden lip, squeezing it with both hands just as Gina had done when she was falling. This time the molding moved.

He slid it to the right and from the front of the bookcase he heard a soft click as the Doric column popped opened. "Yes!" He grabbed the flashlight and knelt down in front of the bookcase, aiming the flashlight's beam into the hidden cavity. At first he saw nothing, but when he leaned closer, eyeing every square inch of the wood, he saw it.

Thomas Hammond had crafted the bookcase from dark English walnut. The inside of the cavity had been roughly sanded and a number of deep chisel marks still remained in the coffee-colored wood. One small section was bleached white, or so it appeared at first glance. Upon closer inspection, Nathan saw that it

185

was a rectangular piece of paper stuck to the sidewall.

He turned his hand sideways and slipped it into the opening, using his fingernail to pick at the edge of the paper. It took several tries, but when it fell away from the side of the cavity he pulled it out and inspected both sides. It was pearl white, roughly the size of a business card and just as thick. On the front was a name, printed in an elegant script.

N. Graf

A short, handwritten message was scribbled on the back.

Nathan's pulse quickened. "This is it," he whispered.

He checked his watch.

Three minutes.

Gotta go.

He slipped the card in his back pocket, swung the column shut, and hurried toward the door. He was halfway there when he turned his ankle on a skateboard wheel, lost his balance, and crashed to the floor.

Just after lunchtime, Ellie and Gina found a bookstore set in a small cluster of shops in Meredith. Across the street was the northern tip of Meredith Bay. Its rippled surface was the color of blue denim, and overhead, the random scattering of thin, doughnut-shaped clouds looked like holes in the sky.

Ellie perused the fiction section while Gina scoured the store's collection of puzzle books. The assortment was just okay, but she managed to find a few that would keep her busy for a time. A very short time. She was that good.

As they emerged from the store, Ellie's phone chirped. When she dug it out of her pocket and checked the call screen, an dark feeling washed over her.

"What's wrong?" Gina asked, when she saw the troubled look on Ellie's face.

"Hopefully nothing," Ellie replied. She connected the call and said, "Nathan? Is everything okay?"

"Hey, Ellie," Nathan said in a pained voice. "Is Gina with you?"

"Yeah, she's right here. Are you all right? You sound different."

"I'm good," Nathan lied. The truth was, he could barely stand after twisting his ankle; he had a shooting pain in his shoulder from colliding with the attic floor, and there was a splinter buried in the fleshy part of his wrist.

"Hold on," Ellie said. She handed the phone to Gina. "He wants to talk to *you*."

Gina took the phone and pressed it to her ear. "What?"

"Where are you?" Nathan said, laboring to speak.

Gina furrowed her brow. He sounded like he was being squeezed in a vice. "Never mind me," she said. "What's the matter with you?"

Ellie pointed across the parking lot, indicating she'd wait in the car.

Gina nodded, then cupped her hand over her ear. "Wait," she said. "Say again?"

"I said…I'm trying to get…into Beck's truck," Nathan said, his words coming out in short painful bursts as he struggled to pull himself up into the back seat.

"Why?" Gina asked. "Are you going somewhere? I thought you were supposed to be staying out of sight. Or did you forget what happened at your house?"

Standing on the running board, Nathan turned and fell backward into the seat. *Stupid skateboard wheel,* he told himself. He let out a pained breath, then said, "I'll explain later. Right now, I have a job for you."

"*You* have a job for *me?* What am I, your secretary now?"

"Relax," he said, "you're going to like this, trust me."

"Trust you? Every time I do that I get into trouble."

He ignored the dig and explained his return trip to the attic, describing the rectangular piece of paper he found in the hidden cavity of the bookcase. He pulled the phone away from his ear and set it in his lap as she launched into a fiery rant about him going back to his house: how it was just the type of behavior she'd expect from him; the kind of stunt that always got him into trouble—got the two of them into trouble; how she couldn't understand why he refused to consider the consequences of his actions, and on and on, her words like the rapid chatter of machine gun fire.

When she finally ran out of steam, he picked up the phone and calmly explained what he needed her to do.

"That was fast," Ellie said a short time later, when Gina opened the car door and slid into the front seat. "Is everything okay? He didn't sound so good."

"He'll live," Gina muttered. She handed Ellie the phone, then stared through the windshield at the boats on the lake, her mind already hard a work trying to decipher what Nathan had told her.

"What is it?" Ellie asked.

"We need to find a library."

With thirty seconds to go, Beck left the front porch and started across the front lawn toward the driveway. As he turned the corner of the house, he heard the truck door slam, and by the time he pulled the driver's door open and climbed in behind the wheel, Nathan was shoving his phone back into his pocket. Beck looked in the rearview mirror and saw him slouching back in the seat, rubbing his shoulder. "What happened?" he asked.

"Nothing," Nathan grumbled, doing his best to ignore the screaming pain in his ankle.

"Did you find what you were looking for?"

"I found *something*," Nathan said, leaning forward to rub his ankle, "but I don't know what it is."

Beck said nothing and started the truck.

As they drove away from the house in silence, Nathan was consumed by the name N. Graf and his cryptic handwritten message. Remember what I showed you. *What does that even mean?* Nathan wondered. By his estimation, it had been scribbled on the card over 160 years earlier, which meant their chances of deciphering it were close to zero.

They were approaching Braden Street when Beck's phone pinged. He grabbed it from the empty beverage holder and pressed the talk button with his thumb. "Beck."

"Beck, it's Jameson."

Beck knew what was coming before Jameson uttered the words.

The urgent tone in his voice was a dead giveaway. Hurried. Tense. He didn't bother to ask Jameson for details, he knew those would come later. "How are we doing it?" he asked.

"I'll meet you and we can go from there," Jameson said. "I've already made the necessary calls."

"Copy that," Beck said. "We're almost back to the house. I'll have Nathan grab his things and then we're good to go. Where am I meeting you?"

"Wait a minute," Jameson said. "Back to the house? Where were you?"

"We went to Nathan's house."

"You took him back to the house?" Jameson exclaimed.

"He said there was something he needed to find," Beck replied.

"And what might that be?" Jameson asked, louder.

Beck eyed Nathan in the rearview mirror. "I'll let *him* tell you."

After Jameson gave him the meeting spot, Beck clicked off the call and slipped the phone back in the beverage holder.

"Let me guess, that was Jameson," Nathan said.

"Correct."

"He didn't sound happy."

"Right again."

"What was that about me grabbing my things?"

"We're moving you," Beck said.

"Moving me? Why?" Nathan asked, sitting up in the seat. "Did something happen? Did Odom show up again? Are my folks okay?"

"Relax," Beck said. "Nothing happened."

Nathan sat back in the seat, only slightly relieved. "It *is* Odom, isn't it?" he asked.

"Don't worry about it," Beck said, as he pulled into the driveway. "Right now, I need you to focus on one thing." He paused momentarily for the garage door to open, and once they were inside he waited for it to go back down. "I'll let you into the house. You grab your stuff and come right back. We have to move fast."

Ay-yi captain, Nathan wanted to say. He climbed down from the truck, gingerly, and hobbled to the door. "Where are we going?" he asked, as Beck entered the code into the keypad.

"Someplace safe."

"Safer than here?" Nathan said sarcastically.

Beck opened the door. "No more questions. Get your stuff and let's go."

It turned out that the Meredith Public Library was so close that Ellie and Gina could've walked there. It was a large brick structure built in the Classical Revival style and set back from the road atop a gentle rise. At first glance it looked like a small castle, with a large attached wing that jutted out at an angle off the back side.

"Are you going to tell me what this is all about?" Ellie asked, after she'd pulled to the curb in front of the library.

"Sure," Gina said. "When I know, you'll know."

"You don't want to tell me just a little?" Ellie asked, gesturing with her thumb and forefinger.

"It's a name, or, part of one," Gina said.

"And that's why Nathan called you."

Gina nodded. *Uh-huh.*

"I see," Ellie said. "Do you want me to come inside with you?"

"No," Gina said as she opened the door. "I won't be that long."

"You've done this before?"

"You might say," Gina told her.

Ellie checked the street in both directions and saw nothing suspicious. "Okay, then," she said. "I'll stay here." She waited until Gina had gone into the library, then picked up her phone and called Jameson. He picked up after the first ring.

"Ellie, my apologies. I meant to call you," he said. "Did you arrive safely?"

"Yes," Ellie replied. "Hey, is Nathan all right? He just called, and he sounded pretty shaken."

"He just called?" Jameson asked. "What for?"

"He wanted to talk to Gina."

"What about?"

"A name," Ellie said.

"A name? What name?"

"Unclear," Ellie said. "But after the call ended, she wanted to find a library in the worst way. That's where we are now."

"Something's up," Jameson said, his suspicion growing.

"How so?"

"Beck told me Nathan wanted to go back to his house, that there was something he wanted to find in the attic."

"When was this?" Ellie asked.

"Within the past hour."

"That fits with the timing of his call," Ellie said.

"If Gina says anything, do nothing," Jameson said. "I'll be seeing Nathan very shortly. When I find out what's going on, I'll call you back and we can compare notes. Also, there are a few housekeeping matters we need to discuss."

"Understood," Ellie said, then disconnected the call. 'Housekeeping' was a code word they'd used years earlier, when they were protecting one of Jameson's contacts from a formidable assailant. The word meant someone was changing location. For their own safety.

She slipped the phone into the front door pocket, an ominous feeling mushrooming in her gut. *Something happened,* she told herself. *They're moving Nathan.*

Beck met Jameson at Birch Meadow. Once Jameson was settled in the front seat of the truck, he turned and addressed Nathan. "You did it again," he said, his face tight with anger. "Why?"

"I had to," Nathan said, defiantly.

"Oh really?" Jameson fired back, reigning in his anger. "Please explain why you would do that. Why you would knowingly put your life in danger...*again!*"

"Because we're nowhere," Nathan said. "I found a piece of sheet music in the bookcase. Big deal. What does it mean? You say it's dangerous? How? No one knows, unless there's something you're not telling me." When Jameson offered no response, Nathan pressed. "Is there something you're not telling me?"

Jameson's expression softened, but only slightly. "No."

"I went back to the attic because I thought there was something I might've missed," Nathan explained. "Something that might explain Thomas Hammond's actions."

"Show him," Beck said.

"Show me what?" Jameson asked.

Nathan pulled the rectangular piece of paper from his pocket.

193

"This," he said. "I found it in the secret cavity where the sheet music was hidden. In my excitement of finding the linen-wrapped roll of paper, I completely missed it."

Jameson reached between the front seats and took the paper, holding it by its edges with his thumb and index finger, as if looking at a photographic slide.

"It's some sort of business card," Nathan said.

"No," Jameson replied, examining both sides closely. "Not a business card. It's a calling card."

"A what?"

"A calling card," Jameson repeated. "Also known as a visiting card. They were popular among the wealthy in Europe and the United Kingdom in the 1800s." His eyes settled on the front of the card. "This name…N. Graf…this is the name you gave Gina?"

Nathan flashed a look of surprise.

"Yes, I know all about that," Jameson said. "I understand she's at the library researching it as we speak."

Nathan nodded his head. *Yes.*

Jameson studied the name, scouring his memory for any recollection of the name Graf. When nothing came to mind he turned his attention to the handwritten message on the back. *Remember what I showed you.* It was very curious, and obviously had significant importance. Why else would it have been included with the sheet music? He took a deep breath and let it out, his initial anger subsided. "The potential danger notwithstanding," he said in a guarded tone, "the risk you took in going back to your house may actually have paid off."

Yeah, no kidding, Nathan thought.

"Only time will tell if this card moves us any closer to understanding the sheet music," Jameson added, "and why Thomas Hammond chose to hide it in the bookcase."

Again, Nathan thought of Gina. At this point, she was their only hope.

Jameson handed the card to Nathan, then turned to Beck. "Let's go."

"Where to?" Beck asked.

"Chelsea."

After 40 minutes, Ellie grew bored. *How long does it take to research a name?* she wondered. She climbed out of the car and surveyed the neighborhood. She saw no immediate threat, no suspicious vehicles parked nearby, and no dangerous-looking characters watching the front of the library. Satisfied that their situation was secure, she walked down the sidewalk to the corner. From there she could see down Lake Street, to the town docks and beyond, where boats of every size were zipping back and forth across the lake, the drone of their motors and the slapping of their hulls against the waves echoing across the water.

She was walking back to the car when she saw Gina emerge from the library. There was an unmistakable urgency in her gate.

"So? How'd you make out?" Ellie asked, once they were back in the car.

Gina was staring back up at the library and didn't respond.

"Hey," Ellie said, snapping her fingers. "You okay?"

"Huh?" Gina stammered, turning from the window.

"Did you find what you were looking for?"

Gina nodded, clearly troubled.

"What is it?" Ellie asked.

"We need to go back," Gina said.

"Sure," Ellie said, starting the car. "I know this great café at Weirs Beach. We can grab some take out and—"

"No, not the lake house," Gina cut in. "My house."

"*Your* house? Why?"

Gina looked at her, spooked. "We have to warn them."

11

Crescent Avenue

Sully sat at his desk sorting through a batch of crime scene photographs he'd taken at a recent jewelry store robbery. As was his habit, he liked to inspect his photos, grouping them by location, subject matter, and type of evidence, before passing them on to the detective in charge of the case. He was so engrossed in the pictures that he didn't notice Christine Reyes walk up behind him.

"Nice shots," she said, from over his shoulder. "Let me guess. The jewelry store on Congress Street?"

Sully recognized her voice and didn't turn around. "Yup, although I don't think the guys that broke in would agree with your assessment," he said, eyeing one photo in particular. He turned in his chair and handed it to her. "Look at this."

Reyes took the picture and held it several inches from her face. "Ooh, a diamond tennis bracelet," she murmured. "And just my size, too."

"Not just any tennis bracelet," Sully explained. "That's a Tiffany Victoria cluster tennis bracelet. Sells for about $50,000. I'm guessing whoever was grabbing things from the case accidentally dropped it. In their haste to leave, no one saw it lying on the floor."

"Too bad for them, but good for me," Reyes said with a grin. She handed Sully the photo. "That means you can buy it for me."

"Nothing would please me more," he said graciously. "I suppose I could sell my house…"

"Keep your house," she said, patting his shoulder. "I have plenty of jewelry. Hey, I've been meaning to ask you. Did you ever find that boat?"

"I did. It's in Westport. Now, if I could only find the owner. He's proving to be harder to track down than his boat. Go figure."

"You said something about looking for him down around Kittery," Reyes said. "No luck, I take it?"

"Nope," Sully said, shaking his head. "If he's there, he's got himself dug in pretty good."

"You searched for any known associates?"

This time Sully nodded, "Yup," then shrugged, "Nothing."

"That seems odd," Reyes said,

"You're tellin' me," Sully groused. "Everything about this guy is odd."

Reyes thought for a moment, then said, "Did you check with the motor vehicle bureau?"

"Uh…actually…no," Sully said with a frown. "I somehow overlooked that."

"Well, don't beat yourself up," Reyes said. "You're an evidence tech, remember? Not a detective." She motioned with both hands.

"Up."

Sully stood at once and let her sit.

She gathered the crime scene photos, arranging them in a neat stack, then slid them aside. He stood and watched, amazed, as she pulled the keyboard closer and began typing, her fingers moving across the keys in a blur. The sharp staccato sounds they made reminded him of January sleet pelting his kitchen window.

"What's this guy's name?" she asked, once she was logged onto the Maine Bureau of Motor Vehicles database.

"Dan Perry."

"Dan…Perry," she said slowly as she entered the name in the system. "Okay, Mr. Perry," she said, pressing the enter key. "Let's see if you have a Maine driver's license."

Several seconds passed.

"Ah, here we go," Reyes said. She quickly read through the information, then pointed to the bottom half of the license.

Sully leaned in for a closer look. "Huh, how do you like that?" he mumbled. "No wonder I couldn't find him."

"Warn them about what?" Ellie asked, as she pulled away from the library.

Gina was mumbling incoherently to herself and didn't answer.

"Hey!" Ellie said loudly. "Warn them about what?"

Gina ignored the question and began frantically searching the center console for Ellie's phone.

"What are you doing?" Ellie asked.

"I need to call Nathan."

"All right, all right, hold on," Ellie said. She dug into the side

199

pocket of the door and pulled out her phone. "Here," she said, handing it to Gina.

Gina quickly navigated through the call history and found Nathan's name. She pressed the recall option and then raised the phone to her ear, tapping her foot nervously on the floor of the car while she waited for the call to connect

It took an eternity.

As she waited, she clenched her fist. *Come on, already.* Seconds later she heard it ringing. "Answer your phone, Nathan," she said anxiously, as if he could hear her.

It kept ringing.

"You've got to be kidding me," she griped.

A voice recording sounded. "Hi, this is Nathan. Wait for the, you know, beep thing, then leave me a message."

She waited for the beep, then said, "Nathan, call me on Ellie's phone the second you get this message. DO IT!" She ended the call and flopped back against the seat, disgusted. *Beep thing. What a jerk.*

"Relax," Ellie said. "He'll call back."

Gina gave her a worried look. "We can't wait," she said. "We need to go back."

Twenty minutes later they reached the lake cottage and Nathan still hadn't called. Gina tried him again and got the same result. This time, she left a different message.

"Nathan! WHAT are you doing? Call. Me. Back. NOW!"

She waited 30 minutes and tried again.

"It's no use," she said, disconnecting when the call went to voice message. "We need to go."

"Not until you tell me what this is all about," Ellie said.

Jameson directed Beck to a neighborhood on Crescent Avenue. Sprawling industrial buildings and warehouses lined either side of the street, eventually giving way to large multi-level apartment houses.

"There," Jameson said, pointing to a narrow driveway up ahead on the left.

Beck slowed, then turned in, snaking past a white three-story apartment building. In the back was a rectangular brick building, separated from the house by a parking area large enough to accommodate several vehicles. The brick building, a former muffler shop, was showing its age. The bricks that were originally tomato red had aged to a soft shade of peach. A steel door was positioned on the front, and the large windows on either side of it had been bricked in, as had the two bay doors set on the right side of the building. Behind the structure was a ragged metal fence that overlooked a pair of railroad tracks.

This is it? Nathan thought, craning his neck to see out the front windshield.

"Nathan, you wait here," Jameson said. "Beck, you'll be our lookout."

They climbed out of the truck and Beck did a visual sweep of the neighboring properties while Jameson unlocked the metal door.

"Good?" Jameson asked.

"Good," replied Beck.

Jameson returned to the truck and escorted Nathan into the building, followed by Beck. Once they were all inside, Jameson closed and locked the door, then flicked a wall-mounted light switch just inside the door. A long row of neon tubes flickered to life over-head, showering the concrete floor with light. Running along one wall was a row of empty metal shelves. In the near corner was a stack of three car tires. Other than that, there was nothing. The building was deserted.

"This way," Jameson said.

They cut across the floor, the scuffing sound of their footsteps echoing off the walls, to a small glassed-in office in the back corner. It was empty, except for an old wooden desk and a calendar from 1965 that was tacked to the wall. It was open to the month of October and showed a cherry red 1964 Corvette Stingray.

"Okay, now I'm confused," Nathan said, eyeing the small space.

"Good. That's the whole point," Jameson said. He stepped behind the desk and reached underneath the top edge, feeling with his fingertips. Seconds later came a discernible click. Using both hands, Jameson pushed against the edge of the desk and it slid forward, along with a section of the floor, revealing a hidden staircase that led to a lower level.

"Whoa!" Nathan murmured, staring into the dark well.

"Indeed," Jameson said. "Follow me."

Nathan and Beck followed him down the dark stairway. When they reached the bottom, they heard the office desk slide back into place with a muffled scraping sound.

Nathan paused to look back over his shoulder. *Okay, that was weird.*

Jameson pushed through another gray metal door, pausing momentarily to feel for the light switch on the wall to his left. Seconds later, a grid of recessed lights in the ceiling lit up, filling the entire room with a soft white glow.

"What is this place?" Nathan asked, as he stepped into the room.

"It's a bunker, of sorts," Jameson explained.

Another secret room? Nathan thought. He was struck by the realization that he truly didn't know Jameson at all. Clearly there was more to the man than met the eye, and despite their time together, there was much Jameson hadn't shared. Nathan wondered why that was.

Jameson saw the curious look on Nathan's face and said, "You'll be safe here, which is why I chose it."

"You *chose* it?" Nathan asked, his eyes wide. *How many more secret places do you have?* he wondered.

"Yes," Jameson said. "The perimeter of the building is monitored by a series of cameras that Beck and I can check at any time of the day or night. That, plus the single entrance will provide you with the highest level of protection until we can put an end to this Dan Perry business."

Nathan slowly surveyed the room. To his left was a Murphy bed, folded up against the wall. To the right of it, a small closet, and on the adjoining wall was a large flat screen TV. Positioned across from it, much like Beck's living room, was a pecan-colored leather couch. In the opposite corner was a small kitchenette and a narrow counter extending outward from the wall. Two wooden stools sat on each side. To the right of that, in the corner, was a doorway that led to a small bathroom.

"You'll find the refrigerator fully stocked," Jameson explained. "While you're here, help yourself to anything."

"Wait! You're leaving me here alone?" Nathan exclaimed.

"No. Beck will be here with you when he's not outside. At night, one of you can sleep on the Murphy bed, the other on the foldout sofa."

"And what I am I supposed to do while I'm here?" Nathan asked.

"I'll leave that up to you," Jameson said. "Play cards. Watch TV. Just remember, you're in hiding from an extremely dangerous enemy. Sully was able to dig up some more information about him and it's not good. Not good at all. Based on what he told me, we had no choice but to move you to a safer location."

"What he told you," Nathan said, prompting Jameson for details.

"He's an international fugitive," Jameson said.

Beck nodded his head slowly, the news hardly coming as a surprise. "That means he's even more dangerous than I first told you," he told Nathan.

Oh, great, Nathan thought. *Just what I wanted to hear.*

"Now, before Beck takes me back to Birch Meadow, do you have any questions?" Jameson asked.

"Yeah," Nathan said. "What about my folks? Do they know I'm here?"

"They know we moved you. I didn't tell them where, but I assured them you'd be completely safe, and that Beck would be with you."

"For how long?" Nathan asked.

"That depends on Sully and his team, but hopefully not long. Their search for Dan Perry is ongoing."

"Ongoing?" Nathan repeated. *Tell them to go faster*, he wanted to say.

"Yes. Sully has been tracking Perry's boat. It was in South

Portland a few weeks ago, then it was spotted in Saco, and earlier today he found it at a marina in Westport."

"Westport? Where's that?"

"An hour north of Portland."

Nathan shook his head, unconvinced. "Perry's just messing with us," he said. "It's just like before, when he drove north with those two trucks after he emptied his store."

"That's exactly what Sully and I think," Jameson said. He turned to Beck. "Ready?"

"Yup," Beck replied, pulling the truck keys from his pocket. "I'll be back within the hour," he said to Nathan. "During that time Rule #3 is still in effect."

Jameson looked from Beck to Nathan, then back at Beck. "Rule #3?"

"Under no circumstances am I to go outside," Nathan droned, like he was reciting it for the hundredth time.

"Yes, of course," Jameson said. "If you go outside, you run the risk of being seen. Is that what you want?"

"No," Nathan mumbled. The memory of Karl Odom lunging at him in the front hallway was fresh in his mind, and he was in no hurry to experience anything like it again. He walked across the room and dropped his duffle bag on the couch, then pulled his phone from his pocket. *At least I have this.*

"Don't bother," Jameson said, when he saw the phone. "There's no cell reception down here."

Nathan gave him an exasperated look. "You're kidding, right?"

Jameson shook his head. *No.*

"What if I need to call someone?"

"Who would you need to call?" Jameson asked.

"Uh, I don't know…my folks. Gina. You!"

"Beck is in charge of all communications," Jameson said.

Nathan shoved the phone back in his pocket. *Great.*

After they left, Nathan sat at the counter and pulled Graf's calling card from his pocket. The very sight of it unleashed another torrent of questions. *Who was N. Graf? Why was his card hidden in the bookcase with the sheet music? Did the sheet music belong to him? If so, why did he give it to Thomas Hammond? And why hide it?*

He flipped the card over and read the handwritten message. "Remember," he said aloud. "Remember what? What did you show Thomas Hammond?" Until he could talk to Gina, he was powerless to find the answers to those questions, which only made him angrier. "I can't call Gina. We have an old piece of sheet music that makes no sense. And I'm a prisoner in an underground bunker because some ex-military psycho is hunting me. What else can go wrong?"

Frustrated, he tossed the card on the counter.

And that's when he saw the thumbprint. It was dark blue, almost black, in the bottom corner of the card, right below the handwritten message. He checked his fingers for any dirt or grime, but they were clean. When he looked back down at the card, he did a double take.

"Huh?"

The thumbprint was gone.

Beck was pulling out onto Crescent Avenue when Jameson checked his phone and saw that Sully had called. He immediately pressed redial and got Sully on the third ring. "Sully, I'm sorry I missed your call," he said. "I'm with Beck. What we discussed last time? It's done."

"What about the other one?" Sully asked, referring to Gina.

"Already done."

"Good. With any luck, those will only be temporary arrangements."

"You have news?" Jameson asked.

"Oh, I most certainly do. I figured out why we're having trouble finding Dan Perry."

"Go on," Jameson said.

"Perry isn't his real name. It's Dampierre."

"Say again?"

"Dam-pee-AIR," Sully repeated, sounding it out. "Edouard Dampierre."

A faint image surfaced from the depths of Jameson's memory. *Could it be?* he wondered.

"You still there?" Sully asked.

"Sorry, I was just thinking of something," Jameson said. "Are you absolutely sure that's the name?"

"Positive."

Jameson's curiosity burned hotter. "Sully, there's something I need to do," he said. "Can I call you back?"

"You know where to find me."

Jameson ended the call and slipped his phone back in his pocket. "Change of plans," he told Beck. "I need you to drive me to Watertown."

"Sure, any place in particular?"

"I'll show you."

Ellie stood at the kitchen counter making tuna sandwiches while Gina paced nervously in the front room. "So, tell me again," Ellie said, "his name is Nick?"

"Nicholas," Gina said. "Nicholas Graf. He lived in London in the 1800s, the same time as Thomas Hammond."

"That's it?" Ellie asked. She capped the mayo and put it back in the refrigerator.

"No," Gina said. "He left London aboard the *Greenwich*."

"How do you know that?" Ellie asked.

"I found a copy of the passenger list."

Ellie flicked both eyebrows…*wow*…then picked up a fork and began mixing the tuna. "And you're sure it was the *Greenwich?*" she said. "The ship that was carrying the second bookcase?"

"Absolutely," Gina said. "But it got diverted on its way to America and there are no records of it arriving…anywhere."

"Okay, that I remember. But what about Nicholas Graf?" Ellie asked, dividing the tuna equally between two thick slices of sourdough bread.

"I checked the immigration records," Gina said. "The last time he was seen was when he stepped aboard that boat. After that, he simply vanished."

"Along with the bookcase," Ellie noted, arranging each sandwich on a paper plate.

"He clearly knew something about what was hidden inside it," Gina said. "And someone made sure he didn't share it."

"Wait," Ellie said. "How is this tied to Dan Perry?"

"I have no idea," Gina replied. "But he began stalking Nathan, trying to lure him to Maine right after Nathan discovered the second bookcase."

208

"And you think, because of what happened to Nicholas Graf…?" Ellie began.

Gina stopped pacing. "Yes!" she exclaimed. "If they were willing to keep Nicholas Graf from sharing what he knew, what makes you think they won't do the same thing to Nathan or anyone else? That's why we have to warn them."

"Warn who?"

"Everyone!" Gina said, nearly shouting. "Don't you get it? Anyone linked to the bookcase is in danger."

"Okay, okay, calm down," Ellie said. "If what you believe is true, then the best thing for us to do is stay right here." She ripped open a large bag of potato chips and loaded up each plate, nearly covering the sandwiches.

"But…" Gina said.

"No. No buts," Ellie said. "Right now, you're safe, and I intend to keep you that way." She picked up both plates and headed for the deck. "Come on," she said. "Time to eat."

Nathan snatched the card off the counter and examined it closely. He held it up to the light, but the paper was free of any markings or blemishes. "It was there, I know it was," he said. "I was holding the card just like this," he said, clamping his thumb and forefinger on the bottom of the card. Graf's cryptic message stared back at him, taunting him.

Remember what I showed you.

"Then I put it down," he said, letting the card fall to the counter. He watching in amazement as the thumbprint appeared again.

Then, just as quickly, it faded away.

12

Bartlett Mills

"Wait a *minute*," Nathan said, staring at the card. He pulled it closer and pressed his palm on it, keeping it there for thirty seconds. When he pulled his hand away, he saw the thumbprint, but only for a second before it slowly faded. He tried again, this time pressing harder and keeping his hand on the card while he counted to sixty. It appeared again, darker, then gradually lightened before vanishing altogether. "Heat," he whispered. "It's activated by heat."

Now, more than ever he desperately wanted to call Gina—to find out what she'd learned about Graf. Maybe she'd tell him something to explain the curious thumbprint on his calling card. But without cell phone reception…

"Hold on," he said, looking over at the door. "They told me not to go outside, but they didn't say anything about going upstairs."

He ran to the door and started up the steps. What little light there was came from the bunker, and he felt along the wall with his hand in search of a light switch. The only thing his fingers met was smooth wallboard, but then he realized he had a much bigger problem—he had no idea how to activate the sliding mechanism overhead. There had to be a switch on this side of the floor, but where was it? He thought back to when they arrived. *Jameson moved the desk...we came down the stairs...we were at the bottom when the desk slid back into its original position.*

"The bottom," he said, then hurried back down the stairs. When he reached the last step, he stopped. "Jameson was right here when the desk slid back into place," he said. "Which means..." He looked to the right, then to the left, searching for a switch on the wall. Finding none, his eyes settled on the handrail. When he ducked down to examine the underside of it, he spotted a small toggle switch. "There you are," he said, smiling. He pushed it and heard a muffled scraping sound as the panel in the floor overhead slid open.

Jameson guided Beck to the industrial building in the woods behind the gravel pit on Pleasant Street. "Wait here," he said, after Beck's truck came to a stop next to the building. Like before, Jameson punched in a numeric code on the keypad mounted next to the door frame, waited for the door to rise, then ducked inside and immediately closed it.

Moments later he was in the underground room, standing in front of a flat wooden cabinet mounted on the wall. It was roughly 4' x 5' and no more than 6" thick, made from white oak and finished with a light stain the color of butterscotch. Two large wooden doors were attached to the front and he opened them to reveal a large cork bulletin board. Attached to it was a map of the world, dotted with colored thumbtacks that marked specific locations in Europe and the United States. Pinned to both sides of the map were photos of giant mansions, museums, and several high-end art galleries.

He perused them, one by one, then turned his attention to the items taped to the inside of each door. There were mug shots, newspaper clippings, and candid photos, taken of individuals waiting on the curb for a taxi, or in line at a train station. Others showed couples talking at an art gallery opening, exiting a grand event dressed in formal attire, or talking casually in an open market, surrounded by an ocean of people and vendor tents.

As he examined each photo, memories slowly began to emerge through the fog of time. Each face, each location, was a piece of unfinished business from another time in his life—words in the final chapter of a book left unread.

His eyes were drawn to one clipping in particular. It was from the Austrian newspaper *Kronen Zeitung*, commonly known as the *Krone*. The picture was dated 1982 and showed four tuxedo-clad men standing on the steps of a museum in Vienna, Austria. The article chronicled the completion of repairs from damage done by Allied bomb attacks during World War II, nearly 40 years earlier.

Jameson remembered the day he clipped the article from the paper. Not for the story, but for the four men in the picture, each one a person of interest to Jameson's associates at the time. Now, as he read the names printed under the photo, they took on a whole new importance.

The second man from the left was Sebastian Dampierre.

Nathan raced up the stairs and stopped in the office to check his cell reception.

One bar.

He moved out into the large open space.

Still, only one bar.

He went to the door, opened it a few inches, and peered outside. The parking lot was empty, and the window shades in the tenement house were all pulled down. He pushed the door open a few more inches and stepped outside, keeping his foot in the doorway as he checked his phone.

Four bars.

"Yes!"

He went back inside and grabbed one of the tires from the stack in the corner, then rolled it over to the door and flopped it down to keep the door from closing. Standing in the parking lot, he punched the preset number for Ellie and put the phone to his ear. Hearing the call connect was the sweetest sound he'd ever heard.

Ellie was sitting on the deck sipping ice tea and watching boats cruise by on the lake when her phone chirped. She picked it up off the arm of the chair and checked the call screen. "Uh, I think it's for you," she said, then tossed the phone to Gina, sitting a few feet away.

"Hey! What are you doing?" she exclaimed, as the phone landed in her lap. She set her plate on the deck, then picked up the phone and pressed the talk button.

"Hey Ellie, it's me Nathan. Is Gina there?"

"Am I here?" she barked. "Of course I'm here. I've been waiting for you to call me back."

"Oh, Gina, good, it's you," he said.

"I called you a million times," she said. "Why didn't you answer? And don't tell me you lost your phone." The words 'I lost it' currently sat at #2 on the *Nathan Cole's Stupid and Highly Improbable Excuses* list.

"I can't go into it right now," he said, hoping that would appease her.

It didn't.

"What's that supposed to mean, you can't go into it?" she said. "Where are you? Do you ever check your phone messages?"

"Uh, no," he said, "I've been a little distracted."

"Distracted," she repeated. *That's new.* She made a mental note to add it to the list.

"Did you find a library?" he asked. As he spoke, an eighteen-wheeler chugged past the end of the driveway, the driver blasting his air horn at another vehicle.

"Where *are* you?" Gina asked again. "At a truck rally?"

Nathan ducked around the corner of the building, clamping his free hand over his ear. "Yeah," he said. "I enrolled in tractor trailer driving school."

"Very funny," she shot back. "And yes, I found a library. Why do you think I kept calling you?"

"Is it bad?" Nathan asked.

"Very bad," she replied. "N stands for Nicholas."

"Okay, good," he said.

"Not so fast," she said. "Nicholas Graf was an apothecary. He apprenticed with Thomas Charles Hope, a leading British chemist, before opening his own shop in London."

"He what?"

"He was an apothecary…" Gina began.

"No, not that. You said he apprenticed with someone?"

"Yes, a chemist named Thomas Charles Hope. Why do you ask?"

Chemist, Nathan thought, nodding his head. That explained the vanishing thumbprint on Graf's card. Only someone familiar with chemical compounds would know how to devise such a thing.

"Nathan? What is it?"

"Nothing," he said. There was no time to explain. By his estimation, Beck would be back at any moment. "What else?" he asked.

"Graf was aboard the *Greenwich*," Gina said.

"Are you sure?"

"Yes, and that was the last anyone saw of him."

Nathan's jaw fell open. "What are you saying? He vanished?"

"Uh-huh. Just like the ship."

Nathan began to pace along the side of the building. "He must've been safeguarding the bookcase as it was smuggled out of England," he said. "My cousin Daniel was aboard the other ship, with the first bookcase."

"But nothing happened to him," Gina said, "or that bookcase."

"Right," Nathan said, trying desperately, and failing, to make sense of it.

"It's tied to the sheet music," Gina said. "Graf knew something about it. Whatever it was, somebody clearly didn't want him to share it. And now, it's happening again."

"You mean, with the two guys in the van…?"

"Yes!" Gina exclaimed, feeling her angst rise again. "And when that failed, Perry sent that thug to break into your house. Remember what Jameson told us? Whatever was hidden in the bookcase is potentially lethal? Well, it's true. And now that Perry knows we have it, we're all in danger."

Nathan heard the unmistakable growl of a truck engine, slowing as it prepared to turn into the driveway. "Gina, I gotta go," he said.

"Wait...don't hang up," she said.

He could hear her shouting as he closed the phone.

"Nathan?...NATHAN!"

Gina calmly set the phone down on the deck next to her plate, then got up from the chair, walked to the end of the deck, and screamed, "AAAAAAAAAAAHHHHHHHH!"

Her voice echoed across the water, drowning out the sound of a passing jet-ski, its bow pounding against the surface of the water.

She closed her eyes, took a deep calming breath, then turned and went back to her chair.

"All better now?" Ellie asked.

"No!" Gina snapped.

"What's the problem?"

"You mean, other than the fact that no one is taking me seriously?"

Ellie popped the last bit of her sandwich into her mouth, brushed her hands together, wiping away the salt residue from the potato chips, then climbed out of her chair and retrieved her phone.

"What are you doing?" Gina asked.

"You'll see," Ellie said. She tapped an autodial number on the phone, and as she waited for the call to connect she turned toward the lake, eyes closed, feeling the warm breeze caress her face. After two rings, Jameson answered.

"Ellie? How is camping?" As he spoke, he taped the article from *Kronen Zeitung* back on the door and swung it shut.

"Couldn't be better," Ellie said, watching a sailboat glide effortlessly down the channel. "There's someone here who needs to talk to you." She handed Gina the phone. "Jameson," she whispered, then went back and sat down.

"Hello? Jameson?" Gina said.

"Hello, Gina," he said. "You need to talk to me?"

"What I *need* is for people to wake up!"

"What are you talking about?" Jameson asked.

She stood and began pacing. "We're in danger," she said. "All of us. We need to warn everyone—"

"Hold on," Jameson said, cutting her off. "Slow down. Take a breath, then tell me what's bothering you."

Gina stopped pacing. Her shoulders sagged and she closed her eyes, took a deep breath and started again. "I went to the library..." she began, calmly.

"To research the name Nathan gave you," Jameson cut in. "The name on the card he found."

"Yes," she said, giving Ellie a firm look. *Really? You had to tell him?*

Ellie gave her an innocent shrug. "What?"

Gina rolled her eyes, then continued. "The card belonged to a man named Nicholas Graf."

"Nicholas Graf," Jameson repeated slowly. The name still held no place in his memory.

"He was an apothecary who lived in London at the same time as Thomas Hammond," Gina said.

"Interesting," Jameson replied.

"No, it's *not* interesting," Gina fired back. "It's worse than that. Much worse. Graf was aboard the *Greenwich* when it left England. After that, he was never heard from again."

Jameson paused momentarily to digest what she'd told him. "You're absolutely sure of this?" he asked.

"Yes. I saw a passenger list for the ship. I checked it against immigration records. He never arrived in America. If he did, there's no record of him anywhere. Don't you see? He knew something about what was hidden in the bookcases, and someone made sure he never passed it on."

Jameson said nothing. While her fears were justified, he needed her and Nathan to remain calm. Moreover, he needed to keep them from doing something drastic, like they'd done a number of times in the past when confronted with a riddle. "I understand your concern," he said. "And I assure you we're taking every possible safety precaution possible."

"Are you?" she said. "What about Nathan? I thought he was supposed to be hidden away somewhere, but he went back to his house. How safe was that?"

"It wasn't, which is why he's been moved to a more secure location," Jameson said.

Good, Gina thought.

"There's something else you need to know," Jameson said. "There's been a significant development in the search for Dan Perry. I can't discuss it now, but suffice to say, we're that much closer to finding him. As far as Nicholas Graf, I'm not sure what to make of him, or his involvement with the bookcases. As soon as we figure it out, I promise you, I'll let you know. Your help in this matter, as always, has been invaluable."

"Thanks," Gina said, less than enthused. She got up from the chair, handed Ellie the phone, and went into the house. If they didn't want to take her seriously, so be it. They couldn't say she didn't warn them. She grabbed a puzzle book and plopped down on her bed, doing her best to ignore the sound of the motorboats whizzing by the dock every three seconds. Didn't these people have anything better to do with their time? What was so exciting about racing from one end of the lake to the other, over and over and over again?

"What do you make of all that?" Ellie asked Jameson, after Gina had gone inside.

"Hard to say," Jameson replied. "There's clearly something we're missing. For the time being, we need to focus our attention on Dan Perry, who, as it turns out, isn't Dan Perry after all."

"Isn't Dan Perry? What are you talking about?"

"His real name is Edouard Dampierre. His family name dates back to the early 1400s in France. Sully discovered it during his investigation."

Ellie sat up in the chair. "Wait. You're telling me he comes from an old European family?"

"Yes."

"And now, he's after this piece of sheet music? Also very old? Possibly quite valuable?"

"Yes."

"And he changed his name?"

"That's right," Jameson said.

"Are you thinking what I'm thinking?"

"Yes," Jameson said. "And there's more."

Sully was like a kid waking up in the morning and suddenly remembering it was Christmas Day. He had a newfound energy after learning Dan Perry's true identity, and he began an aggressive search of the Dampierre name, using various state databases and genealogy websites of families living in Maine. Within minutes he found what he was looking for.

Edouard Dampierre.

Born in Portland, Maine, in 1971.

The youngest of three children, which included two siblings: an older brother Sebastian, and a sister, Ginette, the oldest of the three.

After graduating high school, Sebastian Dampierre's trail ran dry. With no record of his death, Sully assumed the man had relocated out of state. His older sister, Ginette, on the other hand, had stayed in Maine, marrying a local man from Arundel named Emmitt Whitten. Another search revealed that the couple had settled in a small town nearby.

He made a note of the address and grabbed his car keys. On the way out of the building, he passed Detective Jimmy Racine's desk. Racine was several years younger and had recently helped Sully with the sordid Reggie Griffin business.

"Hey, feel like taking a ride?" Sully asked.

Racine was slouched over his desk, studying a list of motor

vehicle warrants. When he heard Sully's invitation, he perked up at once. "Sure," he said, pushing away from his desk. "Where are we going?"

"Bartlett Mills."

On the way back to Birch Meadow, Jameson's thoughts were a hailstorm of names, places, and dead-end leads that stretched over three decades—a tiresome journey that had left him feeling like he was chasing a phantom. But with the new information Sully had given him, could it be that his luck was changing? He was pondering that thought when his cell phone vibrated. When he saw who was calling, he answered at once. "Sully?"

"Hey," Sully replied. "I did some more digging. Dampierre had two older siblings."

Jameson's heart raced. "Was one of them named Sebastian?"

"Yeah, how did you know that?" Sully asked.

"It's a long story," Jameson replied. "Tell me about the other one."

"He's got an older sister, Ginette. I found an address for her right outside of Kennebunk. I'm headed there now."

"Excellent," Jameson said, his excitement building. "Let me know what you find out." He ended the call and stared at the phone, thinking.

"What was that all about?" Beck asked.

Jameson looked over at him, nodding as he spoke. "We're getting closer."

The ride to Kennebunk took 30 minutes. On the way, Sully described in general terms what he knew of Edouard Dampierre, his

Maine roots, how he'd been harassing the Cole family for months, orchestrating the attempted abduction of Nathan, and a subsequent break-in at their home in Massachusetts using a former military specialist. He cleverly sidestepped any mention of the matching bookcases or the sheet music that Nathan had found.

"What is it with that kid?" Jimmy asked, when they came to the Kennebunk exit. "He's always neck deep in something crazy."

"Tell me about it," Sully replied. He came to a stop at the end of the ramp, checked the traffic in both directions, then turned right and headed west. Gradually, the road grew narrower and traffic eased. Ten minutes later he found the street—a dead-end road with a handful of homes on either side, each showing signs of active family life. Sprinklers were on. Lawns and vegetable gardens were rigorously maintained. Barbeque grills and umbrella tables adorned stone patios.

The houses eventually thinned out and were replaced by large tracts of forested land. When they came to the house in question, Sully pulled over, eyeing it through the sparse tree line that ran along the front of the property.

"*This* is what you came to see?" Jimmy asked, looking at the house with disdain. The roof was dotted with moss and was in desperate need of replacement. The drapes in the windows on the second floor were crooked, or missing completely.

Sully pulled the small notepad from his coat pocket and checked the address. "This is it," he said, closing the notepad. "Come on, let's check it out."

"Looks deserted," Jimmy said, as they walked up the driveway.

"I'll say," Sully replied.

"Check that out," Jimmy said, pointing to the relator's sign, barely visible through the mile-a-minute vines.

Sully looked at the sign, then over at the house. Something felt off, but he couldn't put his finger on it. He knelt down and examined the cracks that ran like blood vessels through the tar. They were packed with weeds, and one section in particular caught his eye. "A large vehicle was parked here not too long ago," he said.

"Could've been a moving company truck," Jimmy said.

"Maybe."

"Should we knock on the door?" Jimmy asked. "See if anyone's home?"

"Does it *look* like anyone's home?"

"Hey, you never know," Jimmy said.

"Knock yourself out," Sully told him.

Jimmy gave him a tired look...*really?*...then went to the front door and knocked, the wood like steel beneath his fist. When there was no answer, he tried the knob only to find it locked.

While he was doing that, Sully went to each of the front windows and peered inside, cupping his hands on the glass to block out the sun. Every room was empty. "Well, whoever used to live here is long gone," he said.

His computer search had no other listing for Ginette Dampierre.

The question was, where did she go?

At Birch Meadow, Jameson paced the length of his room, debating how to proceed. The new information Sully had given him about the Dampierre family had recharged his systems, but at the same time he knew it was too soon to contact the authorities. They needed more proof. Undisputable proof. The kind that only Dan Perry could provide. That settled, he turned his attention to Nicolas Graf.

Was he a friend of Thomas Hammond? Was Thomas Hammond one of Graf's customers? Could the message on his card simply refer to some medication he'd made for Hammond? He grabbed his iPad and did an extensive search of the name Nicholas Graf. He wasn't overly optimistic that he'd turn up anything more than Gina had found because her research skills were second to none. But when he changed his search parameter, he discovered something of interest.

During the 1800s, when the symphonies of Beethoven and Berlioz were first introduced to the dedicated hordes of music lovers across Europe, Graf was part of a small group that formed the Philharmonic Society of London. While not a composer or performer himself, Graf was a generous benefactor of the society and a devout patron of the music scene at that time.

When Jameson read that, he put down his iPad and sat back in the chair, thinking. Was Ellie correct? Was the sheet music an extremely rare copy? A document of exceeding value? Could that be Perry's angle? That thought was resonating in his head when his phone vibrated on the desk, breaking his train of thought.

"Fletcher?" he asked, forgoing any formal greeting.

"Jameson," Poole replied politely.

Jameson straightened in the chair. "How are you making out?"

"I'm nearly finished," Fletcher said. His clipped tone made it clear that he was uncomfortable with the urgent timeline Jameson had set forth. "By changing out the blotters hourly, I've managed to remove most of the moisture. Mind you, the document is not entirely flat. If I only had more time…" he said, letting the implication hang in the air.

"No, I fully understand," Jameson said. "And I appreciate your diligence. Really, I do. Will you be at home tonight?"

"Yes," replied Poole. "I anticipate I'll be up until well after midnight, trying to save a rather troublesome postcard, or rather, the stamp affixed to it."

"Oh?" Jameson said.

"It's a 1909 Benjamin Franklin unmarked one cent stamp."

"Is it rare?" Jameson asked.

"It's current value rests at $10,000," Poole replied.

"Then, in that case, I'll be sure to keep my visit brief. Shall we say, 7PM?"

"That would be fine," Poole said. "Until then…" he said politely, then promptly hung up.

Jameson immediately called Kendra, who was busy at the coffee shop cleaning up for the day.

"Yeah," she said, as she gathered carafes from the counter.

"I have two matters that require your assistance," Jameson said. "First, are you free after dinner?"

"I have no plans, why?"

"I'll explain when you get here."

"O-kay," Kendra said slowly. "What's the second thing?"

"I need you to call Elliot right away and see if he can meet with us."

"Meet with us when?" Kendra asked.

"As soon as possible."

"Right," she said, like he was out of his mind. Knowing Elliot, he was probably pulling all-nighters in the studio and sleeping away the daylight hours. "I'll call him," she said, doubtfully, "but don't hold your breath. Elliot's one of those guys who's always on the move. There's not much that slows him down. It's a California thing."

"Tell him I've got something he'll want to see. Be sure to mention the 18th century."

"The 18th century? That's it?"

"That's it."

Odom parked one street away, as he'd done previously. After watching the neighborhood for several minutes to make sure no one would see him, he slipped out the door of his Rover and crossed the street, walking with a slight limp. He cut between two houses, stepping over sprinkler heads and around stray toys, until he came to the tree line. Directly beyond it was Nathan's house. He crept into the trees and waited for several minutes, watching the house for any sign of activity.

Just below the gutter at the corner of the house he spotted a second camera. It was painfully obvious, but he understood why they'd installed it. If presented with the same circumstances, he would've done the same thing, only better—he would've installed it where no one could see it.

He scanned the trees to his left and right. There were several good choices, but in the end he settled on a wolf tree, a monstrous white oak with massive branches, some as thick as his waist. Moving quickly and efficiently, he slipped the sling backpack off his shoulder and went to work.

Nathan rushed back inside the building, pulled the door shut, and returned the tire to the stack in the corner. As he raced toward the small office, he could hear the rumble of Beck's truck growing louder as it came down the driveway. He raced back down the stairs and flipped the toggle on the handrail, resetting the hidden entrance, just as Beck was climbing out of his truck.

Moments later, the door to the bunker swung open and Beck walked in, carrying a large pizza box in one hand and a six pack of soda in the other. "I got dinner," he said. "I hope you like pepperoni."

"Sure!" Nathan exclaimed. He spotted Graf's card on the counter and quickly tucked it in his back pocket.

"Are you okay?" Beck asked, when he saw the frenzied look on Nathan's face.

"Uh, yeah, I'm fine," Nathan stammered, "if you don't count the fact that I'm cooped up in an underground bunker like some kind of laboratory animal."

"Relax. We're leaving in the morning," Beck said.

Nathan eyed him suspiciously. "Is this a joke?"

"No joke. Just make sure you're ready to go…early."

Nathan brightened. "Where are we going?"

"You'll see," Beck said. He flipped open the pizza box and pulled out a giant wedge. Thin slices of pepperoni poked up through a thick blanket of extra cheese.

"How early?" Nathan asked, using two hands to wrestle a slice out of the box.

"Six o'clock," Beck said. He folded the pizza lengthwise and took a bite.

"Excuse me?" Nathan blurted out.

"What would you prefer?" Beck asked, talking as he chewed.

"Oh, I don't know," Nathan said. "Nine o'clock? Ten? Eleven o'clock is a very nice hour of the day."

Beck took a gulp of soda, burped, then said, "No can do."

"Why not?" Nathan asked.

"He'll be gone by then."

13

The Grim Fugue

Nathan was fast asleep on the couch, haunted by a troubling dream where everything he touched faded away before his very eyes. As the nightmare churned on, a hand suddenly gripped his shoulder, rocking him awake. He turned over and saw Beck towering over him like a giant redwood, a ceramic mug of coffee in his hand.

"Time to go," Beck said.

"Very funny," Nathan mumbled, then turned back over and closed his eyes.

Beck grabbed Nathan's earlobe and squeezed.

"Hey, easy does it!" Nathan groaned, brushing Beck's hand away. He exhaled loudly, then propped himself up and rubbed his eyes. *This is criminal.*

"We leave in 20 minutes," Beck said. "Doughnuts are on the

counter, orange juice is in the fridge, and there's hot coffee in the carafe."

"I'd rather drink motor oil," Nathan grumbled.

"That can be arranged," Beck said. "Now, come on, get a move on."

Twenty minutes later, to the second, they were in Beck's truck, pulling out onto Crescent Avenue. Beck still hadn't said where they were going, but Nathan was just happy to be above ground again where he could see the light of day.

Beck stopped to top off the gas tank, and after he climbed back into the cab, he took out his phone and made a call. "We're on our way," he said. "Barring any problems, we should be there in 2 hours, maybe less." After a brief pause, he said, "Yeah, the Regency on Milk Street. I'm familiar with it." Another pause. "He's fine," he said, looking over at Nathan. "A little sleepy but I think he'll survive."

After he ended the call, Nathan asked, "Milk Street? In Portland, Maine?"

Beck nodded. Yes.

Nathan sat back in the seat thinking about his last trip to Portland, months earlier. Most vivid in his mind was a small shop on Wharf Street, just a stone's throw from Milk Street, called Trinidad Traders. It was there that he discovered the *Greenwich* bookcase—a find for the ages, and one that for better or worse would forever be linked to his name. Little did he know at the time that the chain of events to follow would place him in mortal danger.

And the story wasn't over yet.

Not by a longshot.

"You didn't ask why," Beck said, as he pulled onto Rt. 1 North.

"I'm sorry, what was that?" Nathan said, the image of the *Greenwich* bookcase slipping away.

"You haven't asked me why we're going to Portland."

"Let me guess. It has something to do with Kendra's friend, Elliot."

"Very good."

"What's the deal with him, anyway?" Nathan asked. "Kendra didn't say much."

"Couldn't tell you," Beck said, checking the side mirror before jetting into the left lane.

"Is she going to be there?"

"Yes."

"And Jameson?"

"Uh-huh. He'll have the sheet music, too."

Nathan bolted upright in the seat. "He got it back?"

"Sometime last night."

"That was fast," Nathan said.

"Jameson somehow convinced Poole to speed up the process. I guess he really wanted to see that sheet of paper."

So do I, Nathan thought. *So. Do. I.*

Two hours later, as they drove up Market Street past the Regency's circular cobblestone courtyard, they saw Kendra's faded blue Volvo parked near the front entrance. Jameson was sitting in the front seat, lost in thought, while Kendra leaned against the front hood, watching two seagulls fight over a partially eaten hamburger bun. A fast food take-out bag and a crumpled wrapper lay on the ground nearby.

Beck took a right onto Milk Street, then another right onto Silver Street, where he found an open parking space. When Nathan climbed out, he saw Kendra standing several feet away on the sidewalk. "Hey, Kendra," he said, as he walked toward her. A firm breeze carried the salty smell of the ocean, and overhead he heard the all-too-familiar mewing of seagulls. They were sounds and smells that would be forever be riveted to his memory.

"Hey to you, too," she replied. She nodded at Beck. *Hey.*

The three of them were walking to the Volvo when the passenger-side door squeaked open and Jameson climbed out. He had a thin leather portfolio under his arm, clamped tightly against his body like a running back holding a football as he crossed the goal line.

"Good morning," he said, all business.

Nathan sensed something was bothering him.

"He's inside," Jameson said. "Let's not keep him waiting."

"Hold on," Nathan said. "Would somebody like to tell me what we're doing here at 8 o'clock in the morning? And who is this Elliot guy?"

Beck looked at him and smirked. "What is it with you and all the questions?"

"Ask no questions, learn no truths," Nathan said.

"Wow," Kendra said. "Did you just make that up?"

Nathan squinted his eyes and gave her a phony smile. *Very funny.*

"Your questions are valid," Jameson said, "and I promise you they'll be answered very shortly."

As they made their way up the front steps of the hotel, Kendra whispered to Nathan, "Relax, Elliot's a hoot. You're gonna

232

love him."

Nathan gave her tenuous look. *Okay, if you say so.* As they entered the hotel, his eyes were trained on the leather portfolio under Jameson's arm. Each of the questions he had about the sheet music secured inside it began to crackle in his mind like a string of firecrackers snapping and writhing in the driveway.

At the front desk, Jameson consulted with the clerk, a very nice girl named Julie. After a quick phone call, she told Jameson, "He said to go right up." Jameson confirmed the room number, then one of the busboys walked them to the elevator, leading them through a spacious lobby with a broad stairway that led up to the second floor, and another that went to downstairs to additional guestrooms and a private lounge.

Two blocks away, Sully was sitting alone at the end of the counter in a small restaurant on Custom House Wharf. It was his usual breakfast hangout, a place where he could lose himself in the constant chatter of the locals and the steady *whumph* of the swinging door that led to the kitchen.

As he hovered over a mug of hot coffee, he couldn't stop thinking about what he and Jimmy had found at the Bartlett Mills property the day before. Something about the place bugged him, but he couldn't figure out what it was. His cell phone vibrated, breaking his train of thought, and he flipped it open before it could vibrate a second time. "This is Sully."

"Sully, it's Eric Fuller. I won't ask if it's too early to call because I know exactly where you are. That clinking of silverware I hear in the background tells me you're downtown having breakfast. I'm guessing…Custom House Wharf?"

"You got me," Sully admitted. "What can I do for you?" As he spoke he pushed his mug toward the waitress standing nearby and gestured for a refill.

"We need to meet," Fuller said. "Immediately."

"Is this related to our last conversation?"

"It is," replied Fuller. "I need to know everything about Karl Odom. How you found him. Where he was at the time. What he was doing. Who he was with. His physical description. I mean *everything.*"

Sully took in a deep breath let it out. "Well," he said, "I can get that information for you, but it's probably better if you hear it first hand."

"I don't understand," Fuller said.

"How's your schedule today?" Sully asked.

"I can make time."

"Sit tight," Sully told him. "I'll call you back in 20 minutes."

Elliot Kitchens had a suite on the top floor, facing the ocean. As Jameson and the others exited the elevator, they heard a strange sound emanating from his room at the end of the hall. To Nathan it sounded like the deep, throaty croak of a bullfrog.

Kendra rapped on the door.

The bullfrog continued to croak.

She rapped again, harder.

The croaking stopped.

After a momentary silence that stretched for nearly 30 seconds, the door swung open. Elliot Kitchens, the avant-garde and

Grammy Award winning cellist, and current darling of the hip L.A. music scene, stood there dressed in black jeans, a yellow linen shirt, and a gray herringbone vest. He was tall, with a thin frame and a deep California tan. His fade haircut featured a lone mop of hair above his forehead that was spiked forward, and his moustache was neatly trimmed, as was his landing-strip goatee.

"Kay-jay!" he exclaimed, his expression bright. He and Kendra shared a hug, then she stepped back and introduced the rest of the group. "Elliot, you know my dad."

"Jameson," Elliot said, bowing his head politely.

"This is Beck," Kendra said, motioning toward the big man.

"Beck?" Elliot repeated. "Any relation?"

Beck frowned. "Relation?"

"Beck David Hansen?" Elliot said. "American singer/songwriter? Record producer?"

Beck shook his head. "Sorry."

"No matter," Elliot said. "And who might this be?" he asked, looking at Nathan.

Nathan extended his hand. "Nathan Cole."

Elliot shook Nathan's hand, eyeing him intently. "Nathan Cole," he said slowly, trying to place the name. "The Nathan Cole from last year? The one that totally *rocked* all the newspapers and television news shows?"

Nathan gave him a weary nod. *Yup, that's me.*

Elliot's face lit up. "Dude!" he said, fist-bumping Nathan. "What you did? That was *tight!*"

He ushered the group into the room, Nathan first, followed by Kendra and the others.

"Kay-jay?" Nathan snickered, over his shoulder.

"You ever call me that? I'm gettin' my bat," she whispered, then gave him a shove.

Elliot let them past a bed that was bigger than Nathan's bathroom at home, to an open area with a desk on one wall, and a small couch on the other. A row of full-length windows lined the outside wall of the room, and the heavy drapes were pulled back, offering a view across the jagged rooftops of the Old Port and beyond. Set in the middle of the windows was pair of glass doors that had been opened to let in the breeze blowing in off the ocean.

Nathan stared at the ocean in the distance, thinking of his last visit to Portland, and the boat ride that nearly cost him his life.

As the others filtered into the room, Elliot picked up a large black instrument case that was sitting near the edge of the bed.

"What is that?" Nathan asked, studying the curious shape of the case. It had an eerily human form and looked big enough to hold a large child.

Elliot opened the case to reveal a Viole de Gambe. "This," he said proudly, "is Eloise."

"Eloise?"

"Uh-huh. She *speaks* to me," Elliot murmured, flashing his eyebrows as he spoke.

"We heard you playing when we were out in the hallway," Kendra said.

"You *heard* that?" Elliot replied.

The entire Old Port heard it, Nathan was tempted to say.

"I was just noodling," Elliot explained. "Must keep the fingers in shape."

236

Kendra nodded at the open case admiringly. "Eloise...great name."

How about The Bullfrog? Nathan thought.

Elliot closed the case and stood it up in the corner. "Okay, then," he said, addressing Jameson. "What is this thing you want me to see? Kendra said something about the 18th century?"

Jameson went to the desk and opened the leather portfolio. Very carefully, he slid out the packet that Fletcher had assembled, which consisted of two pieces of stiff cardboard, taped together on each side. After peeling off the tape, he opened the sheet music and handed it to Elliot.

"Oh, my...where did you get *this?*" he gushed, poring over every square inch of the paper as if committing each note and musical symbol to memory.

"I'd rather not say," Jameson said.

"Do they have any more?" Elliot asked excitedly.

Jameson and Nathan answered together with a profound, "No."

As Elliot continued to examine the music, Nathan watched his eyes, convinced that he was sounding out each note in his head.

"This is fantastic," Elliot murmured. "Look at this complex voicing. It's no wonder the critics shunned it."

"You know what it is?" Jameson asked.

"Please," Elliot said, with a smirk. "This one's easy."

"Why do you say that?" Nathan asked.

"Right here," Elliot said, pointing. "The treble clef in the first grand staff? That's a dead giveaway. This was written by Franz Eigner."

"Eigner?" Jameson repeated. "I'm not familiar with that name."

"He was a lesser-known German composer in the mid 1700s."

Jameson nodded slowly, his hunch about Elliot Kitchens confirmed. He might be quirky, but his knowledge of music was nothing short of encyclopedic.

"So, wait a minute," Nathan said. "You can tell that by just looking at it?"

"Absolutely," Elliot replied. "Handwritten music is as distinct as a signature. The way this treble clef was written is a perfect example. Many treble clefs swirl gracefully, like calligraphy. Eigner's clef looks more like a hastily scribbled Z with a straight line going down the middle. Compared to other composers, his clefs were abrupt…harsh, even. Still, this was one of his most intriguing compositions. Unfortunately for him, however, it was soundly rejected."

Nathan leaned closer, eyeing the rows of notes. To him it was all a jumble. Like every other piece of sheet music he'd seen, it was nothing but a bunch of lines and notes and strange music symbols. There was nothing he could see to explain why Thomas Hammond had hidden it in the bookcase, or why Dan Perry was so desperate to possess it.

"Why was it rejected?" Jameson asked.

"Despite its intricate complexity, the music was very difficult to listen to," Elliot explained. "Some consider it his most ingenious composition, but the critics of the day didn't agree. They called it *The Grim Fugue*."

"Is it valuable?" Jameson asked.

"Not really," Elliot said. "Don't get me wrong, it's definitely an original, but we're not talking about a Mozart first version manuscript here. Do you have the rest of it?"

"The rest of it?" Jameson said. "What are you talking about?"

"There are two pages missing."

"Are you sure?"

"Uh-huh."

Nathan and Jameson exchanged a knowing look, each one reading the other's mind. Could that be what was hidden in the *Greenwich* bookcase? It would certainly explain why Dan Perry wanted these pages so badly.

"If you want to sell it," Elliot said, "I'm sure I could find a buyer."

"No, but thank you," Jameson said graciously.

"Well, if you ever change your mind, let me know. Hey, is anyone hungry? I'm starving, and they serve an *amazing* brunch in the dining room."

"Brunch?" Nathan said, eyebrows raised. "I vote yes."

"Count me in," Kendra said.

"Then, brunch it is," Elliot said. "On me!"

Several minutes later they were standing at the hostess station in the main lobby, waiting to be seated, when Jameson felt his phone vibrate. He quickly pulled it out of his pocket, saw who was calling, and took the call. "Sully, we're about to sit down to breakfast," he said. "Can I call you back?"

"This won't take long," Sully answered.

"Okay, go ahead."

"We need to meet, right away."

"We?"

"Yes," Sully replied, "We, as in all of us."

"By all of us, who do you mean, exactly?" Jameson asked. He watched Kendra and the others file into the dining room behind a tall gray-haired server holding a stack of menus in his hand.

"You, Kendra, Elizabeth and David, Beck, Ellie, the kids... *especially* the kids. Anyone who's seen or been in direct contact with Karl Odom."

"I see. Is there something you need to tell us?" Jameson asked, as a young couple with two toddlers in tow came walking through the lobby entrance.

"Not me. This is coming from my contact at the U.S. Marshal's Service. His name is Eric Fuller."

"The U.S. Marshal's Service wants to meet with *us?*" Jameson repeated.

The young couple froze, looking at him like he was an armed felon.

"Today," Sully replied.

"Why?" Jameson asked. He saw the look of horror on the young couple's faces and gestured to them with his hand. *It's okay... it's not what you think.* They shot him a nasty look and quickly hustled their kids across the lobby, keeping as far away from him as possible.

"I'll let Eric explain once we're all assembled," Sully told him.

"Got it," Jameson said. "Meeting shouldn't be a problem. Most of us are here in town. We just need to contact Elizabeth and David... and Ellie and Gina, of course."

"Already done," Sully told him.

"Wow, when you said right away you weren't kidding around."

"That's not something you want to do with the Marshal's

Service," Sully replied. "As we speak, Elizabeth and David are on their way. They won't arrive until about 11:30. If you leave town no later than 10 o'clock, you should be there about the same time."

"Leave? Where are we going? And what about Ellie and Gina?"

"They're already there."

"Oh…so we're meeting at…?"

"Yes. It was Ellie's idea. It's quiet. It's remote. And no one will hear us."

"Makes sense," Jameson offered.

"Hey, enjoy your breakfast," Sully told him. "Make sure you leave town by 10 o'clock. I'll text you the address."

Jameson slipped his phone back in his pocket and offered a smile to the young couple who were keeping a watchful eye on him as they climbed the grand stairway with their two kids.

When they saw that, they picked up the kids and hurried up the stairs.

Elizabeth and David took Rt. 95 north toward Portsmouth. From there, they followed a series of roads north and west, through Dover, Rochester, and Farmington, that eventually brought them to the town of New Durham, and Merrymeeting Lake.

As they bounced down the dirt road on the north side of the lake, the irony of the name wasn't lost on David. "Merrymeeting," he said, watching two teenagers paddle-boarding along the shoreline. "Do you think that's why they chose this location?"

"Is that supposed to be funny?" Elizabeth asked.

"Hey, I'm just asking."

"I'm guessing it's a security measure," Russ McCullough said from the back seat. "I mean, just look at this place. Who's going to bother us way out here?"

Any doubts they had about finding the cottage were erased when they came around the bend in the road and saw a slate gray Dodge Charger with the U.S. Marshal's Service emblem on the door. It was parked in the narrow driveway next to the cottage, directly behind Ellie's hatchback. Parked on the shoulder in front of the house was Beck's giant black pickup truck and Kendra's faded blue Volvo.

Elizabeth eased to a stop behind the Volvo and got out, pausing to breathe in the fresh air that carried the earthy aroma of the fir forest across the road. The sound of the motorboats on the lake, and the sun shimmering off the surface of the water, brought back memories of Jewell Lake, 45 minutes to the east, in the town of Crawford. The vivid images of Nathan and Gina's near-death adventure during their last visit there still had the power to jolt her out of a sound sleep.

She followed the sound of voices coming from the far side of the house, to the large deck that overlooked the lake. Everyone was there, along with two men Elizabeth didn't recognize. Jameson was talking to one of them off to the side, both men keeping their backs turned to the rest of the group.

The other man was tall and muscular, with a clean-shaven face and a military haircut. He wore a navy-blue suitcoat, neatly pressed, with a crisp button-down shirt and tailored khaki pants. He was talking with Sully, but when he saw her crest the top of the stairs, he walked over at once. "Elizabeth Cole?" he said.

"Yes?"

He extended his hand. "I'm Deputy Eric Fuller with the United

States Marshal's Service."

"Nice to meet you Eric," she said, shaking his hand briefly. "This is my husband, David, and this is our friend Russ McCullough. Russ has been kind enough to help us with security at the house."

"David, Russ," Eric said as he shook their hands. "Thank you all for coming. Before you leave, we'll need to get your statements."

"Statements?" David asked.

"You'll understand after you hear what we have to say." He turned to the group and said, "Okay people, if I could have your attention."

As the chatter died down, Elizabeth looked across the deck and gave Nathan and Gina a quick wave. They were standing away from the others, near the steps that led down to the dock, looking like a set of mismatched salt and pepper shakers. In unison, they managed a tired smile and a brief, robotic wave.

Right.

Left.

Done.

"I want to thank all of you for meeting with us on such short notice," Eric said. "Given the sensitive nature of what we're about to discuss, I think it's better if we speak inside." With that, he opened the slider and stood aside as everyone filed into the house.

Elizabeth saw Jameson approaching and took his arm, steering him over to the railing. "What's going on?" she asked.

"I guess we're about to find out," Jameson said.

Once they were all assembled in the living room, Eric Fuller stood at the end of the room closest to the road. Directly behind him was a large framed photograph of a breathtaking sunset on the lake. Right below it, pushed up against the wall, was a long narrow table with an assortment of smaller photographs. The man who'd been talking to Jameson stood at Fuller's side. He had the same muscular build as Fuller, but with a chiseled face and short hair the color of beach sand. He was dressed in a gray, custom-tailored Italian suit and stood with his hands folded in front of his body, holding a thin briefcase. The suit, and his serious demeanor, made him look like a defense attorney waiting on the courthouse steps for a client.

"All right, let's get started," Fuller said. "With me today is Mason Bishop, a U.S. liaison for Interpol. He flew up from New York late last night to be with us today. Before we go any further, I need to tell you that what we're going to discuss is classified information, and as such, should not be shared with anyone outside this room. Is that clear?"

The group responded with a collective "Yes."

"Very good. Now, it's my understanding that within the last two days, some of you were in direct contact with Karl Odom. Will those people please raise their hand?"

Nathan and Gina raised their hands. Beck, too.

Russ raised his hand and said, "I saw him from across the street, if that counts."

"It most certainly does," said Fuller. "Anyone else?" he asked.

"David and I were parked at the far end of the street," Elizabeth said. "We were too far away to see him."

"That goes for Kendra and I, too," Jameson added. "We were at the opposite end of the street."

"Okay, thank you for that information," Fuller said.

"The four of you that raised your hand," said Bishop. "I'm not being overly dramatic when I say that you should be glad you're still alive. Karl Odom is a seasoned ex-Marine who offers his services to the highest bidder. He's wanted in connection with a number of violent crimes throughout Europe, including arson, torture, and manslaughter. He's also a suspect in at least another dozen cases here in the United States."

A murmur swept across the room like a hot summer breeze.

"As part of the ongoing manhunt for this international fugitive, I'll be collecting statements from each of you," Bishop said.

Ellie raised her hand.

"Yes?" Fuller said, pointing. "It's Ellie, right?"

"Yes," she replied. "How long have you been after him?"

"Authorities worldwide have been pursuing Odom for 20 years. His appearance two days ago at the Cole residence is the first reported sighting of him in 15 years."

Nathan and Gina exchanged a look of shock. *Fifteen years? No way!*

"So now you understand why it was imperative that we meet with all of you today," Fuller said. "What I'd like to do first is have the four of you that had direct contact with Odom look at some composite sketches. You may wonder why, since we have a confirmed DNA match, but we believe Odom has had plastic surgery to change his looks. In fact, we think he may have done this on more than one occasion. Knowing what he looks like currently will go a long way toward catching him. And make no mistake, it's imperative that we apprehend him before he can harm anyone else."

Bishop opened his briefcase and took out a plain manila folder. From it he removed a handful of artist sketches and placed them side by side on the table. When he was done, Nathan and Gina walked up to the table and examined each one, followed by Beck and Russ.

The first sketch showed a man with bushy black hair and a full beard.

The second was a man with a thinner face and a goatee.

The third was a bald man with small round eyeglasses and a pointed nose.

At the fourth, Nathan and Gina froze.

"That's him," Nathan said, tapping his finger on the sketch.

"Yup," said Gina.

"Are you sure?" said Bishop.

Gina nodded. "Positive. He had snake eyes, just like that."

"And his hair was cut short like that, too," Nathan said.

Bishop looked at Beck, then at Russ, for their input.

"That's him," said Beck.

"I only saw him for a few seconds," Russ said, "but that's him. I'm sure of it."

Satisfied, Bishop collected the sketches, placing the fourth one on top of the pile, and slipped them back into the manila envelope.

"Next, we need to collect statements from each of you," Fuller said. "What you saw, what you heard, anything Odom may have said to you. Remember, every piece of information is important, no matter how small it may seem."

"You know," Nathan said nonchalantly. "If you guys want Odom, you don't need statements."

"Why do you say that?" Fuller asked.

"Because I can get him for you."

Bishop did a double take. "Excuse me?"

Gina elbowed Nathan in the side. "Cut it out," she whispered. "This isn't a joke."

"I'm serious," Nathan said. "In fact, I can guarantee it."

14

Arthur

The room erupted in chaos.

"HEY!" Fuller shouted. When that didn't work, he stuck his pinky fingers in the corners of his mouth and let out an ear-piercing whistle.

The clamor stopped.

"Everyone, please," he said, patting the air with both hands. *Settle down.* He turned to Nathan. "What are you saying?"

Elizabeth stepped forward and said, "Eric, if I may?" She walked over to Nathan and looked him square in the eyes. When she spoke, her words were slow and deliberate, each one glowing hot. "Nathan? This isn't a game. You heard what these men said. This man is a paid killer."

"I know that," Nathan said, casually. "And I'm telling you, I can find him."

"Out of the question," she shouted.

"Wait," Fuller said. "Let him explain."

Elizabeth backed away.

"Go ahead, Nathan."

"What I'm saying is, I can guarantee that Odom will be at a specific place, at a specific time."

Bishop shot him an incredulous look. "How could you possibly do that?" he asked.

"Because that's where I'll be. But more importantly, I'll have Beck with me."

"You lost me," Fuller said.

Beck grinned, realizing Nathan's tactic. It was perfect. "Odom and I had a serious battle on Wednesday," he explained. "It didn't end well for him, and he's going to want another shot at me."

"What makes you say that?" asked Bishop.

"Because Odom's an ex-Marine. He doesn't like to lose. Probably doesn't happen very often. Well, guess what? It happened. And knowing his type, and trust me I do, he's out there right now aching for a rematch."

"This is ludicrous!" Elizabeth exclaimed. "David, tell them."

"Just…wait," David said, gesturing with his open palm. Nathan's comments had piqued his curiosity and he now wanted to hear more.

"Okay," Fuller said to Nathan. "Let's say you're right. How do you plan on letting Odom know where you and Beck are going to be? We have no idea of his current whereabouts. For all we know, he's already left the country."

"Letting him know is the easy part," Nathan said.

"Why is that?"

"Because his boss will do it for us."

"His boss?" Bishop asked.

"Dan Perry," Jameson said, speaking for the first time. "He's the one that hired Odom."

"This is the man you were telling me about?" Bishop asked, keeping his voice low.

"Yes," Jameson said. Then, to Nathan, "How is Perry going to know where you and Beck are? And what makes you so sure he'll contact Odom?"

"Perry is going to know because one of his business associates is going to call him, right after I show him the very thing that Perry is desperate to get his hands on."

"The sheet music," Jameson said, nodding slowly. "Of course."

"This is insane," Gina mumbled.

"Yeah, but it could actually work," Kendra said, the devil in her eyes.

"Absolutely NOT!" Elizabeth yelled. "I will not allow my son to be fresh bait in some crazy scheme to catch a deranged lunatic."

"Mom," Nathan said.

"NO! This man attacked you once and I won't risk that happening again."

"MOM," Nathan said again, louder.

"Don't you get it?" she said. "He's a murderer!"

"MOM!"

She blinked hard. Once, then twice, like her brain had hit the reset button.

"I'm not going to be alone, remember?" Nathan said calmly. "Beck will be with me. And I'm sure the Marshal's Service will have a whole *team* of people there. Won't you?" he said, looking over at Fuller.

"Absolutely," Fuller replied. "I'll bring an entire brigade."

Jameson walked up behind Elizabeth and whispered, "Could I speak with you and David, privately?"

She shook her head, frustrated, then she and David followed him outside. They walked across the deck and down the steps to the dock. For the time being, the boat traffic had subsided, and the surface of the water rippled peacefully in the afternoon sun.

"I know this whole plan sounds crazy, but here's the thing," Jameson said. "Bishop and Fuller want Odom. I want Dan Perry. Nathan's plan, however dangerous it may sound, could very well deliver both men in one fell swoop."

"But how?" Elizabeth asked. "What guarantee do we have that something won't go wrong? This is my son's *life* we're talking about."

"With the help of the Marshal's Service, nothing is going to happen to Nathan," Jameson said. "Odom will be vastly outnumbered in manpower and weaponry."

"You just said you want Perry," David said. "What did you mean by that?"

Jameson paused, thinking of how much to say. "Perry may very well be part of something much more sinister," he said. "But only by catching him can we be sure."

"We?"

"Let's save that discussion for another time."

David looked Elizabeth. "What do you think?"

"Before I agree to anything," she said firmly, "I want to hear the specifics of the plan. Every detail, right down to the part where

Nathan doesn't get harmed."

"Absolutely," Jameson said. "Nathan's safety is the highest priority."

Elizabeth exhaled, then nodded her head. Reluctantly.

"We're in agreement, then?" Jameson asked.

Ten minutes later, Fuller, Bishop, Jameson and Nathan were seated around a card table in the living room. Fuller made notes in a small notepad as Nathan explained the details of his plan. Elizabeth, David, and the others were crowded around the table, listening intently.

"You said something about one of Dan Perry's business associates," Fuller said. "The one who's going to alert him when he sees the sheet music? Who is he, exactly?"

"A couple months ago I went to an antique store in South Berwick, Maine, with my boss," Nathan began.

"Your boss?" asked Fuller.

"Nathan works for Richard Abbott," Elizabeth explained. "He's a well-known bookseller and an old family friend."

Fuller made a note.

"The antique store is called Beale Brothers Antiques," Nathan said. "The owner is Arthur Beale. He and Dan Perry are working together."

"What makes you say that?" Fuller asked, as he scribbled the names in his notepad.

"Months ago, after Perry suddenly vanished, things from his shop began showing up in other antique stores. I saw some of them in Arthur Beale's shop."

"The Green Man desk!" Gina exclaimed, remembering Nathan's description of it, and how it was the same one they'd seen in Perry's former shop on Wharf Street.

Fuller made an uneasy face. "I don't know," he said. "That's a little thin."

"Well, that wasn't the only giveaway," Nathan said. "When Beale and I were talking, he said something that confirmed it. They're in business together, trust me."

"Okay," Fuller said, seeing the sincerity in Nathan's face. So far, the kid had sounded credible, and for that he was willing to give him some latitude. Plus, he seemed to know Dan Perry better than anyone else in the room.

"If I show up with the sheet music," Nathan said, "Beale will immediately contact Perry. And when Beale tells him I'm there, and who I'm with, Perry will call Odom, probably the only person he trusts to bring him the sheet music. When Odom shows up, you guys will be waiting there to arrest him."

"Hold on," Bishop said. "What is this sheet music you're referring to?"

"It's something Perry wants…*badly*."

"Why is that?"

"We're not 100% sure," Jameson said, "but when we say that Perry wants the sheet music, we mean he's completely obsessed with it. He'll stop at nothing to get it."

"You can say that again," Nathan mumbled.

"This past Tuesday, he tried to have Nathan abducted," Sully told Fuller.

"He *what?*" Fuller blurted out.

"We think he was planning to trade Nathan for the sheet music," Jameson explained. "When that failed, he enlisted the services of Karl Odom."

Fuller made more notes. "So, you show up with the sheet music…" he said, prompting Nathan to continue.

"And I pretend I'm trying to sell it. If Beale gives me a price, and he will, I'll stall. I'll say I already have other shops willing to pay me a lot more for it."

"Implying that you've already shown it around," Jameson said, seeing the logic in Nathan's scheme.

"Exactly. And when Perry hears that, he'll go nuts."

"Oh, yes he will," said Jameson, wondering what Perry would instruct Beale to do. It was impossible to predict, which is why they needed to give Nathan an added layer of protection. An idea came to him but he decided to wait and speak with Fuller about it privately.

"I love it," Kendra said, grinning. "You're gonna play Beale, big time."

"Like he was Eloise," Nathan replied.

"Eloise? Who's Eloise?" Gina asked.

"Well, all of this sounds very interesting," Elizabeth said, addressing Fuller directly, "but how do you plan to insulate my son from these thugs?"

"We'll put together a full surveillance team," Fuller said. "Officers surrounding the building, snipers, you name it. We'll have the site completely locked down. When Odom shows up, we'll grab him before he has a chance to enter the building. If Dan Perry shows up, we'll grab him too."

Sully was standing behind Nathan and gave him a pat on the

shoulder. "Nice work, kid. This is a good plan. Everyone gets what they want."

"Except for Odom and Perry," Nathan muttered.

"All right," Fuller said, closing his notepad. He looked up at Sully. "I'm going to need the floor plan of this antique store, a map of the surrounding area, all roads in and out, any neighboring businesses, houses, fire hydrants, you name it. If there's a treehouse, I want to know about it."

Ellie and Gina put out sandwiches and drinks for the whole group, most of whom went back out on the deck to enjoy the early afternoon sun and the view of the lake. Eric Fuller slipped out the front door and stood in the driveway, leaning against his car as he spoke with his assistant, lining up the equipment and manpower they were going to need.

Jameson and Nathan stayed in the living room.

"This is quite an ambitious plan you've cooked up," Jameson said, showing just a hint of a smile. "Your grandfather would be proud of you."

Nathan shrugged. "We have to do what we have to do, right? I mean, they're both evil. Well, maybe not Dan Perry. He's just bad."

"Is there a difference?" Jameson asked. "I haven't told you this yet, but Dan Perry isn't his real name."

"What?" Nathan exclaimed.

"He was born Edouard Dampierre."

"Dampierre?" Nathan repeated, like it was a silly name to have. "Why would he change his name to Dan Perry?"

"I'm working on that," Jameson said. "There's definitely

something he's hiding. Something bad, which explains why he's been so aggressive in his pursuit of you and the contents of the bookcase."

"Oh, speaking of hiding," Nathan said. "What's with all the secret locations and hidden rooms?"

"Rooms?"

Nathan gave him a look. *You know what I'm talking about.* "You take us to a phony auto shop in Watertown, with some kind of underground command center. Then you hide me in a bunker with a secret entrance in an abandoned building in Chelsea."

Jameson hesitated, choosing his next words carefully.

"What's wrong?" Nathan asked.

"When this is all over," Jameson said, "you and I are going to have long overdue chat."

"About what?"

"There are things you don't know…things that…" he said, then paused.

"Things that what?" Nathan asked.

Jameson looked directly at Nathan and said, "Things that I think you're ready to hear."

Before Nathan could respond, Eric Fuller pushed through the front door, phone in hand. "My team is being assembled now," he said. "After I've had a chance to study the area, we'll put together a plan and walk you through how this is going to work."

Nathan nodded his head, feeling a surge of excitement. After months of torment, they were about to catch Dan Perry, and at long last this nightmare would finally be over.

"When do you move?" Jameson asked.

"I can have my team ready to go as early as tomorrow, but I think we should wait until first thing Sunday, just as the shop is opening."

"You're worried about collateral damage," Jameson said. It wasn't a question.

"I am," said Fuller. "I figure if we get there early enough, foot traffic should be light. It's Sunday morning. With any luck people will still be in church...or at home fast asleep."

"What about the other guy?" Nathan asked. "Bishop? Will he have people there?"

"No. Interpol isn't a law enforcement agency. They have no agents or armed officers with the power to arrest criminals. They act as an administrative liaison to law enforcement agencies in a number of countries, providing investigative support and training. Their databases are enormous. They can track criminals around the world." His phone beeped and he checked the incoming number. "I have to take this," he said, then quickly stepped back outside.

"There's one more thing we need to talk about," Jameson said.

"What's that?" Nathan asked.

"The sheet music."

"What about it?"

"I'm not that comfortable with having it so...exposed."

"I agree," Nathan said. "But we have no choice. If Beale suspects the sheet music is fake, this whole plan will die before it gets started."

"You really think he'd notice?"

"Oh yeah. He knows his stuff. You should've heard him talking about the Green Man desk."

"Okay," Jameson said, convinced. "We just got it, that's all. I'd hate to lose it."

"Who's going to take it from me?" Nathan asked. "Beale? With Beck at my side?" He laughed and said, "I'd love to see him try."

An hour later, Bishop had taken everyone's statements and was standing at the kitchen counter arranging them in a pile. Eric Fuller was standing several feet away at the slider, taking in the view of the lake. He stepped back when Jameson slid the door open and stepped inside.

"I wanted to ask you about logistics," Jameson said.

"Sure," Fuller replied.

"How are you going to brief Nathan?"

"I'll set up a video conference for tomorrow," Fuller said.

"Sounds good. I can get everyone together on this end."

"Everyone?"

"Some of these people want to be involved, and honestly, I can't say I blame them. They've all been affected by Odom in one way or another and they want to see him caught as much as you do. I had an idea…"

"Look, I appreciate their willingness to help out," Fuller said, before Jameson could continue. "But we're taking a huge risk as it is using Nathan. We simply can't jeopardize the safety of any other civilians. You understand that, right?"

"I do," Jameson replied, realizing there was no way he was going to change Fuller's mind. But there was another avenue he could take. "What time did you have in mind tomorrow, for the video conference?" he asked, changing the subject.

"Early," Fuller said.

"I can have Nathan and Beck ready at 9 o'clock," Jameson said.

"Perfect," Fuller replied. He pulled a business card from his coat pocket and handed it to Jameson. "Send me your information and I'll forward you the link."

Bishop appeared at Fuller's side, briefcase in hand. "All set when you are."

"Okay, give me a minute," Fuller told him. "I want to speak with Nathan."

As he slid the door open and stepped out onto the deck, Bishop gave Jameson a business card. "I'll wait for your call," he said.

Jameson nodded, then slipped the card into his shirt pocket. No further discussion was required.

Fuller crossed the deck and found Nathan standing next to Gina at the back railing. Both kids were staring out at the water with Gina doing most of the talking. The way she was shaking her head as she spoke indicated how she felt about Nathan's daring plan.

"Nathan," Fuller called out as he approached. "I'm headed out, but I wanted to thank you for your help. I'm going to put together my team and work out all the particulars. Tomorrow morning we'll conference you in on a video call and go over the details. Bottom line, we're going to do everything in our power to keep you safe."

Gina muttered something under her breath.

Nathan elbowed her...*quit it*...then said, "Just do me a favor."

"Anything," said Fuller.

"Make sure your people get Odom before he has a chance to come inside the building."

"Oh, we will," Fuller said, smiling. "Count on it."

After Fuller left with Bishop and Sully, Elizabeth cornered Jameson in the kitchen. "So?" she said. "What's the plan? When do we hear how my son gets out of this alive?"

Jameson looked past her, at the others lounging on the deck. "Come with me," he said.

They stepped outside onto the deck, and Jameson called everyone together. When they were assembled in loose circle around him, he said, "People, we have a couple of tough days ahead of us. Our resolve is going to be severely tested, but know this: the Marshal's Service is very good at what they do. According to Sully, Eric Fuller, whom you met today, runs a very tight ship. His team will throw a net over Beale Brothers Antiques while Nathan and Beck are inside."

"But?" David asked, sensing Jameson had more to say.

We stop this nonsense and nobody dies? Gina thought.

"I mentioned to him that some of you want to help…" Jameson began.

"Yeah, baby!" Kendra exclaimed, pumping a fist in the air.

"Hold on," Jameson said. "When I mentioned that to him, he flatly refused."

Thank you, Gina thought. *You can all go home now.*

"Uh, excuse me?" Kendra said, louder. She turned to Russ. "Can he do that?"

"He can, and he will," Russ told her. "He won't endanger the lives of any innocent civilians, not if he can avoid it."

"He told me as much," Jameson said. "But…I have an idea, one that he might agree to. First, I need to get Sully onboard, but if I can do that, I'm betting he can sell it to Fuller."

Oh, brother, Gina thought, rolling her eyes.

"What's your idea?" Elizabeth asked.

"Fuller has his team. We'll have our team."

"Who are you talking about?" Elizabeth asked.

"Team one will be Sully and Russ," Jameson explained. "Team two will be Ellie and Kendra."

"Doing what, exactly?"

"Let's talk about that tomorrow," Jameson said. It wasn't the time or place to explain why he wanted the teams, where they would be positioned, or what their jobs would entail. The answers to those questions were sure to give Nathan the wrong idea, and if they had any chance of pulling this off, they needed him to be three things.

Focused.

Unafraid.

And most of all, convincing.

Just after 8 o'clock, Ellie finished the last of the dinner dishes. Gina was standing at the slider, staring out at the lake. "You're quiet," Ellie said, as she dumped the dishwater down the drain.

Gina muttered something under her breath.

"What was that?" Ellie said.

Gina mumbled again.

"You have something you want to say?" Ellie asked her.

"I have a lot to say," Gina snipped.

"So say it."

"Nope," Gina said curtly, keeping her back to Ellie. "No one listens to me, so why should I bother?"

Ellie wiped her hands with a dishtowel and tossed it on the

counter, then crossed her arms and leaned back against the sink. "Okay, out with it," she said.

Gina continued to face the glass. "You heard the plan," she said. "They talked about it like they were planning a picnic at the lake." In a mocking tone, she said, "You bring the sandwiches. I'll bring the drinks. Ooh, someone needs to bring bug spray because there might be mosquitos."

"Why didn't you speak up?" Ellie asked.

"I did," Gina snapped, turning from the glass. "I spoke to Nathan, but did he listen to me? No, of course not. Why would he? He *never* listens to me!"

Ellie let her rant. Best to let the fire completely burn out before stirring the ashes.

"They're going to let him *wait around* in that antique shop until an international criminal shows up," Gina said, her voice growing louder. "And then…they think they can *just walk up to him* and arrest him? He's a professional killer!" She pulled at the hair on both sides of her head and shouted, "WHAT IS WRONG WITH THESE PEOPLE?"

She let go of her hair and slumped her shoulders. If only she could snap her fingers and make it all go away. If only she could make a lot of things go away.

"Are you done?" Ellie asked.

Gina gave her a tired nod.

"Let's go," Ellie said, pointing toward the door.

"Where?"

"Outside."

"You're not serious," Gina said.

"Yes, I am. Let's go."

"But...it's *nighttime,*" Gina groaned. "There could be bears out there."

"Oh, I wouldn't worry about the bears," Ellie said, as she slid the door open. "I'm pretty sure you just scared them all away."

She motioned Gina outside, and after a heavy breath and a *you've-got-to-be-kidding-me* eye roll, Gina grudgingly walked out onto the deck. The night air was cool, and the moon's silvery reflection glowed on the surface of the water as if lit from below. The only sound to be heard was the distant gurgling of a motorboat at the far end of the lake.

Ellie leaned on the railing and looked up at the canopy of stars overhead. "Not too shabby."

"What?" Gina asked.

"The stars."

Gina looked up briefly then shook her head. *Stars are stars. Pick your favorite one and let's go back inside,* she wanted to say.

Thirty seconds passed.

Then, a minute.

Gina's explosion had Ellie worried. When Gina was fired up, there was no telling what she might do. Something had to be done to keep her from endangering herself, or the plan that Eric Fuller was putting into place. She was staring up at the night sky when an idea came to her. "Well," she said, pushing off the railing. "Time to call it a day."

"Where are you going?" Gina asked.

"To bed," Ellie said over her shoulder as she walked across the deck.

"To bed? What are you talking about? It's only 8 o'clock."

Ellie reached the slider and turned back. "I know," she said, "but we're leaving before first light."

"Leaving? To go where?"

"Six o'clock," Ellie said, ignoring the question. "Be ready."

Gina opened her mouth to complain when she heard the sound of branches breaking in the bushes nearby. Her eyes went wide and she made a beeline for the slider. "Yup, you're right," she said. "Time for bed."

Jameson had just stepped into his room at Birch Meadow when he took out his phone and called Sully. It was just after 6 pm and Sully was at the Portland Police Department headquarters, a massive brick structure at the corner of Middle Street and Franklin that resembled a medieval castle,

"Jameson?" he said, clamping his phone tightly against his shoulder as he sent Eric Fuller an aerial shot of the retail buildings across from Beale Brothers Antiques.

"Have you got time to talk?" Jameson asked.

"Sure, what's up?"

"We need more manpower."

"Manpower? Where?" Sully asked. He watched the small colored circle on his computer screen spin around and around, letting him know that his information was being sent.

"Inside the antique shop, with Nathan," Jameson said.

"Inside Beale Brothers?" Sully asked, surprise in his voice. The spinning circle disappeared and he sat back in his chair. His work was done for the day. "Why would we need more manpower there?

We have Beck. That's like having three men."

"I know," said Jameson. "But let's assume for a moment that Odom somehow makes it into the building. Beck is going to have his hands full. That leaves Nathan on his own."

"You think Odom won't be alone?"

"I'm not ruling anything out. And neither should Fuller or the members of his team."

"So…what do you have in mind?"

"That's why I wanted to call you. Fuller refuses to include any of us, but if it comes from you, I think he'll have a very different reaction."

"If what comes from me?"

"We position you and Russ McCullough inside the shop. A cop and a former cop. Able to handle themselves in situations just like this."

"Jameson," Sully protested, "I'm not like Fuller's guys. I'm an evidence gatherer for crying out loud. A photographer with a badge."

"And a gun," Jameson said.

"That I keep in my trunk," Sully countered.

"Fuller doesn't know that."

"All right, fine, I'll play along. Let's say he agrees. In this plan of yours, how exactly do you envision Russ and I getting in the building without raising suspicion?"

"Oh, that's the best part of all," Jameson said, smiling.

David Cole sat at the kitchen table, staring out the window into the night. The sky was slate gray, set behind a waning crescent moon cradled in the branches of the towering maple tree next door. In his mind, he envisioned the plan to capture Karl Odom just as Nathan had spelled it out: the sheet music ploy; Arthur Beale's phone call to Dan Perry; the ensuing call Perry would make to Odom; and the legion of U.S. Marshal's that would descend upon him like a swarm of angry bees the minute he drove into the antique shop parking lot. How could it go any other way?

Odom was one guy.

Fuller's team would number at least a dozen.

Probably more.

It was a numbers game, pure and simple. For that reason, his money was on the U.S. Marshal's Service.

Elizabeth was another story altogether. She stood at the kitchen sink, wash cloth in hand, wiping down the fixtures. Next, she cleaned the stovetop, then the inside of the microwave, then the front of the refrigerator. From there she moved on to the cabinet near the sink and began straightening the drinking glasses. The soft clinking noise they made sounded like a wind chime on a blustery day.

David looked over and said, "Honey, you need to relax."

"Relax? How can I relax?" she said, closing the cupboard door. "They're going to offer up my son like a slab of fresh meat, and hope a homicidal nut job comes after him." She moved to the next cupboard and began rearranging the spices.

"Correction," David said. "They're going offer up *Beck* and hope the homicidal nut job comes after *him*."

"Same thing," Elizabeth muttered under her breath. She closed the cupboard door, exhausted, and placed both palms on the counter, eyes closed and her head sagging, as if she'd fallen asleep standing up.

David got up from the table and came over to where she was standing. "Come on," he said, putting his arm around her. "It's been a long day. You need sleep."

"No," she said, turning to face him. "What I need to do is burn that bookcase. And when this is all over, that's exactly what I'm going to do."

"No," David said in a calm voice. "You're not going to do that."

"Oh, no?" she fired back. "Watch me. You're going to come home one day and find a smoldering pile of ash in the back yard."

David shook his head. "You know that's the last thing your father would want you to do. The last thing anyone before him would want you to do."

Elizabeth said nothing. She knew full well that dominion over the bookcase was more than just a family tradition. It was an obligation of honor, one that dated back to the 1800s, when the bookcase first touched American soil. The responsibility that came with it was a tribute to the man who constructed it, only to be wrongly hanged for a crime he didn't commit. Still, ever since Nathan first discovered it hidden away in the attic, the bookcase had proven to be nothing but a source of constant anxiety for her.

What danger would Nathan stumble into next?

Would he live through it?

Or would he be consumed by dangerous forces that he was ill-equipped to overcome?

And what about Gina?

What if something happened to her?

How could she possibly explain it to Gina's parents?

These were the questions that had pulled at the threads of her sanity ever since Nathan and Gina's now-famous trip into the courthouse.

"Speaking of your father," David said. "We need to talk about Nathan."

"What about him?"

"When are we going to tell him?"

"David, please," she said, holding up both hands defensively. "I can't even think about that right now."

"All right," he said calmly. "There's plenty of time. But sooner or later we're going to have to tell him the truth."

She closed her eyes and uttered a silent prayer. *Please, God, no.*

15

Eyes Inside

Ellie and Gina left at 6:30, just as the first light of day was blossoming on the horizon. In the early dawn haze, the surface of the lake looked like polished marble. Gina was still grumpy from the day before, and sat in the front seat, arms crossed, not a word spoken. When they reached the highway, the steady drone of the tires on the asphalt lulled her into a deep sleep. Her eyes didn't open until two hours later when Ellie pulled into the gravel lot off of Pleasant Street, the uneven ground, like a gentle hand, rocking Gina awake.

She sat up just as they passed the collection of archaic excavation equipment, set at odd angles in the tall grass. Blistered with rust and peeling paint, they looked like a scene from a post-apocalyptic movie called, *The Day the Machines Died*.

"You didn't tell me we were going *here*," she said.

"You know this place?"

"Uh-huh. Jameson brought us here after the break-in at Nathan's house."

"That was smart," Ellie said. "He wanted to hide you guys."

Just in case...

"You should've seen him," Gina said, fighting back a grin. "He was pretty worked up."

"Well of course he was," Ellie replied, shooting Gina a disapproving look. "You guys walked into a trap that was designed for a killer. You're lucky you got out alive."

Gina felt bad for making light of it and said nothing more.

They came to the industrial building at the back end of the property and parked next to Kendra's faded blue Volvo. As they were walking to the garage door at the front end of the building, Ellie looked up and waved.

"Who are you waving to?" Gina asked, looking up at the sky overhead. She got her answer seconds later when they rounded the corner of the building and saw the garage door starting to rise. They had just stepped inside when Beck's Dodge Ram came bouncing down the road. The front end was dotted with small blotches of sunlight breaking through the thick canopy of branches overhead, making the truck look like a giant spotted salamander.

Once Beck and Nathan were inside, Ellie punched a number into the keypad next to the door and it slid back down with little more than a whisper.

Nathan and Gina exchanged a baffled look.

"What?" Ellie said.

"You know the code?" Gina asked her.

"No, I'm just really good with numbers," Ellie said, giving them a pathetic look. "Come on," she said as she started across the room, "he's waiting for us."

They followed her to the small office, where she repeated the same steps Jameson had taken during their first visit. Moments later, they were standing at the gray metal door at the bottom of the stairs. Ellie punched in the code, then opened the door and motioned them inside.

They saw Kendra leaning against the edge of the long table that ran down the center of the room, while Jameson was busy working at one of the computers. Directly across from him, affixed to the wall, a large monitor glowed bright white. Running across the middle of the screen was a short message.

Please wait for your host to start this meeting

"Good morning," Jameson said, turning from the computer. "We have some things to cover before the conference call, so let's get right to it." He checked his watch, then began. "In just a few minutes, Eric Fuller is going to detail the plan he's put together to capture Karl Odom. I have no doubt it will be extensive, and with the team he'll have on site, the whole thing should be over in a matter of minutes, bringing an end to this dangerous episode once and for all. Nonetheless, I still want to implement a second tier of protection to help ensure Nathan's safety."

"Did you talk to Sully?" Ellie asked.

"I did. Last night."

"Wait," Nathan said. "You just told us the whole thing should be over in a matter of minutes."

"I believe so, yes."

"Then why the extra protection?"

"Because, as you know, better than anyone else, Dan Perry is not to be taken lightly. After he gets the call from Arthur Beale, I don't think he'll just send Odom. The sheet music is far too important to him."

Nathan nodded his head. Jameson was right. After attempting to lure him back to Maine, sending two goons to abduct him, and then bringing in a hired killer to steal the sheet music, there was no telling what Dan Perry would try next.

"Now, during the call," Jameson said, pointing at Ellie, Kendra, and Gina, "I need you three to wait at the far end of the room, out of sight of the camera."

"Why?" Gina asked.

"Because in Eric Fuller's mind, the three of you aren't involved and don't need to be briefed. Once the call is concluded, I'll explain what I have planned for you."

He looked over at the monitor on the wall. The message had changed.

Good morning

We will get started in just a moment

Thank you for your patience

"Okay, it's almost time," he said. "Ellie, Gina, Kendra…if you'd be so kind as to wait over there," he said pointing at the far end of the room. "Sit, stand, take your pick. Just no loud talking during the call please."

They walked to the other end of the table and took a seat just as Eric Fuller's image appeared on the large monitor. He was sitting next to Sully at a conference room table, each man clutching a large styrofoam coffee cup.

"Good morning, Jameson," Fuller said. "You have Nathan and Beck with you?"

"Yes, they're both right here beside me."

"Excellent. We're just waiting for the others."

There was a brief delay, then a small box appeared in the top corner of the screen as Elizabeth and David joined the call. Russ McCullough followed seconds later.

"Elizabeth, David, Russ...good morning," Fuller said.

Elizabeth and Russ returned the greeting simultaneously, their voices coming through the speaker as a jumbled mishmash of sound.

Elizabeth asked, "Where's Nathan?"

"Right here, Mom," Nathan said, leaning in front of the computer.

Jameson stood up and let Nathan have the seat, then pulled up a chair and sat down next to him.

"Son? How are you?" David asked.

"I'm good," Nathan said, seemingly oblivious to the potential danger that lay ahead. The plan he'd drawn up the day before was nothing more than an action movie in his head, a production of his own imagination. How things would actually unfold was a script waiting to be written. Only time would tell if Eric Fuller's team would succeed or fail.

"You're going to do great, Nathan," Fuller said. "The plan we've put together will effectively lock down the entire area around

273

the antique store. We'll have deputies covering every side of the building. That includes snipers positioned across the street, as well as across the river."

"So, you're concentrating on the building and the immediate perimeter," David said.

"That's correct," Fuller replied. "Like we discussed yesterday, once Odom arrives, we'll be waiting to apprehend him. The only question is when he'll arrive. If things play out as Nathan predicts, we should have a pretty good idea when Odom is on his way. Any questions so far?"

There was another jumble of voices as everyone responded, "No."

"Good," Fuller said. "That brings us to the inside of the building."

Sully handed him a copy of the floorplan and he slid it under a table-mounted document camera, the image instantly filling the screen

"As you can see, the layout of the store is pretty basic," Fuller said, using his pen to point out the different areas of the building. "Entrance in front, exit and loading dock in back. There's a good-sized lobby just inside the front door, with a receptionist's counter, and a short hallway that leads to an office. Beyond the foyer is a large open room. I'm guessing this is where Beale displays his antiques. Is that correct, Nathan?"

"Yes," Nathan answered. "When I was there, he had tables running the length of the room, crammed with all sorts of stuff. There was furniture along one wall, and a row of tall glass cases on the opposite wall, for glassware, jewelry, and stuff like that."

"And what about this small room at the far end of the

building?" Fuller asked.

"I have no idea what that is," Nathan answered. "When I was there, I never made it to that end of the building."

"I'm assuming it's a storage room, because of the proximity to the loading dock," Fuller said.

"Makes sense," Jameson said.

"Now, if I remember correctly, your interaction with Beale will take place in the front foyer. Is that right?" asked Fuller.

"Yes," Nathan said.

"That means the rest of the building shouldn't come into play. Nonetheless, I'll have deputies positioned outside, covering every side of the building, just in case. Now, Jameson, last night Sully shared an idea with me that I think has merit. I'll let him explain it."

The picture on the screen changed from the floorplan to Sully sitting at the table. "Mornin' all," he said with a quick wave. "Got a brainstorm last night. Came to me right around dinner time. It's pretty simple, really, but it may be worth trying. What if I were to show up at the antique store before Nathan arrives, posing as a customer? That would put me inside the building as another layer of protection, so to speak. Then I got to thinking, why not have Russ do the same thing? You know, a cop and a former cop? Both trained to handle situations just like this."

Jameson fought back a grin. "Good idea," he said.

"Russ? Are you okay with that?" Fuller asked.

"Just say where and when," Russ answered. "I'll be there."

Fuller turned to Sully. "You'll work out the details and let me know?"

"Will do," Sully responded.

"Okay, now, Nathan?" Fuller said, his face appearing on the screen again. "I want you to stick to the plan as we discussed it yesterday. You go in, you show Beale the sheet music, you wait for him to call Perry. You're not to leave the building until after Odom shows up and we have him in custody."

"What if Beale doesn't make the call?" David asked.

"Don't worry, Dad," Nathan said. "When Beale sees the sheet music, he'll make the call."

"There's no telling how long it's going to take for things to run their course," Fuller said. "But once the process starts, things outside could get messy, so it's imperative that you stay inside the building where it's safe. You'll have Beck, Sully, and Russ there with you, so you'll have nothing to worry about."

"Got it," Nathan said.

David pulled Elizabeth close and whispered in her ear, "You see? He's going to be fine."

She gave him a hard look. *You'd better hope so.*

Fuller spoke for another few minutes, reviewing the schedule for the next morning. Beck and Nathan would rendezvous with Fuller's command team at 8 o'clock in the parking lot behind the Kittery Trading Post. Obscured by the massive building on one side, and shielded by the trees that separated the lot from the Maine Turnpike, they'd go over the plan one last time. When they were done, Beck and Nathan would make the short drive to South Berwick, arriving at Beale Brothers Antiques a little after 9:30, roughly 30 minutes after Sully and Russ walked through the front door.

With no further questions, Fuller thanked everyone and ended the call.

Once the screen went dark, Kendra pounded both fists on the table. "Oh, baby," she exclaimed, "gonna be a whole lotta shakin' goin' on in South Berwick!" She sprung out of her chair like it was a trampoline and walked over to where Nathan was sitting. "And you think I have all the fun," she said, giving his shoulders a shake that made his head jiggle like a bobblehead doll.

"All right, you've heard Fuller's plan, now it's time to go over *our* plan," Jameson said, bringing an abrupt end to the levity. Beck, Kendra, and Ellie gathered behind him, as he worked the keypad briefly, then sat back, waiting. Now that Nathan knew Eric Fuller's plan, he was confident Nathan wouldn't get spooked when he heard about the additional protective measures they'd be putting in place.

Gina stayed seated at the end of the table, her elbow resting on the arm of the chair and her head tilted into her open palm. Nathan's plan was a runaway train that she was powerless to stop.

Just then, Elizabeth and David reappeared in the same small box at the top corner of the monitor.

"Hello again," Jameson said, leaning forward to work the keyboard.

"Hello," Elizabeth said, looking totally confused. "Is there something you forgot to tell us?"

"Not exactly."

"I don't understand."

"I'm taking additional steps to protect Nathan, and the sheet music, and I wanted you and David to hear them."

"Where's Eric?" Elizabeth asked.

277

"Right now? Probably refilling his coffee cup. He has no knowledge of what I'm about to share with you. If he did, he'd shut it down immediately."

"O-kay," Elizabeth said, intrigued.

"Don't get me wrong," Jameson said. "Fuller's plan is sound. I just want to add to it, that's all."

"Fine by me," Elizabeth replied.

Jameson clicked on the sharing tab and his image was replaced with a detailed street map of the area around Beale Brothers Antiques. "Okay, you can see Beale Brothers there on Mercer Street. Just past it the road takes a sharp turn northward and ends at Sand Spring Road. That's where Kendra and I will be parked. If you follow Mercer Street in the opposite direction, it intersects with Fairlawn Avenue. That's where Ellie will be parked, giving her an unobstructed view of the antique shop. If Odom somehow manages to slip through Fuller's net, we'll have both ends of the road covered."

"And if that happens?" Elizabeth asked. "If he manages to get away?"

"We'll stop him," Jameson said.

"You'll stop him? How exactly do you plan on doing that?"

"You just leave that up to us," said Jameson.

Kendra and Ellie shared a devious smile.

"I've got to go over some things with the others," Jameson said, "but we'll talk later today."

Elizabeth and David signed off the call, and that's when Beck stood up. "Do you need us to stick around?" he asked. They were the first words he'd uttered since he climbed out of his truck.

"Yes," Jameson replied. "I have an important matter to discuss with Nathan and I'd like you to hear it too, since you'll be with him inside the antique shop."

Beck nodded, then sat back down.

Jameson spun his chair around and faced Nathan. "About the sheet music," he said. "From the moment you step into the antique shop, you're not to let it leave your hands. Is that understood?"

"Yes," Nathan said.

"You show it to Arthur Beale, but if he tries to take it, you pull back."

"What do you mean?"

"Here, I'll show you," Jameson said. He reached across the table and grabbed a file folder that was sitting atop a short stack of old newspapers, each encased in a clear plastic bag. He pulled some sheets of paper from the folder, set them face down on the table, then closed the folder and held it away from his body. "You're holding the sheet music like this, then you open it and show it to Beale," he said opening the folder. "Now, try and take it from me."

Nathan sat forward in his chair and reached for the folder when Jameson spun his body away. "Just like that," he said. "If he reaches for it, you pivot."

"Got it," Nathan said.

"If I recall correctly from the floor plan, there's a reception desk in the front lobby."

"That's right."

"If Beale wants to examine the music up close, fine. Set it down on the counter like this," Jameson said, laying the open folder down on the tabletop. "But keep your hands clamped on it." He positioned his hands, palms down, on the folder. One on the top left corner, the other on the bottom right corner. "Beale can look all he wants, but he *cannot* handle the sheet music. It doesn't matter what excuse he gives you. It's non-negotiable. You don't have to say that, but whatever you do, don't let him take it from you."

"He won't," Beck said, cracking his knuckles.

A chill ran up Kendra's spine.

"Now, there's one more thing, and this is important," Jameson said. "When you show the sheet music to Beale, tell him it's from the 1700s. He may have already figured that out, once he sees it, but make sure you tell him. Also, tell him the name of the composer. Do you remember it?"

"Franz Eigner," Nathan said, remembering Elliot Kitchens' description of the music.

"That's correct," Jameson said. "Mention Eigner, and mention the title of the piece—*The Grim Fugue*."

"Why would I do that?"

"Because he'll repeat all of it to Dan Perry. And once Perry hears it, he'll wonder how much more you know. We have no idea what secret the music contains, or why he desperately wants it…"

"But if he thinks I know its secret…"

"Exactly," Jameson said. "It will only hasten his response. He'll send someone to get it immediately."

"Someone he trusts," Nathan said, grinning.

"That's right."

"If he doesn't come for it himself," Nathan submitted.

I hope he does, Jameson thought, eyeing the bagged newspapers on the table.

Ellie cleared her throat, and when Jameson looked over at her, he saw her nod toward Gina, who was slumped back in her chair, arms folded across her chest, staring absently at the edge of the table.

Jameson nodded back. *Almost there.*

"Any questions?" he asked Nathan.

"Nope."

"Well then," Jameson said, standing up. "That brings us to Gina."

Gina looked up, surprised. "What about me?" she asked.

After her tirade in the kitchen the previous night, Ellie had called Jameson with an idea that would include Gina in the plan, not only as a way of calming her down, but also to keep her from doing something drastic. As history had shown, when her emotions were fully engaged, she wasn't afraid to break out on her own to remedy a situation—especially when it involved Nathan.

Jameson had quickly agreed with the idea. Then, after thinking it through, he'd come to the realization that it was something he should've come up with on his own as it addressed an important issue he'd completely overlooked. Not only would Ellie's idea keep Gina preoccupied, but it would make the entire workings of his plan run that much smoother.

"You," Jameson said, pointing at Gina, "have the most important job of all."

Gina looked at each of the others with a quizzical expression. *What's he talking about?*

"Tomorrow morning, all of us are going to have our hands full," he said. "We may have to move fast, and communication will be key. We can't afford to be distracted, trying to share information and making sure everyone received it. Your job will be to direct calls to the group in a quick and concise way, updating us on what's happening inside the building."

"Like an operator," Gina said.

"Yes, exactly like an operator," Jameson replied. "Deploying manpower is important, but managing the situation and relaying critical information when time is of the essence is absolutely critical. Isn't that right, Beck?"

"Without a doubt," Beck said. He had plenty of real-life examples he could cite, but those weren't the kind of graphic stories a decorated soldier with his resume liked to share.

"As you know, Beck, Sully, and Russ will be inside the building with Nathan. Sully will undoubtedly be tasked with sharing on-site information with Fuller. Beck is going to do the same with you. We can't very well ask him to call everybody one at a time—it would simply take too long. Keeping everyone apprised of what's going on will be your job. Beck will call you, and you'll relay that information to the rest of us. If for any reason Beck is indisposed, Russ will be the one who calls. He'll be…the safety net for the safety net, so to speak. With your help, each one of us will have eyes inside the building."

Gina nodded slowly.

"So, what do you say? Will you do it?"

Gina sat up in the chair, fuel tanks at maximum, engines hot. "I will," she said.

"Excellent," Jameson said. "The first thing we need to do is familiarize you with the equipment."

She came over and sat down at the table next to Jameson, and he walked her through the functions of the 10-line phone that was positioned next to the computer. Beck and Nathan stood nearby, watching, while Ellie and Kendra left to get lunch for the group.

"When a call comes in, your job is to share that information with whomever needs to know, as quickly as possible," Jameson explained. "For that reason, I've programmed each person's number into this phone." He pointed to a grouping of small black buttons set in two vertical rows at the base of the phone. "Each of these buttons is assigned to someone in our group. The first row, from to top bottom, is me, Kendra, Ellie, Beck, and Russ. The second row is Elizabeth, David, Sully, and Nathan. To help you remember, I want you to take a few minutes and write in each person's name or initials on the small label next to their button."

He gave Gina a pencil and she wrote each person's first name on the appropriate label. When she was done, he had her practice. She called Ellie, then Beck, then Elizabeth, explaining that she was testing the phone for the next day, before saying goodbye.

No chatter.

No humor.

Quick and concise, just like Jameson instructed her.

When he was satisfied that she had mastered the phone, he sat with her in front of the computer and showed her where to find the various maps he'd saved. From there, he showed her how to use the messaging program to send a message to one person, or the same message to a number of people. "I know you're an expert with research," he told her, "so I won't waste your time explaining the Google Search option."

"Thank you," Gina said, relieved.

"I know this may feel extreme, and if Nathan's trap works, then this entire operation will end very quickly. As you heard me tell

Nathan's dad, the chances are very slim that Odom will get away. Still, I'm glad we'll have you here, just in case anything unexpected happens."

Gina nodded confidently, feeling an overwhelming sense of purpose. She wasn't just a member of the team, she was a *vital* member of the team. People would listen to her. They'd count on her. And that's all it took to change her mind about Nathan's plan.

"Do you have any questions?" Jameson asked.

"Nope," Gina said. She slid her chair closer to the table and got to work, typing on the keyboard. Within seconds, she brought up the street map of South Berwick on the big wall-mounted monitor. Next, a map of Southern Maine that stretched from the state line in Portsmouth, NH, to Casco Bay in Portland. After that she practiced sending messages. First, a single message to Ellie. Then a simultaneous message to Kendra and Jameson. Lastly, a group message to Kendra, Jameson, Ellie, and Beck.

She finished just as Ellie and Kendra walked through the door carrying two large pizza boxes and four take-out bags filled with French fries, onion rings, chicken tenders, mozzarella sticks, and enough ketchup to feed a large farm animal.

After lunch, Jameson stood at the head of table and addressed the group. "Let's go over the timetable for tomorrow," he said. "Beck, you're in charge of getting Nathan where he needs to be. Kendra is with me, as usual, leaving Elizabeth and David."

"What about them?" Nathan asked.

"They want to be kept in the loop at all times," Jameson said. "And for that reason, I think they should be here with Gina. Not only will it save her extra phone calls, it will give your parents first-hand access to everything that's happening."

Gina looked at Nathan and nodded. She hadn't said anything up until then, but the thought of being cooped up alone in a secret basement room was more than a little creepy.

"Ellie? How about you drop Gina off before you head north?" Jameson suggested.

Ellie flashed a thumbs up. "Will do."

Gina looked over at her, forlorn. "Please tell me we're not driving back to the lake."

"No. We're going to your house."

"What about tomorrow?" Gina asked. "What do we tell my folks when we leave again?"

"You let me handle that," Ellie said, with a wink.

Gina gave her a tentative look. *Good luck with that.*

"Okay, then," Jameson said. "Everyone knows where they're supposed to be, and when. I'll have Russ connect with Sully to work out their schedule, which means were done here. Unless anyone has a question?"

Everyone shook their head.

"Good. Now I want you all to remember that what happens tomorrow, happens tomorrow. For the rest of today, free your mind of any preconceived notions. If Eric Fuller's team does its job and we get the expected result, then any worrying we did today will have been a complete waste of energy. So don't worry. Don't second guess. By this time tomorrow we'll all be celebrating."

A short time later, as they were filing out of the building through the open garage door, Beck pulled Jameson aside. "That was a good call, using Gina to work the phones."

"You can thank Ellie," Jameson said. "It was her idea."

"She'll be okay?" Beck asked. "Gina, I mean."

"Very much so," Jameson said without hesitation. "She has my full confidence."

"You think Perry will show up?"

"I certainly hope so," Jameson said. "If he does, don't let him get away. If Odom's with him, you may not have a choice in the matter. I'll tell Sully and Russ to leave Odom to you and concentrate on Perry. If we lose him tomorrow, we may never get another chance at him."

"And Beale?"

"I wouldn't worry about him," Jameson said. "From what Henry Hammond told me, the man is all style and no substance."

"Duly noted."

Nathan walked outside and stopped to breathe in the fresh afternoon air. It was a good day. The soft breeze carried an earthy woodland scent. The sun lit up the canopy overhead. And the plan was set. He felt like the commander of a great army, about to descend upon an unsuspecting foe. A quick and decisive victory lay ahead, he was sure of it.

He turned and looked back at the building, studying its plain metal exterior. He wondered how Jameson came to be associated with it. Was it ever really an auto shop? Was the collection of mechanic's tools just an illusion, put there to fool anyone who might happen to look inside? Who would put an auto shop this far away from the street, at the far end of a gravel pit?

"Hey."

The voice snapped him out of his funk, and when he turned around he saw Gina standing there. He'd been so consumed with questions about the building that he never heard her approaching.

"Are you okay?" she asked.

"Me? I'm fine," he said, as cool as could be.

"Yeah, well, just promise me you won't do anything stupid tomorrow."

"I'll try not to, but you know me, right?" he said playfully, trying to lighten the mood.

"Now, see?" she said, angrily. "There you go, making jokes."

"Sorry," he said, smirking. "I wanted to see how you'd react."

A prolonged silence followed. They both knew the risk he was taking. If Odom somehow managed to get inside the building, there was no guarantee what would happen, federal marshals or not. Nathan would have the added protection of Beck, Sully, and Russ, but Odom wasn't your run-of-the-mill adversary. He killed for a living, and there was a very real chance he could inflict serious, if not fatal harm upon any one of them. Or all of them.

Gina looked down at the ground and kicked at the loose stones.

Nathan watched, waiting for her to speak.

Thirty seconds passed.

He could see that she was twisted up inside, her reasoning and emotions battling it out, each refusing to yield. "Hey," he said. "Don't worry. It's going to be all right."

"You'll be careful?" she said, still kicking at the dirt.

He thought he heard her sniffle. "I will," he said. "I promise."

"And…you'll call me…you know…to tell me…?"

"You know I will," he said.

She wiped her eyes, then stepped forward and hugged him. Before he could raise his arms to hug her back, she peeled herself off him and hurried away.

Any other time, he'd call her back. Find the words to wash her fears away. But this was much bigger and more dangerous than any adventure they'd been on since he discovered the bookcase in the attic. Her anxiety was warranted, but they had this. Easy. The plan they'd constructed was sound; the location was perfect; and the team from the U.S. Marshals Service gave them a decided and overwhelming manpower advantage.

Was it a gamble?

Sure.

Would it work?

Absolutely.

She'd see.

16

Showtime

Jameson and Kendra were already at the house when Beck pulled his truck into the driveway. He killed the engine and checked his watch. "Same as last time," he told Nathan. "Fifteen minutes, no more."

"Let's do it," Nathan said, then opened the door and got out.

Elizabeth and David were in the living room, talking to Jameson. He'd called them the previous afternoon and explained Gina's role and that they were welcome to be in the room with her until Odom was in federal custody. They quickly accepted the offer.

"Ellie's dropping her off and I think it's best that you follow her so you're not stranded there without a vehicle." He glanced over at the mantel clock. "She'll be leaving in 30 minutes."

"Dropping her off where?" Elizabeth asked.

"At an undisclosed location."

In the kitchen, Kendra was busy brewing a fresh pot of

Hawaiian Royal Kona, hand selected from her personal stash at the coffee shop. It was going to be a day for the ages, she could feel it in her bones, and she had no intention of starting it off by drinking some weak, grocery store swamp water filth. As the rich aroma filled the room, she closed her eyes and breathed it in. Was there anything better than beans from the slopes of the Mauna Loa Mountains? She didn't think so.

The front door opened and Nathan came walking in, followed by Beck. "Oh, good, you're right on time," Jameson said, when he saw them appear in the hallway. He stood at once and greeted Nathan face to face. "How are you feeling?" he asked.

"I'm ready," Nathan said.

"Yes, you are," Jameson said. He took Nathan by the shoulders and stared at him intently, his dark eyes, like black onyx, locked onto Nathan's. "If there's one thing you've proven to me, it's that you always find a way to power through, no matter what the challenge. You did it in the basement of the courthouse. You did it in the Whitney Mine. You did it on Storm Island. And you'll do it today." He went to the coffee table and picked up a 12" x 18" Pendaflex folder, held shut by an attached elastic cord. "Guard this with your life," he said, handing it to Nathan. "And don't forget what we discussed."

"The sheet music will never leave my hands," Nathan assured him.

There was a knock on the front door, and seconds later Ellie strode into the living room, dressed in blue jeans, a black tee shirt that read *I'm With the Band*, and an exotic pair of elk skin cowboy boots. "Good morning everyone," she said, like they were going to the beach and not about to take down an international fugitive.

"Where's Gina?" Jameson asked.

"Waiting in the car," Ellie replied. She looked at David and Elizabeth. "Ready to go?"

"We are," said David. He patted Elizabeth on the knee. "Come on."

They rose together, Elizabeth already looking washed out and weary, and went over to Nathan. "Remember what Eric Fuller told you," Elizabeth said. "No matter what happens, stay in the building. You don't need to be a hero. In my book, you already are one."

"Don't worry, Mom. I'll be okay."

"Promise me you'll be careful."

"I promise."

She gave him a long hug, then went to the hallway to get her purse. David gave Nathan a similar hug, then stood back and said, "You got this, Nathan. Just follow the script and it'll be over before you know it."

"Thanks, Dad."

Kendra appeared in the hallway and raised her coffee cup in the air. "Coffee, anyone? It's Kona."

"Oh, that smells so good," Ellie murmured, "but we gotta go."

Beck tapped Nathan on the shoulder, then pointed at his watch.

Nathan started for the front door when Kendra reached out and stopped him. "Hey, what gives?" she said. "No goodbye kiss?"

Nathan gave her a sour look. *As if.*

"Come here," she said, pulling him close. "You're a warrior today," she told him. "Don't you forget that."

"Thanks, Kay-Jay," he replied.

"Get OUTTA here!" she exclaimed. She swatted at the side of his head, but he ducked out of the way and her hand met nothing but air. "Brat," she said, as he walked out the door, smiling.

Sunday morning traffic was nearly nonexistent and Ellie made it to Watertown in record time.

"What is this place?" Elizabeth asked, as they turned off of Pleasant Street into the gravel pit.

"I thought you knew," Ellie replied.

"Jameson has shared some things with David and I, but apparently he left out a few things."

They came to a stop in front of the garage door and Ellie turned to Gina. "You good to go with the phone?"

"Yup," Gina replied.

"Call me if you have any problems."

"I will," Gina said, "but I'm sure that won't be necessary."

As they made their way through the shop, David and Elizabeth exchanged curious looks. Automotive repair equipment? Since when did Jameson know anything about cars? When Ellie led them down the hidden stairway, and through the locked metal door, they were utterly speechless.

An underground room?

Oversized monitors on the wall?

Security feeds from each side of the building?

They stood inside the door, looking like travelers lost in a strange land.

Gina went straight to the computer and got to work. She brought up the street map that showed Beale Brothers Antiques, then picked up the telephone handset, listened for a dial tone, and promptly hung up.

"You've obviously been here before," David noted, watching her work.

"Yup," Gina said. She typed a short message and sent it to the entire group.

Operator is live

When she was done, she spun her chair around and faced Elizabeth and David, who were still standing near the door. "You guys can sit down, you know."

"Uh, no, we'll stand, thank you," Elizabeth said, doing a slow-motion sweep of the room. "This is *not* an auto repair shop," she whispered through her teeth to David.

"Nope," David replied.

Nathan was quiet as they drove north on Rt. 95. In his mind he was replaying his last visit to Beale Brothers, and his conversation with Arthur Beale—a man who looked less like a New England antiques dealer and more like the owner of a Beverly Hills art gallery.

Wild hair.

Flashy clothes.

Eccentric to the core.

Certainly, he would know about the sheet music. Every antique shop owner associated with Perry had to know about it. He would've warned them. Be on the lookout for a young kid with a piece of very old sheet music. No doubt he'd placed a bounty on it, payable to the first person in his network to report it. And given its importance to him, he undoubtedly set forth explicit instructions.

If you see it, call me at once.

Do not let it out of your sight.

Failure to comply will result in serious, if not fatal consequences.

Nathan wondered how Beale would react when he saw it. Would he be unable to mask his exuberance? Wide eyed, secretly counting his reward? Or would he downplay it, feigning mild interest—a ruse designed to lessen its perceived value? However Beale chose to play it, Nathan was ready.

They were approaching the Piscataqua River Bridge, the massive arched structure linking Portsmouth, NH, to Kittery, ME, when Beck broke the silence.

"You know why Fuller set up this meeting, right?"

"Yeah," Nathan said, like it was a no-brainer. "To go over the plan one last time."

"Well, he'll definitely do that," Beck said. "And he'll confirm the assets he's putting in place. But then he's going to ask you a bunch of questions to gauge your state of mind."

"My state of mind? What's wrong with my state of mind?"

"He wants to be sure that you're mentally prepared to go through with the plan."

"He's got nothing to worry about there," Nathan said. Definitely a no-brainer.

Beck gave him an uneasy look. "That may be," he said, "but here's what he won't tell you: Dan Perry has no regard whatsoever for your life. He wants the sheet music. Period. You? You're just a bump in the road in his ongoing attempt to steal it from your family." As he spoke, his agitation grew. "When you meet with Arthur Beale," he said, "you need to remember all the things Perry has done to you. Let your anger be your strength. Let it feed your resolve from the moment you first step into the building. Like Kendra said, you're a warrior. So think like a warrior. Perry had his shot, now you're going to take yours. And today, the warrior will triumph."

It was just after 9 o'clock when Sully made the turn onto Mercer Street in a caramel-colored Jeep Wrangler. The Jeep, on loan from a fellow member of the Portland Police Department, was designed to paint him as an outdoorsman, which fit perfectly with the items he'd inquire about once he was inside the antique shop. His usual ride, an old battered navy blue Crown Vic, was out of the question. It screamed "cop" to anyone who saw it.

As he took the corner, he spotted Ellie's hatchback parked in front of a small clapboarded house turned mom and pop restaurant. The sandwich board on the front lawn read: Voted Maine's Best Brunch! Ellie was sitting on the porch that spanned the front of the building, hunched over an open newspaper like someone scouring the help wanted section. Her hands were wrapped around a bone-white coffee mug that she held close to her chest. From where she was sitting, she had a clear view down Mercer Street, all the way to Beale Brothers.

He slowed, fighting the urge to wave, toot his horn, or better yet, stop in and see if the Maine voters had gotten it right. Instead, he drove on, and 30 seconds later he pulled into the dirt lot in front of Beale Brothers, where a tall man dressed in a lavender sport coat, white shirt, and cherry red pants was hanging a large "Open" flag beside the front door. Sully recognized him at once from the photos he'd seen on the Beale Brothers website. Either Beale had forgotten to brush his mop of gray hair that morning, or he'd recently been staring into a powerful window fan.

"I guess I don't have to ask if you're open," Sully joked, as he shut the driver's door and made his way around the front of the Jeep.

"My friend, your timing is exquisite," Beale replied. He finished hanging the flag, then hastily brushed his palms together, as if the wooden flagpole was encrusted with dirt. "First time here?" he asked, as they went inside.

"Yup," Sully replied, surveying the lobby and the adjoining room. It was just as Nathan had described.

Beale went to the front counter and produced a clipboard and pen. "We like to have our guests sign in so we can notify them about special sales."

"Sales?"

"Auctions and such," Beale said.

"You ever have camera auctions?" Sully asked as he signed the Jeep owner's name.

"As a matter of fact we do," Beale replied, "although not as many as we did years ago. I blame the whole digital craze."

"Oh, don't get me started," Sully muttered. "Why did everyone suddenly abandon the 35mm camera?"

"We have a very nice selection of 35mm cameras, if you'd like to see them," Beale offered.

"That's why I came," Sully replied brightly, sliding the clipboard back across the counter.

When Ellie saw the Wrangler drive by the restaurant, she immediately sent Gina a message.

Guest #1 has arrived

Gina, in turn, forwarded the message to Beck, Nathan, and Jameson.

Jameson and Kendra were parked in a vacant Dairy Queen lot at the corner of Sand Spring Road and Mercer Street. In another two hours the parking lot would be jammed with summer tourists, but by that time Fuller would have Odom in handcuffs.

"Sully just pulled in," Jameson told Kendra.

"And so it begins," she mumbled, watching the road in both directions.

"Indeed," Jameson said, thinking about the night Dan Perry emptied his shop on Wharf Street and vanished in the wind. Would the sheet music be enough to draw him out of hiding? If not the sheet music, then what would it take?

Fifteen minutes later they saw Russ McCullough's pickup appear at the far end of Sand Spring Road. As he approached Mercer Street, he saw Kendra's Volvo, but didn't acknowledge it in any way. He just rolled through the turn and accelerated.

Jameson immediately messaged Gina, echoing Ellie's choice of words.

Guest #2 has arrived

Gina, in turn, passed the message on to Ellie, Beck, Nathan, and Sully.

Arthur Beale was showing Sully a selection of old cameras that took up two of the tall glass cases along the back wall of the main room. When he saw Russ enter the building, he handed Sully the case key, invited him to examine any of the cameras he liked, and then excused himself.

"Good morning," he said to Russ as he walked through the arched entryway that separated the lobby from the main room.

"This is quite the place you have here," Russ said admiring the original rafters overhead.

"Thank you," Arthur said. "You sound like a first timer here at Beale Brothers."

"Yes. I'm in town for some rest and relaxation, and to spend as much time fishing as humanly possible."

"A fisherman, huh? Could I possibly interest you in some vintage fishing gear?"

"Well that depends," Russ replied. "Do you have any old B.F. Meek & Sons reels?"

He'd spent the previous evening searching the Beale Brothers website and knew exactly what fishing tackle they currently had in their inventory. B.F. Meek & Sons reels were a prominent listing.

"As a matter of fact we do," Beale said. "Along with some other treasures as well. The whole lot came from an estate up in near Rangeley."

He explained the sign-in procedure and waited patiently as Russ scribbled down the name Ron McCallister, the watch commander during his days with the Brookline Police Department. Beale glanced at it briefly, then set the clipboard down behind the counter and walked Russ to the back corner of the main room, where a huge selection of fishing gear was spread out across two entire tables. "As you can see," said Beale, "we have some very nice B.F. Meek reels, along with some Shakespeare Free Spool models, a very nice Pflueger and Seminole set, and…oh…when was the last time you saw one of these?"

"Wow, will you look at that," Russ said, feigning astonishment. "A Sidewinder Sidecaster Bakalite & Brass fishing reel."

"Right you are."

"The 'knuckle buster'," Russ said, remembering the online description.

"Right again," Beale said with a polite nod. "Very rare, and highly collectible."

Russ took it from him gingerly and carefully examined it. As he flipped it over, he glanced at the time on his watch. *Any minute now,* he thought.

Ellie was on her second cup of coffee when she heard the distinct growl of a truck engine. She looked over her shoulder just as Beck's black Dodge turned onto Mercer Street, the meaty tires chirping on the pavement. As he powered down the street past her, she reached for her phone and sent Gina an update.

Cue the band

Gina read Ellie's message and shook her head. "Ellie, Ellie,

299

Ellie," she said, smirking at her aunt's endless fascination with music.

"What is it?" Elizabeth asked, when she heard Gina's comment. She and David had finally grown tired of standing and had taken a seat at the table.

"Beck and Nathan just arrived at Beale Brothers," Gina said. She retyped Ellie's message, in her own words, and sent it to Jameson, Sully, and Russ.

Showtime

Eric Fuller was sitting next to a sniper on the roof of the woodstove shop, directly across the street from Beale Brothers. Mason Bishop sat three feet away, envisioning a handcuffed Karl Odom being led away to a waiting police cruiser.

Fuller had chosen the rooftop location for the optimum view it afforded him—a place where he could easily direct his team as needed. Martin Bishop was there strictly as an observer.

The building to their left was a children's clothing store. To the right, a discount shoe store. A sniper was positioned on each roof, and a pair of deputies waited inside, watching the street from behind the front window displays, ready to storm the antique store when directed by Fuller.

To some it might seem excessive, but Fuller wasn't taking any chances. If he'd over allotted his assets, so be it. The prize would be worth the price. His radio squawked and he heard the sniper atop the children's clothing store say, "Friendly vehicle approaching. Black pickup truck."

"Copy that," Fuller said. He took a deep breath and let it out. The game was on. Sometime within the next few hours they would have Karl Odom in custody. Just thinking the words 'Karl Odom in custody' gave him chills. "Okay, people," he said into the mic. "Stay alert. Things are about to get interesting."

Arthur Beale was working at the front counter when Nathan and Beck walked through the front door. He looked up, did a double take, and immediately dropped the papers in his hand. He hurried around the end of the counter, straightening his suit coat as he walked. "Mr. Cole," he said, a nervous tremor in his voice. "This is an unexpected surprise."

Nathan said nothing. Following Beck's advice, he was replaying the moment when he was unceremoniously thrown into the back of the van, only to have his bike hurled at him moments later. Sometimes anger is good.

"I believe the last time we spoke you were here with Richard Abbott," Beale said. He sized up Beck from head to toe. "I see you brought a rather...uh...large friend with you today."

If Beale was expecting an introduction, Nathan wasn't in the giving mood. Beck's name wasn't important, only his physical description. Once Odom received word that Nathan was in the building, accompanied by a colossus, his damaged pride wouldn't allow him to stay away.

"Is there someplace we could speak...in private?" Nathan asked.

"Why certainly," Beale replied. "Right this way." He led them past the front counter and down the narrow hallway, stopping several feet from his office door. "What can I help you with?" he asked.

Here goes, Nathan thought. He took the Pendaflex folder from under his arm, removed the elastic cord holding it shut, and pulled out the sheet music. When he opened it and turned the sheet so Beale could see it, the shopkeeper instinctively reached for it, just as Jameson had said he would. Nathan, in turn, spun his upper body away. "Uh-uh," he said. "Eyes only."

Russ saw Nathan and Beck enter the shop and immediately set down the reel. He moved to the center of the room where he could better monitor Nathan's interaction with Beale at the front counter. After Beale led them away, he moved to the front corner of the room and stood at the edge of the wide entryway. From there, he had a clear view of the hallway. When Nathan opened the Pendaflex folder, he turned toward the wall and typed out a quick message to Gina.

Nathan is showing Beale the SM

"Nathan's showing Beale the sheet music," Gina said, reading the message aloud. She quickly forwarded the message to Jameson and Ellie, and when she was done, she sat back in the chair, admiring the computer, the multi-line phone, and the array of monitors on the wall. "This is so cool," she said.

"What's so cool?" Elizabeth said, in a testy voice. "That my son could fall prey to a bloodless killer?"

David rested his hand on her forearm. "Easy, honey. She's just doing her job."

"What I mean is, we have eyes inside the building,"

Gina explained.

"Oh…right," Elizabeth said apologetically. "Yes, that's very helpful."

Beale could hardly contain his excitement. This was it. Just as Perry had forecast: a kid with a very old piece of sheet music. Beale never imagined that it would be *this* kid—the most famous 12-year old in the country. For reasons that Perry had never fully disclosed, the boy posed some kind of threat to their business dealings. What that threat was, he couldn't fathom. He was just a kid, for crying out loud. And now, here he was, sheet music in hand, standing three feet away.

But he knew he had to proceed carefully. The last thing he wanted to do was scare the kid off. He laced his fingers together as if praying and held them against his chest as he leaned down to study the music.

"It's from the 1700s," Nathan said. "The composer was Franz Eigner. It's called *The Grim Fugue.*"

"Interesting," Beale said, appearing to be fascinated by the intricate pattern of notes. In truth, he couldn't care less. What's more, he couldn't understand why Perry was dead set on acquiring this ancient scrawl. It looked like it was penned by a raving lunatic. Still, Perry's mandate was crystal clear, and Beale knew what he had to do next.

"We're on our way to Portland to meet with a classical music collector," Nathan lied, reciting the words he'd practiced on the drive north. "He plays for the Portland Symphony Orchestra. Apparently, he's a big fan of Eigner's work."

Beale didn't like where this was going.

Then Nathan set the hook. "We'll see what he's willing to pay," he said. "A collector like that? I'm guessing he'll pay a lot more than the others offered."

"The others?" Beale asked nervously. He could feel his monetary reward slipping away.

"Yeah, but I have no idea what's fair and what's bogus," Nathan said, pointedly. "I don't want to get ripped off...know what I mean?"

Beck nodded his head in agreement, his firm expression suggesting that anyone who tried to short Nathan would face the consequences.

Beale saw that and stammered, "Yes, uh, I mean no...uh...of course not."

"We were in the neighborhood," Nathan explained, in a more casual tone, "so I figured I'd stop by and show it to you. See if you could tell me what it's worth before we drive north."

Beale's heart was racing now. "Uh...yes...well, um, I'd be more than happy to help you with that," he said, nearly out of breath, "and I...um..."

He paused, nibbling the edge of his lip, and raised his index finger in the air.

"Could you excuse me for just *one* moment?"

17

Crown Linen

Beale darted into his office and closed the door. With jittery hands he dialed Dan Perry's number, fumbling with the phone like it was coated in bacon grease.

"Yes?" Perry said, picking up after the second ring.

In the background, Beale heard the thud of a heavy object being dropped on the floor.

"Hey, easy with that!" Perry yelled, at Romero and Foss, who were loading sealed crates onto a wooden pallet. Then he was back. "Okay, Arthur," he said impatiently. "What is it?"

"Y-you won't believe it," Beale stuttered. "He's here...in my shop."

Nathan walked over to the office door and leaned in, listening.

"I was standing at the front counter," he heard Beale say, "and when I looked up, he was walking through the door."

Then, as if someone had slipped a burlap bag over Beale's head, his words became muffled and Nathan could only make out bits and pieces.

"Yes…kid…sheet music…"

Nathan guessed that Beale was pacing back and forth as he spoke—walking toward the door, then turning and walking in the opposite direction. Nathan looked over his shoulder at Beck and flashed a thumb's up. *It worked!*

Beck immediately took out his phone and fired off a short message to Gina.

Beale's calling Perry

Romero and Foss were hoisting more boxes onto a pallet, chattering like a pair of cowbirds, when Perry lowered the phone and yelled, "QUIET!"

They immediately froze, looking like two mannequins drenched in sweat, holding heavy boxes.

Perry put the phone to his ear. "Say again?" he asked Beale.

"Nathan Cole is here…in the building," Beale repeated slowly, enunciating each word. "He just walked in with some behemoth of a man."

"And he has the sheet music?"

"Yes. He said it's from the 1700s. Something called *The Grim Fugue*, by Franz Eigner."

Perry nearly dropped the phone.

"From what he told me," Beale said, "he's already shown it to some other people. He wants an appraisal done before he goes to Portland to meet with a classical music collector."

Perry's body stiffened. "Arthur? Listen to me closely," he said calmly. "You're not going to let that happen. Do you understand? You're going to quote him a price, I don't care what it is, and then you're going *pay* him that amount. Is that clear? You give him a number, and then you…"

Perry's words fell off, and for a moment Beale thought he'd lost the connection.

"Hello?" he said.

"On second thought," Perry told him. "I have better idea."

Russ went to the entryway and peeked around the jamb. He saw Beck standing against the wall, and a few feet away, Nathan had his ear pressed to the office door. Beale was nowhere in sight.

"Hey!" Sully whispered, from the camera case. "What are they doing?"

Russ pulled back. "Nathan showed Beale the sheet music. Now Beale's in his office with the door closed."

Sully didn't have to ask what that meant. He pulled out his phone and messaged Fuller.

Beale took the bait
He's making the call

Fuller's response was immediate.

Copy that

307

Martin Bishop peered over the parapet. Other than the three vehicles parked in front of the antique store, the street was like a ghost town. The sun was starting to cook the pavement, and the flag on the front of the antique store hung motionless. "Not a creature was stirring, not even a mouse," he muttered, his anticipation starting to hum.

He looked left, then right, wondering which direction Odom would come from. Not that it really mattered. Odom would pull up to the antique shop in a hurry, anxious to settle the score with Beck. He'd jump out of his vehicle, only to be swarmed by armed federal marshals. It might not happen for another hour, but Odom would be there, he was sure of it, and a 20-year manhunt would come to a glorious conclusion.

As Nathan continued to listen, he could tell that Beale was growing frustrated with Perry. It was evident in his sharp tone and the increased volume of his words.

"Why?...wouldn't it just be easier for me to...yes, I know that, but..."

Then, like before, his words faded into muffled bits and pieces.

"Who?...fine...Hamilton...yes, I will..."

The conversation ended and silence filled the room. Nathan darted back across the hall and assumed his original position just as the office door swung open and Beale stepped out into the hallway.

"My apologies," he said, pulling the door shut behind him. "Now, where were we?"

"You were going to give me a price?" Nathan said, holding up the sheet music.

"Ah yes, the Eigner piece."

Nathan read Beale's sudden lack of memory as a ploy. *He's going to downplay its significance, and its value*, he thought. He wondered if Perry told him to do that, or if Beale cooked it up on his own. No matter. Nathan was ready with a counter proposal that would send Beale into a panic.

"Sheet music is very unique," Beale said. "Every piece holds its own distinct value based on a number of criteria." He pursed his lips and tapped them with his index finger, like a man trying to decide which bottle of wine to open for his dinner guests. "I've got some auction catalogs in my office that might be of use," he said. "If you'd care to wait in the lobby, I'll get them and join you shortly."

"Sure," Nathan said. He slipped the sheet music back into the folder, and then he and Beck walked back to the lobby and waited at the front desk. "So far, so good," Nathan said softly.

"We'll see," Beck replied, his expression as hard as quarried stone. He knew things could go off the rails at any moment, but he didn't tell Nathan that.

Fuller had just sat back down when his radio squawked.

"Vehicle approaching."

The report came from one his deputies positioned around the corner, in a patch of woods that separated Mercer Street from the river.

"Identify," Fuller said.

"It's a uniform delivery truck, sir. Crown Linen."

"Copy," replied Fuller. Crown Linen. Those guys were everywhere. He turned to the sniper sitting several feet away. "Does

Crown Linen deliver on Sunday?" he asked.

The sniper shrugged. "Beats me. I got a buddy who works for them. Says they're crazy busy."

"Huh," Fuller said. He turned to look as the truck came around the corner, slowed, and then swung into the Beale Brothers parking lot, coming to a stop next to Sully's Jeep Wrangler.

Dan Perry ended the call with Beale and immediately dialed Karl Odom.

"Yeah," Odom said.

"The boy and some big guy are at Beale Brothers Antiques in South Berwick, Maine."

"I know."

"*What?*" Perry replied. "How could you possibly know that?"

"I'm on site," Odom replied.

Perry's eyes went wide. "You're on site?" he exclaimed.

"Yes."

Perry's face broke into a rare display of euphoria. "I can be there in 15 minutes," he told Odom.

"Stay where you are," Odom replied. "It's a trap." He checked the outside mirror on the passenger side of the truck and saw movement on the roof of the building directly behind him.

"A trap? Are you sure?"

"Yes."

Trap or no trap, Perry wasn't about to let this opportunity slip away. "The boy has the package," he said. "Can you retrieve it?"

Odom was still watching the mirror when he saw a sniper rise up from behind the parapet, his rifle pointed directly at the truck.

He was either using the scope to get a closer look, or he was preparing to fire.

"Can you retrieve it?" Perry said again, his voice straining.

"Gotta go."

"No! Wait!" Perry shouted. I need to know if—"

Click!

Perry exhaled heavily and lowered the phone. He closed his eyes and took a long deep breath, envisioning the layout of the antique shop and contemplating his options. If the boy's sudden appearance at Beale Brothers was, in fact, a trap, there was sure to be a platoon of police waiting nearby. Odom might be good. The best, even. But outnumbered and outgunned? No one could survive those odds. The situation called for a different strategy, and one in particular came to mind—taught to him by his chess tutor when Perry was only 9 years old. It was called the "double attack."

His eyes snapped open and he called to Romero and Foss. "Stop what you're doing," he said. "Beale Brothers Antiques. Go there now. The boy just showed up with the package. Be careful, it could be a trap. I suggest you take the truck."

Romero nodded, then shook his index finger at Foss. *Go get the keys, hurry.*

Ten minutes later, after a change of clothes, the two men drove away from the building, the leaf springs squeaking loudly as the truck bounced and swayed.

A bad feeling came over Fuller as he watched the truck sitting idle, the driver still inside.

"What's he doing?" he mumbled. He keyed the radio again. "Does anyone have a visual on the driver?"

A reply came from Bennett, the deputy in the building next door to the antique shop. It was an old shoe factory that was undergoing renovations, and from one of the first-floor windows, Bennet had a clear view of the driver's-side door. "He's still inside the truck," he said.

"Can you see his face?" Fuller asked.

"Negative," replied Bennett. "He's wearing sunglasses, and he's got the brim of his hat pulled down."

"What's he doing?"

"Talking on his phone."

"Copy," Fuller said. He looked over at Bishop. "He's talking on his phone."

Odom slipped the phone into his pocket, never once taking his eyes off the side mirror. So far things had been a breeze. Earlier in the day, his preparation had paid off when the tiny camera he'd hidden in the wolf tree behind Nathan's house picked up Beck's truck pulling into the driveway. From there, he followed Beck to Kittery and watched from the far end of the parking lot as Beck and Nathan met with Fuller and three of his deputies.

Odom's gut told him something was about to happen. Something nearby. Why else would the kid and his protector drive this far north to meet with the U.S. Marshals Service? On a Sunday of all days? When the meeting was over, he followed Fuller's Dodge Charger to South Berwick, staying far enough back to avoid arousing suspicion. When Fuller turned onto Mercer Street, Odom drove as far as the intersection and then pulled over onto the shoulder. He watched Fuller's Charger slow in front of Beale Brothers, brake lights flaring, then turn into the alley between the shoe store and the woodstove shop. *There's plenty of open spaces on the street, but he parks behind the building*, Odom thought. It could only mean one thing: he wasn't parking, he was hiding.

Odom slipped the binoculars back in his travel bag and crept along the shoulder, to a narrow dirt road that snaked back into the woods. Not long after he backed in, using the trees as cover, he saw Beck's truck appear in the distance. That's when his hunch was confirmed, and with that realization came a plan. He knew he'd be walking straight into the trap, but he'd beaten traps on numerous occasions. All things considered, it wasn't that hard to do, and deep down he enjoyed the adrenaline rush it gave him. This time would be no different.

He pulled out of the dirt driveway and turned right. Two blocks later he spotted a linen delivery truck parked in the driveway of a small ranch-style house. There were no other vehicles in the driveway and he assumed the owners were at church, or enjoying a leisurely Sunday morning breakfast at the local diner.

Perfect.

Fuller's radio squawked.

It was Bennett, again.

"We have movement," the deputy said. "The driver is exiting the vehicle through the driver's door." There was a brief pause. "He's walking around the front of the vehicle."

Fuller saw the driver appear in the short space between the nose of the truck and the front door of the antique store. In his hands was a freshly laundered shirt, encased in a long thin plastic bag that trailed behind him like the tail of a kite.

Beck and Nathan were still waiting for Beale to return when the front door opened and a man walked in carrying a laundered business shirt on a hanger. He was tall, dressed in a pair of black coveralls with a white patch sewn on the breast.

Crown Linen & Uniform Service.

Beck looked over briefly and then dismissed him. Beale would be out any second, he could deal with the guy. Probably needed a signature, or payment, or both.

The man crossed the lobby and stopped five feet from Beck. "We meet again," he said.

Beck turned to face him. "Do I know you?"

"You don't recognize me?" Odom replied. He dropped the shirt on the floor and pulled off the baseball hat and sunglasses that he'd found in cab of the truck. "How about now?"

The realization struck Beck like a war club. He straightened his stance, keeping his arms hanging loosely at his side, ready for whatever Odom might throw at him. And throw at him he would.

Without another word, Odom flung the hat and glasses aside, reached into his coveralls, and pulled out a Ka-Bar fighting knife.

Russ heard the exchange and peered around the casing of the entryway. A delivery man was standing in front of Beck, probably asking for the owner. When the man suddenly tore off his hat and sunglasses, Russ recognized him at once. He pulled back and motioned to Sully, who was still standing in front of the camera case.

"Pssst."

"What?" Sully asked.

Russ jabbed a finger in the direction of the front counter.

Sully looked past him and saw Odom standing across from Beck with the Ka-Bar in his hand. *Where did he come from?* he thought, his pulse quickening. He ducked under a nearby table and called Fuller. "Suspect is in the building," he said quietly. "Again, suspect is *in* the building."

While he was doing that, Russ was busy on his phone, typing a message to Gina.

Odom is inside the building

Fuller jumped to his feet and keyed the mic. "The driver of the linen truck is Odom," he said. "Repeat, the driver is Odom. He has entered the building through the front door. "Ayers, Pruitt, take a position on either side of the front door and see if you can get a visual through the sidelights." To the sniper he said, "If you get a clean shot, take it."

The front door of the discount shoe store burst open and deputies Ayers and Pruitt bolted across the street. As they approached the front door of the antique shop, they split up, Ayers going left, Pruitt going right. They eased up to the sidelights on either side of the front door and peered through the glass.

Pruitt had a better angle. He saw Odom, from the back, holding the knife at his side. "The suspect is in the front lobby," he said into his shoulder-mounted radio. "He is armed. Repeat. He is armed."

315

"Identify," Fuller said.

"Looks like a Ka-Bar, sir."

Just then, another deputy came on the radio. "Be advised, we have another vehicle approaching, travelling west from Fairlawn Avenue."

"Please identify," Fuller said.

"It's a UPS truck."

Gina felt a stab of dread when she read Russ' message. "Oh no."

"What's wrong?" Elizabeth asked.

"He's in the building," Gina said as she feverishly typed a message to Jameson and Ellie.

"Who's in the building?"

Gina looked over at her, but didn't speak. The look of fear on her face said it all.

"NO!" Elizabeth shouted. She looked at David. "How did he get in the building? I thought there were U.S. Marshals everywhere."

When Jameson read Gina's message, he clenched his teeth and pounded his fist on the armrest.

Kendra leaned over, trying to see the screen. "What happened?"

"Odom is in the building."

"What? How can that be?" Kendra asked. "Beale just made the call."

"Who knows?" Jameson said, shaking his head.

"So what do we do?" Kendra asked.

"We stay right here, as planned."

When Ellie got Gina's message, she paid the bill and went to her car. Odom had mysteriously gotten inside the building, which meant he could mysteriously get away. Her job was to stay and watch, but if Odom came her way, she'd use any means possible to stop him.

A UPS truck rattled past. She considered it briefly, then eyed the Crown Linen truck parked in front of the antique shop. That had to be the way Odom got into the building. The simplicity of it was as impressive as it was deeply troubling.

Drive right up to the front door in an everyday delivery truck.

Walk inside, easy as you please, under the watchful eyes of an armed team of U.S. Marshals.

This guy Odom was very daring.

Or very stupid.

"Looks like you got a new job," Beck said to Odom. As he spoke he reached out and gently steered Nathan behind him.

"This?" Odom replied, tugging at the coverall. "Funny thing. I found it in the back of a delivery truck. Fits me perfectly, don't you think? The truck keys were in the visor, so I figured, what the heck, why not take it for a spin?"

"Let me guess," Beck said. "The truck just happened to steer itself here."

"Something like that," Odom said. "Just think of what I would've missed if it hadn't."

Out of the corner of his eye, Beck saw two armed deputies ease through the front door without so much as a sound. Feathers in the wind. "What's your play here, Odom?" he asked, trying to stall for time.

"We have unfinished business," Odom replied calmly.

"Oh, really," Beck said. "How's the knee?"

A spark of anger flickered in Odom's eyes. "Never better," he said defensively.

"DROP THE WEAPON! DO IT NOW!" Ayers yelled.

Odom grinned. *Right on time.*

"WE *WILL* SHOOT."

Odom didn't move.

A loud metallic *chikk-chikk* sound echoed through the lobby as Pruitt jacked a round into his Remington 12-guage pump shotgun.

With that, Odom released the Ka-Bar and it landed on the floor next to his foot.

"YOU TWO!" Ayers shouted to Beck and Nathan. "MOVE AWAY!"

Too late.

In the time it took to blink, Odom turned and dropped to the floor in a crouch, then kicked out his leg and delivered a powerful Tiger Tail Sweep aimed at Beck's ankles.

Beck anticipated the move and hopped back, knocking Nathan to the floor in the process, then dove forward and plowed into Odom, knocking him backward.

Nathan sat up slowly, feeling like he'd been hit by a bulldozer. When he saw the two deputies with their guns pointed at Beck and Odom, he waved his hands frantically in the air, yelling, "Don't shoot...don't shoot!"

Beck climbed atop Odom, pinning him to the floor, then turned to Nathan. "WHAT ARE YOU DOING?" he shouted. "GO!"

With Beck momentarily distracted, Odom wrestled one hand free and reached up, grabbing Beck's ear. He pulled down violently, dragging Beck sideways onto the floor. As he rolled with him, he spotted the Ka-Bar lying on the floor just inches away.

Nathan scrambled to his feet and froze. *Go? Go where? Out the front door?* Fuller had made it clear that he was to stay inside the building. From beyond the entryway he heard someone call his name.

"NATHAN!"

He looked over and saw Russ gesturing to him wildly with both hands.

"Get over here!"

Nathan cut a wide path around Beck and Odom and ran into the main room. Russ grabbed him by the shoulders and steered him down the center aisle. "Find a place to hide," he told him. "And don't come out until we tell you."

Odom was reaching for the Ka-Bar when Beck grabbed his wrist with one hand, his elbow with the other, and twisted sideways. Odom's arm exploded in pain and he rotated his body to keep his shoulder from breaking.

As the two men rolled across the floor, Pruitt yelled to Ayers, "You got 'em?"

"Got 'em," Ayers shouted back, keeping his gun trained on Odom and Beck.

Pruitt tapped the mic on his shoulder radio and gave Fuller an update.

"They're *fighting?*" Fuller exclaimed.

"Affirmative," said Pruitt.

"Do you have a shot?

"Negative, sir."

Fuller shook his head in disbelief. "They're fighting," he told Bishop. "Can you believe it?" He got back on the radio to Pruitt. "I'm sending you more people."

"Copy that," Pruitt replied.

Elizabeth paced back and forth, fuming. "He looked me right in the eye and told me he'd have a whole *team* of deputies waiting to catch that man. So where are they? Can someone please answer that for me?" she shouted. "And where is Nathan? Did he say?"

"No," Gina said. "Hold on." She attacked the keyboard with both hands, typing a message to Russ as fast as her fingers would move.

Where's Nathan? Is he all right?

Russ read the message and responded at once.

Don't worry Nathan is safe

Romero stopped the truck in the middle of the street, then backed into the overflow parking area at the end of the building. The truck was an older UPS model, purchased years earlier by Dan Perry at a vehicle auction. It still had all the markings of an actual UPS truck, but it belonged to no fleet—people just assumed it did, including members of law enforcement, which was the whole idea. It helped eliminate suspicion when Perry's men were picking up or dropping off packages at odd hours of the day or night.

Romero parked at the end of the loading dock, a square concrete slab with a short ramp on the front side. Foss went to the back of the truck and pulled out a dolly while Romero extracted his massive body from the driver's seat. Then, like any other package pickup, Foss wheeled the dolly up the ramp, with Romero lumbering along behind him.

Nathan sprinted down the aisle toward the back corner of the room. When he reached the storage room, he pulled the door open and ducked inside. To his right was a narrow shipping table, covered with packing tape, labels, and a pile of shipping manifests. To his left, the room extended for 40 feet, and was packed with assorted pieces of antique furniture and stacks of wooden crates.

He leaned back against the door, catching his breath, when the rear exit door suddenly opened and Romero stepped inside. Directly behind him, pushing a steel gray dolly, was Foss. Both men were dressed in brown UPS uniforms.

"There he is," yelled Foss. He saw the folder in Nathan's hand and said, "Grab him!"

Romero stormed forward, but Nathan ducked left and Romero's meaty fingers merely grazed Nathan's shirt sleeve. Romero let out a chuckle, like they were two kids playing a game of tag. "Ain't no friends around to help you this time, boy," he said.

When Foss heard the commotion in the lobby, he set the dolly aside, went to the door, and eased it open a scant inch. Through the narrow opening, he saw the federal marshals, guns up and ready to shoot as two giants wrestled on the floor in front of them. He closed the door and said, "We don't have much time. Just grab the kid and let's go."

Nathan backed away from Romero slowly, looking to his left and right for something he could use as a weapon. Oh, what he'd give for Kendra's baseball bat.

Romero hunched down, hands forward, stalking Nathan like a seasoned cage fighter. Nathan waited until he was almost on him, then faked to the right. Romero lunged, grabbing at nothing but air as Nathan ducked down and darted the other way. He was almost past Romero when the brute flashed his arm out and grabbed Nathan by the shirt collar. In one smooth move he jerked him backward, ripped the Pendaflex folder from his hand, then flung him headlong at Foss, who flipped him up in the air and dropped him onto his stomach like a champion calf roper.

"Quick," he shouted to Romero. "Toss me that tape."

18

Just Another Day at the Office

Fuller radioed for two more deputies to enter the building through the front door. As they were going inside, he looked at the far end of the building and saw the nose of the UPS truck pointing out at the street. "Bennett," he barked, into the mic. "You gotta get that UPS truck outta here."

"They're leaving now, sir," Bennett reported. He had moved outside and was standing 20 feet from the loading dock, watching the driver hold the door open for his helper, who emerged from the building with a large cardboard box strapped to a dolly.

"Copy that," Fuller replied.

Bennett watched the two men slide the box into the back of the truck. Then, as if they were behind schedule, they quickly closed the rolling steel door and climbed into the cab. The engine came to life and the truck roared out into the street, creaking and rocking on the rutted pavement.

Beck and Odom were tangled like a knot as they continued to roll around the floor, each man trying to vanquish the other. Two of the marshalls kept their guns trained on the pair, while the other two attempted, without luck, to apprehend Odom. It wasn't until Beck got Odom in a chokehold that they were finally able to cuff him, which took nearly a minute as Odom continued to thrash violently with his hands and feet.

When he was finally subdued, Pruitt stood up and radioed Fuller. "Suspect is in custody. We got him, sir."

Fuller pumped his fist in the air…"YES!"…then hurried down to the first floor with Bishop. They emerged from the woodstove shop just as Ayers and Pruitt were dragging Odom outside. His hands were cuffed at his belly and his legs were shackled. But it was the look on his face that gave Fuller pause. It was chilling. He was studying every person he saw with menacing eyes, committing their faces to memory for the next time they met, when he would exact his revenge in slow, excruciating doses.

Beck stood at the front counter doing a neck stretch, tilting his head down toward his left shoulder, then slowly rolling it toward his right shoulder. Russ and Sully were standing nearby, and when they heard the sharp cracking of bones coming from beneath Beck's shirt, they exchanged a painful look.

A loud voice erupted from the far end of the hallway and two deputies appeared, escorting a handcuffed, and very angry Arthur Beale toward the door. His hair was in disarray, as was his suit, and he was squirming like a fish, loudly declaring his innocence and threatening legal recourse if they didn't release him at once.

Beck waited until he was outside, then called Gina.

"Hello?" she said tentatively. It was the first time Beck had ever called her.

"It's over," he said. "Odom and Beale are both in federal custody."

From the other end of the phone he heard shouts of delight as Elizabeth and David's nightmare had finally come to an end.

"So, that's it?" Gina asked.

"That's it," Beck replied. He looked over as Eric Fuller and Mason Bishop walked through the front door. "Gina, I have to meet with Eric Fuller now, but we'll talk later, okay?"

"Okay," Gina said. She disconnected the call just as Elizabeth and David descended upon her, smothering her with hugs. "All right…thank you…yes, I know…it's great…" she said, craning her neck to see the keyboard as she typed a quick message to Jameson and Ellie.

"Are you all right?" Fuller asked, as he approached Beck.

"Fine," Beck said, like it was just a routine day. Get up. Duke it out with an international criminal. Go home. Have a beer. Maybe watch a movie. Order some take out.

"I hear it was touch and go there for a few minutes," Fuller said playfully.

"Who told you that?" Beck said, pretending to be insulted.

A smile broke out on each man's face and they shook hands. Fuller did the same with Sully and Russ, thanking them for their help. "Hey, where's Nathan?" he asked.

"Nathan!" Russ exclaimed. He tapped the side of his forehead with both hands. *Silly me.* "In all the confusion, I completely forgot about him."

Sully took several steps backward and looked through the entryway. "The last I saw, he ducked into the storage room."

"Well, let's bring him out here and tell him the good news," Fuller exclaimed. "That kid deserves a medal."

"You can say that again," Russ said as he turned to go. He walked into the main room, then broke into a sprint, running along the back wall of the building, past the glass cases that were just a blur in his peripheral vision. When he got to the storage room, he pulled the door open, calling out as he stepped inside. "Nathan, it's over!" He stopped short when he saw a roll of packing tape lying on the floor. Right next to it was a razor knife. "NATHAN?" he shouted.

Beck knew something was wrong when he heard Russ shout.

"What's wrong?" Sully asked, seeing the look of concern on Beck's face.

"I'm not sure," Beck said, as he pushed past Fuller and Bishop.

"Did I miss something?" Fuller asked.

Sully was hurrying after Beck and didn't answer.

Russ emerged from the storage room just as Beck got there, unable to mask the dread he was feeling.

"What is it?" Beck asked.

"He's not here."

"Not here? What are you talking about?"

Beck made a move for the storage room when Russ grabbed his arm. "Wait," he said. It was a potential crime scene now, and he pulled the door open and pointed at the packing tape and the razor knife on the floor. No further explanation was needed.

"NO!" Beck shouted. This wasn't happening. Not today. Crime scene or no crime scene he shoved Russ aside and stormed into the room, yelling. "NATHAN! Come on out. We got him."

Sully stopped at the door, slightly out of breath. "What's goin' on?"

"Go check the main floor," Beck told him. "Make sure you look under every table."

Sully leaned in, surveying the room. "I thought he was in here."

Beck pointed. "Main floor. GO! NOW!" Then, to Russ, "You're with me."

Sully worked from back to front, starting with the center aisle. He pulled up the linens that draped each table, looking underneath briefly before running another ten feet to repeat the process. All he found were empty cardboard boxes and wooden crates.

"Sully, what's going on?" Fuller asked, from the entryway.

"We can't find Nathan," Sully replied. He reached the end of the center aisle and moved to the next one.

"He's gotta be here somewhere," Fuller said.

The front door opened and Jameson walked in, Kendra following right behind him. When he saw Fuller, he walked over to offer his congratulations.

"Jameson?" Fuller said, surprised. "What are you doing here?"

"We were in the area," Jameson replied. Then he noticed the concerned look on Fuller's face.

"What is it?" Jameson asked. He looked past Fuller, into the main room, and saw Sully checking under the tables, frantic. "Eric?

What's wrong?"

"They can't find Nathan," Fuller replied.

"What?"

The front door opened again and Ellie stepped inside. When she saw Jameson and Kendra, she walked over to them, smiling. "Hey, I heard the good news," she said to Kendra. "Just another day at the office, right?"

Kendra shook her head solemnly.

"What's wrong?" Ellie said.

The front door burst open and Beck and Russ ran in, both men out of breath. When Jameson saw Beck's face flushed red, a wave of panic rose in his chest.

"He's gone," Beck said. "We just checked the perimeter and he's nowhere to be found."

"The sheet music?" Jameson asked.

Beck shook his head. "Gone."

Jameson staggered backward, like the ground had suddenly shifted beneath his feet, and Kendra and Ellie grabbed his arms to keep him from collapsing on the floor.

"Did you see anyone leave? Ellie asked Kendra.

"Leave? No. How about you?"

"Just a UPS truck, that's it."

"Are you sure?" asked Beck.

"Positive."

Beck and Russ exchanged a worried look.

"What?" Jameson asked.

Russ told him about the packing tape and razor knife lying on the floor, five feet from the back door.

"Where were you?" Fuller asked Ellie, unsure how she'd come to be in South Berwick at that particular moment.

"At the corner of Mercer and Fairlawn," she said.

"And you're sure it was only the UPS truck that left?"

"Yes," she said, picturing the two men she saw through the windshield as the truck passed her car. "Big guy behind the wheel," she said. "Small weasely guy in the passenger seat."

"Big guy, small guy—it has to be the same two goons that tried to abduct him on Tuesday," Kendra said.

"I'll put out a bulletin," Fuller said, then hurried toward the door. "Don't worry," he called back over his shoulder. "We'll find him."

Ellie muttered something under her breath, then pulled the car keys from her pocket and raced to the door. Moments later, she tore out of the parking lot, tires screeching on the pavement. She raced up Mercer Street toward Fairlawn Avenue, filling the air with the acrid smell of burning rubber.

Jameson walked slowly into the main room and sat down in the corner, in an antique mahogany chair with blood red velvet upholstery and sculpted lion paw feet. He sat forward, his elbows resting on his knees and his head lowered. Praying. Then, slowly, he took his phone from his pocket.

It was time to tell Elizabeth and David.

19

The Legacy of Nathan Cole

When Nathan came to, he was slumped over on the floor. Gone was the tape binding his hands and feet, and the strip covering his mouth. His eyes blinked open and he saw a wall of black. His shoulder and hip throbbed from being dropped on the floor like a bag of garbage, and with great effort he pushed himself up into a sitting position.

The air around him was old and musty, as if the windows hadn't been opened in years. In fact, they hadn't. He reached out, feeling in the dark, but his finger touched nothing but air. He listened for any kind of sound: a car passing by outside, a plane flying overhead, a neighbor mowing the lawn. He heard none of those things. Only a deafening silence.

The last thing he remembered was Romero grabbing him and pulling the Pendaflex folder from his hands, then flinging him effortlessly at Foss. Beyond that was nothing but a series of fuzzy images, smudges of gray and brown and black. Mostly black.

He wrestled his flip phone from his pocket and opened it, using the light from the screen to illuminate his surroundings. He was in the room of a house. Through the dim haze he saw a front door, and directly across from it, a stairway leading up to a second floor. There were three windows that he could see: one on the wall to his left, two more to the left of the front door. The shades had been pulled down, blocking out any light from the outside.

There was no furniture. No pictures hanging on the walls. The only sign of human occupation was a small throw rug placed near the sill of the door. He labored to stand, doing his best to ignore the ache in his hip and shoulder. "Hello?" he called out. "Is anyone here?"

He waited, listening, but heard nothing.

One by one he pressed the preset numbers on his phone: first Beck, then Jameson, then Ellie, then his mother. Each time, nothing happened. The screen stayed lit for several seconds, then went dark. He shoved the phone back in his pocket and shuffled over to the closest window. He felt along the sides and bottom, searching for the edge of the shade, but he couldn't find one. What he thought was a window shade was, in fact, a fixed steel panel, painted black. Solid and unyielding. His confusion quickly turned to fear and he hobbled over to the door. He grasped the doorknob and tried to turn it when the floor suddenly gave way beneath his feet.

He dropped straight down, landing hard on a concrete floor. He rolled over onto his back, his entire body wracked with pain, and stared blindly into the darkness.

"Mr. Cole, welcome" came a voice from somewhere overhead. It was Dan Perry. Or Edouard Dampierre. Nathan wasn't sure what to call him anymore. But his voice was unmistakable—eerily calm and conniving—the voice of a man with evil thoughts running amuck in his head.

"Let me out of here," Nathan said in a weak voice.

"You want to leave?" Perry said. "Go ahead. You can leave anytime you like. Of course, you just have to figure out how. But that shouldn't be too difficult for a clever boy like you."

Nathan rolled onto his side, then eased himself up, grimacing. "I wouldn't get too comfortable," he said, laboring to speak. "The federal marshals are on to you. They'll be here any minute."

"Is that a fact? Are you referring to the federal marshals that let my men walk right in and take you? Never stopped them? Never checked their identification? I heard one of them even stood in the parking lot and watched them drive away. Stood and watched. Can you believe that? No, right now I imagine they're running around in circles trying to pick up your trail. Unfortunately for you, however, they won't succeed."

"I wouldn't count on it," Nathan mumbled, anger bubbling up inside him.

"Well, let's just say the odds are in my favor," Perry said.

Nathan could hear him smiling. An evil, twisted smile. "How's that?" he asked.

"Because they have absolutely no clue where to start looking," Perry said, chuckling. "There are no suspects to question. No vehicle to track. My men took care of that detail five minutes after they grabbed you. So as you can see, you're on your own."

"They'll come," Nathan insisted.

Perry said nothing.

"Did you hear me?" Nathan shouted. "They'll come!"

Still no reply.

"THEY'LL COME!"

With great effort, he climbed to his feet. Using the light from his flip phone, he surveyed the room. The walls were barren, and there were no doors or windows. The ceiling was covered with sheets of corrugated steel, and directly overhead he saw the opening of the shaft that had dumped him where he now stood. Without something to stand on, it would be impossible to reach. Not that he had the strength to climb up it.

In the silence, Perry's words taunted him.

"You can leave anytime you like… you just have to figure out how."

That meant there was a way out. Something Perry had installed in the room. But why? Was it a test? A challenge of wits? A childish taunt: I know something you don't know. Or was it a lie? Something to get his hopes up, only to drive him into a fit of desperation and rage.

On the wall to his right, set down near the floor, was wood-framed panel roughly three feet square. He limped over to it, ran the light from his phone over every square, then leaned against the panel with his shoulder.

It wouldn't budge.

He sat down and pushed it with the bottoms of his sneakers.

No good—it still wouldn't give.

He was climbing to his feet, using the top of the frame for support, when he felt it move. He pulled on it with both hands and it folded down like a truck tailgate. Using the light from his phone, he peered inside and saw a narrow crawl space. What it was for

333

or where it led was irrelevant; it was the only option he had for getting out of the room, and if it led nowhere, he'd simply turn around and come back. What choice did he have?

He had just cleared the opening when the panel snapped shut behind him. When he reached back to push it open, it wouldn't move. It was locked in place. *Just go forward*, he told himself. *Forward is the way out.* Those five words became his inspiration and he repeated them like a chant as he laid on his stomach and did an Army crawl, using his forearms and knees in unison to propel himself forward.

Forward is the way out..

Forward is the way out...

The words gave him energy and helped him overcome the pain that beat like a drum through every muscle and bone in his body. At the same time, a nagging voice in the back of his head warned him that there could be more booby traps like the one on the first floor.

But what would they be?

Another collapsing panel in the floor?

Or something worse?

What other evil was Perry capable of?

He continued on, stopping every few feet to check the floor, the walls, and the top of the crawl space. When he was certain there was no danger, he advanced.

He'd gone six feet...or was it eight?...when the crawl space took a 90-degree turn. He turned on his side and snaked around the corner, feeling the floor for any unwanted surprises. Four feet later he came to another panel. He opened his phone, the light from the screen starting to weaken, and felt the eerie sensation of being trapped inside a casket. The thought made his breath quicken, and he pointed the phone at the panel seconds before the screen went black. He shoved it back in his pocket and pushed against the panel. It wouldn't move. Did it fold down like the last one? He checked along the top for something he could get his fingers around, but all he felt was smooth steel.

Forward is the way out...

He pressed both palms against the panel. It was cool to the touch, and with as much force as he could generate, he pushed upward. No good. He tried again, this time pushing sideways when the panel slid three inches to the right, then abruptly stopped. Something was jamming it, keeping it from opening all the way.

The muscles in his arms ached and he laid them on the floor to gather his strength. That's when the panel began to slide shut, all by itself. "No!" he said, raising his arms to stop it. He was too late and the panel closed with a soft click. He took a deep breath, raised his arms, and pressed his palms against it again, pushing sideways just like before.

The panel wouldn't move.

No! It just worked.

He dropped his arms again, feeling another twinge of panic. He thought of Gina and her dire warning on the phone about the sheet music and Dan Perry.

"He knows we have it, and we're all in danger!"

Gina had always been the wise one. Think first, jump second. Unlike him: jump first, deal with the consequences later. Now, lying entombed in the narrow crawl space, trapped by a madman, he was faced with the gruesome prospect that he'd never see her again.

Never tease her about her puzzle books.

Never feel the sharp sting of her fingers when she flicked his ear. Or hear her scolding tone.

"That's not going to happen," he growled. He hoped Dan Perry was listening. "I'm not giving up," he shouted, his voice filling the cramped space like a loudspeaker. "You hear me? I'M NOT GIVING UP!"

With renewed purpose, he pressed his palms against the panel. This time, when he pushed sideways, it slid open again. Three inches, just like before. Why it worked now and not moments earlier was a question for another time, and he quickly thrust his left hand into the narrow opening just as the panel began to close. It pressed against his forearm right below the wrist, but instead of stopping like an elevator door, it kept pressing. Harder and harder.

He reached up with his other hand and grabbed the edge of the panel, trying to pull it back, but he was powerless to stop it. It pinned his arm against the side of the crawl space, and he felt his wrist starting to numb. As he flexed his hand, trying to restore the circulation, his fingers brushed against a small switch on the inside edge of the panel. There was soft click, and then it stopped moving and slid all the way open. The cruelty of the design only fueled his anger.

He let out a weary breath, then crawled through the opening. Once past it, it slid shut again. He continued for another five feet when the floor suddenly gave way, tilting downward at a sharp angle, sending him sliding downward through another narrow chute. He shot out the other end, falling helplessly through the air for what seemed like an eternity before slamming onto a packed dirt floor. As he lay twisted in a heap, pain coursing through his entire body, a panel at the end of the chute slid shut. There was no going back.

He looked up and saw thin rays of light, like silver needles, breaking through the wall. What little light they provided allowed him to see his surroundings. He was at the bottom of a deep circular well, lined with stone. At the top, the crawl space continued. Directly below it, affixed to stones with metal brackets, was a wooden ladder that extended downward, stopping several feet from the dirt floor.

He climbed to his feet, teetering, and stood beneath it.

Forward is the way out.

The bottom rung was at least eight feet from the floor. When he reached for it, his hand fell short by over a foot. He jumped up once, twice, and then a third time, but fell short each time. After a brief pause, he took in a deep breath, summoned what strength he had left, and leapt up, grabbing the bottom rung. He was pulling himself up when it snapped, sending him plummeting back down to the ground. As he lay there crippled by the pain that burned through his body like molten steel, Perry's voice sounded from a small speaker overhead.

"Oh, too bad," he said. "You were doing so well."

Nathan gritted his teeth, fighting desperately to remain silent.

"Nothing to say?" Perry asked. "Don't worry, there'll be plenty of time for conversation. We're just getting started."

Nathan closed his eyes and focused his thoughts. This wasn't the first time he'd been in a tight spot with no hope of escape. Each of those earlier episodes was far worse than this one, and one by one he replayed them in his mind: trapped in the basement of an abandoned building that was moments away from being demolished; being nearly buried alive in a hollow cavern deep inside a mountain; stuck in a small cave on an island in Maine, held hostage there by a violent Spring tide. The images faded and that's when he realized that Perry had been talking the whole time.

"…affairs to attend to, so I must take my leave…but don't worry, we'll speak again. There's lots more fun to come."

And with that, he was gone.

Nathan eyed the ladder, devising a new strategy, and then stood.

Forward is the way out…

He jumped up and grabbed the sides of the ladder, then slowly pulled himself upward, reaching up with one hand, then the other, advancing an inch at a time—left, right, left, right. It was painfully slow, and when he came to the second rung, Perry's treachery was revealed. A narrow cut had been made in the center of the wood to weaken it. The higher he climbed, the deeper the cuts became, but by keeping his hands and feet to the outside edge of each rung, he was able to reach the top of the ladder, where streams of sunlight poured in through a series of small holes where the sill had rotted. The sight emboldened him, giving him renewed energy, and he grabbed the edge of the crawlspace and pulled himself inside.

He'd gone ten feet, possibly more, the darkness made it impossible to tell, when he saw the end of the crawl space. Just beyond it was a short flight of stairs encased in bright sunlight. Like a siren's song they called to him. His pulse quickened and he crawled faster, all the while keeping his eyes trained on the stairs.

Suddenly he stopped. Something wasn't right. *This is too easy*, he thought. The air had grown noticeably cooler, and he reached out and felt the ceiling, the side walls, and the floor directly ahead.

Satisfied that there were no booby traps, he continued on. He'd gone another ten feet when the crawlspace abruptly ended. He stopped short and reached out into an empty black void. There was no floor. No ceiling. No walls. Only cool, moist air.

Through the darkness he saw an open doorway, and beyond it, a narrow hallway that led to the stairs. At the top, through an open bulkhead door, he could see the forest that lined the edge of the property—the leaves of the trees, like a thousand tiny hands waving him onward. He was almost out.

He ran his fingers along the floor of the crawlspace, to where it ended. Several inches below the edge his fingers grazed cold stone. He slid forward until his shoulders cleared the end of the crawl space, then rested his hand on the stone for support.

From somewhere overhead, a small bulb flickered to life, creating an eerie fog-like glow. Through the dim haze he saw the room for what it was. The walls were packed dirt and granite stone. What he thought was a stone floor was nothing more than a narrow ledge, barely 6" wide, encircling an open pit. At the bottom were long shards of razor-sharp steel, set at random angles that protruded upward like the teeth of a giant shark.

He was teetering unsteadily on the edge when Perry's voice echoed through the room. "Ooh, careful now," he said. "You don't want to fall into the pit. We have *so* much to discuss."

Nathan slid back into the crawl space, his heart pounding.

"What? No snappy comeback?" Perry asked.

Again, Nathan held his tongue. Fighting evil with rage was like dousing a house fire with gasoline.

"I must say, Trask really outdid himself with this room," Perry said. "It used to be a wine cellar, but I think it looks much better now. I can't decide which part I like better: the vanishing ledge, or those pieces of jagged steel at the bottom of the pit."

Nathan looked past the pit and eyed the open doorway on the opposite wall, wishing he could magically sprout wings and fly.

"He calls it the Basking Pit," Perry explained. "Has something to do with the way Basking sharks open their jaws to capture their food. The likeness is uncanny. Anyway, since you'll be here for quite some time, are there any questions you'd like to ask me?"

Nathan closed his eyes, slowly breathing in and out, in and out. *Say. Nothing.*

"No?" Perry said. "Certainly, you must be wondering about the sheet music."

"I know all about it," Nathan spat, the words escaping his lips before he could stop himself from saying them.

"Oh, I doubt that very much," Perry countered. "Nonetheless, there was a chance, however slim, that you might've discovered the truth, accidentally or otherwise."

"You mean, like Nicholas Graf did?" Nathan shouted.

Perry said nothing.

"What?" Nathan said. "No snappy comeback?"

When Perry spoke again, his words simmered with hatred. "I'm not sure how you came to know that name, but the two of you have something in common. He stuck his nose in where he shouldn't have and it cost him everything—a fate that will soon be repeated."

Nathan knew he'd struck a nerve but remained silent.

"Graf was a guest of my family," Perry said. "And how did he show his appreciation? He stumbled into the wrong place, saw things he shouldn't have seen, things that didn't *concern* him. Instead of simply ignoring what he discovered, he planned to use that knowledge to expose us, and we couldn't have that happen, now, could we? Little did he know, after his intrusion, we had him watched."

Then, Perry's voice took on an introspective tone.

"It was all very curious," he said. "The bookcase, the way he arranged to have it concealed aboard a ship bound for America, under the cover of darkness. Why all the secrecy, we wondered? Well, we found out soon enough. I *will* give him credit, he was very clever: choosing a piece of classical music that no one cared about, then having it hidden in a seemingly ordinary bookcase. What Graf didn't know was that we had a man aboard the ship. What was that name of that boat, again?" he said, taunting Nathan. "The *Greenland?...the Greenbriar?...*"

"*Greenwich!*" Nathan shouted, another wisp of anger slipping out.

"Ah, yes, the *Greenwich*. You'd think someone would've warned Graf about the perils of sailing across the ocean. Such rough business, sailing. The high seas. The moonless nights. You could fall overboard and no one would be the wiser."

Nathan's mind was spinning as the truth was gradually revealed to him. The rumored danger hidden within the bookcase was no fanciful tale. Gina was right, and Perry had just confirmed it—Graf had learned something that ultimately cost him his life.

"It took some doing," Perry said, "but we recovered the sheet music. Half of it anyway. By the way, let me be the first to thank you."

"What are you talking about?" Nathan hissed.

"You don't know?" Perry asked, genuinely surprised. "And to think, they call you the most famous 12-year-old detective in the world. That's laughable. All this time, we assumed that the missing pages were lost or destroyed, but then you came along and led us straight to them."

"That's a lie!" Nathan shouted.

"Is it?" Perry asked calmly. "You really don't get it, do you? Allow me to spell it out for you. Your first mistake was wandering into my office at Trinidad Traders. Ordinarily, I would've paid it no mind. People were always wandering back there with a question about some item in the shop. But after you left, I noticed that the blanket covering the bookcase had been removed. That was your second mistake."

Nathan pictured that exact moment two months earlier, when he pulled the thin blanket from the bookcase, recognizing the design at once. It was identical to the bookcase in his attic—a perfect twin. Only later did he discover the truth, that Thomas Hammond had built two bookcases.

"The blanket was the only thing out of place, and it got me thinking," Perry explained. "I asked myself, why would a 12-year-old boy be interested in my bookcase? But then again, you're no ordinary 12-year-old boy, are you? You're the grandson of Henry Hammond. So then I asked myself, why would the grandson of Henry Hammond, owner of a world-renowned bookshop, be interested in my bookcase? There was only one logical answer: you were looking for the pages that had been hidden inside it. But why? Because you had the missing pages, that's why. Graf didn't lose them, or misplace them as we had assumed. And that led to the biggest question of all:

how did you acquire them? Could it be that Thomas Hammond built not one, but two bookcases? Did Graf separate the sheets, then smuggle them out of England inside matching bookcases, aboard two different ships? You were kind enough to answer that question for us. And now, after years of wondering, the sheet music is safe once again. Unfortunately for the Hammond family, however, the legacy of Nathan Cole, much like that of Nicholas Graf, will be very short lived. Goodbye, Mr. Cole."

At that, the light that had cast an eerie glow down into the pit went out, leaving Nathan a prisoner of the darkness once again. Perry's voice faded away and didn't return. He'd inflicted the final, crushing blow, words that would haunt Nathan's every thought, tormenting him until the light slowly faded from his eyes.

For the Dampierre family, it was a fitting end for the boy who had threatened to bring down their empire. And unlike the notoriety he'd gained the year before, after his startling discovery in the courthouse, Nathan Cole's epitaph would be as baffling as it was tragic.

The boy who simply vanished.

Massive searches would be conducted. Pleas to the general public for any information about his whereabouts would saturate social media sites, television stations, and newspapers from coast to coast. Months would pass. Years. But he would never be found. His broken body would slowly rot to dust as it was slowly picked apart by rodents.

In the basement of an ordinary house.

At the end of an ordinary street.

On the outskirts of an ordinary town in southern Maine.

20

Global Air Freight

Nathan lay inside the crawl space, shattered by Perry's words. Every one of them was true. He'd foolishly charged into Trinidad Traders, Perry's shop on Wharf Street, never once considering that by doing so he was showing his hand and putting himself and his entire family at risk.

He looked across the pit. Through the gloom he saw the open doorway, the hallway, and the flight of stairs. They were less than twenty feet away, but call it a mile. Call it ten. If he could somehow reach the stairs he'd be free of this nightmare. But with no light to guide him around the treacherous pit, it was an insurmountable distance. A bridge too far.

But he was out of options.

Going back was out of the question.

Forward is the way out…

He sat up and turned his body sideways. With his left hand, he reached up and grabbed hold of the wall overhead to steady himself, then slowly eased out onto the stone ledge.

Forward is the way out...

He hugged the rock wall and started inching his way along when the ledge began oozing a thick oily substance. His left sneaker shot out from under him and he clutched the boulders to keep from falling.

Was this more Trask madness?

A narrow ledge coated in oil?

At first glance a means of escape, but in actuality a path to certain death?

You want to leave? Go ahead. You just have to figure out how.

Afraid to move his feet for fear of falling into the pit, he grabbed hold of a boulder and pulled himself forward, keeping his muscles rigid and his legs locked in place. His sneakers slid easily over the oil-soaked stone, and when he reached the corner he took a step onto the adjoining ledge and immediately pulled his foot back.

Something about the ledge was different.

It was barely four inches wide.

Suddenly, he understood what Perry meant by "the vanishing ledge."

He reached out with his left hand and took hold of a football-sized boulder, then placed his sneaker sideways on the ledge. It slid across the oily stone and he nearly fell. As he clutched the boulders in the wall, his heart pounding wildly, he took a deep breath and tried again. *Short steps,* he told himself. *Nothing but short steps.*

Working at a snail's pace, he grabbed hold of a rock and took a short step onto the next ledge. Next came his right hand, and then his right foot. Once he was set, he pulled himself along, making sure he had a firm hold of the rocks each time before moving forward.

When he reached the final corner, he tested the next ledge with the tip of his sneaker. It was only two inches wide. He turned his foot and set it on the narrow stone, but as he put his full weight on it his sneaker slipped of the edge. He tried again, with a shorter step, and got the same result. The edge was too slick, and there simply wasn't enough surface area to accommodate the width of his sneaker.

His arms began to ache, and his fingertips were tingling from the lack of blood from holding his hands up over his shoulders for so long. He dropped one arm, letting it hang by his side until he felt the blood flowing back to his fingertips, then repeated the process with the other hand. With circulation restored to both hands, he eyed the open doorway. It was only six feet away, but the ledge was too treacherous. One wrong step would seal his fate forever. But the wall...

"Yes!" he whispered.

He reached up as far as he could and hooked his fingers over the top of a thick slab of granite. He did the same thing with his right hand, then hung from the wall just long enough to lift his feet and stick the toes of each sneaker into a gap between the rocks just above the ledge.

After that, it was just a matter of repeating the process.

Left hand grab – left foot stick.

Right hand grab - right foot stick.

Stone by stone he used his hands and feet to maneuver his way across the rock wall in the dark. When he reached the doorway, he gripped the top of the casing with his left hand, then his right, and dropped down onto the floor.

Standing on solid ground never felt so good.

He started down the hallway, the sunlight beyond the bulkhead like an invisible lariat pulling him forward. Up ahead on the left was a small furnace room. Directly across from it, an alcove with a chop saw, a grinding wheel, welding tanks, piles of lumber, boxes of unused screws and bolts, and several cases of motor oil.

The madman's workshop.

He was passing the furnace room when a hand reached out grabbed him. Another hand covered his mouth to keep him from calling out as he was yanked sideways into the room and pushed up against the wall. In the weak light he saw Ellie staring back at him, her index finger pressed to her lips. *Shhh!* When she saw the recognition in his eyes she pulled her hand away from his mouth.

"How did you...?" he started to say.

She clamped her hand back on his mouth and put her finger to her lips again, this time shaking her head violently. *DO NOT SPEAK!* She tapped her ear, then pointed to the ceiling. *They're listening.*

Nathan looked up, then nodded. *Got it.*

She took him by the arm and led him out of the room and down the hallway, keeping close to the wall. When they reached the bulkhead stairs, she stopped and pointed at a rubber mat positioned in front of the bottom step. It had a black bubble surface with no sign of dirt or wear.

She looked at him and shook her head. *Don't step there.*

He gave her a thumbs up. *Understood.*

She stepped over the mat, onto the first step, then turned and offered him her hand. That's when she noticed the dirt and grime covering his clothes, the cobwebs and dead bugs in his hair, and the oil that stained his sneakers. The sight sickened her and she could only imagine what kind of hell he'd been through.

Once he was safely on the stairs, she knelt down and gave the rubber mat a sharp kick. The floor fell away and the rubber mat plummeted downward into a black hole lined with more pieces of razor-sharp steel shards. Nathan looked down into the abyss, horrified by the twisted thinking behind such a brutal deathtrap. Was there no end to Trask's insanity?

The open bulkhead door.

The forest in plain sight.

Sunshine.

Fresh air.

Were they all part of a deadly ploy?

You're almost out…just run up the steps and you're free.

Ellie tugged on his shirtsleeve. *Let's go.*

In Watertown, Elizabeth was pacing the length of the room, her body shaking as she muttered uncontrollably. In the previous hour she'd spoken to Jameson, Beck, Kendra, and Sully, each of whom had tried their best to console her, telling her that it was only a matter of time before Eric Fuller's dragnet would catch Nathan's abductors, and that he would be returned alive and unharmed. The words had given her a feeling of optimism for a time, but now any hope of Nathan's safe return was melting away. Making matters worse: no one had heard from Ellie.

Gina hadn't moved from her chair. Other than working the

phone, she didn't speak. There were no words that could quell the fear that consumed her. What she wanted to do most of all was shout at the top of her lungs into the phone, to the whole group, "I TOLD YOU THIS WAS A STUPID IDEA!" Instead, she folded her arms on the table and laid her head down, too scared to utter a single word and too horrified to think about what Perry was doing to Nathan.

"That's it," Elizabeth shouted. "We've waited long enough." She stopped pacing and made a beeline for the door. "My son is missing and we have no idea what they're doing about it."

David was leaning back against the edge of the table, his head lowered in thought. Or in prayer. He sprung up and intercepted her just as she was reaching for the door handle. "Stop," he said. "You heard what Sully told us. They've got every law enforcement agency in Maine—"

"Doing what?" she shouted, before he could finish.

The ringing of the phone cut through the room like an air raid siren. When Gina looked up and saw Ellie's name on the screen, she dove for the handset. "Ellie, where have you been?" she yelled.

"Gina, it's me, Nathan."

"NATHAN?" she shouted. She looked over at David and Elizabeth. "OH MY GOD! IT'S HIM!"

They raced over to the table and Elizabeth wrenched the phone out of Gina's hand. "Nathan? Where are you?" she said, her words exploding out of her mouth. "Are you okay? Are you hurt?"

"I'm all right, Mom," he said. "I'm with Ellie."

"With Ellie? But how...?"

"There's no time to explain. Put Gina back on. Better yet, put me on speakerphone."

Elizabeth leaned down, staring at the phone through a veil of tears, her finger shaking as it hovered over the keys in search of the speakerphone button.

"Right there," Gina said.

Elizabeth punched the button, and when Nathan spoke again, his words filled the room.

"Gina, are you there?" he asked.

"Yes, I'm here, with both your parents," she said, her voice choked with emotion.

"Son, are you all right?" David asked, his heart beating wildly.

"A little banged up, Dad, but alive…thanks to Ellie. I'll explain everything later, but right now, Gina, I need you to work your magic."

"I'm ready," she said, placing both hands on the keyboard.

"I need you to find something or someone called Hammington, or Hammilon," Nathan said, trying to remember Arthur Beale's muffled words.

"Do you mean, Hamilton?" she asked.

"Yes! That's it…Hamilton."

"Give me a second," she said. She typed in the name and watched as a seemingly endless list of possibilities appeared on the screen. "Okay," she said, reading from the screen. "There's a Hamilton College in Clinton, New York; a Hamilton Company that makes laboratory equipment; Alexander Hamilton; Hamilton, Massachusetts; Hamilton Jewelers in Princeton, New Jersey; Hamilton Township, also in New Jersey."

"No," Nathan said, tapping his fingers nervously on the armrest.

"Try limiting your search to the state of Maine."

"On it," she said.

David and Elizabeth watched in amazement as her fingers flew over the keyboard.

"All right, here we go," Gina said, reading from the new list of possibilities. "There's a Hamilton House Museum in South Berwick, the Hamilton Audubon Sanctuary in West Bath, the Hamilton Mill in Saco—"

"Stop!" he blurted out. "That has to be it."

"Are you sure?" Gina asked.

"Yes. Jameson told me Perry's boat was seen in Saco. Can you send the address to this phone?"

"Doing it now," Gina said.

Nathan watched the screen on Ellie's phone until he saw the notification appear. "Got it," he said, then lowered the phone. "Do you know how to get to Saco?" he asked Ellie.

"Do I ever," she replied, starting the car.

After they'd left the house in Bartlett Mills, she'd driven straight to the interstate. Nathan had her pull into the rest area in Kennebunk where they could hide amongst the rows of tractor trailer trucks while he used her phone to make his calls. His flip phone lay spent in the center console.

"Gina, you're the best," he said. "Now, can you patch Jameson into this call?"

"I thought you'd never ask," she said, a smile finding its way to her lips.

Jameson was waiting at the counter while Eric Fuller's deputies conducted a full search of the antique shop and the surrounding area.

Kendra and Russ were standing outside with Beck, next to his truck.

"They'll find them," Russ said, when he saw the look of fury in Beck's eyes.

"Not if they switched vehicles," Beck countered. With an ongoing search by local and federal authorities, he'd been instructed to stay put—not his preferred course of action.

Nathan had been taken on his watch.

It was his responsibility to make things right.

Once the deputies cleared the building, Jameson went to the storage room and took pictures of the sealed crates. As he neared the back of the room, his phone rang and he answered it without checking to see who was calling. "This is Jameson."

"Jameson, it's me," Nathan said. He chose the speakerphone option and held the phone over the center console so Ellie could listen in.

Jameson stumbled backward against a stack of crates, nearly knocking them over. "Nathan," he exclaimed, gasping for words. "Where are you? Are you hurt?"

"I'm fine," Nathan said. "I'm with Ellie."

"Ellie?" Jameson said, confused. "No one's heard from her."

"I'll explain later," Ellie said.

"Where are you?" Nathan asked Jameson.

"We're still at Beale Brothers."

"Good. I'm going to send you an address. Ellie and I will meet you there."

"Address? What address?"

"If I'm not mistaken, it's where Dan Perry is hiding."

"How do you know that?"

Nathan gave him a 30-second recap: how he listened in on Beale's conversation with Dan Perry; how he overheard Beale mention the name Hamilton, and Gina's search that revealed a historic mill in Saco by the same name.

"Saco? That's where Perry's boat was spotted," Jameson said.

"Exactly," Nathan replied.

"Listen to me," Jameson said, relieved to have Nathan back, unharmed. "Don't do *anything* until we get there. Is that understood?" The last thing he wanted was to lose Nathan again. "I'll have Sully call for backup—"

"No," Ellie shouted. "No police. The minute Perry sees them he'll vanish before we even step foot in the building."

"Along with the sheet music," Nathan added.

"We're 20 minutes away," Ellie said. "After we scout the location, we'll call you back with a place to meet."

"Good idea," Jameson said. He checked his watch. "We'll see you in 45 minutes."

"And Jameson?"

"Yes?"

"Make sure you bring Beck."

"Oh, don't worry," Jameson said. "Knowing him, he'll insist on driving."

"Jameson?"

It was Elizabeth.

"Elizabeth?" he said. "I didn't know you were on the call."

"You'll keep us apprised of what's happening?" she said.

"I will. You have my word."

He slipped his phone in his pocket and hurried out the back door. When he got to the front of the building, he pulled Kendra, Russ and Beck into a tight circle, then checked to make sure no one was within earshot. "Okay, listen," he said quietly. "Nathan just called me..."

"WHAT?" Kendra exclaimed.

"Easy," Jameson said, throwing another quick glance over his shoulder. "We need to keep this quiet."

"Was it a ransom demand?" Russ asked.

Kendra began flexing her fingers like she might tear the siding off the building.

"No," Jameson said. "He's with Ellie. They're headed to Saco. Nathan thinks that's where Dan Perry is hiding."

"He's with Ellie?" Kendra asked, fighting to keep her voice low. "How did that happen?"

"I'll explain on the way, but right now we need to go."

They were piling into Beck's truck when Sully emerged from the building. He hurried over and spoke to Jameson through the open window just as Beck fired up the engine. "What' up?" he asked.

"We have to leave," Jameson told him.

"What happened?" Sully asked, picking up on the urgency in Jameson's voice.

Just then, Kendra ran up to the side door and climbed into the back seat.

"Uh, is there something I should know?" Sully asked, when he saw the baseball bat in her hand.

Jameson gestured to Beck. *Let's go.* As the truck began to move, he leaned out the window and said, "Wait for my call."

Ellie sped north on the Maine Turnpike, staying in the left lane and ignoring the posted speed limit.

"Thank you," Nathan said, breaking the silence. In all the excitement, it was the first chance he'd had to speak the words.

"No thank you required," Ellie said. She saw flashing blue lights in the rearview mirror, a half mile back, and pulled into the right lane, wedging in between two large Winnebagos. Ten seconds later, a state trooper flew past and disappeared in the distance.

"How did you do it?" Nathan asked.

"How did I do what? Find you?"

"Yeah."

"I almost didn't," she said, as she pulled back into the left lane and accelerated. "Thank the young kid that ran the light at the Rt. 9 intersection."

"Huh?"

"When those two guys in the UPS truck drove past me, I got a good look at both of them. Big ugly guy at the wheel. Short weasely guy in the passenger seat."

"Yup, that's them," Nathan said, recalling the look of elation in their eyes when they cornered him in the storage room. They were like two ravenous animals closing in on a helpless prey.

"They had a fifteen-minute jump on me," Ellie said, "but when I came up on the accident, traffic was stopped in both directions. Try hiding a UPS truck in the middle of a line of cars. Can't be done. Once traffic was finally allowed through the intersection, I followed the truck to an old brick garage in North Berwick. The UPS truck went in one side, the overhead door closed, and five minutes later the other door opened and a white delivery van came out. Talk about stupid."

"What are you talking about?"

"They should've used a less obvious vehicle. You know, something plain that would blend in with traffic? Instead, the van they used had the graphic of a jetliner taking off, and the words Global Air Freight plastered across the side."

"They switched vehicles," Nathan said. That explained the memory flashes he'd been having—the squeak of brakes, being jostled about inside the cardboard box, muffled voices, tense, rushed, then more jostling as the engine raced and the tires chirped on the pavement.

"Where was that house?" he asked.

"Bartlett Mills. It's a little town just west of Kennebunk."

"The two drivers didn't see you following them?"

"No, they were in too much of a hurry," Ellie explained as she took the Saco exit. "I'm sure they didn't want a repeat of what happened the first time they tried to grab you."

"So, what did you do?"

"I parked in a driveway up the street and watched them haul a large box through the front door. It took them nearly a minute."

"There was a trap door in the floor," Nathan said.

"Ahh," Ellie said. "That explains why they were being so careful."

"By the way," Nathan asked. "How did you know about the trap door at the bottom of the bulkhead stairs?"

"Something about it wasn't right," Ellie said. "An old house like that? Abandoned? With a brand new rubber mat? Then I noticed a thin seam cut into the floor all the way around it. If the mat had been bigger, I never would've seen it."

"Well, all I know is, if you hadn't been there…" Nathan began.

"Don't think about that," Ellie said. "You're out now. You survived. Now it's time to end this thing."

She took the downtown exit and followed Main Street until they crossed the bridge onto Saco Island. From there, the road snaked past two immense brick mills, built in the early 1800s, before crossing over another bridge into Biddeford. Once they cleared the first bridge, Ellie took a quick right onto Gooch Street, then another right into the Saco Transportation Center parking lot. She parked in a vacant spot next to the Amtrak building, then grabbed a pair of small binoculars from the glove box.

Standing on the edge of the platform at the back of the building, they could see a third mill, much smaller than the other two, built on the southern edge of the island facing Biddeford.

"Well, what do you know," Ellie said, examining the structure through the binoculars.

Nathan craned his neck to see. "What is it?"

"Here, take a look," Ellie said.

Nathan took the binoculars and scanned the building from left to right. On the near end was a square loading dock, and just beyond it, a huge rolling steel door. Backed up to the door was a white delivery van. On the side was the graphic of a jetliner taking off, and the words Global Air Freight.

Ellie watched him lower the binoculars, his mind already hard at work plotting a way to get inside. "Okay, breathe," she said. "We need more information." She eased the binoculars out of his hands and steered him across the platform toward the car.

"Where are we going?" he asked.

"To get a closer look."

She pulled out of the lot and took an immediate right, following the narrow lane that ran between the two massive brick mills. She parked at the end of the largest one and they walked around the end of it, to a thicket of trees and shrubs. From that vantage point, they had a straight-on view of the Hamilton Mill.

The left side of the building, roughly a third of its overall length, was four floors. The windows on the first three levels had been papered over from the inside, blocking out any view through the glass. The right side of the mill was two floors, and the glass in those windows had been replaced with boards that had aged to the color of cinnamon toast.

After several minutes, Ellie had seen enough. "Okay, let's go," she said. They went back to the car, and this time when they left the lot she drove south, over the bridge into Biddeford. Three turns later they were parked at the end of Pearl Street, behind a short stand of trees along the edge of the river. Directly across the water was the south-facing side of the Hamilton Mill.

"Huh," Ellie said, eyeing the boarded-up windows that overlooked the river. Without counting them, she put their number at well over fifty. But because the mill had been built at the very edge of the water, there was no way to gain entry from the river, short of having a boat. Even then, they'd have to scale the brick and find a way to break through the boarded windows without being seen or heard.

"Are you thinking what I'm thinking?" Nathan asked.

"Yup."

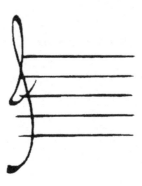

21

Rotterdam

The Saco Transportation Center had two parking lots. They sat on either side of the Saco Station Amtrak building, and when Beck turned in, he saw Ellie's car in the eastern lot, parked at the curb facing the track. He pulled up next to the passenger side and spoke to Nathan through the open window. He had no idea what Nathan had been through since he last saw him in the lobby at Beale Brothers, but now he looked like a kid who'd been cleaning chimneys all morning.

Messy hair.

Dirty face.

His tee shirt soiled with grime.

"Are you okay?" he asked.

"Much better now," Nathan replied.

Kendra picked up the bat lying across her lap and squeezed it with both hands. "Just wait 'til I find the creeps that took him," she growled.

Russ gave her a fearful look, then patted her forearm. "Easy, now."

Ellie got out of the car and walked over to Beck's window. In her hand was a hand-drawn map she'd made after they'd finished scouting the mill building. "Here's what we have," she said, holding up the map so Beck could see.

Jameson leaned over the center console for a closer look. "Are you sure this is the place?"

"Positive," Ellie replied. "The van they used is parked at the end of the building."

"So they *did* switch vehicles," Beck said. *I knew it.*

"Nice work, Ellie," Russ said, from the back seat.

"Yes, nice work," the others said in unison.

"Had to be done," Ellie replied matter-of-factly. "Nathan can tell you the whole story later. It's pretty sickening."

Beck eyed the map, then said, "How do you want to do this?"

"The back side of the building is out, unless you're in the mood for a swim. Along the front are a couple of doors, here, and here," she said, tapping the map with her forefinger as she spoke. "I'm guessing they're locked, but that shouldn't be a problem."

Beck looked at her, eyebrows raised.

"What?" she said. "You never picked a lock before?"

"Picked? No. Blew up? Yes."

She gave him a look. *Yeah, I bet.* "It's a pretty big place so I suggest we split up into three teams," she said. "Kendra and I will approach from the opposite end and enter through one of the front doors. Beck, you and Nathan go in through the loading dock.

361

Jameson, you and Russ can monitor the outside from the parking lot."

Jameson shook his head uneasily. "I'm not sure having Nathan go inside is such a good idea. He's been through enough as it is."

"Don't worry about Nathan," Beck said. "He'll be with me." His tone made it abundantly clear: they may have fooled me once, but it won't happen again.

"Agreed," Ellie said. "We need him to identify the two guys that grabbed him. Wouldn't want to rough up the wrong people."

"Speak for yourself," Kendra muttered, tapping her foot impatiently on the floor of the truck.

"What if they're armed?" asked Russ.

"They won't have guns," Nathan said. "They think I'm dead."

"What?" Beck blurted out.

"They think I'm dead."

"Dead? What are you talking about?" Jameson asked.

"The house where they took me was a torture chamber, built by some guy named Trask. Perry taunted me the whole time I was there. Right now, he thinks I'm still trapped there, or dead."

"That's it!" Kendra said, her anger boiling over. "We need to go, right now. Someone is going to answer for this."

"Hold on," Jameson said. Then, to Nathan, "Did you say Trask was the builder?"

"Yeah, that's the name Perry used. It sounded like he was the architect of the whole thing."

Jameson looked at Beck, troubled.

"What's wrong?" Beck asked.

"You all need to be extremely careful once you're inside."

"We'll be careful," Beck assured him. "If they think Nathan's dead, the last thing they'll expect is all of us showing up on their doorstep."

"All right, then," Ellie said, eyeing the group. "Any questions?"

There were none.

"Then we're set," she said. "Beck, you take Nathan, Russ, and Jameson to the lot on the other side of this building. It sits kitty corner to the mill, and depending on how close you park, you and Nathan should have a 60-second walk to the loading dock. Give Kendra and I a few minutes to get in position, then we'll coordinate a simultaneous entry by phone."

Beck turned to Jameson. "Once we neutralize Perry and anyone else we find, I'll contact you to let you know it's safe to enter the building."

"Neutralize…I like that word," Kendra said, smacking the end of the bat on her open palm.

"Everyone be careful," Ellie said, then leaned in and said to Beck, "First one to Perry wins."

Beck started the truck. "You're on."

As Kendra and Nathan switched vehicles, she stopped him and put her hand on his shoulder, a mix of anger and excitement radiating from her body. "Don't forget what I told you at the house," she said. She reached out and drew an imaginary zig-zag line across his forehead with the tip of her finger, then did the same on her own forehead.

"What was that?" Nathan asked.

"A lightning bolt," she said. "It's an old Indian war paint symbol, meant to give warriors great power and speed." She tapped his arm lightly with the tip of her bat, for luck, then climbed into Ellie's car.

Beck drove slowly past the front of the Amtrak building, to the lot on the far side. He parked halfway down the outer edge at the end of a short row of cars and looked over at the mill. Ellie's assessment was spot on. Walking at a brisk clip, he and Nathan could easily reach the loading dock in a minute, tops.

After he and Nathan got out of the truck, Russ moved to the driver's seat, giving him a better view of the building. Jameson took advantage of the lull to dial Sully.

"Jameson? Is everything okay?" Sully asked. "You guys tore out of here like a Texas twister."

"I'm going to text you an address," Jameson said. "For now I need you to keep it to yourself."

"I can do that. Do you want to tell me what's going on?"

"We may have found Dan Perry. If things get out of hand, I'm going to need you to call in the cavalry."

"Why? What are you planning to do?"

"Right now, we're just going to have a look around…see what's what."

"Are you sure you want to do that?"

"There's six of us," Jameson said. "And Beck counts as two."

"Uh, try three," Sully quipped. "Plus, Kendra and her bat count as two."

"True," Jameson said. "Now listen, if you come, it's got to be in something that doesn't arouse suspicion. That means no cruiser, and definitely not your Crown Vic."

"I still have the Jeep. Does that count?"

"Perfect. I'm sending you the address now." He sent the message, then typed another that he sent to Elizabeth, as promised.

On site now. Going to have a look around.

Elizabeth's reply was two words.

Be careful!

Ellie drove between the two long mill buildings and parked in the same spot as earlier. From there, she and Kendra walked down a short asphalt roadway toward the Hamilton Mill, using a thick row of trees and shrubs as cover. When they reached the end of the building, they worked their way along the front, past the papered windows, until they came to the first door. It was old but solid, covered with riveted strips of metal and painted lima bean green. Three massive iron strap hinges held it in place, and right below the cast iron door handle was an old single-cylinder deadbolt. When Ellie saw that, she looked at Kendra and smiled.

At the opposite end of the building, Beck and Nathan had stopped behind a tall patch of bushes twenty feet from the loading dock. From there they could see through the open door, where several shrink-wrapped pallets sat, waiting to be loaded onto a truck. There wasn't a person in sight.

"Let's go," Beck said.

They ran to the corner of the building and vaulted up onto the loading dock platform. Beck stood at the edge of the door, his back against the building, with Nathan right next to him. To their left was the Global Air Freight delivery van. Beck briefly considered disabling it, should anyone try to use it to escape, but he wasn't planning on letting anyone leave the building.

From somewhere inside, they heard a pair of voices and the thud of a heavy box. Beck peeked around the corner and did a quick scan from left to right, making a mental list of everything he saw. *Six pallets. Pale yellow forklift. Long workbench on the left wall.* The right half of the room was an open bay, big enough to park a large box truck.

He looked beyond the pallets, at a wide brick archway that led to the next section of the building. Two men were standing at a long steel table, opening a large wooden crate. He pulled back and guided Nathan toward the edge of the door. "Recognize those two guys?" he asked.

Nathan leaned forward and looked into the building briefly, then stepped back and nodded. "Yup, those are the guys that grabbed me."

"Good," Beck said, taking out his phone. "I can't wait to meet them."

Ellie knelt down in front of the metal door, examined the lock briefly, then pulled a lock-pick set from her back pocket. Thirty seconds later she stood up and cracked the door open, to make sure there wasn't a slide bolt on the inside, then eased it shut. She felt her phone vibrate and checked the incoming message from Beck.

Ready when you are
2 visible targets

She showed the message to Kendra, then typed a quick reply.

Count to five then go

Beck tucked his phone back in his pocket and flashed five fingers at Nathan.

Then four.

Three.

Two.

One.

"Stay close," he whispered, then crouched down and ran into the building.

After a silent five count, Ellie looked at Kendra and whispered, "Go time." Once inside the door, they stopped sort. Directly ahead of them, less than five feet away, was an enormous steel pallet rack, painted dull orange, extending up toward the ceiling three levels. Each level was lined with wooden pallets that were packed with cardboard boxes and heavily shrink wrapped.

They moved closer to the rack and peered between two of the pallets. Through the narrow gap they saw Romero and Foss standing on either side of the steel table, removing the top of a wooden crate.

"The big guy was driving the van last Tuesday," Kendra whispered.

"Today he was driving the UPS truck," Ellie said. "That short guy was with him."

As they spoke, Romero dug a small oil painting out of the crate and peeled off the bubble wrap. The thick gold leaf frame glistened in the bright light of the halogen bulbs overhead as he carefully inspected it. When he was done, he handed it to Foss, who rewrapped it and packed it in a waiting cardboard box.

Ellie ducked down and looked to her right. The steel rack stretched for another 20 feet, stopping just short of the brick archway that lead to the loading dock area.

"Follow me," she whispered.

Beck and Nathan watched from behind one of the shrink-wrapped pallets as Romero and Foss finished with the wooden crate and went over to a nearby pallet to retrieve another one. Once they were out of sight, Beck darted to the right, past the forklift, to the corner of the room. Moving slowly, he crept up to the brick archway, stopping next to a steel strapping cart. From there, he could see the end of the steel pallet rack in the next room. Standing behind it, in the shadows, were Ellie and Kendra.

When Romero and Foss returned to the steel table with a new crate, Beck motioned to Kendra, then tapped his chest and pointed at Romero. *I'll take the big guy.*

She flashed a thumbs up and pointed at Foss. *I'll take the little guy.*

That settled, Beck grabbed a band cutter from the steel strapping cart and dropped it on the floor, sending a loud clank echoing across the room.

Romero and Foss froze.

"What was that?" Foss said.

"Probably another river rat," Romero grumbled. "How many times have I told you to shut the door?" He set his pry bar on the table, disgusted, and walked toward the shipping area. "I swear, it's like I'm dealing with a child!" he griped as he walked through the brick archway. Out of the corner of his eye he detected movement, and as he turned to see what it was, Beck's tactical boot caught him square in the face. The reverse roundhouse kick knocked Romero out cold and he toppled to the floor like a falling tree.

Foss dropped the wooden lid and picked up a razor knife. He had just cleared the end of the table when Kendra came bounding in from behind the pallet rack, went low, and knocked him to the ground. Beck moved in to help when she waved him back. "No," she shouted. "He's mine."

Foss was staggering to his feet when she unleashed a crushing blow to his shoulder, sending him stumbling backward in agony. "That's for Tuesday," she said, spinning the bat at her side like an airplane propeller.

"You don't understand..." Foss mumbled, struggling to stand.

"Oh, I understand perfectly," Kendra said. She reared back and hit him again, this time in his midsection. "That was for today."

Foss buckled over, wobbling like a top. "You have no idea...what he'd do..." he said, his words coming out in painful bursts, "if we didn't..."

"Shut up!" Kendra barked, then drove her foot into the side of his knee. When he collapsed on the floor, she jammed her foot on his chest, pinning him in place. "Nathan? Is there anything you want to say to this creep?" she said.

Nathan grabbed the razor knife off the floor and stood over Foss, eyeing him with contempt.

"No," Foss snarled. "It's impossible."

"I thought I told you to shut up," Kendra said, grinding the tip of the bat into his shoulder.

As he writhed in agony, Beck took a roll of packing tape from the table and offered it to Nathan. "I think you should do the honors."

"You better believe it," Nathan said, snatching the tape out of Beck's hands.

With one hand, Kendra lifted Foss off the floor like a throw rug and flipped him over onto his stomach. She knelt down, pressed her knee in his back, and growled in his ear, "Nobody does that to my friend."

While Nathan went to work with the tape, Beck texted Jameson.

First floor secure

2 trophies

Jameson responded immediately.

On my way

Just then, Ellie appeared, slightly out of breath. "We good here?" she asked. She looked down at Foss, then over at Romero, who was still lying on his side, unconscious, his arms and legs bound with tape, with another strip covering his mouth. "Nice work you guys," she said.

"Where did you go?" Kendra asked

"In there," Ellie said, pointing at the far end of the room, where a giant steel door was suspended on a rolling track. "It's a storage area. There's also a staircase leading up to the second floor."

"Well, what are we waiting for?" Kendra said, itching for more action.

"Hold on," Beck said, when he saw Jameson appear at the loading dock door.

He walked through the maze of sealed pallets, surveying the room as he went. When he got to the archway, he eyed Romero, then Foss. "Are these the two guys from this morning?" he asked Nathan.

"Uh-huh," Nathan replied.

"And from Tuesday," Kendra added.

Jameson nodded approvingly. Good. "Are there any more?"

"Not here on the first floor," Beck said. "Upstairs? Who knows?"

"Let's get these two out of sight in case any more of Perry's men show up," Jameson said. He took out his phone and texted Sully and Elizabeth.

We have the two UPS drivers

Sully's reply arrived first.

On my way - in the Jeep

Elizabeth's message came seconds later.

Did you find Perry?

Jameson wrote back.

Not yet

As Beck and Kendra dragged Romero and Foss behind the pallet rack, Jameson went over to the steel table and examined the wooden shipping crate. The bill of lading attached to the top matched some of the others he'd seen in the storage room at Beale Brothers.

"There's a whole room full of shipping crates beyond that rolling door," Ellie told him.

Jameson glanced at the door briefly, then pulled the lid off the crate. He dug down through the packing peanuts and dredged out a rectangular frame roughly 16" x 13". After he'd removed the bubble wrap, he could only stare in disbelief.

Ellie blinked hard. "Is that what I think it is?" she asked.

"Yes," Jameson replied. "An original Picasso, stolen from a museum in Rotterdam two years ago."

He carefully rewrapped the painting and returned it to the crate, his mind racing with a singular explanation. *Could it be?* he wondered. Without more substantial proof, it was just wishful thinking. "Okay, listen up," he said, motioning for the others to gather around him. "We need to search the whole building. We'll start on this floor and work our way up. Russ is covering the front and Sully will be here shortly to assist as needed."

"Just Sully?" asked Beck.

"Just Sully."

"What will you tell Fuller?" Kendra asked.

"Unknown," Jameson replied. "I guess we'll cross that bridge when we come to it."

Ellie and Kendra exchanged a look. *Okay, then.*

Ellie led them over to the rolling steel door and into a darkened room littered with pallets. Each was loaded with unopened wooden crates of every size. On the north side of the building sat an old freight elevator, its wooden gate raised as if inviting passengers to climb aboard. "This looks like an overflow area," she said, keeping her voice low. "If I'm reading it right, they store the incoming crates here, then move them into the room we just left for processing. Once the contents are repackaged in cardboard boxes, they store them on the pallet rack. From there, they go to the shipping area." She looked at Jameson, eyebrows raised. "After that...?"

"Precisely," he said, digesting her meaning.

While they were talking, Beck and Kendra did a quick sweep of the room. When they were done, Ellie walked the group over to the corner, where a wide metal stairway angled upward to the second floor. Beck went first, followed by Kendra. At the top of the stairs they paused, watching for any more of Perry's men. Seeing none, they waved the others upstairs.

Unlike the room below, there were no wooden pallets loaded with boxes. Running along the far wall was a row of metal storage containers. Another group of six were grouped together in the middle of the room. Each unit had a metal pull-down door that was shut and padlocked.

"You notice anything different about this room?" Jameson asked.

"It's cooler," Nathan said.

"That's right. These are climate-controlled storage units,"

Jameson said.

"Climate controlled?" Nathan asked.

"Storing certain items requires a steady temperature and humidity level, to protect them from extreme heat or cold."

"What kind of items?"

"Antiques, fine art, important papers…"

Ellie went to the closest unit and worked the padlock with a pick. When it popped open, she raised the door to reveal several large pieces of antique furniture.

Jameson stepped inside and inspected the closest piece—a rosewood parlor cabinet from the late 1800s. As he knelt before it, examining the fine inlays and painted decorations, he began to nod. After too many years, he was very close now—he could feel it.

"You know what that is?" Kendra asked, when she saw the look of recognition on his face.

"I do," Jameson replied. "I also know the estate it was taken from in Burgundy, France."

As Ellie pulled the door back down, Beck went to the near wall where there was another rolling door. It was made from thick wooden boards and hung on a heavy iron track, a leftover from many years earlier when the building was a nail factory. Beck rolled it open slowly, the steel wheels emitting a soft squeaking sound, and saw a long empty room that stretched the length of the building. Two rows of thick hand-hewn wooden posts ran at intervals from one end to the other, and the heavy plank floors had buckled in spots beneath a thick coat of dust.

They climbed the stairs to the third floor and found more temperature-controlled storage units. After a quick search of the room, Jameson and the others waited as Beck crept up the stairs to the fourth floor. Moments later he came back down, stopping halfway. He put a finger to his lips...*shhhh*...and gestured for the others to join him.

22

Not Who but What

Beck went up the stairs first, then Kendra, followed by Ellie, Jameson and Nathan. At the top of the stairway was a small landing, roughly ten feet square. To the left was a plain wooden door. To the right, a second door made from industrial metal with a gray finish and a brushed steel handle and rose plate. Beck went to the wooden door, placed his ear against it and listened for several seconds, then twisted the doorknob and stepped inside.

The room was a large open-concept apartment, fully furnished, with signs of human inhabitation everywhere. Dirty dishes filled the sink. There were several takeout food containers in the refrigerator. In the bathroom, a toothbrush lay on the sink next to a crinkled tube of toothpaste, and a used bath towel hung on a peg next to the shower. Beck did a thorough sweep of the premises, then stepped back out into the hallway and shook his head.

No one there.

He stepped up to the second door, and like before, placed his ear to it, listening. When he heard a voice, he gestured to Nathan with a quick wave of his hand.

Nathan went to the door and leaned in, his ear barely touching the metal. The voice he heard was one he knew all too well. Soft. Measured. Eerily calm. He looked up at Beck and nodded slowly. *That's him.*

Beck pulled him away from the door and motioned for Kendra to join him. "You take Perry," he whispered in her ear. "Leave any others to me."

Kendra gripped the bat with both hands, ready for action. "Let's do it."

Beck turned to the others and raised an open palm…*wait here…* then slowly turned the handle and pushed the door open.

Perry was sitting at his desk, talking on his phone as he reviewed a shipping manifest. Other than a few nautical items and a 1950s articulating desk lamp, the desktop was spotless. Bright sunlight streamed in through the unpapered windows, making the polished hardwood floor shine like bronze. Rare antiques were scattered around the room, creating a museum-like atmosphere. When Perry saw Beck's massive frame come through the door, followed by Kendra, wielding her bat, he lowered the phone at once. "Who are you, and what are you doing in this building?" he demanded.

Beck ignored the question and shifted to the right.

Kendra went left.

Perry eyed them both, a look of confusion on his face. When he saw Nathan enter the room, he dropped the phone and jumped to his feet. "No," he hissed, his face burning with anger. "You're dead." He moved to the end of the desk, as if it might offer him some measure of protection.

Nathan ignored him and surveyed the room. The *Greenwich* bookcase was several feet away, positioned between two large windows that overlooked the Saco River and the historic mills of Biddeford. He walked over to it and ran his hand up the side, feeling the smooth dark wood. "This belongs to my family," he said. He turned and faced Perry. "We're taking it back."

"Oh really," Perry replied. "How do you plan to do that?"

"There's five of us and only one of you, Edouard," Jameson said.

"Bravo," Perry said, in a mocking tone. "You know my real name."

"We know a lot more than that."

Perry inched away from the desk, sweeping his eyes from left to right like a field general assessing his enemy's position. "What do you think you'll gain here?" he said. "Do you honestly believe it will change anything? I assure you, it won't. You can't stop us. Nobody can."

Kendra and Beck moved with him, keeping pace with his retreat. Several feet behind him, pushed up against the wall, sat a 19th century Renaissance library conference table with six barley twist column legs and an intricately hand-carved apron. To the right of that, taking up the corner, was a tall bleached-oak housekeepers cupboard from the late 1700s, with four full-length paneled doors.

"Look around Edouard," Jameson said. "There's nowhere for you to go. And no one is going to come to your aid. The federal marshals have Odom, and we have your two men downstairs."

Perry showed no emotion as he continued to move backward. Odom could take care of himself. Romero and Foss? They were nothing more than tools, meant to be used and then discarded. Such was life. He'd have two replacements by the start of the next business day. "That was a neat trick at Beale Brothers," he said, buying time as he took another short step backward. "Whose brilliant idea was that?"

"It was mine," Nathan said proudly. "And you fell for it, just like I told them you would."

"How do you figure?" Perry asked, watching Kendra and Beck as he continued to back away.

"Simple," Nathan said. "All I had to do was show Arthur Beale the sheet music and he did the rest. We knew once he called you, you'd send somebody to pick it up. So, let me be the first to thank you," he said, using Perry's own words. "Those two 'somebodies' you sent led us straight here."

"Such a bright boy," Perry replied, with a look that was pure evil. "Too bad you didn't die in the basking pit like you were supposed to." He took another step backward. "And you!" he said, eyeing Jameson with disgust. "We should've dealt with you long ago, just like we did with your companion at Whitehall."

Jameson's eyes burned as if the flesh had been ripped from his bones. "Take him," he growled.

Kendra and Beck moved in, and that's when Perry turned and ran to the housekeepers cabinet. He opened one of the doors and ducked inside, closing it seconds before Beck and Kendra got there.

They pulled at each of the doors only to find them locked from the inside.

Ellie sprinted to the cabinet and shouted, "Move!" As Beck and Kendra backed away, she ran her fingers along the edge of each door, pulling at the raised panels. "Nathan, look in the desk," she said. "See if you can find a paperclip."

He ran to the desk and rummaged through the center drawer until he found a thin pile of papers held together by a large paper clip. "Found one."

"Straighten it for me," Ellie said, continuing to check the edges of each door.

Nathan removed the clip, letting the papers fall to the floor, then worked the wire until it was as straight as he could make it. When he handed it to Ellie, she bent it into a rough "z" and slipped one end under the edge of the door just below the small wooden doorknob, then worked it upward until it flipped the small latch holding the door closed.

When they pulled it open, there was nothing there.

No shelves.

No boxes of supplies.

No Perry.

"You've got to be kidding me!" Kendra shouted.

"Hold on," Beck said. He bent down and examined the bottom of the cabinet, running his fingers over the rough wood, side to side and front to back. In the back corner he saw a small hole, no bigger than a dime. At first glance it looked like a knothole, a rustic feature of the pine boards used for the base of the cabinet. But when he slipped the tip of his finger into the hole and pulled, a section of the floor came loose, revealing a darkened shaft below. At less than 30 inches square, it just large enough to accommodate Perry's slender body. Bolted to one side was a narrow steel ladder.

Jameson went to the cabinet door and leaned in, staring down into the opening. When he saw the steel ladder descending into the darkness, he shook his head in disgust. Of course Perry had an escape option, he told himself. A man that cunning? Working with a madman like Trask? It was a safe bet that Perry had other built-in contingencies strewn throughout the building as well.

But he wasn't out yet.

Jameson pulled his phone from his pocket and called Russ. "We're on the fourth," he said. "Perry just escaped and is likely headed your way."

"Understood. We'll watch for him."

"We?"

"Sully just arrived."

"Put him on,' Jameson said.

There was a momentary rustling sound and then Sully came on the line. "Jameson, talk to me," he said.

"We had Perry cornered but he managed to get away," Jameson told him. "I need you to contact Eric Fuller and have him lock down the island. If we lose Perry, we may never find him again."

"Understood," Sully replied. He clamped Russ' phone against his shoulder and began typing in Eric's number on his own phone.

"And Sully?"

"Yeah?"

"If Martin Bishop is still around, tell Eric to bring him too." Jameson clicked off the call and turned to the others. "All right, listen up," he said. "Sully and Russ are watching the outside of the building. We need to search the *inside*, floor by floor, leaving no area unchecked. Perry has roughly a five-minute jump on us which means he couldn't have gotten very far."

As they rushed toward the door, Nathan grabbed Jameson's arm. "Wait," he said, then went to Perry's desk and began rummaging through the drawers.

"What are you looking for?" Jameson asked.

"This," Nathan said, pulling the Pendaflex folder from the deep filing drawer. He removed the sheet music and laid it open on the desktop, then pulled Graf's calling card from his back pocket. "Remember this?" he said.

"Yes," Jameson replied, unsure why Nathan was showing it to him again—now, of all times.

"Check this out," Nathan said. He slid the articulating desk lamp closer, turned it on, and tilted the spherical brass shade downward. He held Graf's card up to the bulb and waited. At first nothing happened. Several seconds passed. Then several more. Then, slowly, the thumbprint materialized on the paper.

Jameson leaned closer, awestruck.

"Now, watch," Nathan said. He lowered the card and the thumbprint gradually faded away. "I think that explains this message," he said, tapping his finger on Graf's scribbled note.

"Remember what I showed you," Jameson said softly, the words taking on a startling new meaning. "But...how did you...?"

"Figure it out?" Nathan said. "By accident. I found out something else, too. Nicholas Graf learned something about Perry's family—something very bad that they didn't want anyone to know."

"That's what Gina said."

"Well, as always, she was right," Nathan replied, "and Perry confirmed it when I was trapped in his house of horrors. He said that Graf had seen something he wasn't supposed to see, something he intended to use to expose them."

"Them?"

"Actually, the word he used was 'us'."

Jameson's expression intensified.

"I think Graf wrote down what he'd learned on the sheet music using some kind of disappearing ink," Nathan said, "and this thumbprint on his calling card proves it." He set the card aside and lifted the sheet music up to the light. Starting at the top, and working from left to right, he passed the paper within an inch of the bulb, taking great care not to let them touch. Every few inches he stopped and counted to ten to give the paper a chance to warm.

In the first grand staff he saw it.

A single name.

It was written in the same scrawl as the message on the calling card.

Bernstein

"Bernstein," he said, reading it aloud. He had no idea what it meant and moved the paper another few inches. Halfway through his ten-count another name slowly appeared.

Rosenburg

"Rosenburg?" He looked over at Jameson, who stood in stunned silence, the names all too familiar.

In the second grand staff, Nathan found a third name.

Acker

And to the right of that, a fourth.

Ravenhof

But they didn't end there. In the third grand staff was a fifth name.

Saint Germaine

And several inches to the right of that, another one still.

La Roche

With each name, Jameson's expression grew more assured. The pieces of a very old puzzle were falling neatly into place, and he pulled his phone from his pocket and hit the speed dial number for Sully. "Tell me you have him," he said, after Sully answered.

"Not yet," Sully replied. "Russ is covering the north corner. I'm watching the south corner. Don't worry, he's not going anywhere."

"We *cannot* let him escape," Jameson stressed. "If it helps, he escaped through a trap door at the southern corner of the building."

"A trap door? What is it with this guy?" Sully asked.

"It's bigger than we thought," Jameson said. "As we speak, I've got Beck, Ellie, and Kendra searching every floor. Once they're done, I'll send them outside. Until then, you two have to lock down the perimeter."

"Will do," Sully replied. "I just heard from Eric. His team should be here any minute now."

"Good. We need all the manpower we can get," Jameson said. "Let me know when they arrive." He clicked off the call and gestured to Nathan. "Wrap that up and bring it with you. We need to go help the others search the building." He went to the door and held it open as Nathan carefully slid the sheet music back into the folder. Where the second sheet was would have to wait, because time was of the essence now. With every passing second, Perry was getting that much farther away.

"What about those names?" Nathan said, as he walked to the door. "Do you know what they mean?"

"Yes. Come on," Jameson said, herding Nathan out the door and across the landing.

"But…who are they?" Nathan asked, scrambling down the steps. With Jameson rushing him, it was everything he could do to keep from falling headlong down the stairs.

"Not who, but what," Jameson said.

"Huh?"

"They're not people."

Kendra did a full sweep of the 3rd floor, starting with the enclosed shaft in the corner. She checked to make sure there were no hidden openings that would allow Perry to get out before he reached the bottom floor, or wherever the ladder ended. When she was done, she went downstairs to the second floor to help Ellie. Just like the floor above, the shaft extended from ceiling to floor with no visible openings. They were just finishing their search when Jameson and Nathan came down the stairs.

"Anything?" Jameson asked.

Ellie shook her head. "Nothing. The shaft continues down to the next floor. His only option is to go back up or keep climbing down."

"Agreed," Jameson said. "My guess is he'll continue downward, which means we have to hurry."

They rushed down the stairs to the first floor and saw Beck standing in the corner next to the shaft, his ear firm pressed firmly against the wood. As they approached him, he pressed a finger to his lips...*shhh*...and waved Jameson closer. "Listen," he whispered.

Jameson put his ear up against the wood and heard a soft brushing sound. Something was rubbing against the inside of the chute. He looked at Beck and whispered, "Is that him?"

Beck nodded. *Yup.*

Jameson quickly gathered the group near the freight elevator and said, "Perry's headed for the basement. Ellie, you take the next room. Beck and I will take the shipping area. Kendra, you and Nathan you have this room. Look for stairs or any other access to the lower level. If you find something, call out and wait for us to join you. No one is to go into the basement alone. I repeat, no one is to go into the basement alone."

Ellie raced to the processing room, where Romero and Foss were flopping around on the floor like two fish out of water, struggling desperately to free themselves. Without success. Beck and Jameson went to check the shipping area, while Kendra and Nathan remained behind.

"I'll check between the pallets," she told Nathan. "You take the perimeter."

"Got it," he said, then started along the end wall of the building, examining the heavy plank flooring for any gaps or seams that would indicate a removable section. He reached the corner and continued along the back wall when he found a large wrought iron hatch roughly three feet by four feet. The thick hinges and crudely fashioned handle, along with the discoloration of the iron, indicated it was part of the original building construction.

He set the Pendaflex folder down on the floor, then grabbed the handle and lifted the hatch, the hinges emitting a soft squeak as he pulled it open. The iron was heavy, and he had to use both hands to push it upright where it abruptly stopped, refusing to move any further. "Found something!" he called to Kendra, who was on the opposite side of the room.

Through the opening he saw a set of wooden steps that disappeared into a black void. He leaned down for a closer look when Dan Perry suddenly appeared and grabbed the front of Nathan's shirt. "Looking for me?" he growled through clenched teeth, unable to contain his anger.

Nathan swatted his hand away, but Perry was too quick. He clamped on to Nathan's ankle with both hands and pulled him toward the hole. "What a fitting end for the famous Nathan Cole," he snarled. "I get to finish you myself."

"Guess again," Nathan said. He grabbed hold of the iron hatch, and pulled it forward. The hinges sang out a cruel warning as the hatch crashed to the floor, snapping the bones in Perry's forearms and pinning him in place.

The blood curdling scream that followed brought the others racing back into the room, where they saw Nathan standing atop the steel hatch, hands on his hips.

Smiling.

"I got him."

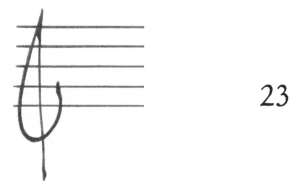

23

Châlucet

E ric Fuller's deputies pulled Dan Perry from the hole in the floor and ushered him outside. He walked unsteadily, hunched over, his arms hanging at awkward angles and his shirtsleeves ringed with blood. He had the look of a beaten man, wracked with pain, too stunned to utter a single word. How could this have happened? They had the boy. They recovered the sheet music. The threat had been neutralized. Where did it go wrong?

As Jameson stood on the loading dock watching him hobble across the parking lot to a waiting ambulance, a flood of memories washed through his mind, ripping open a scar that no amount of time would ever heal.

"Dad?"

He turned and saw Kendra standing behind him, her face somber. A shared feeling of sadness lived within them, and in the hug that followed, no words were spoken. Words couldn't change the past, and though justice for what had transpired years earlier would finally be dispensed, it wouldn't be enough.

Not all tradeoffs hold equal value.

"I need to call Elizabeth," Jameson whispered. He tightened his embrace then pulled away. It had been nearly two hours since he last spoke to Elizabeth, and she and David had waited far too long to hear the news he was about to give them.

Kendra composed herself then looked back into the shipping room. "I seemed to have misplaced my bat."

"Go," Jameson said, taking his phone out of his pocket. "I'll join you shortly." He pressed the speed dial number for Elizabeth and within seconds the call connected. One ring later, she answered, the faint echo of her voice telling him she'd pressed the speakerphone button so David and Gina could hear.

"Jameson, what's happening?" she said, frantic.

"It's over," Jameson said. "We got him."

"You got him?" Elizabeth shouted. She and David hugged.

"Actually, it was Nathan," Jameson said.

Gina couldn't contain her curiosity. "How did he do it?" she asked.

"I think it's best if he tells you himself," Jameson replied.

"Is he all right?" Elizabeth asked.

"He's fine. Although I think relieved might be a better word."

"You're still in Saco?" David asked.

"Yes."

In the prolonged silence that followed, Elizabeth sensed there was something Jameson wasn't telling them. "Jameson, what is it?" she asked.

His words came out cold and hard. "He was part of it, Elizabeth. At Whitehall."

"Are you sure?"

"Positive."

Elizabeth closed her eyes and let out a pained breath. "Jameson, I'm so sorry."

Gina stared at her, confused. *What are you talking about?*

A loud, shrill whistle broke the silence, and Jameson turned to see Eric Fuller motioning to him from the processing room. Standing near him in a loose circle were Beck, Ellie, Kendra, Sully, Russ, and Nathan. Jameson waved back...*be there in a minute*...then said, "Elizabeth, I have to go. It looks like we're all going to be here for a while so you should probably take Gina home. You'll have to think of something to tell her parents..."

"Don't worry," Elizabeth said, giving Gina a wink. "I'm sure the three of us can come up with something. You'll be okay?"

"I'll be fine," he said, "but let's talk later. There's still a lot to do." He gave her the code to the door, then clicked off the call.

"All right," Fuller said calmly, once he had everyone assembled. "Who'd like to tell me what happened here?"

Ellie spoke first. She explained her pursuit of the UPS truck after it left Beale Brothers Antiques, how she witnessed Romero and Foss switching vehicles before driving to the house in Bartlett Mills, and how she snuck inside and guided Nathan to safety.

"Bartlett Mills?" Sully asked. He had her confirm the address, then said, "We went to that house on Thursday. It looked deserted."

Nathan shook his head sadly. "Not quite," he said.

"Well, thankfully, the two of you got out," Fuller said. "How exactly did you end up here?" he asked, gesturing at their surroundings with both hands.

Nathan explained the phone conversation he overheard between Arthur Beale and Dan Perry, the curious word that Beale uttered, and how Gina identified it as the Hamilton Mill on Saco Island.

Fuller looked over at Jameson, astonished. *Wow.*

Jameson raised an eyebrow. *Indeed.*

Beck went next, explaining their entry into the building, including their takedown of Romero and Foss, and what followed on the fourth floor with Dan Perry. By the time he was done, Fuller looked like he'd just stepped off a rollercoaster.

"A ladder, inside a chute, hidden in the floor of a cabinet?" he said, with a dizzy expression.

"No doubt the work of Trask," Jameson said.

"And so…he climbs down the ladder all the way to the basement," Fuller said, piecing together the bizarre chain of events. He turned to Nathan. "And that's when you found the hatch in the floor?"

"Uh-huh," Nathan replied. He recounted how he searched the room, found the hatch along the back wall, and his ensuing struggle with Perry, who attempted to pull him down into the basement to "finish him."

"He said that?" Fuller asked.

Nathan nodded triumphantly.

"The warrior rules," Kendra said. She traced a lightning bolt on her forehead and Nathan did the same. Going forward it would be their secret, unspoken sign.

Fuller checked his watch, then said, "Okay, everybody get comfortable. We've got a lot to get through. Are there any decent pizza shops around here?"

As the group dissipated, Jameson walked up to Fuller and said, "Nathan and I have some unfinished business on the fourth floor. Martin Bishop is going to want to join us."

"Be my guest," Fuller said. "My men are done up there."

Jameson said very little as they climbed the stairs to the top floor. Once they were in Perry's office, he told Bishop about the stolen items they'd found downstairs and Perry's cryptic warning that he and his associates couldn't be stopped—a subtle admission about his criminal network. He went on to explain the sheet music: how Graf had used it to hide the information he'd obtained about the Dampierre family, passing it on to Thomas Hammond, who hid it in two matching bookcases; smuggling them out of England aboard separate ships, and how Nathan not only unearthed the sheet music, but also discovered the hidden information they contained.

"Show me," Bishop said.

Standing on either side of Nathan, he and Jameson watched as the names slowly reappeared under the warm glow of the desk lamp.

"Bernstein...Rosenburg," Bishop said, reading the names aloud.

"You know them?" Jameson asked.

"Yes," Bishop replied. "Austria."

Jameson nodded his agreement. *Yes, they are.*

As Nathan moved further down the page, Bishop pulled a small notepad from his jacket pocket and began scribbling notes. "Acker, Ravenhof," he said, adding the names to his list. "Belgium."

Again, Jameson nodded.

"Saint-Germain, La Roche," Bishop said, writing faster now. "France."

Nathan continued to the fourth grand staff, where two more names blossomed into view.

Grunwald

Rastede

"Grünwald and Rastede," Jameson said. "Germany?"

"That's right," Bishop said as he jotted down the names. He had the troubled look of a man standing helplessly by as a brush fire streaked across the forest floor, consuming everything in its path.

Nathan moved to the facing page and worked his way across and down. Like before, each grand staff contained two, sometimes three names. Jameson and Bishop took turns reading them aloud, confirming their country of origin, which included Italy, Spain, Denmark, and the Netherlands.

When he reached the bottom of the page, Nathan set the sheet music down and turned off the lamp. "You told me these aren't people," he said to Jameson. "So what are they?"

"Castles," Jameson answered.

"Castles?" Nathan repeated, with a confounded expression.

"Given what we now know about Perry, or Edouard Dampierre, along with the things he said to you, and to us earlier, I'm certain these castles were the original storehouses for stolen art, used by a criminal network called the Covin."

Bishop looked down at the sheet music, thunderstruck.

"Interpol has been investigating the Covin for decades," he said. "But they're a ghost."

"Agreed," Jameson said. "These castles are very old, and it's a safe bet that some of them have fallen into disrepair. Still, they might shed new light on the Covin's operation."

Bishop picked up the sheet music and looked underneath it. "Is this it?"

'No," Jameson replied. "There's a second page."

"Where is it?"

"Unknown," Jameson replied.

"He'd want to keep it close by," Nathan said. He looked around the room, considering each piece of furniture, before his eyes settled on the desk. One by one he pulled out the drawers and rifled through their contents, then removed them completely and held them overhead, checking the bottom panels.

While he was doing that, Jameson and Bishop went around the room, examining the walls and floor for any more hidden compartments. Bishop was checking the wall across from the desk when he stopped to look at a framed picture hanging on the wall. The image held his attention for nearly a minute.

"What is it?" Nathan asked.

"The Château de Châlucet," Bishop replied, without taking his eyes from the painting. "After our discussion at the lake on Friday, I researched the Dampierre family. This castle was originally built in west-central France as a medieval fortress. Years later it was acquired by the Dampierre family and served as their home for generations." He paused to look back at the sheet music, lying open on the desktop, a thought forming in his mind.

"What?" Jameson asked.

"According to what I read, the Dampierre family actively supported the music of the time and held regular house concerts."

"Nicholas Graf was a devout music patron," Jameson added. "He could very well have attended those concerts."

"He did," Nathan said.

Bishop gave Nathan a dubious look. "What makes you so sure?"

"Perry said Graf was a guest of his family, and that he somehow wound up in the wrong place and saw things he wasn't supposed to see."

Jameson envisioned a grand ballroom filled with guests; a classical quintet playing the latest offerings from Haydn, Mozart, and other noted composers of the day; Nicholas Graf in the crowd, held spellbound by the music, until something draws him away. A trip to the privy chamber, perhaps? A search for one of the wait-staff?

Jameson imagined him wandering away from the main hall, eventually finding himself on a lower level where he wanders into a vast storeroom filled with stolen art treasures. At that point Jameson's vision grew murky, eclipsed by a seemingly endless barrage of questions.

Did Graf examine each piece of art?

Were they grouped and tagged with their destinations clearly marked?

Did he write down the names on a scrap of paper, or did he commit them to memory, only to embed them later within the pages of Eigner's melancholy fugue?

He snapped out of his reverie when Nathan abruptly stepped forward and pulled the painting off the wall. He flipped it over and found a large manila envelope taped to the back. Tucked inside it was the second page of The Grim Fugue.

He rushed back to the desk and turned on the lamp. Just like the first page, more names appeared within each grand staff—castles that Bishop and Jameson placed in England, Scotland, Sweden and Norway, joining a network that spanned the whole of Europe.

"These pages are a roadmap of the Covin's network as it existed in the mid 1800s," Jameson said.

Bishop reviewed his list, stunned, then looked down at the sheet music. "I'm going to need those pages," he said.

"Yes, by all means," Jameson said, handing him the Pendaflex folder. "Take them."

Bishop gathered both sheets and slipped them into the folder, then addressed Nathan with a look of heartfelt appreciation. "That was excellent work young man," he said. "It would appear the news reports I heard about you are true."

"Yeah…well…" Nathan said, sheepishly, "do me a favor and don't tell anyone."

"On that you have my promise," Bishop said. He shook Nathan's hand, then addressed Jameson. "We have a monumental task ahead of us," he said. "Can we count on your help?"

"Absolutely," Jameson replied. "I have an extensive collection of files that I'd be happy to give you."

"Thank you," Bishop said. "You'll hear from me within the next day or two."

And with that he hurried out of the room to make a series of calls that would keep him occupied well into the night.

After he was gone, Nathan sat back in the chair, eyeing

Jameson suspiciously. "How is it that you know so much about this criminal network? What did you call it?"

There was a time when Jameson would've dodged the question, earmarking it for some vague time slot in the future. But that time had passed. The long arduous journey he'd begun years ago was nearing its completion, thanks to Nathan's discovery of *The Grim Fugue* and Nicholas Graf's invisible list of names. For those reasons, Nathan deserved to know the truth. He'd more than earned it.

"They call themselves the Covin," he said. "Years ago, I was part of a group who were tracking them. At the time they were rumored to have a global network through which they moved millions of dollars of stolen artwork each year. We're talking everything from estate robberies, gallery thefts, museum heists, you name it. That number has undoubtedly stretched into the billions."

"You were part of a *group?*" Nathan asked, giving Jameson a curious look.

"Yes," Jameson said, offering no further explanation.

Nathan, in turn, didn't press.

"It became my life's work," Jameson said. "I collected vast amounts of information, chased down hundreds of leads, spoke to countless criminals, some of whom refused to talk to me unless I could guarantee their safety."

"That explains the secret rooms," Nathan muttered under his breath.

"It was during that time that I met your grandfather. Much like you did today, he was instrumental in helping me uncover the truth about a high-ranking member of the Covin—a man known as the

Eidolon. For years he had existed as nothing more than a ghost, all the time living just over an hour from here on the North Shore."

"My *grandfather* did that?" Nathan asked, awestruck.

"He did. And right after that I went to work in his bookstore."

"Wait," Nathan said, eyebrows furrowed. "You were tracking a criminal network, and then you went to work in a *bookstore?*"

Jameson turned from the desk. "I didn't have much choice," he mumbled as he walked over to the *Greenwich* bookcase.

"What did you say?" Nathan asked, getting up from the chair and following after him.

Jameson stood before the bookcase, eyeing the books on each shelf. "It was complicated," he said.

"Does this have something to do with what Perry said…about your companion?"

"Yes," Jameson replied. "The person he was referring to was—"

His words fell away when a book on the middle shelf caught his eye.

"You were saying?" Nathan asked.

Jameson pulled the book from the shelf and stared at the front cover like a man in a trance. When he pulled it open and saw the inscription on the title page, a jolt racked his body and he staggered backward, nearly dropping the book on the floor.

Nathan reached out and grabbed hold of him. "What's wrong?"

Jameson stared at the inscription, his jaw hanging open in shock. "This was hers," he said, his voice barely above a whisper. He closed the book and stumbled over to the conference table, collapsing into one of the chairs.

"Who are you talking about?" Nathan asked.

"Claire."

"Claire? Claire who?" Nathan asked.

"My wife," Jameson replied, sadness swimming just below the surface of his words.

Nathan couldn't remember Jameson ever mentioning his wife before, and he never found cause to ask him. Until now. "*That's* who Perry was talking about?" he exclaimed.

Jameson nodded.

"You're telling me Perry, or this Covin organization, killed your wife," Nathan confirmed, anger taking hold of him.

"I suspected it was the Covin, but I had no proof," Jameson said. "Not until today, when Perry mentioned it. This book is further confirmation."

Nathan's rage surged and he suddenly wished he'd jumped up and down on the cast iron hatch while he had Perry trapped beneath it.

Pain for pain.

Blood for blood.

"She was an avid history buff," Jameson said. "Not long after I gave her this book, she told me she'd found something in it that linked the Covin to a property in Portsmouth, New Hampshire— a sprawling estate called Whitehall."

Perry's words stung Nathan's memory like a barb.

"We should've dealt with you long ago, just like we did with your companion at Whitehall."

Jameson was deluged with pain and regret. "It was the night before I was scheduled to fly back from Europe," he said. "She called to tell me what she'd found, that she was certain of its connection to the Covin, and that she was planning to visit Whitehall the following day. I begged her not to go until I returned, but..." He shook his head sadly as his words fell off.

Nathan didn't ask what happened after that. It was all right there in Jameson's eyes.

"It was meant as a warning," he said. "Stop, or you'll be next."

"Or Kendra," Nathan offered.

Jameson shook his head. "No. This was before she was born."

O-kay, Nathan thought, another question springing into his mind.

"I had to convince them that I'd given up my pursuit of their organization, so I took a job with your grandfather. Looking back now, Hammond Books saved my life, and for that I'm forever indebted to your family."

Then, like a switch had been thrown, his mood shifted.

"And now, years later, lo and behold, you discover the sheet music in the bookcase, and Graf's cleverly disguised list of Covin storehouses, and we catch their prize fish."

Nathan's thoughts were still focused on Whitehall. "Was she right?" he asked. "About Whitehall? Was it part of the Covin network?"

Jameson shrugged. "Unknown," he said. "I couldn't follow up, not without risking my own life."

"So, you just dropped it?"

"I made some subtle inquiries over the years, with Ellie's help, but nothing came of it."

Nathan slid the book off the table and examined the image on the front cover. It showed a palatial 19th century Victorian mansion, surrounded by expertly maintained hedges and flower beds that were bulging with color. A 2-tier spill fountain carved from fine Italian marble sat in the center of the large circular driveway. "This was her book?"

"Yes."

"Why is it here, in the *Greenwich* bookcase?" Then it dawned on him. "Unless…"

"Go on," Jameson said.

Nathan gave him an uneasy look, afraid to speak the words for fear of the pain they would inflict.

"It's all right," Jameson said. "You can say it."

"She had the book with her when she went to Whitehall," Nathan said gently.

"Correct. And I never saw it again," Jameson said. "Not until just now."

Nathan looked down at the book, confused.

"I know what you're thinking," Jameson said. "The book ties the Covin to Claire's death, so why keep it here of all places…in plain sight?"

Nathan nodded his head. *Exactly.*

"Arrogance," Jameson said. "You heard what Perry said when we confronted him. He thinks his organization is untouchable. For the longest time they were, but their luck is about to run out."

Nathan opened the book and turned to the title page.

Castles by the Sea
The Grand Estates of the New England Coast
by
Margorie Crandell Hicks

In the bottom corner was a short inscription.

All my love,
J.

He stared at the page as questions flooded his mind.

"What is it?" Jameson asked.

Nathan closed the book, his thoughts still churning.

"Do you mind if I hold onto this for a little while?"

24

Monday

Nathan slept in. Not only was he exhausted from the tumultuous events of the previous day, questions about Claire Jameson's book from the *Greenwich* bookcase were ruling his every thought. Try as he might, he couldn't let it go.

What did she find in the book that led her to Whitehall?

Why did she ignore Jameson's plea to wait for him?

What compelled the Covin to keep the book, knowing full well that it could implicate them in her death?

Was it arrogance as Jameson had suggested?

Or was it something else?

Sitting up in bed with the book propped open in his lap, he had begun a careful examination of each page, until the weight of his questions became too much and exhaustion pulled him into a deep sleep.

He didn't toss or turn.

He didn't dream.

The aches and pains that had wracked his body slowly drifted away, taking with them the horrifying memories of the Bartlett Mills house.

His mother waited until eleven o'clock, then went upstairs and knocked on his bedroom door. Hearing no answer, she eased it open and looked into the room. Nathan was fast asleep on his bed, sprawled out on his back like a shipwreck survivor washed ashore by the waves. An open book was tucked under his arm. She hesitated, debating whether to wake him or let him sleep, then went over to the bed. She was gently working the book loose when his eyes snapped open. "Don't!" he exclaimed, grabbing the book with both hands.

"Okay, okay, relax," his mother said, letting go of it. "I was just going to put it on the table."

Nathan pulled the book to his chest and slid off the opposite side of the bed. With eyes half open from the bright morning sunlight, he hobbled over to his bureau and tucked the book in the middle drawer, then went back and climbed under the covers.

"You have visitors," his mother said.

"Who is it?" he grumbled.

"Come downstairs and see."

Moments later, when he reached the bottom of the front hall stairs, he saw his father sitting on the living room couch. Beck and Jameson were seated across from him in the matching red chairs.

"Ahh, there he is," David said brightly.

Nathan walked into the living room and dropped onto the couch.

"How you doin', kid?" Beck asked.

Nathan yawned, then blinked hard, like he'd been doused with a bucket of cold water. "Uh, I don't know. Good, I guess."

"Jameson was telling us about his conversation with Martin Bishop," David explained. "He wanted me to pass along his gratitude for everything you did. He said you're the bravest kid he knows."

Nathan had never given it much thought and could only offer a weak shrug. He knew if Gina was there, she'd have a very different opinion on the matter.

"Martin couldn't divulge everything that's happening," Jameson said, "but he did say that Karl Odom and Dan Perry, or Edouard Dampierre, if you like, will be prosecuted to the full extent of the law. I suspect both will remain behind bars for the rest of their lives. As far as the Covin is concerned, a number of law enforcement agencies, including Interpol, are actively pursuing them. They're moving very quickly, and according to Bishop they've already located Edouard's brother, Sebastian. The search for their older sister Ginette is ongoing."

"You're helping them, right?" Nathan asked.

"I am. But given the scale of the investigation, which will likely span several continents, it's going to take us time to locate everyone associated with the criminal enterprise. The good news is, the information you found in the sheet music gives us an excellent place to start."

"So, Nicholas Graf's efforts will achieve their intended purpose after all," David said.

"Yes, thanks to Nathan," Jameson said. "But it's going to take time, and until we find every Covin member it's imperative that we exercise extreme caution."

"What do you mean?" Nathan asked.

"The list that Nicholas Graf made dates back over 160 years. Since that time, the Covin's network has undoubtedly grown. How big? We won't know until we round them all up, which could take years. Until we do, we have to assume that Covin members are everywhere."

"Great," Nathan mumbled under his breath.

"On a brighter note," David said, changing the subject, "there's something I want to show you." In unison, he and Beck stood, followed by Jameson.

"What is it?" Nathan asked.

"You'll see," his father said.

Nathan followed them through the kitchen, down the stairs, and outside to the garage. Beck's truck was backed up to the door so they entered through the side. There, sitting in the middle of the floor, was the *Greenwich* bookcase.

"Beck and Jameson delivered it early this morning," David said.

Nathan stood motionless, staring at it in awe. After all the years the Hammond family had spent searching for it, wondering who had taken it, and what had become of it, the bookcase was finally home. "Where are the books that were in it?" he asked.

"There," Beck said, pointing to a pile of cardboard boxes in the corner.

Elizabeth came up behind Nathan and wrapped her arms around him. "I've dreamed of this day ever since my father first told me about Thomas Hammond and the two bookcases," she whispered in his ear. "I wondered if I'd ever see the *Greenwich* bookcase, and now, here it is… thanks to you. Your grandfather would be so proud."

"I did have some help, Mom, remember?" he countered.

"The question is, where should we put it?" David said.

"Well, I guess that's something we need to talk about," Elizabeth said. "But first, who's ready for lunch?"

Beck, Jameson, and David nodded their heads, then followed Elizabeth back into the house.

Nathan stayed behind.

He'd never seen the bookcase in the attic without books. Seeing its identical twin with empty shelves brought about a vision of Thomas Hammond in his workshop: standing before the two bookcases, inspecting his craftsmanship; sanding out any rough spots; wiping them down with a rag before applying the dark chocolate-colored stain.

Years later, both bookcases would be filled with books. And while Nathan understood the nature of the collection in the Hammond bookcase, why his family members had saved them, he wondered what kind of books had been stored in the *Greenwich* bookcase. What literature would interest the likes of Dan Perry and the Covin members that came before him? Criminals, one and all.

He went to the corner and opened one of the boxes. The books were an assortment of hard and soft covers, packed with their spines up. He chose one at random and read the title.

The Reflection of Light and Color
A Study of French Impressionism in the 1860s
by
Gilles-François Vignaud

He was flipping through the pages when he found a slip of paper. It was less than an inch wide and roughly three inches long. The rough edges indicated it had been torn from a small notepad. Written at the top was the number 124. He inspected it briefly then tucked it back into the book and reached for another.

The Antique Collector's Guide, Volume 3
Southern Maine from Kittery to Cape Elizabeth
by
Everett Ingersoll

It was much older than the first book, with a scruffy cover, a broken binding, and ancient pages that looked like they'd been soaked in mud. As he carefully thumbed through them, a narrow strip of paper fell out and fluttered to the floor. When he picked it up and examined it, he discovered the number 70 written at the top.

His curiosity soared higher and a pulled out a third volume—not a book, but a thick catalog with a glossy cover that showed a 19th century French gothic desk with ornately carved front panels and turned columns at the corners.

Steiner Galleries
Fine Arts & Antiques Auction
Saturday, September 19, 2009

He was fanning the pages with his thumb when he discovered another strip of paper wedged into the binding. Before he could take it out, the side door opened and his father stepped inside.

"Are you going to join us for lunch?" he asked.

"Oh…uh…no…" Nathan stammered. "I'm not hungry."

After his father left, he quickly checked the rest of the books in the box. Each had a narrow strip of paper marking one of the pages, and written at the top of each one was a number.

He repacked the box and raced back into the house, using the front door to avoid going through the kitchen where lunch was being served. In his bedroom, he took Claire Jameson's book from his bureau drawer and sat on the edge of the bed, carefully checking every page.

In one of the middle chapters he found it. Had he not fallen asleep in the wee hours of the morning he surely would've seen it.

The paper was no wider than his finger, with rough edges. At the top was the number 490. He ran to the window and checked Gina's driveway. The garage door was open and her parents' car was gone.

Perfect.

He grabbed his flip phone from the bedside table and called her. It took several rings, but she finally answered.

"Hello?"

"Hey," he said, unable to contain his excitement. "What are you doing right now?"

"Whoa, slow down," she said. "First of all, welcome home. Secondly, how *are* you?"

His reply came out in a rapid stream, as if the words were fighting one another to escape his mouth. "Me? I'm fine, a little sore, but not bad, hey, you like number puzzles…"

"Yes, I know that," she groaned, rolling her eyes.

"Well," he told her, "I just found a huge one."

Epilogue

Standing in the back room of Hammond Books, Maria Garza opened the book of watercolors by Francesco Bassetti and showed Daniel a painting of the Basilica di San Marco, its onion-shaped Byzantine domes backlit by a stunning peach-colored sunrise.

"This painting was stolen two days ago from an estate in Waltham," she said.

"How do you know that?" Daniel asked.

"Because I heard the thieves talking about it."

Daniel leaned closer and studied the image. "That's odd," he said softly. "I've heard of no such theft."

"That's because the authorities are keeping it quiet," Maria explained. "The family that was robbed is very well-to-do, and exceedingly private. If word were to get out…"

"Yes, of course," Daniel said. "Where did you overhear this conversation?"

Maria explained that she worked as a housekeeper for a wealthy merchant on Chestnut Hill—a man with excessive holdings and considerable influence. "Two days ago, two men came into his private library," she said. "They had no idea I was cleaning the adjoining bathroom and could hear every word they said."

"By 'they'," Daniel said, "are you referring to the two men who were pursuing you?"

"Yes. That's why I've been on the run since I last saw you."

"What are you saying? The thieves know you heard them talking about it?"

"Yes," Maria replied, fear returning to her eyes.

Daniel pulled up a chair and motioned for her to sit, then took a seat across from her. "Tell me more," he said.

"They were talking about the painting, laughing about how easy it was to steal it," she said. "I peeked around the door frame and saw one of them pull this book out of his jacket and slip it in the desk drawer."

"Go on," Daniel said, confused.

"I couldn't understand why they would be leaving a book in the library, in the owner's desk of all places. After they left I took it from the drawer and examined it. And I found this," she said, pointing at four words scribbled in the margin next to the picture of the painting.

Daniel took the book from her and studied them for several long seconds.

Front foyer left side

"Is this what I think it is?" he asked.

"It was the location of the painting," Maria replied. "Apparently, the house is full of artwork. The thieves were given that book with a picture of which painting to steal, along with the exact description of where to find it. I took the book, and as I was leaving the room, they must have seen me with it."

Daniel's expression darkened. "When we first spoke," he said, "you said you stole the book to save your father."

"My father is employed as a groundskeeper at that same estate in Waltham. His name is Tullio. I heard the two thieves bragging about planting evidence that would implicate him in the theft."

"Evidence?"

"A pair of leather work gloves, taken from the gardener's shed and left in the foyer, right below where the painting was hung."

"But…why him?" Daniel asked.

"He has very little money and speaks almost no English," Maria said. "A valuable painting like that would be impossible to resist for such a simple man, or so they want the authorities to believe."

Daniel shook his head, unconvinced. "I don't know," he said. "Those gloves could belong to anyone."

"No," Maria said. "He's the only groundskeeper."

"Then we have to move quickly," Daniel said, closing the book. "Before anything happens to your father."

Tears welled up in Maria's eyes. "It's too late," she said, her voice breaking as she spoke. "He was arrested the day after the theft. I honestly don't know what's going to happen to him."

A burning rage consumed Daniel. Just like his brother Thomas, an innocent man had been arrested for a crime he didn't commit, his honor and his family name disgraced. Fueled by that injustice, Daniel vowed he wasn't going to let that happen again. He gave Maria back the book, then stood. "It's not safe for you to go outside," he said, "so I need you to wait here."

"Wait here? Why? Where are you going?" she asked, alarm in her voice.

"I know someone who can help your father," he said. "Don't worry, I'll only be gone a few minutes."

When he returned 10 minutes later, he was accompanied by a tall, clean-shaven man dressed in a dark suitcoat, with a crisp white shirt, pinstriped vest, and maroon tie. A charcoal-gray bowler hat sat atop his head.

"Maria, this is Charles Flannery," Daniel said. "He's a member of a newly established law enforcement agency in Chicago called the Pinkerton National Detective Agency. Why don't you tell him what you told me?"

Flannery was in the Boston area tracking three fugitives suspected of robbing a train in Montgomery, Alabama. He had visited Daniel's shop earlier in the week where the two had become instant friends. He listened with great interest as Maria recounted the conversation she'd overheard in the library, which she punctuated by showing him the writing in the book.

After that, with Flannery's help, things happened very quickly. Within the hour, Tullio was set free and the two men who had been pursuing Maria were apprehended on suspicion of robbery. Maria's employer was subsequently arrested when the stolen painting was found in a closet of his home on Chestnut Hill.

With Tullio's release, Daniel felt an overpowering sense of satisfaction. Not only had he righted a wrong, he'd kept an innocent man out of prison and saved his reputation in the process. The experience made Daniel wonder what other secrets existed, hidden away inside seemingly ordinary books. All one had to do was look for them—and that's exactly what he did.

From that day forward, he began scouring every book he brought into the shop, looking for unsolved mysteries that had implicated the innocent, wrongfully shaming or degrading them in the process. Then, very quietly, not for material gain or public tribute, he went about uncovering the truth and correcting those wrongs. As the books grew in number, he stored them in the bookcase that sat in his office, a fitting tribute to its builder, Thomas Hammond.

In time, the bookcase would be passed on to another family member, designated as the keeper of the case of secrets, thereby establishing a Hammond family legacy that would stand for generations to follow.

A silent force for good.

Careful.

Watchful.

Unseen.

Notes

THE GROSS FUGUE, also known as the Great Fugue or Grand Fugue, was a single-movement composition written by Ludwig van Beethoven in 1825 as the final movement of his Quartet No. 13 in B— major (Op. 130). It was universally condemned by contemporary music critics, but since the beginning of the 20th century, it is now considered among his greatest achievements.

INVISIBLE INKS, also called sympathetic inks, contain one or more chemicals and require the application of a specific "reagent" to be activated. Some will reveal their message when heated. At one time, their use and composition were considered classified government information.

COBALT CHLORIDE turns blue when heated and becomes invisible again as it cools.

"NOWHERE TO RUN TO" was written by the Motown team of Holland-Dozier-Holland and released in 1965 on the Dance Party album by Martha and the Vandellas.

PHILHARMONIC SOCIETY OF LONDON was formed in 1813 and is the oldest classical music performing body in the UK.

LINEN, from the Latin word for flax, *linum*, is the world's strongest natural fiber. It comes from the inner part of the flax plant and has been used for thousands of years in thread, shirts, sheets, embroidery, and many woven fabrics. Its natural color varies from ivory to ecru, tan and grey.

COWL INDUCTION HOOD is a backward-facing scoop in the hood, designed to draw cool, high-pressure air that collects at the base of the windshield at speed. The air is forced directly into the air inducers, and in turn, the combustion chambers, helping to increase horsepower.

SACO ISLAND began the industrial history of the Saco-Biddeford area in the 1760s. Since that time, it has undergone numerous name changes, including: Indian Island, Cutts Island, and Factory Island. Two of the buildings on the island are noted for their length: the York Mills #1 and #4, which are more than 500 feet long.

THE HAMILTON MILL is a fictitious structure and was based on a box factory that existed on Factory Island (now Saco Island) in the mid 1800s, producing boxes for the nearby textile mills. The Hamilton name was inspired by the B.F. Hamilton store, a dry goods emporium that also operated on Factory Island at that time, dealing in silks, fabrics and woman's accessories.

THE CHÂTEAU DE CHEVRON is an ancient castle in the commune (administrative division) of Mercury, in the Savoie départment of France. It was owned by the powerful Chevron Villette family and has no connection to the fictional Dampierre family.

THE CHÂTEAU DE CHÂLUCET was a medieval fortress built in the 13th century by Bishop Eustorge at the confluence of the Briance and Ligoure rivers, in the commune (administrative division) of Saint-Jean-Ligoure in the départment of Haute-Vienne. The fortress was trapezoidal in shape and consisted of two parts: a castle built on the summit of a rocky outcrop (upper Châlucet, 13th century), and a square keep called "Tour Jeanette" (lower Chalucet, 12th -16th century). Throughout its history is has been alternately inhabited by lords and bandits and is considered one of the most beautiful ruins in France.

"MY GRIEF LIES ALL WITHIN, AND THESE EXTERNAL MANNERS OF LAMENT ARE MERELY SHADOWS TO THE UNSEEN GRIEF THAT SWELLS WITH SILENCE IN THE TORTURED SOUL. THERE LIES THE SUBSTANCE," is from Richard II (4.1), by William Shakespeare. It was believed to have been written around 1595 and chronicles the downfall of King Richard II of England and the schemes of his nobles.

DORIC COLUMN is an architectural element developed in the western Dorian region of Greece in about the 6th century BC, and represents one of the five orders of classical architecture. In public and commercial applications, it is a defining feature of Neoclassical style buildings.

TISCH LIBRARY, originally Wessell Library, is the principal library for the Medford/Somerville campus of Tufts University. With 2.7 million volumes, it serves as the main branch of the Tufts library system.

MUNROE TAVERN, in Lexington, MA, was built in 1735 and served briefly as a field hospital for the British Army during their retreat back to Boston from Concord on April 19, 1775. The house was added to the National Register of Historic Places in 1976 and is now operated as a museum by the Lexington Historical Society.

TEK-WIPE is a highly absorbent non-woven textile made from a blend of hydro-spun cellulose and polyester. It's durable, reusable, extremely strong when wet, chemically stable and highly absorbent, making it ideal for a large range of conservation treatments, including the humidification of sensitive media.

WESTPORT ISLAND, MAINE, formerly Westport, is located on Maine's mid-coast (Lincoln County) in Sheepscot Bay. Incorporated as part of Freetown, now Edgecomb, in 1774, it flourished as a fishing and farming community in the early 1800s.

THE GRAND STAFF originated somewhere around the 13th century and features two five-line staves that span the complete range of pitches. The top stave uses a treble clef while the bottom staff uses a bass clef.

MERRYMEETING LAKE is a 1,233-acre body of water in the town of New Durham, NH. The lake is a nesting place for common loons and ducks, and the deep, cold water allows for a variety of game species to thrive, including brook trout, lake trout, rainbow trout, whitefish and landlocked salmon. Warm water fish include largemouth bass, smallmouth bass, northern pike, walleye, pickerel, horned pout, white perch, yellow perch, crapple and bluegill.

SHIRE is a British breed of draught horse, named for the British shires (countryside) where the breed was developed. At various times, they have held world records for both the largest horse and the tallest horse. Prior to the use of machinery in agriculture and industry, the Shire horse was used for its immense pulling power. Despite their imposing size, they are typically calm, docile, and eager to please.

SULAWESI COFFEE comes from an island by the same name in the Republic of Indonesia. Coffee was first brought to Indonesia in the late 1600s by the Dutch, who, by the mid 1800s, had begun cultivating crops on the islands of Sulawesi, Bali, Timor and Sumatra. Located in the bean belt just south of the equator, the Indonesian islands, with their ocean mist, volcanic soil, soaring heights, and natural old-growth forests, produce coffees that are prized for their unique, unmistakable flavors, velvety feel and earthy tones.

FORT DODGE, KANSAS is an unincorporated community in Grandview Township, Ford County, Kansas. From 1865 to 1882 Fort Dodge was an outpost on the Santa Fe Trail. At its greatest capacity, the fort boasted four companies of infantry.

CALLING CARDS, also called visiting cards, visiting tickets, or compliments cards, originated in France in the 18th century. They became essential social accessories for the fashionable and wealthy in Britain, Europe, and the eastern United States during the 19th and 20th centuries, serving both as a utilitarian object and status symbol.

BARTLETT MILLS is a fictitious town. The name was based on a parcel of land near Kennebunk, ME, known as the Bartlett Mills area, once the site of a mill and farm owned by the Bartlett family.

"LIKE THE CLAPPERS," is a British phrase that means very fast or very hard. It originated in the slang of the Royal Air Force during the Second World War.

APOTHECARY came from the word apotheca, meaning a place where herbs, spices and wines were stored. During the 13th century it referred to a person who sold these substances from a shop or street stall. A ruling by the House of Lords in 1704 accepted apothecaries as part of the medical profession and allowed them to legally prescribe and dispense medicine.

THOMAS CHARLES HOPE (1766-1844), was a British physician, chemist and lecturer. By 1820, his lectures at the University of Edinburgh reached profound popularity, attracting over 500 attendees, including numerous foreigners, from princes to ancient historians.

WOLF TREES are defined as tall forest trees with a large diameter trunk and widely spreading crown. Many are over 150 years old and are commonly found along the edges of rock walls.

VIOLE DE GAMBE, translated as "viol of the leg," is a stringed and fretted musical instrument played upright between the legs with a bow. They first appeared in Spain in the mid to late 15th century and were most popular during the Renaissance and Baroque periods (1600-1750).

INDIAN WAR PAINT was made from the natural materials that were available to the American Indians, including clay, berries, plants, minerals and tree bark. Warriors believed that it gave them strength and protection, and would strike fear into the enemy. Various symbols were painted on warrior's faces and bodies, such as circles, stripes, triangle, and zig-zag lines representing lightning, which they believed gave them great power and speed.

"NOT A CREATURE WAS STIRRING, NOT EVEN A MOUSE" is from a poem, "A Visit from Saint Nicholas," published anonymously on December 23, 1823, in the Sentinel, the local paper of Troy, New York. Known as "Twas the Night Before Christmas," after its famous first line, its authorship is in question, although many believe it was penned by New York writer Henry Livingston.

BENJAMIN F. MEEK was a jeweler and watchmaker in Frankfort, KY. In 1883 he moved to Louisville and established the B.F. Meek & Sons reel shop with his sons Pitman and Sylvanus. He is credited with making the first fishing reel to incorporate spiral-cut gears, jeweled pivot bearings, and oil holes for the bearings.

DOORKNOB ROSE PLATES are decorative backplates (rectangular or oblong) that fit around a doorknob and have an opening for keys.

"WHOLE LOTTA SHAKIN' GOIN' ON" was written by Dave "Curlee" Williams and James Faye "Roy" Hall. It was first recorded by Big Maybelle in 1955, and later popularized by Jerry Lee Lewis in 1957 for Sun Records. His rock and roll/boogie-woogie version reached number one on Billboard Magazine's R&B chart, and number one on the country charts, making him an instant sensation.

EASTERN PHOEBES are a plump songbird and the most tame and well-known member of the flycatcher clan. They are very active and flick their tail upward restlessly while perched. They often build their nests under an eve, on a window ledge, or above a doorframe.

AND FOR THE RECORD...

The police protocols used in the story do not reflect the actual procedures used by the U.S. Marshal's Service, or any other law enforcement agencies in the United States.

Acknowledgements

Once again, it was a collection of incredible people who gave of their time to help me craft the next book in the Third Floor Mystery Series. Without their assistance, such a tale would never have been possible, and to each of them I offer my heartfelt appreciation.

I'd been kicking around the storyline where Nathan Cole discovers a sheet of classical music with a mysterious code hidden among the notes. It was only after a conversation with Michael Mahadeen, music educator and freelance music composer/engraver with Montclair State University, that the plot took shape. His enthusiasm was equal to, if not greater than, my own. He schooled me in the fugue musical form and shared a wealth of historical information that fed effortlessly into the story as well as the chapter page illustrations. For his amazing music knowledge and passion I am forever grateful.

The character of Fletcher Poole, as well as the humidification procedures he employed, were developed with the divine guidance of Kathryn Boodle, an associate conservator with the Northeast Document Conservation Center in Andover, Massachusetts. Her deep knowledge of paper, ink, and document restoration is nothing short of astounding, and the detailed information she shared was instrumental to the plot.

The fight sequences were developed with the help of John Boudreau, U.S. Army Sargent, retired, whose expertise in hand-to-hand combat helped define the characters of Beck and Karl Odom. I thank him for not snapping me in half when we were choreographing each of the fight scenes.

The town of Bartlett Mills is fictional and grew out of conversations with Cynthia Walker, Director of the Brick Store Museum in Kennebunk, ME, and Carrie Weeman, Deputy Town Clerk. Historical details about Saco Island (and the mills that were built there) were provided by Anatole Brown, Education and Program Manager of the Saco Museum in Saco, ME, who has a profound knowledge of the area.

The phrase "Sometimes anger is good," came from a conversation with pastor and friend, Joseph Mabe, who used those words to characterize the creation of his hyperbaric chamber, a journey he undertook in the face of adversity.

Huge thanks go out to the good folks at Gem Graphics in Keene, NH, who helped with first reader copies, layouts, covers, and bookmarks; to Joe Bills at Escape Hatch Books, for believing in a haunted bookcase in the attic, and who wrangles with the legal stuff when not urging me onward: the staff at the Toadstool Bookshops for the superb work they do inspiring readers of all ages; Marcia Lusted, my "hawk eye" content and line editor, and my first readers, those brave souls who peruse the chapters in their unvarnished form.

Profound thanks to the devoted followers of the Third Floor Mystery Series, who keep me up late at night, scheming. And to the librarians and teachers throughout the world, you may hide your capes well, but I know that you're superheroes one and all.

Illustrations

The chapter page illustrations were taken from autographed manuscripts of classical composers from the Renaissance, Baroque, Classical, Romantic, Late Romantic, and 20th century eras. They are the actual clefs penned by those composers and were processed using the Torn Edge filter in Photoshop.

Chapter 1   Claudio Monteverdi (1567-1643)
Chapter 2   Johann Sebastian Bach (1685-1750)
Chapter 3   George Frideric Handel (1685-1759)
Chapter 4   Wolfgang Amadeus Mozart (1756-1791)
Chapter 5   Ludwig Van Beethoven (1770-1827)
Chapter 6   Gioacchino Rossini (1792-1868)
Chapter 7   Franz Schubert (1797-1828)
Chapter 8   Hector Berlioz (1803-1869)
Chapter 9   Frédéric Chopin (1810-1849)
Chapter 10   Giuseppe Verdi (1813-1901)
Chapter 11   Theodore Döhler (1814-1856)
Chapter 12   Albert Becker (1834-1899)
Chapter 13   Anton Bruckner (1824-1896)
Chapter 14   Johannes Brahms (1833-1897)
Chapter 15   Pyotr Ilich Tchaikovsky (1840-1893)
Chapter 16   Antonín Dvořák (1840-1904)
Chapter 17   Ernest Chausson (1855-1899)
Chapter 18   Edward Elgar (1857-1934)
Chapter 19   Gustav Mahler (1860-1911)
Chapter 20   Claude Debussy (1862-1918)
Chapter 21   Richard Strauss (1864-1949)
Chapter 22   Samuel Coleridge-Taylor (1875-1912)
Chapter 23   Joseph Maurice Ravel (1875-1937)
Chapter 24   George Gershwin (1898-1937)

About the Author

Alfred M. Struthers lives in Peterborough, New Hampshire. In addition to crafting books that inspire, entertain and make a difference in the lives of readers young and old, he is a singer/ songwriter, woodworker, and avid collector of fossils that line the streambeds around Cooperstown, New York.

Coming Soon!

The Watchman's Keep

The floorboards gave way with a thunderous crack. The resulting implosion swallowed Nathan as if caught in the jaws of a mammoth beast, sending him plummeting downward in an avalanche of dust, debris, and splintered wood. He landed hard amid the rubble on a packed dirt floor, and for several long seconds he lay there dazed, pain shooting through his entire body.

Until he heard the rats.

At first, they were just vague shapes, scurrying about in the shadows. But as his eyes adjusted to the dim band of light streaming down through the ragged hole in the floor overhead, their size and numbers became more defined. Some were as big as house cats.

Waiting.

Watching.

Neither fearing nor attacking him.

Like a gathering army their numbers continued to grow, and it was only a matter of minutes before they would advance in a ravenous swarm.

Eat up, friends. Don't be shy. There's plenty here for everyone.

He scrambled to his feet and slid his backpack off his shoulder, ignoring the pain that gripped his body. From the center compartment he dug out his flashlight, and with a flick of a button it came to life, filling the cramped room with light. He turned slowly and took stock of his surroundings, running the beam over every square inch, through the thin veil of dust that hung in the air.

It was a small cellar, barely twelve feet square. To his right, a pair of old wooden barrels were pushed up against the stone foundation, suggesting that the room had once been used to store potatoes and carrots and other root vegetables—maybe even a keg of ale or two. To his left, a rickety wooden staircase led up to the first floor.

The eerie silence that followed his fall was gone, replaced by the squeaks of the ever-growing horde of rats. Where they were coming from Nathan didn't know, but what had started out as a half dozen quickly doubled, then tripled. And still they came.

As if signaled by a silent bell that only they could hear, they began moving in unison, tightening the circle around their prey. Nathan kicked pieces of broken boards and debris at them, scattering them long enough for him to make a run at the stairs. But just as quickly they mobilized, and as he scaled the steps they charged after him in a frenzied wave, hissing and chattering.

Time to eat.

He had just cleared the top step when he spotted something nestled between two studs on the wall to his left. Even under a thick blanket of spider webs, its size and shape were unmistakable. It was the cast bronze figurine known as *The Lady of Florence*, crafted by Umberto Caracci.

Five years earlier, in a daring home invasion, it was stolen from an estate in North Cambridge. The robbers were never caught, and according to the account Nathan read in a book from the *Greenwich* bookcase, they had stashed some of their stolen loot somewhere in the area in an attempt to hasten their escape. To date, some of those items had never resurfaced, and it was believed that the robbers never returned to retrieve them.

Included on the list was *The Lady of Florence*.

He pulled it off the fireblock and shoved it in his backpack when the rats swarmed the landing.

And he felt the first bite.

Made in United States
Orlando, FL
09 September 2023

36843409R00241